A note on the author

Denzil Meyrick was born in Glasgow and brought up in Campbeltown. After studying politics, he pursued a varied career including time spent as a police officer, freelance journalist and director of several companies in the leisure, engineering and marketing sectors. Previous novels in the bestselling DCI Daley thriller series are *Whisky from Small Glasses* (Waterstones Scottish Book of the Year, 2015), *The Last Witness*, *Dark Suits and Sad Songs* and *The Rat Stone Serenade*. Denzil lives on Loch Lomond side with his wife, Fiona.

WELL OF THE WINDS

A D.C.I. Daley Thriller

Denzil Meyrick

First published in Great Britain in 2017 by Polygon, an imprint of Birlinn Ltd.

Birlinn Ltd
West Newington House
10 Newington Road
Edinburgh
EH9 1QS

www.polygonbooks.co.uk

1

ISBN 978 1 84697 372 7
eBook ISBN 978 0 85790 923 7

British Library Cataloguing-in-Publication Data
A catalogue record for this book is available on request from the British Library.

Typeset by Hewer Text UK Ltd, Edinburgh

To Mary Anderson, our neighbour and friend

'He who was living is now dead,
We who were living are now dying . . .'

T. S. Eliot, *The Waste Land*

PROLOGUE

Kinloch, 1945

He'd always known this moment would come. He reached into the deep pocket of his gabardine raincoat, feeling the reassuring heft of the blade, and closed his fist over the wooden handle.

Out on the loch, beneath the full moon, a dozen grey warships loomed, framed by the roofs and spires of Kinloch and the hills beyond that cocooned the town. Elsewhere, a bright night like this was dreaded: cities, towns and villages picked out in the moonlight, prey to waves of enemy bombers, or, worse still, the spine-chilling whine of the new super weapon – the doodlebug. Not so on Scotland's distant west coast – here, there was a safe haven.

Crouched behind a boulder down on the causeway, he could hear the breeze tugging at the rough grass that fringed the rocky shoreline, and the hiss and sigh of the sea.

The stuttering engine of a car could be heard winding its way along the coast road, which skirted the lochside before disappearing into the hills. The headlights cast a low, weak golden beam, sweeping across the field behind him. The engine stopped with a shudder and the lights flickered out as the vehicle pulled up to the causeway.

The man held his breath as a car door opened and then slammed shut.

It was time.

The beam of a torch flashed across the waves. A rat scurried away from the light. He inhaled the cool air, tainted by the stench of rotting seaweed. The footsteps were getting closer now, scuffing across the rocks in his direction.

'Hello? Are you there?' The voice was deep and resonant with no hint of trepidation. For a heartbeat, he wondered how the end of existence could creep up so suddenly. Was there no primeval instinct at work, protecting frail flesh, bone and breath?

He stepped out from behind the boulder, shielding his eyes from the glare of the torch.

'What in hell's name are you doing here?'

Though the question was brusque, the voice was calm, almost uninterested. He watched as the man turned the beam of the torch back along the way he'd come and firmly pulled down his trilby when a gust of wind threatened to send it spinning into the waves.

Ignoring the question, he rushed him from behind, hooked his left arm around the man's neck and snaked his right arm across the man's waist. Up and twist, right under the ribcage, as he'd been taught – plunging into him again and again. There was only fleeting resistance as the sharp blade did its job. The man had been completely unprepared for the attack – just as they'd said he would be. His victim tensed, convulsed, and then went limp. A gurgle –a plea – came from the depth of his throat as his life drained away.

Aided by his assailant, who took his weight, the dying man slipped gently to the ground.

He dragged the body behind the boulder that had been his hiding place, almost losing his nerve when a deep sigh – the last sign of life – issued from the victim's gaping mouth. Leaving the corpse propped up behind the boulder, he got to his feet and took deep gulps of the tangy sea air.

He waited, with only the thud of his heart in his ears and the restless surf for company. It had been as easy as they'd predicted.

In what must only have been minutes, but seemed like hours, he heard another car making its way slowly along the causeway road towards him.

His job was done. The greater good had prevailed – the greater good must always prevail.

1

Gairsay, an island off the coast of Kintyre, the present day

Malcolm McAuley whistled along to the radio. It was his last delivery of the day and he was feeling cheerful. He collected the mail off the first ferry at seven every morning in his guise as the island's only postman. When he'd taken on the job, almost ten years ago, his task had been the delivery of letters, but now that his fellow islanders were taking advantage of online shopping, he delivered mainly parcels. With fewer than two hundred souls on Gairsay, an island just over five miles long and one and a half broad, his daily routine rarely took more than an hour.

It was how he liked it. McAuley had many other tasks to perform in the course of his day.

He turned the Royal Mail van onto the rough track that led to Achnamara, the farm belonging to the Bremners. He'd known the family all of his life, as he had most of the island's residents. He always remembered old Mr Bremner fondly. Though the man rarely spoke about his past, everyone knew he'd escaped the Nazis by the skin of his teeth. The rumour was that, with his wife, he had made the hazardous journey across war-torn Europe, before reaching safety and a new home on this tiny island off the west coast of Scotland.

Though they made little of it, ornaments and other religious paraphernalia in their home made it obvious that the family were Jewish. However, keen to play their part in the community, they soon began attending the kirk like everybody else, treating the services as more of a social event than an act of religious devotion. They were good, kind people, who had quickly become part of the tight-knit island community.

Achnamara, like the rest of the farms, had once belonged to the company who owned the island. In the main, they were benign landlords, though through a series of tough factors they made sure that the land they owned yielded all it could. Back in the forties, when old Alex Grieve and his wife – childless and worn out by years of hard toil – had become unable to work the farm to its full potential, they'd been quietly retired and a place found for them in a small cottage in Gairsay's main settlement, the village of Prien. The Bremner family had moved in to Achnamara and had been there ever since, eventually buying the farm from the island's proprietors in the sixties.

Though similar offers had been made to other tenant farmers, they'd been unable to find enough cash, so the six other farms on Gairsay had remained in the hands of the company, until the island was bought by its population in 1999, a landmark purchase in Scotland that heralded similar transactions by remote communities across the country.

Old Mr Bremner, big, strong and jovial, had died in the eighties, but his wife Jan was still thriving despite her advanced age. The work of the farm had long since been taken on by the next generation. Though farming was the family's main livelihood, they also fished for crab and lobster, using a small boat they kept tied up to a rickety pier by the shore.

The package McAuley was carrying today was addressed to Jan, so he looked forward to a chat with the old woman over a cup of tea and a slice of the delicious cake that always seemed to be in plentiful supply.

The main farmhouse was newly whitewashed and looked as pristine as ever. Unusually, there was no sign of life in the yard, though McAuley heard a cow lowing balefully in an outbuilding.

He collected the small parcel from the back of the van and rapped on the front door, which was painted bright red. As was his habit in almost every dwelling on the island when there was no reply, he turned the heavy brass knocker, engraved with the family name, and opened the door.

'Hello! It's the post. Is anybody about?' he called, expecting to be greeted by a family member. All was quiet, so he called again.

He looked into the large, bright lounge, where, because of the chill of the March morning, a fire blazed in the hearth. However, nobody was there.

Down the hallway, he was sure he'd find someone in the kitchen, but, worryingly, though two plates of bacon and eggs were sitting on the large wooden table, the room was empty. A pan of milk had boiled over, and dark smoke was issuing from the range, filling the room with an acrid smell. Wrapping his hand in a tea towel, he removed the blackened pan from the stove, then placed it in the Belfast sink, sending clouds of steam into the air when he turned on the cold tap.

He almost tripped over a chair, pitched over on the far side of the table. He set it back upright and made his way out of the kitchen, calling again in the hope that someone would reply.

Nothing.

After climbing the stairs and checking the bedrooms, he thudded back to the ground floor and made his way to the back door of the farmhouse. He turned the old brass key in the lock and pushed the door open, scanning the fields beyond. The grass was a dull green under the grey sky, with only a few sheep dotted here and there on the pasture. An old mare whinnied at the sight of the postman and trotted expectantly to the fence.

It was as though the family had been in the house only minutes before his arrival, then vanished.

Across the fields was the bungalow where Jan's grandson and his wife lived. They ran the farm, so it was likely that some kind of meeting was taking place, he thought. After patting the horse, he set off quickly along the lane towards the dwelling, certain that he would find the Bremners there.

2

DThe Glasgow cemetery sprawled untidily over the hillside. Daley shivered as he made his way through ranks of grave-stones and other, more elaborate monuments to the dead.

Thoroughly lost, he stopped a maintenance man and asked where the most recent burials were to be found.

'Up there, big man,' he replied, jerking his thumb over his shoulder. 'The newest graves are on the top o' the hill.'

Daley walked slowly in that direction. He paused at a grave upon which a white teddy bear had been placed on top of some toys and a huge wreath: *Miss you for ever, Toby. Deepest sadness, Mum and Dad xx*, the card read.

He knelt down to read another tribute, written in a child's hand and placed in a clear plastic bag to protect it from the elements. The rain had got in, blurring the ink, but Daley could still read it.

You were my wee brother, and I love you. You were taken away to heaven. Now you're an angel. Please watch over me.

The big policeman got stiffly to his feet and sighed.

He'd wanted to go to the funeral, but had been dissuaded from doing so by a phone call. 'I know what you did, and you're not welcome.' The words had echoed in his head ever since.

He watched a crow hop along the path ahead of him, then

rise in flight, squawking as it came to land on a black marble headstone. The bird's cry, harsh and intrusive, echoed amongst the graves. Though Daley could see cars, factories, roads and people in the distance, none of the sounds of the city seemed to reach this place. Only the wind whining through the gravestones, punctuated by the cawing of the crow, filled his ears.

He stopped at a gleaming grey granite headstone, brand new and carved in the shape of a heart.

MARY ELIZABETH DUNN, TAKEN TOO SOON was all he could read before the breath caught in his throat.

Though it had been weeks since her funeral, the sods of green turf used to cover the grave of DC Mary Dunn were still a patchwork, like squares on a chessboard. The winter had been cold, but spring was on its way. Soon the soil would seal her in the tomb in which she would lie for eternity.

Faded red roses lay at the foot of the stone. *Love you for ever, Angus x.*

Daley had a bouquet of yellow roses. Through his tears, he could make out the message he'd written on the card: *For what should have been.*

He wasn't sure how he'd expected to feel. But, in the end, the emotion was the same as the last time he'd gone to place flowers on his mother's grave: emptiness – the absence of being, a void where once had been the warmth of love. Despite himself, he thought of the bodies he'd had to watch being exhumed in the course of his duties as a police officer. The thought of the beautiful, fresh-faced woman he'd loved so much rotting away under his feet almost made him scream out loud.

It was really over. Something in him now, silently,

reluctantly, accepted she was gone. The pain in his heart brought more stinging tears to his eyes and he wanted to sink to his knees and sob.

He turned and walked away from the grave, tossing the flowers into the first waste bin he came to.

The block of flats stood near the centre of Milngavie, an upmarket suburb to the north of Glasgow. As he parked in the street Daley looked up to the second floor, his destination. Should he do this? He felt he had to.

He trudged up two flights of stairs, feeling his age, feeling more than his age. In the last few weeks, he'd barely been able to function. Everything in his life had changed. All the things he'd felt were certain and permanent had disappeared in an instant. Though he found it hard to give his feelings voice, he felt as though he wanted to give up, to put an end to it all. As was his way, though, he kept quiet and let silent cries fill his head, cries that were slowly driving him mad, sending him spiralling into a pit of despair.

The nameplate on the door read MRS G DUNN. He rang the bell and stepped back. As he heard movement inside the flat, a voice in his head screamed at him to run, to flee this place. Despite this, he stood his ground, swallowing heavily as he heard a key turn in the lock.

The woman was in her fifties, slightly built, with shadows under her blue eyes. Daley saw the echo of her daughter in her face, and was instantly lost for words.

At the same moment, she realised just who her visitor was and crossed her arms tightly over her chest, looking at the ground at Daley's feet and frowning.

'What do you want?' She gave each word its own space, as

though she was speaking to a person for whom English was a foreign language.

'Can I come in?'

She hesitated for a moment and stood back from the door, opening it just wide enough to admit her visitor.

At the end of the hallway, Daley could see the lounge door ajar, so headed automatically towards it.

'Not in there. Here,' she snapped, directing him into the kitchen. 'I need a coffee.'

He stood awkwardly as she boiled the kettle and deliberately filled only one mug.

'What do you want from me?'

'I couldn't leave things the way they were,' said Daley, shuffling from foot to foot like an errant schoolboy in front of the headmaster. 'I had to speak to you face to face. Do you understand?'

'For what reason? So that you can explain to me why you took advantage of a young woman who was in your charge? So that you can tell me why you made her life a misery, running back and forward to your tart of a wife while she pined for you? Wasting her life, what there was left of it. So you can feel better about yourself?' She paused. 'Mary should have been having the time of her life with a young man of her own age, instead of mooning after a fat, selfish, washed-up excuse for a human being like you.'

'That's not how it was.'

'Oh, really, just how was it, then?'

'I loved her.'

'You used her. She was young and pretty, and you used her. Don't give me your midlife crisis shit. I had a husband just like you. Instead of being a father to his daughter, he spent

11

his time chasing girls not much older than her. It's pathetic!'

'I just had to come and say I was sorry.'

'Sorry? To hell with your "sorry". She meant the world to me. She was my life, you bastard!' She slammed the coffee mug onto the kitchen table, slopping the contents over her hand.

'It was an accident, Gillian. You can't blame me for that.'

'An accident? The way I understand it, she'd just left her boyfriend's after telling him their relationship was over. The roads were treacherous, she'd been working all night, yet she decided to pick that moment to finish it with a clever young man who would have made her happy. I wonder why that was?'

'I shouldn't have let her go, I know that. But she wanted to be honest with him . . .'

'What do you know about honesty?' Gillian Dunn slumped onto a chair and held her head in her hands. 'We had no secrets, you know. She told me everything . . . everything about *you*.'

'Well, you'll know that we'd decided to make a go of it.'

'You bastard! Do you know how you sound? Like a little boy – a stupid little boy. If she'd gone home and stayed there that morning, she'd still be alive. Instead, to please you, she took her car out in the ice and snow to tell poor Angus that it was over. You don't have to be a fucking detective to work out how things worked out.'

'I'm sorry. I am so sorry. I've thought of nothing else for weeks.' Daley walked towards the woman and tried to touch her shoulder, to do something – anything – to ease the situation.

'Get your hands off me, you creep. In fact, get out. Get out before I call your colleagues and have you flung out.' Daley was momentarily rooted to the spot. 'Get the fuck out of my house!' she yelled, flinging the coffee mug at him.

3

Detective Sergeant Brian Scott was sitting in Daley's glass box in Kinloch Police Office, trying desperately to complete yet another new Police Scotland form. He cursed as the screen jumped again without letting him type in the box he wanted to.

His boss, and best friend, had taken a short leave of absence, and it was Scott's job to hold the fort. In the main, the policing of Kinloch was easy. Most of those intent on dealing serious drugs in the community had been rounded up by Daley and his detectives, so now the main staples of a police officer's life occupied the CID team: road traffic accidents, breaches of the peace, assaults, petty theft, domestic abuse and drunkenness. Meat and drink to someone of Scott's experience.

However, anything to do with IT did not fall into that category.

He swore again as the machine in front of him refused to obey his commands. He was about to try again when his phone burst into life.

'DS Scott. If you want tae speak aboot computers, away tae PC World.'

'No, Brian, not computers,' said Sergeant Shaw from the front desk. 'I've just had the special constable from Gairsay on the phone. Seems as though a whole family have just disappeared.'

'Where the hell is Gairsay again?'

'It's that wee island just off the coast as you're driving down the main road to the town, you know, the one with the wind turbines. Half an hour on the ferry. I think we should get someone over there.'

'Aye, right away. I'm your man – never as happy as when I've got tae get on a boat. Come through and gie me the gen on this.'

Two hours later, Scott and a youthful detective constable, Ian Potts, were boarding the ferry to Gairsay. Scott sighed as he looked at the darkening sky. 'Oh great, we're just about tae get a storm. I hope this bucket is seaworthy.'

'I wouldn't worry if I was you, Sergeant,' Potts replied. 'I don't think the ferry to Gairsay has ever sunk.'

'No time like the present. Here, make yourself useful and away and get the tickets.' Scott handed the DC a credit card. 'And mind and get a receipt.'

As he watched the young officer thread his way through the cars parked nose to tail on the small ferry, he rubbed his chin. He was worried about Daley. He hadn't heard from him for almost a week, and the big man was seriously depressed – as down as Scott had ever seen him. He'd phoned his mobile a handful of times, but there'd been no reply. Desperate to hear anything about his friend, he'd even resorted to contacting Liz, though he wished he hadn't. Her ex-husband had failed to pick up his son, James junior, as arranged, and she didn't care if she never saw him again. Before Scott could ask her if she'd any idea where his DCI was, the phone had gone dead.

Scott had hoped that the couple would get back together somehow. He'd watched them bicker for more years than he cared to remember but still manage to keep the spark of their relationship alive. Daley's admission that he'd loved his young colleague Mary Dunn had probably made any kind of reconciliation impossible.

Scott had been called to the scene when Mary's car was discovered. She had skidded on ice, ploughed through a wall, then hit a tree. Despite the trauma of the accident, save a trickle of blood from her nose, there hadn't been a mark on her. Her pale blue eyes had stared blankly into space in exactly the same way so many dead people he'd come across in the course of his career had done.

It had been his job to tell Daley. After that, things had changed. The big detective became sullen and withdrawn. He did his job – functioned, more or less – but any sign of the man he knew had all but disappeared.

Disappearing was becoming a habit, he thought to himself, trying to concentrate on the new job in hand. Yet another riddle to be solved. He sincerely hoped the outcome would be an easily reached, happy one.

'Here, Sergeant.' Scott jumped when the car door opened and Potts handed him the credit card. 'Were you having a wee doss?'

'Naw, son. I was just wondering why you were taking so long.'

'See that guy there?' said Potts, pointing at a tall man with tanned skin and a military-style haircut who was making his way along the car deck.

'Aye, what about him?'

'Reckon he's a cop? I was standing behind him in the queue for tickets. Looks like one.'

Scott had to agree; with the straight back and the shaven head, the man could well be a policeman. 'Too old, though. If he was in the job, he's well retired now.'

'What age do you think he is?'

'Mid sixties, easily,' Scott replied. 'You'll need tae get better at recognising ages if you're going tae make progress in this line of work, son.'

'I'm okay with folk my own age. Can't get the older ones, though. I mean, that guy would be ages with you, right?'

'My arse, ages wae me! Dae you think I'll still be ploughing this furrow when I'm sixty-five?'

'What else will you do?'

Scott had to think for a minute. What would he do? He'd been almost three months off the drink, and had discovered to his dismay that it was his only hobby. In a desperate attempt to fill the time he'd normally have spent standing at a bar or in an alcoholic stupor, he'd decided to get fit. He'd been to the gym a few times – even been out for a run or two – but still couldn't understand what people got out of it. His reward had been a twisted ankle and aching knees – where was the joy in that?

'I'll be sitting on a beach somewhere hot, wae a long drink, son,' he replied.

'A long drink of what, Fanta?'

'I'll gie you Fanta, you bugger.' Despite himself, Scott smiled. He was well aware that his recent conversion to sobriety had prompted much speculation amongst his fellow officers, not to mention a sweepstake just when he'd fall off the wagon. He was determined to prove everyone wrong. In any case, he never again wanted to feel the way he had done in the months leading up to signing the pledge. He shuddered at the thought. A drink-free existence may be boring, leaving time heavy on his hands, but at least he didn't wake up every morning feeling sick, with a thudding head and a feeling of impending doom. Not to mention the things he'd imagined he'd seen.

His phone rang. Daley's name was flashing on the screen. 'Jimmy, how are you, pal?' The reply was indistinct, though he thought he caught the word 'shit'. 'You're breaking up, big man. Listen, I'm on a boat heading for Gairsay ... Hello?' The fragmented tones of Daley's voice were replaced by a long whine. 'See these bloody things,' he said, clicking off the call. 'Bugger all use.' He began redialling the number, squinting at the screen without his reading glasses.

'You'll not get a signal now.'

For the first time, Scott felt the pitch and roll of the vessel. Even though he couldn't see the sea, he knew he was on it. 'Dae they work on this Gairsay?'

'Yeah. I was over there a few weeks ago after that man had a heart attack on the golf course, remember? I got a signal no bother.'

'Aye, okay. I'll leave it till we get there, then.'

Daley dialled again. *The mobile number you have called is temporarily unavailable. Please try again later*. He threw the phone onto the passenger seat of the car and leaned his head back on the rest.

He shook his head at the reaction he'd had from Mary's mother; the look of pure hatred in her eyes. He cursed himself for being stupid enough to pay her a visit in the first place. He cursed his life.

Everything was hopeless.

He looked at the narrow road snaking up the steep hill ahead of him. The mountains towering above him were dark and menacing – no sign of the sun, just grey, grey, grey, turning to black. It seemed as though nothing would be bright again.

Cars swished past in the rain, their red rear lights bright in the gloom, getting smaller as they made the climb up the hill, until they were mere pinpricks showing faintly above the Amco barrier, the only thing between them and the sheer drop on the other side.

He'd felt it before, this pull to oblivion. The little voice that whispered in the high places: *Do it, just do it, go over the edge.* He'd never liked heights. The dreams that had terrified him most since he was a child were those in which he was falling. Had they just been dreams, or were they the ghosts of times past, or visions of what was to come? Voices from another universe only a sliver away, where instead of being tucked up in bed, he fell through the air, only for everything to stop. He wondered if Mary had ever had those dreams.

He gunned the engine, pulled out of the layby and sped up the steep hill. Knuckles white, gripping the steering wheel, he peered into the gloom ahead.

The first few hundred yards were flanked by thick pine trees. A river frothed in spate, coursing its way down the hillside, bolstered by melting snow from the places high above. The car's engine strained as he chose a lower gear.

He was getting higher now. In the distance he could see a line of traffic crawling at snail's pace behind a large

HGV. This road – the pass – was known as the 'Rest and Be Thankful'. Though he'd driven it often since his posting to Kinloch, this was the first time the name had made sense.

Far, far below now, he could see a tiny white cottage nestling at the bottom of the valley. A burn, a ribbon of silver water that had probably carved out its path over millennia, snaked along the valley floor in a lazy 'S' shape. The barrier to his left looked insubstantial; any car driven at it would be sure to break through and somersault down the sheer hillside. Impossible to survive, he reasoned.

He thought of Mary and tugged the wheel sharply to the left.

Scott felt the ferry judder as the ramp lowered onto the slipway at Gairsay. It had been a short crossing, lasting less than half an hour, but half an hour was more than enough to spend at sea, as far as he was concerned.

Soon, a low hill adorned with three tall wind turbines came into view, and the vessel juddered as the ramp lowered onto the slipway. A man in a high-vis jacket waved the cars off the ferry, saluting each driver with a broad grin.

'They're a happy lot o'er here, eh?' remarked Scott as the car bumped off the ferry.

'Aye, great wee place in the summer,' replied Potts. 'I've been over a few times with my girlfriend. Gardens, white sand, a nice wee hotel – relaxing, you know.'

'You missed your vocation, son. You should've got a job wae the tourist board. Here, pull over while I try tae get a hold of Jimmy.' Scott retrieved the mobile from his jacket pocket and was pleased to see that he now had a strong signal.

He scrolled down to Daley's name and pressed it. The phone rang out.

The mobile number you have called is temporarily unavailable. Please try again later.

'You're like ships in the night, gaffer,' said Potts.

'Is that all you think aboot doon here? Boats? Right, let's find this farmhouse and this McAuley bloke. Special constable, yeah?'

'Aye, amongst other things.'

'What other things?'

'Och, you'll see.'

4

Daley wound down the window and gulped mouthfuls of fresh air. In two hours or so, he'd be back in Kinloch. Once again he'd have to wander the corridors of the police office, where all he could do was hear her, see her and smell her. He saw her shy smile, her smoothing out of imaginary creases in her skirt, her cornflower-blue eyes. He hadn't had the courage to do what he'd wanted to do – to turn the steering wheel and plummet into oblivion. He knew that he never would. He was marooned in this existence – this limbo – until he died by other means.

Thoughts of his son brought hot tears to his eyes. Would he too be plagued by the melancholy that so tormented his father?

Reluctantly, he started the car and pointed it in the direction of Kinloch.

'That'll be three sixty, Tommy,' said the shopkeeper. He held out his right hand for the money, while with his left he pressed buttons on the ancient till. 'You have a good day, now, and we'll see you tomorrow.' The customer shuffled past the men in suits who had been standing behind him. 'No need to ask who you are, gentlemen,' observed the shopkeeper, carefully rearranging a few strands of hair over his balding head.

'I'm DS Scott and this is DC Potts, Mr McAuley.'

'Please, Sergeant, Constable McAuley, if you don't mind. You're now talking to me in my official capacity as a special.'

'A man o' many jobs, I see.'

'Och, just the ones nobody else wants to do. I run the shop and the post office here, which of course makes me the island's postman. I'm retained by the police and the fire brigade, too.'

'Busy man.'

'And the water board. Oh, and the Met Office as well. You'll quite often hear my reports if you listen to the shipping forecast on the radio. A vital function for those at sea.'

'Aye, well, I know all aboot that,' said Scott. 'We'll need you tae take us tae this farm, if you would. You can fill us in on the way there. We'll take oor car. Are you ready?'

'I'll just be a few moments. I'll have to get the wife to come and man the shop.' With that, he disappeared through a door at the back of the shop, calling for his wife.

'What does everyone else dae for a job here? Your man seems tae have everything sewn up.'

'Mainly fishing and farming,' replied Potts. 'Though there's a fish farm at the south end of the island that employs half a dozen or so. Then there's the hotel, and the gardens. Great place for a wander in the summer.'

'Righto, Alan Whicker. Save it for the tourists.'

'Who's Alan Whicker?'

'Dae they no' have tellies where you come fae, son?'

'Aye, but maybe not the black-and-white ones you're used to, gaffer.'

Before Scott could reply, a thin-faced diminutive woman appeared behind the counter. Her short bobbed hair was steel-grey and she bore a strained expression. 'Himself will be with you directly,' she said in a sing-song Highland accent. 'He's just getting his stab-proof vest on.'

'His what?' asked Scott.

'When he's on duty he never goes anywhere without it on. Dreadful things happen to policemen these days. Besides, it's Force Standing Orders.'

'You'll likely know mair aboot Force Standing Orders than me,' muttered Scott, watching the woman open the till and count what looked like meagre morning takings.

'Right, Sergeant.' Malcolm McAuley appeared from behind the door, in full uniform, complete with the afore-mentioned stab-proof vest and a fluorescent jacket, with POLICE emblazoned across it in a blue-and-white flash. 'I'm good to go. I'll be back when I'm back, Jean. You know what the job's like,' he continued, as though he was a dyed-in-the-wool beat cop from Glasgow.

'Right, RoboCop,' said Scott, stifling a smile. 'Let's get up tae this farm, and hope that there's somebody at hame and this is all just a wild goose hunt.'

'Chase, Sergeant,' remarked DC Potts.

'If there's any chasing tae be done, that's your job, son. Let's get going. I hope you don't get a rush of customers, Mrs McAuley.' Scott opened the front door of the shop and headed for the unmarked police car.

'You be careful, Malcolm,' said Mrs McAuley, biting her lip. 'I hate seeing you as the thin blue line.'

'Yellow line, d'you not mean,' said Potts cheekily. 'Don't

23

worry, we'll get him back home safe and sound. Come on, Constable McAuley.'

'Have you got your pepper spray?' shouted Mrs McAuley, but it was too late. She watched as her husband got into the car, almost knocking his hat off in the process.

From the village, which was situated in the middle of the island, they turned right, heading roughly north. The road was single-track, and they were frequently forced to slow down behind sheep taking a leisurely stroll along the route.

'Right, gie us the background on these Bremners,' said Scott to McAuley, using their slow progress to learn something more of the missing family.

'Well respected on the island, Sergeant. Old Mr Bremner and his wife arrived just after the beginning the war, as you maybe know. They're Jews. Managed to escape the Nazis in the nick of time. Their son, Randolph, came over a wee bit later. He must have been a tiny baby when his mother and father made it out of Germany. A dangerous journey, I dare say. They left him with a family friend who passed him off as her own and got him to the island. Easier, I suppose, though I still don't know how they made it in those dark days.' He sighed.

'That's a long time ago. Who's still alive?' Scott was more interested to discover who was missing than in having a history lesson.

McAuley, though, was undaunted. He drew in a deep breath. 'Oh, old Mr Bremner died in the eighties, but Jan, his wife, is still alive. Nearly a hundred, you know. Randolph, the son, shares the house with her. Always been a bit of an oddball. He was educated on the island by a private tutor

– another German, though I don't know much about him. Randolph went back to Germany in the late fifties. To rescue his parents' fortune, so they said. Anyhow, he came back a couple of years later with a German wife and stayed put after that. He and his father didn't get on – that was plain.'

'What about his wife?'

'Lovely woman, by all accounts. Died in her forties. Cancer, I think. I barely remember her. She was Dougie's mother.'

'Who the hell is Dougie?'

'Well, Gunther is his real name, but he always hated it. He asked us all to call him Dougie, and Dougie he's been ever since. He's just like one of us; likes a pint and manages the farming and lobster creels. He and his wife live in the bungalow across the field from Achnamara. He runs the farm now. Randolph used to, but not very well. Made a hash of it when the old boy died. His idea of farming is bees. Been stung a couple of times by them in the course of my duties.'

'Right, we've got this Randolph and his mother. He was born sometime around the beginning of the war. His mother, who's a kick in the arse aff a birthday card fae the Queen, and then there's this Dougie and his wife. Is that it?'

'Yes . . . well, no, actually.'

'Make up your bloody mind,' said Scott as they ground to a halt, this time behind a queue of cows who were crossing the road.

'They have a son, Alex. He'd be in his twenties now, I think. He's not on the island. Never liked it here. After primary school on Gairsay he went to some private place near Glasgow. Another case of father and son not seeing eye to eye. A cruel boy, bullied other kids when he was young.

Cheeky in the shop when he came back for holidays – arrogant, you know?'

'Where's he now?'

'Now, that's an interesting question. Last I heard, he was at Glasgow Uni, but then he decided he wanted to go to Europe, so he moved elsewhere to complete his studies. Another one who didn't like his name.'

'What's he called?'

'An odd one – foreign – sounds like Alice?'.

'Alice? Are you sure?'

'Well, something like that. Anyhow, I've not seen him for a few years, though there's the odd postcard from him. I recognise his handwriting. You have to be vigilant in this job, Sergeant Scott.'

'Aye, right,' said Scott, raising one eyebrow. 'So, basically, we have four missing persons in total?'

'Yes. Jan and Randoph from the farm itself, and Dougie and Eva from the bungalow.'

Soon, the three conical mountains that were the Paps of Jura soared hazily out of the blue. They passed by some small steadings and a couple of cottages before the road turned up a small hill, and McAuley told Scott to take the first left onto a farm track leading to Achnamara.

Gulls squawked overhead as the occupants of the car alighted in front of the farmhouse. Scott took in the scene, noting with dismay that there still seemed to be no sign of life.

'So, what time did you get here, Mr ... Constable McAuley?' he asked, deciding to humour their local guide.

'Now, let me see,' replied the special constable, fishing a notebook from the pocket of his fluorescent jacket. 'Just to let you know, I didn't make these notes at the time. Well, for a start, I was in my postman's uniform, so it wasn't appropriate. But I jotted what I found in my official notebook as soon as I got back home – after I'd called Kinloch Police Station, of course.' He flicked through the pages slowly, making Scott sigh, until he stopped and, with a note of triumph in his voice, announced that he'd visited Achnamara at about 07:35 hours. 'I then proceeded to knock on the door. When there was no reply, I took it upon myself – observing the custom of the island, mark you – to open the door, shouting to see if anyone was home.'

'And there wasn't,' said Scott, anxious to hurry things along.

'Wait now, Sergeant.' McAuley cleared his throat, again consulting his notebook. 'First off, I turned left into the hall, then—'

'Okay, we get the drift. Tae cut a long story short, there was naebody aboot, right?'

'Yes, that's correct,' replied McAuley, clearly disappointed that he'd not been able to take this rare opportunity to disclose the full set of notes he had meticulously written earlier.

'Did you move anything?' asked DC Potts.

'Well, I took a burning pot of milk off the stove and uprighted a chair. But apart from that, I just left everything the way it was.'

'Let's take a look,' said Scott, turning the brass door handle and entering the hallway.

'How long do you intend to stay, Mr Feldstein?' enquired the plump woman behind the reception desk of the Gairsay Hotel.

'I'd prefer to leave that open. I'm here researching a book and I'm not sure how long the work will take.' The man spoke with an ostensibly American accent that overlaid a slight, but distinctively foreign, inflection. 'I'm willing to pay extra, of course.'

'Oh, that won't be necessary. We've just opened for the season. It's a quiet time of year. Gets much busier come late May and June when the gardens are at their best.' She paused. 'A writer, did you say? How interesting.'

'Not that interesting, I'm afraid. Just boring old history. But it's a living,' replied Feldstein. 'I'll give you my credit card details, then if you could show me to my room? I've had a long journey.'

'Of course, Mr Feldstein.' The receptionist took her new guest's details, then led him through a door and up a flight of carpeted stairs and along a corridor. She stopped at room nine, opened it with a key on a long wooden tab, and handed it to her new guest. 'This is one of our nicest rooms. There's a great view across the bay towards Kintyre. The phone's there on your bedside table, so just call reception if you need anything. Breakfast is between seven and nine, served in the dining room across from reception, and we do lunch and dinner if you book ahead.'

'Thank you,' he said, flashing the woman a smile as she left. It swiftly faded to a blank expression as he flung a large case onto the bed and unzipped it. He removed some clothes and hung them in the wardrobe. When the case appeared to be empty, he pushed a tiny lever on its side, revealing a false bottom which he pulled free from the case. A small handgun and a box of ammunition were strapped to the inside. He pulled the tape away roughly and cocked the weapon, checking and rechecking it, before loading it and tucking it into the waistband of his trousers. He taped the ammunition box into the case, before reassembling it and stowing it in the wardrobe.

He sighed as he looked out of the window. Under a grey sky, the sea looked dark and restless. A small boat with two fishermen aboard was puttering slowly across the bay. Seabirds were swooping and diving on the breeze. He stood for a few minutes, seemingly transfixed by the scene, then took the smartphone from his pocket.

'I'm here. Now what?' He listened to the voice on the other end before hanging up without a word.

It didn't take long to ascertain that the Bremner family hadn't returned to Achnamara. Scott opened a drawer in an old oak sideboard in the lounge. He found a well-thumbed address book and handed it to Potts.

'Lots of addresses of folk on the mainland, and abroad, Sergeant.'

'Well, use your initiative, son. I'm sure the Bremners had plenty of friends on the island. We can contact them easily. We want tae find oot where this Alex bugger is – the boy needs tae know his family have been beamed up. He might even know something aboot it. So, look for his address. And we'll need tae find out who was the last person tae see them. Have you any idea?' He glanced at McAuley.

'Well, I was here two days ago with another parcel. But Dougie usually enjoys a pint or two in the local hotel most evenings. I can check if he was there last night.'

'Don't you enjoy a drink or two yourself?' asked Scott.

'Och, no. By the time my working day's finished, I just relax in front of the telly for a couple of hours.'

'Unless there's a fire, or you've got tae arrest someone, eh?'

'We have little crime here, Sergeant Scott. Some of the young folk get a bit rowdy at the weekends, but it's mainly good-natured stuff.'

'So the stab-proof vest stays in the wardrobe?'

'I like to get out on a Friday night and let folk see the uniform. A reassuring presence, don't you think?'

'I'm sure everyone sleeps like babies here, knowing you've got their backs,' said Scott, seemingly without a hint of sarcasm.

Without warning, there was a loud crack like a firework or the discharge of a rifle. Scott could smell cordite on the air.

'It came from out in the hall,' whispered Potts, crouched behind a leather sofa.

'Was it a gun? It sounded like one.' Scott was almost rooted to the spot. It wasn't that long since he'd been the victim of a shooting, and the memory of it was sharp enough to make his mouth dry.

'Look!' McAuley was pointing out into the hallway, from where issued a thick pall of blue smoke.

Scott rushed out of the lounge. The smoke was coming from under a door on the opposite side of the hall. 'What room's that?'

'It's just a cupboard, I think,' replied McAuley.

Scott ran into the kitchen, Potts at his back. 'We'll need tae get water, son.'

'Here,' replied Potts, pulling a blue plastic bucket from under the sink and handing it to his superior.

Scott banged the receptacle into the deep sink and filled it with cold water. When it was about three-quarters full, he heaved it back out, slopping water on himself and the floor. 'You get the door handle, son. Quick!'

Potts tugged at the brass handle on the cupboard door, but it wouldn't budge.

'There's a key in the lock!' shouted McAuley.

Potts turned the key and pulled the door open. A cloud of acrid smoke billowed out of the cupboard, causing Potts to cough and splutter.

Scott pushed past him with the bucket and poured the water onto the floor, from where the smoke was now coming. 'Quick, get me more water! We need tae get this pit oot.'

McAuley found a large cooking pot after the young detective had refilled the bucket and raced back to Scott with it. After a few trips, the smoke began to peter out. Scott poured another bucketful over it for good measure, then stood back, coughing and choking, his trousers soaked and his face blackened with soot.

'What the hell was that?'

Potts edged into the cupboard, his feet squelching on the wet carpet. He took a flashlight from his pocket and directed its beam to the floor. 'Looks like a hatch, Sergeant. A cellar, maybe?'

Scott looked at McAuley, who was looking in dismay at his sodden trousers. 'You know anything about a cellar here?'

'No. I've never seen it before.'

Scott peered at the floor of the empty cupboard, still illuminated by Potts's torch. 'Right enough, there's some kind of hatch here.' He poked tentatively at the floor with his left shoe, then squatted over the hatch and grasped a brass handle.

'If this is the door tae the cellar, we better take a look. The family might be down there.'

'Shouldn't we wait for the emergency services?' said McAuley, his voice wavering.

'We are the emergency services,' replied Scott. 'From now on, you can be the fireman.'

McAuley shook his head for a few moments, then looked despairingly at the detective. 'But . . . I don't have the right uniform on.'

5

With a feeling of dread, Daley pulled into the car park behind Kinloch Police Office. He let the engine idle and closed his eyes. He took deep breaths, trying to calm himself and muster the strength to go into the office.

It was mid afternoon now. His journey to the town had been spent in total silence. He could no longer bear listening to the radio as he drove. Silly pop songs got on his nerves, classical music was too melancholy, and he couldn't concentrate on chattering voices. He'd spent two hours with his own thoughts; they hadn't made for good company.

He jumped when someone knocked on the window by his side. Daley pressed a button on the door and the window wound itself down.

'Sorry to disturb you, sir. I saw you parking up on the CCTV,' said Sergeant Shaw.

'What's the hurry?'

'It's DS Scott, sir. We have a bit of a situation on Gairsay. Chief Superintendent's been looking for you.'

'Gairsay? What's Brian doing over there?'

'I'll brief you on the way in, sir.'

Daley followed Shaw into the office. By the time he was

sitting behind his desk in the familiar glass box, he had a rough outline of what was happening on the tiny island.

The phone on his desk rang.

'Chief Superintendent for you, sir.'

Daley took the call.

Symington listened, her eyebrows arched in surprise. 'Not to stop you, Jim – I know you're fresh to this yourself – but to recap: basically, a whole family were reported missing on Gairsay early this morning, and DS Scott went to investigate. Am I right?'

'Yes, ma'am.'

'Since then, they've had to put out a fire and they've discovered something untoward in a cellar. Not this family, I hope.'

'No, ma'am. DS Scott has just called for the assistance of the Bomb Squad. Apparently the door to the cellar was booby-trapped in some way.'

'Is everyone okay?'

'Fine, though no sign of the Bremner family. DS Scott is there with DC Potts and the island's special constable. The Bomb Squad are making their way from Glasgow in a helicopter as we speak.'

'Tell Scott I don't want him taking any risks.'

'I haven't spoken to him directly yet, ma'am. My understanding is that everything has been secured now, and the squad are merely a precaution. But something's up, ma'am.'

'Please, Jim, it's Carrie. We agreed, didn't we?'

'Yes, Carrie, we did. I'm just about to call Brian now. As soon as I have an updated sitrep from him, I'll call you back.'

She hung up. Daley still sounded flat, exhausted, haunted by recent events. Had it been any other officer, she would have insisted that he take proper leave. However, she knew he was on his own now, his private life a mess. Only the discipline of the job was keeping him going.

She knew that feeling – knew all about loneliness.

She picked up the phone again. 'Get me a car and a driver. I'm going to Kinloch.'

Feldstein had borrowed a bicycle from the hotel. He now stood on top of the highest hill on Gairsay, which conveniently overlooked Achnamara. He folded the map and returned it to his backpack. Using his expensive Swarovski binoculars, he peered at the farm, assessing all the activity that now surrounded it.

He'd seen the blue helicopter flying low over the island from his hotel room. Deciding to tap into local gossip, he'd spent half an hour in the hotel's tiny bar. Apart from wild speculation about the disappearence of the Bremners – something he already knew – he gleaned little new information. A drunken old woman had persistently tried to engage him in conversation, but the barmaid had managed to stop her from annoying him. Soon realising he'd discover very little within the cramped confines of the public bar, he decided to take to the hill.

He scanned the sea surrounding Gairsay. He could see the white sails of a yacht as it glided across the grey waves in the distance, most likely heading for the isle of Islay. The day had brightened slightly, and the dim disc of the sun could be seen through light cloud. It wasn't warm though, and he was glad he'd decided to wear a thick polo-neck under his Barbour jacket.

The phone in his pocket rang.

'Yes,' he said curtly.

'The farmhouse, what is the situation?' The voice on the other end was deep, with a similar accent to his own.

'The Bomb Squad are at Achnamara now. The property is still intact.'

'That is good news. I'm surprised that you're not looking at a pile of smouldering ruins by now.'

'We've been betrayed.'

There was a long pause on the other end of the line before he received a reply. 'Maybe. Maybe it was just luck.'

'How could it be luck? Only you and I knew that I'd be here today. You, me and Berkovic. One of us is a traitor.'

'Do you know what you're saying? This organisation has been working for the last seventy years to shed light on this. Why would there be this problem now?'

'You tell me,' Feldstein replied flatly. 'We won't make any progress here until after dark.'

'You'll have to be careful. Remember, you're in the UK, not some corrupt South American republic or festering Arab cesspool.'

'I know where I am. You concentrate on your responsibilities. Find out who has betrayed us and eliminate them.' He hung up.

He counted three policemen in uniform now. He focused the binoculars on the front door of the property. A man with short dark hair, wearing a suit, was smoking a cigarette and talking on his mobile. He studied the man for a few moments, turned, and began to make his way back down the hill.

He would need to get some sleep. It promised to be a very long night.

*

'The boys fae the squad reckon it was an incendiary charge, Jimmy. They're just making a last sweep, then I'll be able tae get in there and have a look.'

'Good. Why on earth would someone rig such a thing to their cellar?'

'Your guess is as good as mine, big man. I'm sure we'll find oot mair when I manage tae get in there.'

'Just you and Potts. Leave McAuley where he is. We don't want the whole island talking about this. Symington's on her way. I'm meeting her at the ferry.'

'This place is full of surprises, Jimmy. I'll see you when you get here.' Scott ended the call and breathed in the salty air. He heard footsteps and turned round.

'All clear, Sergeant Scott,' said Watts, the head of the Bomb Squad. 'You're in for a treat down in the cellar.'

'How so?'

'I'll not spoil the surprise, but it's like stepping back in time.'

Scott followed Watts back into the farmhouse, where three members of the Bomb Squad, all in protective gear, were packing away their equipment.

'We've swept the rest of the house. No more nasties to report,' said Watts. 'We're off to take a look at the bungalow nearby. Here, this is what caused your problem.' He handed Scott a small, blackened box, from which wires extruded, their plastic coating melted to reveal the copper wire underneath.

'Oh aye. I'm sad tae say my knowledge o' this kind o' stuff is very limited, my friend. Tae be blunt: what the fuck is it?'

'It's an incendiary timer – a bloody old one, at that. Probably made sometime in the thirties.'

'So it didn't work very well?'

'Luckily for you, no, it didn't. The charge was probably damp. It would have sparked off more spectacularly if you hadn't doused it in water.'

'No' just a pretty face, eh?'

'Indeed,' replied Watts with a smile. 'Oh, one more thing. It's German.'

'What is?'

'The timer. I'll have to take it back and consult the books, but I think it's an old Wehrmacht device.'

'What's this, the bloody Eagle Has Landed?'

'In your case, more like the pigeon, eh? It all fits, I suppose.'

'Fits how?'

'Wait till you get into the cellar, then you'll see what I mean.' Watts walked off, leaving Scott puzzled.

'What now? Are we going down there, Sergeant Scott?' asked McAuley.

'Time you got back tae your shop, Constable McAuley. We'll take things fae here. Thanks for your help.'

'Oh, I see. I was kind of hoping I'd get to go down to the cellar. The bomb boys tell me it's interesting.'

'I'll let you know what it's all aboot,' said Scott. 'Mind now, this is police business, keep it to yourself.'

'I think you'll find I'm professional in all things, Sergeant.'

'You've got a lot o' things tae be professional aboot.'

'I hope they're okay – the Bremners, I mean. I've known them all my life.' He walked away, his fluorescent jacket, blackened in places by soot, vivid against the dim sky.

Scott loped up the front steps, back into the farmhouse. 'Right, DC Potts, let's get doon there.'

With Potts behind Scott, both holding torches, the detectives descended a short metal ladder that led from the open hatch down into the cellar. Though the ceiling was low – there was just enough room to stand up – Scott was surprised by the extent of the space he was now in. It was clear that the cellar ran the full length of the house, with various nooks and crannies.

To his right sat a Chesterfield-style couch, its burgundy leather worn to bright pink in places. Facing it was a wooden bureau, of the type his granny might have given pride of place to in her best room. An anglepoise lamp sat above a blotting sheet, beside an ink well and a selection of pens and pencils. Everything looked decades old – out of place.

'Look at this, Sergeant,' said Potts. He'd walked deeper into the cellar, and was now out of sight around a corner.

Scott followed the beam of Potts's torch. On the wall in front of them was a huge map of the world, faded and yellowed with age. Various areas had been marked with red stars and white circles. Scott ran his finger across the bottom of the map, dislodging a line of thick greasy dust.

'Dae you notice something strange aboot this, son?'

'It all looks strange to me.'

Scott pointed the beam of his torch over the European section of the map. A huge black swastika was plastered across a large swathe of the continent.

6

Kinloch, 1945

The vessel lay on its side on the shingle of the ancient causeway. The good people of the town were well used to seeing naval craft. Since the beginning of the war, their loch had been filled with vessels of all shapes and sizes – most of them clothed in the battleship grey favoured by the Royal Navy and their allies. They had seen the population of their small town more than double; sailors, soldiers and airmen became a regular sight in the shops, pubs and hotels. The world had become a different place. Their country was locked in a life-and-death struggle against people of whom they knew little; people governed by a philosophy that seemed as at odds with the way they ran their lives as it was possible to be. The locals could still remember stories of the blood, gore and filth of the trenches. To those who had been caught up in it, it seemed such a short time ago. To those who followed events in the newspapers and hung on the words of those who returned, it had been a conflict fought at a remove. This war, however, was more personal to those who hadn't signed up. In years gone by, soldiers trooped off on trains and ships to another land to take on an enemy. In the last few years, the enemy had come to them.

Every man, woman and child on the causeway watched the sailors in silence as they clambered warily onto this strange vessel, now almost completely above the waves, with only the tapered beam partially covered by the grey water of the loch. The crowd stared as two seamen took the ladder up the conning tower and disappeared into the body of the craft.

One small boy turned to his father. 'Whoot's that black cross a' aboot, Faither?'

His father sucked on his pipe before answering. 'It's a German submarine, son, a U-boat.'

The boy bit his lip for a few moments, his eyes searching along the superstructure of the vessel. 'Should we no' run away? Whoot if they Germans come oot and start shooting?'

'Their shooting days are o'er, son,' replied his father pragmatically. 'There's no man left alive on that boat.'

'How dae you know?'

'How long have I been at the fishing for?'

'For ever?'

'Aye, it seems like that sometimes.' He nodded, tapping the used tobacco from his pipe with the palm of his hand. 'Mind whoot happened to your uncle Billy?'

'He drooned.'

'Aye, he did that, son.'

'My auntie Sheena was greetin' for weeks.'

His father turned away from his son, blinking away tears at the memory of his drowned brother. 'She did, aye. So did we all.' He looked down at the boy, ruffled his hair with his big, calloused hand. 'The men aboard that boat are drooned, tae. Like your uncle Billy.'

The boy looked, wide-eyed, at his father, just as a burst of laughter came from a group of young men standing a few yards away. 'How come there's naebody greetin' jeest noo?'

'These men were Germans, son. The enemy.'

'So there's some folk we want tae droon?'

'Put it like this: if they men were still alive, they'd try and kill us. Noo that they're deid they canna dae that.'

The boy bowed his head. Before long, he started to sniff copiously, a muffled sob coming from his closed mouth.

His father knelt down and lifted the boy's chin gently with his forefinger. 'Whoot's the matter, Hamish? Why are you crying?'

'It's no' right they boys are laughing,' he sobbed. 'They men are drooned, jeest like my uncle Billy. We didna laugh when he died. We shouldna laugh at they men, neithers.'

His father looked up just in time to see one of the sailors who had disappeared into the U-boat poke his head over the conning tower and wave frantically. Soon, more sailors could be seen scrambling into the submarine.

Daley stood beside his car, hands in pockets, at the ferry terminal. In the distance, the peaks of Jura towered over Islay. Much closer, across a short stretch of water, lay Gairsay, a strip of green land with a couple of low hills and houses and farm buildings dotted about it. He watched the lazy sweep of the wind turbines for a few moments, finding it hypnotic. Gazing back at the sea, Daley could see the black-and-white ferry making its way towards the mainland, almost halfway through its journey. The weather had improved, and weak late-afternoon sunshine glinted off the water. Daley watched a crow hopping along the car park, pecking at the ground, looking for pieces of discarded food. It reminded him of his visit to Mary's grave, and he tried to force the painful memory from his mind.

The phone rang in his pocket, and, expecting it to be Scott, he answered it without looking at the screen.

'You don't deserve to see your son.' The voice was as cold as it was familiar: Liz.

'Liz, please. I've had a lot on. I'm sorry. I'll make time to see him in the next few days, I promise. We can get this sorted out.'

'Don't bother. I've been to my lawyer, and he agrees with me. We'll have to make this formal. You'll have to go to court to apply for access. It's obvious that you can't be trusted with a more informal arrangement.'

Daley paused before answering. It was as though she was a complete stranger; that nothing, no warmth or affection, had ever passed between them. He could hardly blame her, though. 'I'm sorry that things have come to this, Liz.'

'This is the last time I'll be in touch. If you have anything to say to me, I want you to do it through the lawyers. There's a letter on its way to you from mine.'

The phone went dead.

It had been short, but most definitely not sweet. He could think of a time when a phone call like that from his wife would have devastated him. Now, it only registered as a minor irritation. He missed his son, though, and felt guilty that he'd been too wrapped up with his own grief to have seen the boy. That had been thoughtless and wrong. Still, he couldn't let her dictate terms, not now. He resolved to call his own solicitor as soon as he had a moment.

He heard a car pull up behind him. Chief Superintendent Carrie Symington was sitting in the passenger seat of an unmarked police car. She waved and smiled. He watched as the driver removed her bag from the boot and, after a brief exchange, got back in the car and drove off.

'I'll go over in your car, Jim, if that's okay?' She walked over to his vehicle and waited for him to open the boot. 'I took a call on the way down the road.'

'Oh, who from?'

'The MOD, some bureaucrat called Timothy Gissing. Wants to be kept informed, if you please.'

'How do they know anything about this?'

'Your guess is as good as mine, Jim. Their involvement in anything makes me twitchy. What's this all about?'

'I don't really know. They've managed to disable some kind of booby trap in the farmhouse and now they're searching the cellar.'

Symington let Daley lift her bag into the car. 'So, not just a missing persons enquiry?'

'It would seem not, ma'am.'

She studied her colleague. He'd lost weight and looked pale and drawn. The vitality she'd first noticed in him had disappeared under the weight of grief. 'You're just back from some leave, am I right?'

'Yeah,' replied Daley with a drawn-out sigh.

'These feelings won't last for ever, Jim. I know it's hell just now, but it will get easier.'

'I'm not sure I want it to get easier, ma'am.'

'Carrie, remember.'

Daley smiled weakly. 'We better get going. Ferry's nearly here.'

7

'It's like stepping back tae the war,' said Scott, looking at a dusty typewriter. 'Reminds me of my auld granny's hoose. She never redecorated after my grandfaither got killed in a Lancaster bomber. The hoose was frozen in time. I used tae go there when I was a boy. This is just the same.'

'Some kind of hobby, do you think?' considered Potts. 'A fascination with the military?'

'Maybe, son, maybe. What's through here?' Scott turned the handle of a heavy oak door. The room was spacious, holding a pair of camp beds, two chairs and a table, and old filing cabinets. On the wall above an ancient electric fire a painting stood out in the gloom. Scott whistled through his teeth. 'If it's a hobby, it's a strange one.' The woman in the painting seemed to be staring straight at him. Whoever had painted her had been good; the piercing cold blue eyes seemed almost illuminated.

'Who's that, gaffer?'

'I've no idea, but I wouldn't like tae bump intae her on a dark night.'

'One of the family, maybe?'

Scott stared up at the painting and shivered involuntarily. 'Maybe. The painting's quite old, by the look of it.'

Scott forced his gaze away from the woman in the painting and took in the rest of the room. The cream paint on the beds was chipped, with spots of rust bubbling through. The faded striped mattresses looked thin, old and well used, with no sheets or blankets to hide their stains.

Against the far wall sat the filing cabinets, each with three deep drawers and, like the beds, dotted with rust. Scott was surprised to find the top drawer of the first cabinet he came to unlocked, so he pulled it fully open and delved inside. Under the beam of his torch, reams of yellowed paper nestled in cardboard files. He pulled one out and studied the typescript. 'We're going tae need a translator.'

'I suppose there's nothing unusual about a German family having documents in their own language,' observed Potts, peering over Scott's shoulder.

'Naw, not at all, son. But look at this.' He pulled out one sheet of paper, which crackled with age. Emblazoned at the top of the page was a black swastika contained within a white circle on a red background.

'Did McAuley not tell us that the family were Jewish?'

'Aye, he did that. Not the kind of headed notepaper you'd expect to find in the hoose o' somebody of that persuasion, would you no' say?'

As advised by Sergeant Shaw, Daley stopped off at the village shop to speak to McAuley. The special constable was standing behind the counter, now dressed in a brown hand-knitted cardigan and fawn corduroy trousers. Though he'd spoken to him by telephone in the past, it was the first time the pair had met. As they exchanged pleasantries, Daley noticed that McAuley's hands were shaking slightly. 'Did you get a bit of a fright?'

'Aye, a wee bit, sir,' confessed McAuley. 'I've been the special over here for a number of years now, and this is the first time I've felt in any kind of real danger. Your sergeant was very professional, mind. Made sure we were all safe.'

Daley pondered the professionalism of DS Brian Scott for a few heartbeats before smiling. 'He's been in the job a long time now, an old hand. Sergeant Shaw in Kinloch tells me that you knew this family reasonably well.'

'I thought I did, sir. But you know what thought did,' replied McAuley ruefully. 'Stuck a feather up its arse and thought it was a chicken, if you'll pardon the expression. I can't understand why the Bremners would rig up a device like that to their cellar – doesn't make sense.'

'This job rarely makes sense. In any case, we don't know if the family were responsible for that. Could all be something to do with why they've disappeared, but best we don't jump to any conclusions.'

'No, no, of course not. On that subject, my wife took a call when I was up at the farm with your colleagues – from a newspaper, if you please.'

Daley cursed silently. Any involvement with the press was the last thing he needed. Just after Mary's death, he'd been snapped by a photographer on his doorstep, while personal questions were fired at him by a spotty-faced journalist, anxious to know just what his relationship had been with the deceased woman. Symington had managed to suppress the story, but at the moment – like most times in his career – he wasn't particularly well disposed towards the gentlemen of the press. 'How on earth did they come by this so quickly?' he asked.

'This is a wee island, sir. I'm sure you know how quickly gossip spreads in Kinloch – well, it fair gallops on an island this size. The Bremners were well liked, but that won't stop someone trying to make a few bob with the papers.'

'No, I guess not. Could you direct me to their farm, please? I've got the chief superintendent in the car and I want to get up there and see what's what, especially now that we know the press are on their way.'

Outside the shop, McAuley watched the two police officers drive off in the direction of Achnamara. To him, Superintendent Symington looked little more than a girl, and he marvelled at the fact she was the divisional commander.

He was distracted from his ruminations when he heard footsteps from behind. A tall man of late middle age, with a deep tan and a shaven head, approached him and asked if he stocked postcards. He spoke in perfect English, with only a hint of a foreign accent.

'Now, you can rest assured that you've come to the right place for postcards,' replied McAuley.

The man followed the special constable into the shop, pausing for a moment to look around before ducking through the door.

After being shown round the cellar and examining the rest of the farmhouse, Daley, Scott and Symington stood in the yard. Scott was patting the old horse. 'We'll need tae get somebody tae look after the livestock, ma'am.'

'Yes, it's in hand. The other farmers on the island are going to take it in turns to make sure everything's in order. We'll have to secure this house overnight, until we can get more bodies over here tomorrow,' she said, looking at Daley, who appeared to be sniffing the air absently. 'Can you arrange that, DCI Daley?'

'Yes, sure,' he replied. 'DC Potts can take the first shift, then we'll work something out . . . It's one of the strangest things I've ever seen,' he said, referring to the cellar and its unusual contents. 'Once we get a translator over tomorrow, hopefully we can make more sense of it. What do you think, Brian?'

'Seems tae me there's been much mair going on here than farming. But why would a family like the Bremners have all the Nazi stuff?'

'If they are Jewish, I think it's quite obvious,' replied Symington. 'There was a lot of activity here during the war. Kinloch was a main port for the Royal Navy – handy for the Atlantic approaches and so on. Maybe the Bremners just took a keen interest in it all. A lot of exiled families did, terrified that the Nazis might win.'

'You're very well informed, ma'am,' said Daley.

'My grandfather was in the army back then – in intelligence. His stories got me hooked from a young age. Been a kind of hobby ever since. I read about it all the time.'

'Despite what we've discovered in the cellar, and the unusual circumstances, the family have to be our main priority. I've circulated their descriptions to the Royal Navy as well as all the usual suspects. Finding out what's happened to them could go a long way to explaining all of this,' said Daley.

'I agree. I want to set up a temporary incident room in the hotel. Potts has been down there sorting it all out. They have a room they can let us use, plus accommodation, phones, broadband. We'll hold the fort overnight, then get going in earnest tomorrow. Who knows, maybe the Bremners will have turned up by that time,' said Symington.

'I widnae hold my breath if I was you, ma'am. Whoever rigged that booby trap wanted tae set the whole place ablaze. If not the family, who else? If you ask me, they're off on their toes – I've seen enough moonlight flits in my time. Used tae happen in oor street near every week,' said Scott. 'We'd nowhere tae go, so when the tally man came, my mother used tae make us lie on the floor under the window until he gave up. Either that, or my faither piled him o'er a hedge.' Scott grimaced at the memory.

'Sometimes I wonder just how you ended up in the police, DS Scott,' remarked Symington with a smile.

'Aye, me tae,' he replied honestly.

The night was cold, with low cloud obscuring the heavens and a breeze that cut through DC Potts every time he set foot outside the car to check the environs of Achnamara. He had another two hours until he was relieved, which meant trudging round the property twice more to make sure everything was secure.

He turned the dial on the car radio in search of something more uplifting than a chat about economics. He settled upon a station playing hits from the eighties, drumming his fingers to a one-hit wonder.

After listening to another couple of songs, he decided it was time to brave the elements and go through the routine checks DCI Daley had outlined. *Make sure all the doors and windows are secure, and nobody is hanging about. If the press appear, refer them to me at the hotel.* He zipped up his ski jacket and left the warmth of the car.

The old mare whinnied as he flashed his torch around. A distant oystercatcher called plaintively against the backdrop of the restless ocean, which washed back and forth on the rocky beach a few hundred yards ahead, its tang ever-present.

Potts was whistling tunelessly to himself as he rounded the corner of an outbuilding to check the rear of the property. A scraping noise made him direct the beam of the torch across a paddock, where something flitted out of sight. He hurried towards a fence, leaning on it as he waved the torch about. He jumped when the eyes of a sheep reflected the light, then smiled at his racing heart.

As he turned, a blow caught him full in the face, sending him crashing to the ground. The torch spun through the air and landed with a crunch on the stony ground, shattering the tiny bulb and returning the farmyard to darkness.

Daley lay in his hotel bedroom in the dark, staring at the ceiling. He'd passed a pleasant enough evening with Symington and Scott. First, dinner, with a delicious turbot that he had enjoyed as much as anything he'd eaten in months, then a few drinks in the cosy bar. With Scott drinking orange juice and Symington on soda water and lime, he'd felt awkward drinking alcohol, but had had three pints nonetheless, in the hope that they would help him sleep. They hadn't.

The few locals who populated the bar were inquisitive, but not obtrusively so; just asking politely about the Bremners and if there was any word from them. When the police officers answered in the negative, heads shook; the islanders appeared to be as mystified by the disappearance of the family as those investigating it.

Only one wizened old woman, three sheets to the wind, caused a scene, screaming unintelligibly at no one in particular. She was soon dealt with by the bar staff, who spirited her away, back to her home in the hills above the village, much to everyone's relief. From what the detectives could understand, it seemed she was no friend of the Bremners.

Daley switched on his bedside light, looked at the time, and considered picking up the paperback he had found on a bookshelf in the hotel lounge. He read a few pages before trying to sleep, but the book – about a divorcee who fled her mundane existence to make a new life on another continent – failed to capture his imagination, and he gave up after the first chapter.

This, now, was the pattern of Daley's life: an hour-by-hour struggle to sleep, to soothe his mind, to distract it from the grief, guilt and sadness. It felt like a wall of insurmountable difficulty, stretching as high as the eye could see.

Initially, he'd regretted his promise to Mary about staying in his job. Now, though, he wondered just how he would have coped in the months since her death without the daily grind of police work to occupy him.

He eased himself out of bed, his back stiff from lying on a new mattress and the twinge in his right knee a testament to middle age, and switched on the kettle.

As the water boiled, he looked at his watch – just after 3 a.m. He decided to have a strong coffee and then head over to Achnamara to relieve DC Potts earlier than planned. At least one of them might be able to get to bed and get some rest.

Before long, he was padding downstairs in the silent hotel. He unbolted the front door and made his way to his car, shivering as he crossed the road. Turning the heater on full, he turned away from the sea and towards Achnamara farm.

It took Feldstein seconds to drag the unconscious body of DC Potts behind a barn. He held a chloroform-soaked cloth against his mouth for a few moments, making sure he'd remain unconscious while he entered the farmhouse. He'd been surprised at how lax the police officers in the hotel had been, talking openly about their plans to watch the Bremners' property overnight. He had plenty of time to do what he had to do.

He took out a large jemmy from his backpack and went to work on the front door. In a few moments, it splintered open. He caught a whiff of the smoke from the bomb as he moved down the hall. Soon, he was descending the stairs to the cellar.

Daley saw Potts's empty car as he drove into the farmyard. Assuming his DC was busy checking the property as instructed, he made his way around the corner of the house, cursing the fact that he'd left his torch in the hotel. He called out to Potts, waiting for a reply that didn't come.

As he fumbled along the rear of the house, his foot caught on something bulky. He cursed loudly as he landed heavily on his knees, wincing as he tried to pull himself back to his feet.

He could smell something – a chemical smell. He was surprised when he heard a groan coming from the object he'd tripped over. He edged towards the noise and leaned down. 'Potts, is that you?'

The reply was indistinct, but he could discern the strong odour of chloroform now. In the darkness, knee twinging painfully, he dragged Potts back around the building to his car. As he struggled to get the young DC out of the cold, he picked up the mobile phone lying on the dashboard. He listened for a few moments before a familiar tired voice answered the call.

'Brian, get yourself up to the Bremner farm now! We've got a situation.'

Before Scott could reply, Daley hung up and, using the torch on his phone, looked around. The farmhouse door was ajar, the shattered lock visible.

Daley took a deep breath, then, as silently as he could, made his way up the front steps. Even with the little torch on his phone, it took him a few moments to become accustomed to the gloomy interior of the farmhouse. He stopped in the hall for a few moments and listened. There was definitely movement, muffled footsteps, the sound of something being dragged across a floor. It was hard to pinpoint from exactly where the sound was coming, until he noticed a sliver of light from under the door in the hall. Someone was in the basement.

Scott yawned as the car engine spluttered into life. 'The bloody press – any bets,' he muttered under his breath as he pulled away from the Gairsay Hotel.

He had been irritated by the brevity of Daley's call, but not surprised. His old friend still wasn't himself. It was as though he was on automatic pilot, just going through the motions at work, keeping going. He'd noticed that Daley was drinking more heavily then he'd ever seen him, but he had no right to comment. Besides, in all the years he'd known the man, he'd rarely seen him the worse for booze. He supposed that it took a lot to intoxicate someone with a frame like Daley's. He thought back to his own battle with the bottle: the blackouts, the pounding head, the upset stomach, the feeling that the world was about to collapse around him. Yet he still missed a drink.

He accelerated up the single-track road to Achnamara.

8

Kinloch, 1945

Inspector Urquhart stared at the slender youth, who was standing alongside his rotund father, turning a Homburg hat over nervously in his pale hands.

'I take it that you've heard from Chief Constable Mathieson, Inspector Urquhart?'

'Yes, I have.'

'Well, glad to hear it.' Retired procurator fiscal Thomson McColl ignored the curtness of the inspector's reply. 'I'm sure that my son here will prove to be a fine asset. You want to do your bit, don't you, Torquil?' he said, nudging his son with his elbow.

'Y-yes, y-yes, of course,' came the stammered response.

'Why didn't you join the army or navy to do your bit like the rest of the lads your age?' asked Urquhart, pointedly addressing the son rather than the father.

'He is prone to headaches, Inspector, migraines, in fact. The admission board felt—'

'Are you a coward, Torquil?' Urquhart didn't give McColl time to finish his sentence.

'That's an outrageous accusation, Inspector!' Thomson McColl's face turned crimson, a thick vein pulsing in his temple.

'Answer the question, boy,' said Urquhart, again ignoring the lad's father.

'No, of course not,' mumbled Torquil.

'I can't hear you,' said Urquhart.

'N-no. I'm n-not a coward,' stammered Torquil, his voice thin and cracking.

'Rest assured, Inspector Urquhart, the chief constable will hear about this. You shall not insult my family. I don't care how many medals you can pin to your chest.'

'You may leave now, Mr McColl. Your son can stay here. I'll let you know my decision in due course.'

'*Your* decision! The decision has been made, Inspector, I can assure you of that.'

'Please, F-father. I-I'm a m-man now. I can stand up for myself.' Torquil clenched his fists, crushing his hat further.

There followed a heavy silence. McColl, still red-faced, stared at his son, mouthing words that refused to form sounds, while Urquhart casually signed a document on his desk with a flourish of his fountain pen. He looked up, gazing between father and son.

'Well, I think you should do as your son asks, Mr McColl. I'm not too old to forget my father telling me that I should stand on my own two feet. I think it's time you let your son stand on his, don't you?'

McColl, puffing heavily, shook his head at the inspector, nodded peremptorily to his son, turned on his heel in military fashion, then left the office, slamming the door behind him.

'I'm s-so s-sorry. M-my father is used to getting his own way.'

'High time he learned some manners, then.' Urquhart put down his pen and massaged his temple wearily. 'I don't like being told what to do when it comes to my job, Torquil. Not by your father, the chief constable, anyone.' He stood up, a solid broad-shouldered presence behind his desk. 'But you can hardly be held responsible for the actions of those who should know better. I have a simple rule, though.'

'Y-yes, sir.'

'Do what I tell you, no matter the circumstances. Do you understand?'

'Y-yes. Absolutely.' Torquil gave the detective a weak smile.

'Absolutely, *sir*. I'll give you a fortnight to prove your worth. If you can, well, then we'll see if we can turn you into a police officer. If not, I don't care who your father thinks he is, or what favours he asks of his friends. You will have no future in the job. Do you understand me?'

'Y-yes, sir,' replied Torquil in the strongest voice he could muster.

'And another thing – stop bloody stammering!'

Taking care to do so as quietly as possible, Daley lifted the hatch and made his way tentatively into the cellar, pausing only when one step creaked under his weight. When the sounds from below continued, undisturbed by his footfall, he carried on until he reached the bottom, where he paused, heart thudding.

The immediate area was empty, so he followed the pale light further into the cellar, trying to recall the layout he'd seen only a few hours before.

The door to the room with the beds and the filing cabinets lay open, but the movement – a shuffling noise, like something heavy being dragged across the floor – ceased. Daley stopped dead, hardly breathing in case whoever was in the cellar heard him.

Silence. He could see that one of the filing cabinets had been dragged into the middle of the floor. An open drawer revealed a rank of yellowed files, each marked in neat, faded German handwriting. The door to the next room – a small kitchenette, as far as he could remember – lay wide open, though no light issued from within. Assuming whoever was in the cellar must be in this room, he tiptoed towards it, pausing just behind the doorframe to listen for signs of life.

'Don't move.' The voice was deep and authoritative. 'Turn around slowly.'

Daley did as he was told. The man facing him was older than himself, muscular with close-cropped hair. He was holding a pistol, which was now pointed at the detective.

'I was hoping you would arrive,' he said casually. 'It makes things easier. Of course, I'm sure your colleagues won't be far behind, so we don't have much time.' The man's accent was hard to place, but he spoke clearly and with precision.

'My detective sergeant is on his way. Whatever you think you'll achieve here, let me assure you, you won't. Please put down the gun.'

'You should have been more careful, checked behind the filing cabinet. A rudimentary error, if you don't mind my saying.'

Daley didn't reply, but knew he should have made sure the room was empty before pursuing his quarry into the next. He wasn't thinking properly. He had to get his head straight. 'Just put down the gun,' he said eventually, with more confidence than he felt.

To his surprise, the man laid the pistol on top of the filing cabinet and picked up something else as he did so. 'Take this, and take my advice. Keep it to yourself, or soon it will be removed from your possession. Read it and understand it. It is the key to what happened here.' He handed Daley a leather-bound notebook. The cover felt rough and brittle with age. 'What do you mean, keep it to myself? I'm a police officer, and this is evidence.'

'I know who you are, DCI Daley. And, as I said, in a way, I'm pleased you have stumbled into this on your own. Otherwise, we would have had to work out a way of getting this to you without raising suspicion. From what I know of you, you are a straight, determined man – much like the person who wrote this.' He gestured towards the notebook and moved closer.

Suddenly, Daley realised that he'd seen the man before – briefly, in the hotel bar. 'You are under arrest, Mr . . .'

The man smiled. 'My name is Feldstein, and you may place me under arrest if you wish. But I can assure you that it will be short-lived.'

'I'll leave that for the procurator fiscal to decide,' replied Daley, suddenly aware of a commotion coming from the ground floor.

'Your colleague has arrived. Sergeant Scott, I think I'm right in saying?'

Daley's brow furrowed. 'How are you so well informed, Mr Feldstein?'

'Being well informed has been my business for very many years, Mr Daley. Far too many, in fact.'

'Jimmy, are you doon there?' Both men raised their eyes to the ceiling at the sound of the call. Scott's footsteps above sounded deafening in the low-roofed cellar.

'Your colleague has a less subtle approach, no?' Feldstein smiled.

'You could say that.'

'If you are not accustomed to listening to advice, DCI Daley, I urge you to listen to mine. Take this journal and keep it safe. You will learn much. Make it subject to your evidence protocols and it will be spirited away, and what happened here, and in many other places, will remain hidden for longer than it has been already. And let me assure you, what happened here is not just dusty old history.' He held up the journal. 'I was lucky to find it so quickly, but I don't suppose Bremer ever thought we'd get this close.'

'Don't you mean Bremner?'

'I meant what I said.'

Scott burst into the room, an extendable baton clutched in his right hand. 'What the fuck's going on? Is this the bastard that did for DC Potts? He's up there in the motor, spark oot.'

'It's okay, Brian. Please place Mr Feldstein under arrest. Attempted theft by OLP should be an adequate charge for now,' said Daley.

'Come here, you big bugger,' shouted Scott, grabbing Feldstein and handcuffing him in one smooth, well-practised movement. 'Here, there's a shooter on top o' that filing cabinet!'

'Remember what I said, Mr Daley.' Feldstein smiled as Scott pulled him roughly out of the room and upstairs.

Daley fanned the pages of the journal in his hand. Tiny spidery writing, in faded fountain-pen ink, neatly covered the pages, so tightly spaced it was hard to decipher. He closed the journal, and followed Scott and his prisoner out of the cellar at Achnamara.

9

The mortuary was filled with bodies. Thirty, Urquhart counted. The smell was putrid, and he could hear McColl gagging. He turned to see the lad cover his mouth and nose with a freshly ironed white hanky. 'Are these the first dead bodies you've seen?'

'Y-yes, sir,' spluttered McColl. 'I-I saw my grandmother when she died, but she didn't smell like this.'

'If you make it as a police officer, rest assured you'll see the dead nearly every week. If it's any consolation, it took me time to get used to it. It's only natural.'

'Why are they that colour?' McColl was pointing at the bloated face of a man that looked distinctly green.

'Hypostasis. Caused by a mixture of asphyxiation and sea water. Though these poor souls have been dead less than two days, I reckon, the sea has still had time to do its bit.'

Urquhart lifted a white sheet that was covering a young bearded man. His naked body was a pale grey colour, making the dark hairs on his chest look black. 'This is the captain, so I'm told.'

'He's very young.'

'Mid twenties, I'd say, not much older than you. People grow up quickly in war.'

Urquhart made his way along the line of corpses, taking a brief look at each in turn. 'What do you know about U-boats, Torquil?'

'They've been sinking our ships in the Atlantic throughout the war. My father says that anyone who serves in a submarine is a brave man, though.' The expression on Urquhart's face made him stop.

'There's nothing brave about taking people's lives the way they do. Nothing brave about war, full stop. It's just a hell that everyone gets flung into – the innocent, the guilty, the brave, cowards, all alike. It makes no difference.' He paused. 'One thing is strange, though. The crew should be larger.'

'How so?'

Urquhart lifted the sheet covering the last sailor, then replaced it. 'They were in a Type Twenty-one U-boat. The usual crew would be nearly sixty men yet there are only half that number here.'

'Maybe the Germans don't have many sailors left, sir. My father says that they have children fighting for them now.'

'Yes, I'm sure that's true. For once, he seems to have the right of it.' Urquhart rubbed his chin. 'Come on. I want to see their personal effects.'

They left the mortuary, crossed a yard, and entered the main building that housed the Kinloch Cottage Hospital. A pretty nurse with dark hair, wearing a blue uniform and stiff white apron, was pushing an old man in a wooden wheelchair.

'Nurse, do you know where the possessions of the men from the U-boat have been stored?'

'I'll take you to Matron,' she replied, a smile lighting up her face. 'Are you a policeman now, Torquil?'

'S-sort of,' McColl replied. 'Well, I'm hoping to be.' His face reddened as he looked warily at Urquhart, hoping he would say nothing to add to his embarrassment.

'This way, please. She's on her rounds.' The nurse led them down a corridor and into a large men's ward. Rows of beds faced each other, a patient occupying every one. At the end of the room, Matron, resplendent in a dark blue uniform and an elaborate hat, greeted the policeman and took them to her office where she took a large bunch of keys from a drawer.

'Just their uniforms and whatever personal effects they had, I'm afraid. Anything of a sensitive nature – letters and the like – was retained by the navy.' She selected a key then took them down a long corridor to the room where the men's possessions had been stored. She switched on a light that revealed a pile of soaking sea boots, thick woollen jerseys, oilskins and caps. The stench was nearly as pronounced as it had been in the mortuary, but seemed not to bother either the matron or Urquhart.

'Here,' she said, handing the inspector a blue duffel bag. 'Everything the navy left is in this bag. Mainly rings and so on. Their identity tags have been taken away.'

Urquhart took the bag and thanked her. 'I'll ask the navy for access to the other items, though I doubt I'll get anywhere.'

A quizzical look crossed her face. 'Why should you? I would have thought this was purely a naval matter.'

Urquhart smiled pleasantly. 'I like to think that anything that happens in Kinloch or its environs is at least partially my business.'

'Well, if you're speaking to anyone in authority in the RN, please ask them if I can burn these uniforms. This is a place of healing, not a dumping ground. I really must get on with my rounds now. The doctor will be here soon, and he doesn't like to be kept waiting, especially when he's spent the morning at the golf club.' She rolled her eyes. 'Good day to you, Inspector Urquhart.'

The Ministry of Defence,
Whitehall, London, the present day

Timothy Gissing stared at the memo and sighed. He had less than a year to serve before he could retire to the little cottage in Cotswolds he and his wife had purchased just before Christmas the previous year. The communication he'd just received from his section chief was the nightmare he'd been hoping to avoid for almost every day of his thirty-year career. Ironic, he thought, that it had to happen right now, just as he was about to leave. 'One last hurrah,' he said to himself as he put the memo to one side and lifted his phone.

He hated being called into the office early, and chided the secretary for taking four rings to answer the internal call. 'Get me the ACC in charge at Police Scotland,' he ordered. 'Quickly.'

He pictured the roses that framed the front door of his cottage, and smiled wistfully. A photograph of his wife took pride of place on his desk. She still turned heads. He found it impossible to believe that the woman with whom he had shared so much of his life was now in her sixties. She certainly didn't look it, despite her rather extravagant lifestyle.

He looked across the room and studied his reflection in the large gilded mirror facing his desk. His hair was thinning now, grey, and his face looked more lined than usual. Those dark shadows under his eyes. If his wife looked ten years younger than her actual age, he looked at least ten years older than his. Too much time stuck in here, he thought to himself. Too much time dealing with the things that had to stay out of sight, yet had to be managed every day, swept under the carpet if possible, or made to disappear if necessary. The nation's dirty washing, laundered and hung out to dry every day. If the stains wouldn't come out, the garment had to be burned, all trace of its offending presence obliterated.

The seriousness of the memo he had just read firmly pointed to the latter.

The phone interrupted his thoughts. 'ACC Dixon on the line, Mr Gissing,' said his secretary.

'Put him through.' He listened to the clicks as the call connected. 'ACC Dixon, so sorry to disturb you this early in the morning. Tim Gissing here, Section One at MOD. I spoke to one of your colleagues yesterday, a Chief Superintendent Carrie Symington.' He waited as the voice on the other end went through the normal pleasantries. 'The outlook has changed, however. We now have a Category Five problem and I'll have to pull rank, I'm afraid. On you and the Scottish legal system, as it happens.'

He listened as the senior police officer raged and spluttered on the other end of the line. 'Sorry, old boy. The paperwork's on its way via the usual channels. Make sure it's dealt with as a priority. I'll check in with your local office in a couple of hours.' He heard the policeman attempt a reply, but decided to end the call. 'Life's too short, Jock,' he said to himself.

Scott shook his head. 'So we've tae let this guy go, ma'am?'

'Yes, Brian. He has diplomatic immunity.'

'But he has to leave the island, right?' asked Daley.

Symington raised her eyebrows. 'No, he doesn't. He has to undertake to stay away from Achnamara, but that's all. I've made my feelings known to the chief constable, but it won't make any difference.'

Daley thought about the journal he'd been given by Feldstein. It was at the bottom of his suitcase, and he didn't quite know why he hadn't lodged it as evidence. He supposed that instinct was at work again, and he rarely ignored his instinct – in his career, at least. Having not had time to study the journal's contents, Daley puzzled over what could be gleaned from its pages.

'Penny for them, Jim?' asked Symington.

'Nothing, ma'am. Just daydreaming.'

'Makes a difference fae mooning aboot wae a face like a wet weekend, Jimmy,' replied Scott. 'If this bugger is tae walk free, can I go for another couple o' hours o' shut eye? I'm fair puggled, ma'am.'

'Off you go, then,' said Symington, watching as Scott trudged out of the room. 'What about you, Jim?'

'It all depends on your movements, ma'am. I know there's a lot to do here, but I need to make sure things are adequately covered back in Kinloch.'

'No problem. I'm expecting a visit from an ACC, so I'm staying put. I'm also told that the media are on their way in force, so someone will have to be here to fend them off. Not your favourite task, I suspect.'

'No, most certainly not. What about the farmhouse? Any joy contacting this young man – Alex, or whatever his name is?'

'We're still looking for any evidence of contact with him. Old letters, address, emails, but nothing yet. A specialist team are being sent over from Glasgow so hopefully they'll have more success. Then there's the imminent arrival of our ACC. Can of worms, Jim. This Feldstein character takes the biscuit.'

'Yes. Can I ask what diplomatic immunity he's working under? It all seems a bit cloak and dagger, from what I can gather.'

'He's an Israeli.' She let the information sink in.

'Okay . . . I think I'm right in saying that the Bremner family are Jewish?'

'So we're led to believe.'

'If that's their real name.'

'Sorry, what do you mean?'

'Nothing, ma'am, just idle speculation. I'll head to the mainland on the first available ferry. I can get back here quickly, if there are any problems.'

'Very good. I'll keep you up to speed. Go and tend to our flock in Kinloch.' She stopped, biting her lip. 'And, Jim, try not to dwell on the past. It's a fruitless exercise, trust me.'

'Yes . . . Carrie. I'll keep in touch. Good luck with the ACC and the press. Rather you than me.'

She watched him slouch along the hotel corridor. Again, she wondered at the wisdom of letting him carry on without a proper break. He'd functioned perfectly well in the last twenty-four hours, so she reconciled herself to the fact that her decision was the correct one. Let him work on, exorcise the ghosts with the sheer effort of being a detective.

Her phone rang. She didn't recognise the number, but answered the call nonetheless, expecting a senior officer or, worse still, a member of the press.

'Hello, ma'am, hope you haven't forgotten about me?' The voice was mocking and painfully familiar.

'How did you get this number?' she asked, flustered.

'Aren't you forgetting? I'm a detective. You didn't think you could hide for ever up in Jockoland, did you? Time we had another little chat, don't you think?'

10

Daley looked on as the Forensic Investigation team left the ferry he was about to board to return to Kinloch. Inspector Stoddart, the head of the unit and an old friend of Daley's, caught sight of him and stopped his car. 'Jim, I knew this was part of your new kingdom. Bit of a mystery, is it not? From what I've read in the background report, anyhow.'

They chatted for a few moments. The last time they'd worked together had been in a murder squad in Glasgow almost ten years before. Stoddart asked after Liz, and not being able to face explaining his depressing domestic situation, Daley replied that she was fine, thriving, in fact.

'We'll take the place apart and see what we can find. Fascinating, really – a change from the normal shit, at least. If I have to deal with another drug dealer's mini-mansion in the leafy suburbs, I think I'll resign.'

The ferryman was waving to Daley to board, so he wished Stoddart good luck and fired up the engine. 'Oh, Brian's on the island.'

'Brian Scott? Well, at least I'll have someone to sink a few with at the end of the shift,' replied Stoddart brightly.

'If you mean ginger beer and lime, yes, you will.' Daley

waved vaguely and drove down the ramp towards the vessel, leaving Stoddart with a puzzled look on his face.

Kinloch, 1945

Urquhart was astonished that the cigarette lighter burst into life, issuing a strong blue flame when he flicked the ignition wheel. Maybe it was true what they said about German engineering; certainly, for this to work after being submerged under the sea for several days was impressive. Extinguishing the flame, he examined its silver casing. The German eagle embossed on the side of the device was clutching in its claws a red roundel containing a black swastika. This was the second such device he had pulled from the dead sailors' belongings, and for some reason it fascinated him more than the gold rings and cigarette cases that made up the rest of the haul.

There was an inscription, engraved in tiny writing beneath the eagle. Urquhart peered at it through his steel-rimmed glasses, but still couldn't make it out. 'McColl, you have youth on your side, what does this say?' He handed the lighter to his new charge, noting the lad's trembling hand as he took it from him.

'I-Ich liebe dich, E.' He handed the lighter back to Urquhart. 'I love you. His sweetheart, probably?'

'Yes, no doubt.' Urquhart looked at the other cigarette lighter, but the eagle and swastika emblem on it were not accompanied by any inscription. 'I want you to log all of these items, with a brief description in here,' he said, handing McColl a thick blue ledger. 'Date and time we took them into our possession, along with the details of any engraving et cetera. Take it through to the general office. You'll find all you need there.'

He watched McColl go and shook his head. He disliked patronage of any kind. He'd served with enough sons of the gentry in the last war to realise that it was a system that weakened any institution, whether it be a military regiment or a police force. He believed in meritocracy; that said, he had taken to McColl, and hoped the young man would thrive away from the overbearing presence of his father.

He thought of his own parents for a few moments. His mother, kind and hard-working, his father, remote and ill-tempered. He knew he should be married and settled down with children by now, but shuddered at the thought. His life was one of rented rooms in shared houses or cheap hotels. After the all-embracing life of the army, the police had seemed the natural choice. He was ready to move from town to town at a moment's notice, his possessions fitting easily into two stout suitcases.

In his mind's eye, he saw her again: her dark hair and twinkling brown eyes came back to him with little effort. It hardly seemed any time since he'd waved her goodbye on the bridle path beside the brook in the small Normandy village. In reality, it was long ago, and a very different world. Yet he could still see the wrinkle of her nose as she angled her face into his to kiss him.

Evelyn. Beautiful Evelyn. He resisted the desire to take out his wallet and stare at the faded image of her that dwelt there, next to his heart, and instead turned the key of his right-hand desk drawer. He reached in and removed the leather-bound journal. It was new, smooth to the touch. Placing it on his desk, he opened it at the appropriate page. He picked up his

silver fountain pen, and then, in a slow precise hand, began
to write.

Monday, 7th May, 1945

*With regret, I have been forced to take on a young assis-
tant, one Torquil McColl, the son of the retired Procurator
Fiscal. I will do my best to train this young man in the ways
of the police service, but I fear – even at this short exposure
– that he will prove too highly strung to become an effective
police officer. I have not lost hope, though.*

*This afternoon I attended the local hospital, where I
examined the corpses of thirty dead German sailors, an
unfortunate U-boat crew.*

*Note: the crew seemed depleted. The complement of the
vessel should be circa sixty. As yet, the RN has made no
comment as to the reasons for the vessel's sinking. Amongst
the sailors' possessions are two silver cigarette lighters, about
a finger's length and thickness. Both bear Nazi regalia . . .*

Daley went through his correspondence: memos from headquarters, routine emails and even some letters. He read a
request from the local high school that he might give a talk
to fifth-year students as to the merits of a career in the police.
Much as he liked to encourage the young, he made a mental
note to make his excuses and leave the task to someone else.
How could he try to persuade someone with their whole life
in front of them to devote it to staring at dead bodies and
dealing with the worst that humanity had to offer?

Wondering who to send, he thought briefly of Brian, but
instantly dismissed the notion with a smile. The thought of
his friend being a role model for anyone was a bizarre one.

He then worried that, for entirely different reasons, he was an equally unsuitable mentor.

With no conscious effort, his mind drifted to his son. What did the world have in store for his little boy? He shuddered at the thought and reminded himself to call his lawyer.

Forcing himself out of his chair, he brought his holdall over to his desk, unzipped it and fished about in the depths. His hand alighted upon the dry leather of the journal. He removed it from the bag and opened it on his desk, the furtive nature of its acquisition prompting him unconsciously to glance at his door before starting to read.

The cover bore the words, *The Journal of Inspector Wm. Urquhart M. M. Volume 4, commencing Monday, 7th May 1945.*

It took time for Daley to become accustomed to the cramped writing, but soon he could read it quite quickly. The first page covered the sinking of a German U-boat on the causeway next to the island at the head of the loch. He read on with interest, wondering just why this object had been taped to the back of a filing cabinet in the cellar of a remote farmhouse on an even more remote island off the coast of Kintyre.

The keeping of a journal was a rare event amongst police officers now, but he'd seen the day when young detectives were encouraged to do so by their wily older colleagues. *Cover yer back, son. Write it a' doon. Aye, but not in your official notebook, or every defence lawyer this side o' the High Court will know what's been going on.*

Resolving to give his predecessor's journal his full attention away from Kinloch Police Office, Daley closed it and replaced it in his holdall. He thought of Feldstein. How had he known of the journal's existence, and what could he discover about the disappearance of the Bremners and the strange contents of their farmhouse from its pages?

He realised that, in what seemed like the first time in months, his mind was focused, not partially labouring on events of the all too recent past.

He looked at his watch – almost one thirty. He deserved some lunch. He pulled on his jacket, left the office and took the short walk to the County Hotel.

Carrie Symington could hear Brian talking to Stoddart, but she couldn't concentrate on what was being said. She kept hearing that sly Cockney voice. Her heart thudded in her chest.

'Would that be okay, ma'am?'

She raised her eyes to see both Scott and Stoddart looking at her intently.

'Sorry, what . . . would what be okay?'

'We need to get the advice of a military expert, ma'am,' replied Stoddart. 'It's just that so much stuff in the cellar looks like it's from the Second World War. The translator's busy as we speak.'

'And mind, you have that press conference this afternoon,' said Scott.

'I'm sure you'll be able to assist me there, Brian,' replied Symington with a forced smile.

'Aye, well, if you knew my track record wae these things, you'd soon work oot that you'd be better off on yer ain. I'm no' so good at anything tae dae wae the press, ma'am.'

Stoddart snorted, subduing a laugh. 'You can say that again. That press conference you did down here a few years ago is still required viewing on YouTube. Remember, the one where the victim's husband kicked off?'

'Oh, I remember it fine, okay. Oor Jimmy left me holding the baby there, and no mistake.'

'What?' asked Symington.

'Are you feeling okay, ma'am? You're looking a wee bit peaky, if you don't mind me saying so,' said Stoddart.

'I'm absolutely fine. Now, let's get on with this, or we'll be stuck on this island for the duration.' Symington noticed the detectives glance at each other, and regretted her sharp tone. 'I'm just a bit tired. All this bloody sea air,' she continued, this time with a smile. 'So, get on to HQ and see who they recommend, Inspector Stoddart. And, Brian, I'd like to have a word with the special constable here. What's his name again?'

'McAuley, ma'am. I'll gie him a phone so that he can get the right uniform on.'

'Yes, that's a good idea,' replied Symington, again distracted. 'I better get prepared for this press conference, so if you'll excuse me . . .' She eased herself out of the chair and walked out of the incident room.

Scott shrugged his shoulders. 'Women, eh, who knows?'

Daley walked into the hotel, past the sweeping staircase with the well-trodden carpet and faded wallpaper, and opened the door to the small bar he'd become so accustomed to over the last few years.

He bought a pint and stood at the bar, looking at the selection of filled rolls on offer.

'Would you no' be better wae a proper lunch? We've got some lovely haddock in the day,' said Annie. 'You're needing tae get some meat back on they bones o' yours.'

76

'I've been trying to lose weight for years. Now's my big moment,' replied Daley.

'Whootever you think, Mr Daley. If you ask me, you've got the frame tae carry it off, so I'd no' be so keen tae let yersel' go.'

'I'll have a tuna roll, please, Annie.'

'Here, have two,' she said, fishing the rolls from the basket, unwrapping the clingfilm and putting them on a plate. 'Are you sitting doon?'

'Yeah, the usual.' Daley nodded to the back of the room, lifting a newspaper from the bar. The headline was bold: ISLAND FAMILY VANISH – POLICE BAFFLED. He groaned, tucked the paper under his arm and walked to a table at the back of the quiet bar, Annie following with his plate.

'Here, you enjoy your lunch,' she said, fetching a napkin from a neighbouring table. 'At least you'll have your paper for company. We're deid the day.'

'Cheers,' said Daley, opening the newspaper to read more speculation about the Bremners.

Annie made to walk away, then hesitated. 'I got a phone call the other night,' she said, rather sheepishly.

'Oh, who from?' asked Daley, suspecting he already knew the answer.

'Fae Liz. She was asking for you. Sounded a wee bit doon, if you ask me.'

'She certainly didn't sound down when I talked to her yesterday. In fine form, in fact.' Daley recalled the acrimonious conversation he'd had with his estranged wife.

'Aye, well, jeest sayin'. Don't you go cutting off your nose tae spite your face. We a' know you've had a bloody hard time . . . whoot wae . . . well, you know.' She wiped some crumbs from the table. 'Life's too short, is a' I'm saying.'

She turned round on hearing the bar door open. 'Talking aboot life being too short . . .'

'How ye, Annie, Mr Daley?' The old man smiled, his slanted eyes crinkling. 'They telt me at the station you were oot for your lunch. I thought you might have taken a wee wander in here.'

'Good to see you, Hamish,' said Daley, meaning it. 'Take a seat. What can I help you with?'

'Well, now, you see, jeest maybe I can help you.' Hamish sat stiffly on a stool opposite the detective, took a pipe from his pocket and sucked at it unlit.

'I'll leave yous to it. And mind, one whiff o' pipe tobacco and you're oot on your arse, Hamish.' She bustled off, grinning to herself.

'I hope you've not been breaking the law and smoking in a public place.'

'Ach, I was in last week. Jeest had a few too many and forgot where I was. Lighting up efter a' these years – it's automatic if you're no' thinking aboot it. Now, forbye that. I've come tae tell you something aboot Gairsay.'

11

Timothy Gissing read the report twice to make absolutely sure he'd got the gist of it. He opened the laptop on his desk, studied his contacts list, and dialled the number in Brussels on his mobile, not wanting to route the private call through the main switchboard.

He waited anxiously for a reply, and was about to end the call when a breathless voice sounded in his ear. 'Timothy, you have been a stranger. Give me two minutes and I'll call you back. The same number, yes?'

Gissing drummed his fingers on his desk, waiting impatiently for his call to be returned. He answered as soon as the smartphone buzzed in his hand. 'Hans, sorry to call. We have a potential problem.'

'Don't we always have potential problems? It is the way of the world for people in our profession. Tell me, what have we to cope with now?'

'T2304. If you don't remember, I'll give you time to look it up.'

Hans repeated the reference slowly, and sighed. 'For this, you do not have to aid my failing memory. Bremner, yes?'

'Yes, absolutely. Very impressive, old boy. They have been compromised – compromised in the worst possible way.'

'Are they in custody?'

'No, thank heavens. Not yet, anyhow. But they had to bail at very short notice – literally minutes. The whole property is under scrutiny now by the local police. A unit is on the way. Some damage has already been done.'

'Tell me it's not Feldstein.'

'Yes, I'm rather sad to say that it is.'

Gissing could hear his caller breathing heavily, but he didn't want to interrupt his thinking, so waited patiently.

'Let us hope that they followed the agreed protocols. Do you think they have?'

'My information is negative in that regard. My operative will do his best to consolidate certain . . . certain delicate information. But, as you know, to keep those on the ground interested and not to raise further suspicions, we'll have to follow our own compromise protocols. I'm sure you know what I mean.'

'Then we better hope that the Bremners are found soon, and by the right people. I don't need to remind you of their particular relevance. Your intelligence services, are they mobilised?'

'Yes, as discreetly as possible, and the CIA have been informed. We're all aware of the significance here.'

'How were we caught off guard so quickly, in this, of all cases?' The German's voice had an edge of impatience.

'Pure chance. Before we could get boots on the ground, some local plod had stumbled on the whole sorry mess.'

'Timothy, it is vital that we resolve this to our mutual satisfaction. A scandal of this nature could destroy all that has been worked for, especially in the current climate, and the EU is a fiasco as it is. Keep me informed. An alternative outcome, well, it doesn't bear contemplation. The only blessing we have is that the future is, at least, secure. We all know what the potential consequences are here.'

Before Gissing could reply, the line went dead. Oh, to be in the bloody Cotswolds right now, he thought to himself. He placed the smartphone in his pocket and reached across the desk. 'Get me Section Three at MI6,' he barked.

'First of all, Hamish, how do you know about Gairsay?'

'Och, you know fine nothing's a secret for long roon aboot here. It jeest brought something back tae mind. When I heard aboot it, you understand.'

Daley looked at the old man as he took a sip of the beer he'd just bought him. More wrinkles, he thought. More loose flesh on his neck. For a man who seemed always to have a tan, he was paler than the detective had seen him. It had been a long winter, of that there was no doubt. 'What was brought back to mind?'

'My faither had a wee lobster boat during the war. Ach, there was so much activity in Kinloch then, you wouldna recognise the place – full o' sailors and that. I canna mind much o' it noo – save for the chocolate ye used tae get fae some o' the servicemen. The auld man got tae know a few o' the senior blokes – officers – who had a taste for lobster. Aye, an' they weren't feart tae put their hands in their pockets, war or no war.'

'So your father was as resourceful as you?'

'He always kept us fed and watered, wae a roof o'er oor heads, tae. They were hard days, Mr Daley. We expected tae see Nazi soldiers in jackboots marching up Main Street at any time.'

'I'm sure that wouldn't have gone down well here.'

'No, nor would it. The Kinloch folk wid have taken tae the hills. We wouldna have collaborated wae the enemy, and that's a fact. They'd have bitten off mair than they could chew.'

Daley saw the look on the old fisherman's face, and somehow didn't doubt that the wartime population of Kinloch would have been hard to subdue, if the current residents were anything to go by. 'So just what did your father do?'

'There was a German sub went doon on the causeway, you know, at the island thonder.' Hamish took another sip of his pint. 'I can mind it, a horrible business. Well, tae cut a long story short, for some reason, the local police inspector got tae looking intae this. Don't ask me why, I wid have thought it was a military matter.'

'And?'

'There was something aboot Gairsay. My faither had tae take this inspector oot on his boat a few times. I canna mind the bloke's name noo.'

'William Urquhart?'

'Yes, yes, that's it,' replied Hamish with a grin. 'I should've known you'd be ahead o' me, as usual.' He sucked thoughtfully at his unlit pipe.

'So, what did your father and this Urquhart get up to?'

'Well, that's what I can't jeest mind. I know one thing for sure, right enough. He held a grudge against a family on Gairsay for the rest o' his life. I mind – och, years later – every time we sailed past them, he'd spit oot the wheelhoose.'

'Who were they, do you remember?' asked Daley, already knowing the answer.

'I mind that, no bother. The Bremner family, that's who he couldna stand. Don't ask me why, for he'd never talk aboot it. But I never saw him take such a dislike tae anybody, and he was an easygoing man, my faither.'

Daley took a bite of his roll and thought about Inspector Urquhart and his journal.

The boat was small and cramped. The young skipper peered out through the squall that had blown up out of nowhere. He hated jobs like this. He was more used to taking tourists on little jaunts in the height of summer. Sailing down the west coast of Ireland in these seas was a treacherous business, especially considering his small vessel was overloaded. Still, the money was good, and he always needed money. *Don't ask any questions*. The man in Belfast had said that more than once. But he was worried about the old woman. She looked frail, and the rough weather had made her sick. She was standing at the back of the tiny wheelhouse, glad, he thought, to be out of the cramped cabin below deck. A man – perhaps her grandson – had his arm wrapped around her, speaking to her softly in a language he didn't understand, but reckoned was German. An elderly man – maybe this old woman's son, he thought, certainly too young to be her husband – stood apart from them. He stared out at the squall, his eyes keen in a sharp face, displaying no emotion, no sign of fear, or any compassion for the woman.

'We don't have too far to go,' he shouted over his shoulder. 'Maybe another half an hour, though this squall might hold us back a bit. Pity we had to lay up for so long.'

'Okay, cheers. We'll be fine. Just get us there as quickly as you can.'

The skipper was surprised by the broad Scottish accent. He'd expected him to sound like the old woman, who had encouraged him to keep them safe on the high seas. 'The high seas'; it was such an old-fashioned term. He watched her nestle into the chest of her comforter.

Come to think of it, he'd only exchanged a few words with the elder passenger, who was still staring out to sea blankly, almost as though he had accepted that their lives were in danger and the thought was of no consequence. The skipper hadn't thought to wonder about how he'd spoken – no discernible accent, from what he could remember. He felt sorry for them; their safety was a great burden on his shoulders.

He gripped the wheel and looked through the window; the wiper was working hard but afforded him barely any view at all.

The boat ploughed on through the heavy sea.

Daley breathed in the salty air as he walked back to Kinloch Police Office. He always found it strange that there seemed to be one particular day – at the beginning of spring and again of autumn – that you could feel the season ahead. As he neared the top of the brae, he swore he could feel the first gentle intimations of summer: a slight change in the light, the scent of grass, birdsong. Today was that day.

He longed to put the darkness of winter behind him. It had been the worst of his life. Never the most carefree of men, he'd plumbed – was still plumbing – the depths of his being. All the old certainties were gone or had morphed into something he didn't recognise. The last time he'd felt anything like this was when his parents had died.

He could feel Mary's warm skin next to his, he could hear her breathing as she slept, he could feel her caress. Her scent filled his head, as though she was actually there, not rotting in a cold grave on a Glasgow hillside.

Sergeant Shaw was busy talking to a youth at the front desk as he entered the office. Before Daley reached the door that would take him to the CID suite, Shaw called to him. 'Just had a message from Gairsay, sir. Chief Superintendent Symington will be holding a press conference at three. Thought you'd want to watch it.'

'Do you know if Brian is involved?' replied Daley with as much levity as he could muster.

'He'll be assisting, apparently.' Shaw grinned.

'Thanks for letting me know.' Daley opened the door to the CID suite, but stopped, turning on his heel. 'Would you mind looking out the service record of one of my predecessors, if you have a moment?'

'No problem, sir. Who in particular?'

'An inspector by the name of Urquhart.' Daley could see that the name was unfamiliar to Shaw. 'He was here towards the end of the Second World War. Do you think you can lay your hands on anything?'

'I'll have a go. It'll be a request for information from HQ, sir, so I'll need to give a reason.'

'Tell them I'm giving a talk at the high school about the life of a cop during the war. Just say I'm looking for a bit of background – good PR and all that jazz. That usually works.'

'Good PR, the magic words. That'll do the job. I'll get on to it now.'

Daley went into his office. He needed cheering up, and the sight of Brian Scott as part of a press conference could almost be guaranteed to lift the spirits. He remembered watching him at Machrie, with the bereaved husband of Izzy Watson. It didn't seem that long ago.

'Remember, you're just there to look the part, Brian.'

He nodded obligingly. Whatever had been troubling Symington seemed to be behind her now.

They were watching a cameraman set up his lights in the dining room of the Gairsay Hotel. A group of journalists were in a huddle, sharing anecdotes and glancing furtively at the detectives.

'You cannae trust that mob, ma'am. They'll dae anything tae get you on the wrong foot.' Scott eyed the press warily. 'I'll be fine as long as I've no' tae say anything.'

'Just nod when I introduce you, and look as though you're focused on the task in hand. Come on, Brian, you must have done a few of these in your time.'

'Aye, but I'm no' getting any better at them – worse, in fact. It's just a piece o' nonsense anyhow. I mean, what's it going tae achieve?'

'It'll keep those vultures at bay for a while,' said Symington, looking at the journalists. 'There's too much speculation about this one. Gossip on the island, mainly. We'll pour some oil on troubled waters, then try and find out what actually happened to the family.' She smiled conspiratorially, all silver braid and shiny buttons. 'And please do up your tie, Brian,' she continued, with mock exasperation.

'Typical of oor Jimmy tae duck this. It would've looked better if you'd been sitting alongside him.'

Symington shrugged her shoulders. 'We can't all be encamped over here. Daley has the sub-division to run.'

'As well as sitting there gettin' a' maudlin aboot everything,' said Scott with a grimace.

'Well, he's been through a lot. I don't think I'd have been able to just carry on at work. He's being very stoical, if you ask me.'

'He's got naethin' else in his life, you mean. It was always like that. Apart fae him and the wife, the job was everything. Mind you, she kept him on his toes. I wish she was back, for a' her faults.'

'I don't really know anything about that side of things,' said Symington, looking around the room impatiently. 'What time is it?'

'Ten tae three, ma'am. No' long noo till we're on display. At least I've no' tae think aboot John Donald giving me a critique when we're done.' Scott raised his eyes to the ceiling.

'I get the impression that you and my predecessor had some issues?'

'Aye, you could say that. But that probably doesn't cover it . . .' Before Scott could go into more detail about his tortuous relationship with his late boss, a harassed-looking PR officer made his way towards them, clearing his throat to interrupt the police officers' conversation.

'We'll get you and Sergeant Scott seated, ma'am. Oh, and Special Constable McAuley.'

Scott followed his eyeline to the back of the room. Sure enough, McAuley was there, in full uniform and stab-proof vest. 'Are you having a laugh?' joked Scott. 'That bugger will likely forget whether he's the butcher, baker or the candlestick maker. He's no' the sharpest tool in the box, you know.'

'He'll be fine,' Symington interjected. 'Besides, it'll take the heat off us. He's local. Have faith, Brian.'

'I didnae think you'd go for a daft idea like that, ma'am.'

'It was my idea, DS Scott. Now, let's get up there and get this over with,' she continued brightly as they pushed their way through the knot of journalists to the end of the room where a Police Scotland backdrop had been set.

'Here we go,' muttered Scott, as he struggled to straighten his tie.

The two boys were running at full pelt along the sand, a terrier barking at their heels. The sun was out, and the beach, near Derrybeg in County Donegal on the Republic of Ireland's north-west coast, glinted white in the early spring sunshine. Disturbed by the boys' antics, gulls wheeled and squawked overhead.

Detritus washed up on the beach by the storms that had lashed the Atlantic coastline all winter was strewn everywhere. Old plastic fish crates, the gnarled branch of a tree bleached by sea and sun, juice bottles by the dozen, discarded netting, and the twisted frame of a plastic chair: all washed up by the restless sea and part of a playground of infinite possibilities for children now that the winter gales and short, dark days were over.

The little dog stopped beside a cluster of rocks at the water's edge, and started to whine, digging up the sand with its paws.

'Hey, Rooney!' shouted one of the boys, anxious not to leave his pet behind. 'What are you playin' at?'

The terrier paid him no attention and continued to whine, backing away from the rocks.

'What's up, Declan?' shouted the second lad, from further along the beach.

'It's Rooney. Maybe found a crab or something. Wait there, and I'll go and fetch him.' The boy retraced his footsteps to the little dog, which was now growling and barking excitedly.

'Come on, you daft bugger,' he said, leaning down to pat the animal. 'Sure, we've to get back home, or Mammy will send for the Guards.'

The dog raced back towards the rocks, confident now that his master was with him.

The boy shook his head and jogged forward, intent on pulling his pet away from the distraction. He stopped in his tracks.

The old woman lay on her back. The only eye she had left stared blankly at the sky; a tiny hermit crab made its way from a deep gash in the half of her head that remained intact.

The boy screamed, making the little dog howl.

12

Symington, Scott and Special Constable McAuley took their seats. Scott ran his finger round the collar of his shirt; he felt as if he was being slowly strangled. McAuley, who had been persuaded to remove his stab-proof vest, took a gulp of water from the glass in front of him and looked out of the corner of his eye at his chief superintendent, who was listening intently to what the well-groomed PR officer in front of them had to say.

'I would like to introduce Special Constable McAuley, resident here on Gairsay and the man who discovered that the family were missing, DS Scott from Kinloch, and Chief Superintendent Symington, Divisional Commander.' The man cleared his throat. 'Chief Superintendent Symington will begin with a brief summary of what has happened to date, followed by a Q and A. When you're ready.' He nodded to a floor manager wearing headphones, who held out his hand, then counted backwards from ten, indicating the last three numbers with his fingers only.

Symington straightened her back and began to read from the script in front of her. 'Ladies and gentlemen, welcome to the Isle of Gairsay. As you know, we are investigating the disappearance of the Bremner family. They are local farmers, well known and liked within the island community . . .'

Daley was watching the proceedings in the AV suite. On the huge screen, his colleagues looked surreally larger than life. He was especially impressed by Symington, but not surprised she was delivering such an assured performance in front of the gathered cameras and journalists. In full uniform, replete with braid, she sounded well briefed and confident, while giving the press only the barest overview of what had been discovered at Achnamara.

He couldn't help smiling at Scott's obvious discomfort. His face was flushed and he looked to be breathing heavily, even though he was only really there for moral support. Likewise, McAuley looked like a fish out of water, glancing frequently around the room, his mouth gaping.

In what seemed like no time at all, Symington had finished her summary of the facts and handed back to the PR man, who asked the assembled press corps if they had any questions.

'David Lynne, BBC News,' a young journalist called out. 'Am I right to assume that no intimation of their possible whereabouts was left by the family?'

'Yes, that is correct, though we are continuing with a thorough search of the Bremners' properties in case this yields any clues as to their whereabouts,' replied Symington with a polite smile.

'Linda Watson, *Daily Record*. We have information that some surprising items have been found amongst the Bremners' possessions – is that correct?'

Daley watched Symington carefully. She looked unfazed by the question, replying only that the contents of the house appeared to have little bearing on the family's disappearance, but were being investigated just in case. Though he knew this wasn't strictly true, he smiled at the easy way his boss minimised the true nature of what had been discovered at the farmhouse. Already, she was doing a much better job than he could have hoped to.

A few questions followed about the individual family members and their history and position within the small island community, all of which Symington handled with ease, constantly underlining the need for information in order to make sense of their disappearance.

Just as it appeared that the proceedings were winding down, a disembodied voice sounded from the back of the dining room. 'Tell them the truth! It's time everybody knew whoot went on!' The voice was slurred and heavily accented, and as the camera jerkily refocused on who was causing the interruption, Daley recognised the dishevelled woman who had been swiftly removed from the hotel the night he'd been in the bar with Scott and Symington. Her clothes were ill-fitting and dirty, and her lank grey hair hung limply over her face.

Before she could call out again, she was escorted from the venue, protesting loudly and incoherently. As the buzz of interest from the gathered journalists died down, the PR man brought the press conference to an end, with a brief apology for the interruption.

Daley grimaced and flicked the screen off just as Sergeant Shaw hurried into the room.

'Sir, we've just had this from the Irish Coastguard. A body's been washed up on the shore in Donegal. Matches the description of Mrs Bremner senior, though it's been pretty knocked about. They're sending images as soon as they have them. They seem pretty convinced it's her.'

'Donegal?' Daley thought about the geography involved. County Donegal was part of the Irish Republic, but it was visible from the Kintyre peninsula if the weather permitted. What could possibly have happened at Achnamara that would result in the old woman's body ending up in Donegal?

'Have we established the whereabouts of Alex Bremner? Finding him must be a priority now – especially if this body does turn out to be that of Mrs Bremner.'

'Last heard of in Austria, sir. Part of some EU student delegation. We've passed it on to Interpol, but they report that the trail has gone cold. He's taking some kind of sabbatical, sir.'

Daley shrugged. 'Keep at them, please. And keep me up to speed.' Whatever the Bremner family had been involved with, it looked likely that their youngest member would have to cope with the loss of his relatives, prior to being asked some difficult questions.

The sins of the father, thought Daley. All too often the offspring of those who involved themselves with crime, or some other unwanted notoriety, found that they bore a taint of those who came before. He'd seen the children of criminals bullied, ostracised, bad-mouthed, or taken down the wrong path simply because of who their family happened to be.

It looked as though Alex Bremner – once they'd found him – ran the risk of such judgement.

Kinloch, 1945

Inspector Urquhart could see four big destroyers and half a dozen ancillary vessels at anchor as he made his way from his lodgings to Kinloch Police Station. He'd become used to the sight of the loch filled with warships and the streets of the town bustling with servicemen and women, but there was something brutal and unsettling about these great instruments of death in the warm spring sunshine. He'd been posted to Kinloch in 1944 and had little knowledge of the community in peacetime, but he had often tried to picture the pre-war community. There was no doubt that, with its rolling hills and white beaches, the area was idyllic.

Come to think of it, he found it hard to remember what peacetime was like anywhere. He was originally from a small village in Ayrshire and, though he didn't return there very often, the last time he had visited his elderly mother, the small community had borne little resemblance to the place he'd grown up in, thronged as it was with soldiers from the temporary army barracks.

He remembered his time in the army – latterly in the military police – and unconsciously rubbed his right thigh, hoping to ease the pain there that still made him limp. As he stared out over the loch in front of him, the sunlit scene was replaced by the smoke-filled chaos of the beach at Dunkirk. The sheer cacophony, the frightened horses, the men screaming; the smell of blood and cordite that mixed with the tang of the ocean as thousands of soldiers waited on the beaches to be saved by the flotilla of small boats that had braved the Channel to rescue them.

He held his breath as the scream of the Luftwaffe's dive-bombers sounded again in his head. He could feel the spray of blood and gore splattering his face as his fellow soldiers were blown to bits beside him by a bomb blast. A head, ripped from the body at the neck, rolled along the sand, its remaining eye hanging by a bloodied stalk from a now empty socket.

'Fine day, Inspector,' said an old woman as she passed, making him jump and come back to the here and now. 'I see McArthur's the bakers are selling torpedo-shaped loaves the day.'

'Sorry?'

'You know, bread in the shape of a torpedo tae celebrate the sinking o' thon U-boat. Good for them, says I. If I hadna bought a new loaf yesterday, I'd buy one mysel'. Bloody Nazis, don't know when they're beat. No' even wae Hitler deid.' She walked on, tutting and shaking her head. Wartime or not, the community of Kinloch was never short of an opinion – normally trenchant ones.

Urquhart continued his walk along the esplanade, pausing to watch a small fishing boat and her crew leave the harbour. An old fisherman with a pipe clenched between his teeth poked his head from the wheelhouse window as the vessel made its way out into the loch, threading incongruously between the warships that dwarfed it.

Hitler or no Hitler, the war wasn't over yet. He'd faced the German army and fled for his life along with the rest of the British Expeditionary Force. He'd marvelled at the ruthless efficiency of the Nazi war machine. No, despite all that had happened, he found it impossible to believe they were beaten.

He walked on up Kinloch's Main Street. Sure enough, a queue had formed outside the bakery. A young woman, her hair tucked into a knotted scarf, passed him with a torpedo loaf in her basket, smiling shyly at a group of sailors who were laughing their way up the street in their baggy uniform trousers and black caps, the name of their ship embroidered in gold along the headband.

'Inspector, a word, if you please.'

Urquhart turned round to see Thomson McColl. 'Yes, Mr McColl, how can I help you?'

'My son tells me you've had him cataloguing the personal effects of dead German sailors.'

'Yes, and what about it?'

'Surely that's the job for some clerk or a wee lassie, not a trainee detective?'

Urquhart stepped towards McColl. 'His job is whatever I see fit. Any more interference from you and he won't be a trainee anything. I thought I made myself clear yesterday. Good day to you, Mr McColl.'

As Urquhart climbed the hill to his workplace, the pain in his leg made him wince. 'Arrogant bastard,' he said under his breath, as a dark blue RN truck thundered past him in a haze of belching engine fumes.

Daley looked at the image on the computer screen and compared it with a photograph of Mrs Bremner. There could be little doubt, despite missing half of her face, that this was the woman they were looking for. 'Do we know anything else, Sergeant Shaw? Was she the only one found?'

'Not really, sir. They're searching the shoreline, but nothing yet.'

The Bremner family had disappeared from their farmhouse on Gairsay, and now one of them had turned up on a beach in the Irish Republic. Daley looked at the map on the wall. The distance involved was relatively small, the journey taking just over an hour or so, depending on the vessel. He stared at the empty desk in the CID suite. DC Mary Dunn wasn't coming back, and neither was Mrs Bremner.

In her hotel room, Symington listened carefully to Daley's report. She thanked her DCI, then ended the call. She would have to seek the advice of her superiors; it wasn't what she'd been hoping for.

She looked at her reflection in the long wardrobe mirror. She looked tired and was sure that the fine lines around her eyes hadn't been there a few weeks ago. She supposed her mother's warnings were right. She would age prematurely in the police force. It would drain her self-worth and vitality and then spit her out. She seemed destined for a lonely old age, forgotten and discarded by the society she had served, forced to take desperate singles' holidays for the want of something to do, with a dwindling hope of finding a partner with whom she could spend her final years.

Choices, my dear, choices. Her mother's mantra echoed in her head louder and louder. She hadn't worried about it in her twenties; now she was in her late thirties, it was already beginning to haunt her.

She thought of the Bremner family. On the surface, they were farmers, living a quiet rural life on a tranquil island. But what had their lives *really* consisted of? Already, the discovery of documents from as far back as the early days of the Second World War indicated that they were involved in some way with Nazi Germany. The contradiction was breathtaking. Soon, she realised, this case would be passed on to another department, probably the Security Service. But it fascinated her. Her job was to make the best of the resources at her disposal and to do her best until she and her colleagues were relieved of responsibility. She intended to do so.

The phone on her bedside table rang. 'Hello, Symington,' she replied, almost forgetting that she was in a hotel and not a police office.

'Oh, sorry to disturb you,' said the woman at the reception desk. 'I've got someone on the line from your headquarters. Says it's urgent. Will I put him through?'

'Yes, yes, please,' replied Symington, slightly irritated that the woman hadn't seen fit to ask for a name. But, she reasoned, she couldn't expect the staff of the Gairsay Hotel to conform with Police Scotland communication guidelines. She waited for the call to be connected.

'Very good show, ma'am . . . apart from that bit at the end.' The voice made her freeze. 'You're still looking as fit as you did ten years ago.'

'I'm going to have this call traced, you bastard.'

'We both know that's not going to happen. You could have had me strung up by the balls a long time ago, if you'd wanted. But we've still got our little secret, haven't we?'

'This is a public line – anyone could be listening.' She was dismayed to note that her hands were shaking.

'Yeah, that's the thing. I want you to answer my calls on your mobile, otherwise I'll have to think up new ways of getting in touch. Know what I mean?'

'Why on earth do you want to speak to me? I've got nothing to say to you.'

'I don't know. Seeing you again – in the flesh, so to speak – has brought it all back. Made my heart flutter. You haven't forgotten our little deal, have you? I used to look forward to our *meetings*.'

'I'm not so wet behind the ears now, I can assure you.'

There was laughter on the other end of the phone. 'It wasn't your ears I was thinking about, love. Now, be a good girl and shut up. I'm going to call you tonight, about seven, okay? We'll be meeting up again very soon. I've always loved it up there in Scotland.'

The line went dead. Symington continued to listen for a few moments, worried that she would hear the click of another receiver being put down, but only the dial tone sounded in her ear.

She fell back on the bed and stared at the fire alarm on the ceiling, feelings of disgust and dread her only companions.

13

Kinloch, 1945

'Sir, we've had a report of wreckage found on the beach at Glensaarn. A fisherman found it. He's here now.'

'Give me a few moments then bring him to my office,' said Urquhart to the young constable, striding past him and through the main room, where two secretaries were bashing away on their typewriters. He almost jumped in surprise when he caught sight of someone sitting in his chair.

'Sorry, sir. I-I was just waiting to see what you wanted me to do,' said Torquil McColl, jumping out of the chair.

'You can start by not discussing what we do here with your father. He just stopped me in the street and harangued me about your duties. I warn you, I won't put up with any interference, and if it means your finding somewhere else to spend your time, so be it.'

'S-sorry, sir. He asked me what I'd been doing. I-I didn't see the harm—'

'Well, you see the harm now! Wait for me at the bar office. Someone is coming to see me.'

Blushing furiously, McColl left the office, shutting the

door quietly behind him. Urquhart removed his trilby and placed it on the hat stand. He hadn't bothered to bring his raincoat and was dismayed to see a dark cloud obscuring the sun as he stared down Kinloch's Main Street through the thick panes of his office window.

'Come in,' he called, on hearing a tentative knock at his door.

The door opened slowly to reveal a tall, thin man in a navy-blue fisherman's jumper, a pair of filthy dungarees, and a flat cap pulled down low over his eyes. 'Your constable jeest asked me tae knock,' he said, removing the cap to reveal a tanned face with inquisitive, slanted eyes.

'Yes, sit down, please, Mr?' said Urquhart, pulling the visitor's chair out from the desk. 'I think I've met you before.'

'Jeest call me Ranald, Inspector. Everyone else does. I fish around these parts. I'm here aboot the wrecked vessel I seen at the Largiebank thonder, jeest on the shore at Glensaarn.'

'When did you come across this?'

'Oh, no mair than a couple o' hours ago. I didna know whether tae come tae the polis or report it direct tae the navy. Tommy Deans – you know, the harbour master – says I should come tae you, in the first instance, anyhow.'

'Yes, well, he had the right of it there. I'll inform the Royal Navy if it concerns them. I want you to take me to where you found this wreckage. We can get there by road, yes?'

'Och, aye,' replied Ranald. 'We'll jeest have tae loup o'er the dunes once we get there, but you'll be used tae louping o'er things, I shouldna wonder, Inspector.'

'Good. I'll organise a car.' Urquhart put his head round the door and called down the corridor, 'McColl, McColl! Find me a vehicle.'

His young charge scurried from the bar office in search of transport.

'If you want a wee fill o' baccy, I've plenty in my pouch,' said the fisherman, setting a match to a briar pipe clenched between his teeth.

'No, thanks, I'll stick to the coffin nails.' Urquhart produced a packet of Craven 'A' from his pocket and took out a cigarette. 'Let's see if we can make any sense of this wreckage.'

The fisherman nodded and sent a puff of blue smoke heavenwards, his eyes crinkling in a smile. 'I'll leave that tae you, Inspector.'

Brian Scott opened his bag and rummaged through his underwear. He pulled out a pair of garish lime-green running shoes with fluorescent yellow stripes and examined them carefully with a leery eye. Next, he found a pair of grey jogging pants and a sweatshirt.

In minutes he'd donned the sports garb and was stretching his legs the way the instructor at the Kirkintilloch gym had shown him.

As he was leaving the room, he caught sight of himself in the wardrobe mirror and almost burst out laughing, but then recalled the horrors of the DTs and the anxiety he'd felt, and smiled at his reflection, reassuring himself. After decades of self-destructive boozing he was now on the right track.

He trotted along the corridor and downstairs, then past the reception desk and out of the hotel onto the main road. He bounced on his toes for a few seconds, coughed, and set off at a gentle running pace.

It was a bright day on Gairsay, with a hint of springtime warmth. He jogged past a row of cottages, then the village hall, and was soon out in the countryside, heading the two miles or so to the southern tip of the island.

He was impressed by how fresh he felt. He was breathing easily as his feet thudded along the tarmac road, which rose slightly as he passed the entrance to the gardens for which Gairsay was well known. He could smell the soil and the sea, and birds were twittering in the hedgerows. Despite a slight throb in his right knee – a throwback to an old football injury – he ploughed on, getting more and more into his stride.

This is the life, he thought to himself. He glanced up at the wind turbines towering over the island and turning languidly in the light breeze. They rotated just enough to mean that the island was self-sufficient when it came to the provision of electricity, even making a little capital on a surplus exported to the national grid.

In his wildest imaginings, DS Brian Scott had never thought he'd become a convert to fitness and good living. But, as his heart thudded in his chest and he fought to keep his breathing steady, he couldn't help feeling that he'd happened upon the secret to a happy, contented life, and he resolved to encourage Jim to take up a similar fitness regime. There was little doubt that the overweight, depressed DCI was in need of some attention and TLC.

As he turned a corner, he was unable to avoid colliding with a dark figure who emerged from the hedgerow, sending him crashing painfully to the ground on his tender knee. Struggling to his feet, swearing and gasping for air, the hot stench of alcohol replaced the healthy scents of land and sea.

'You need tae listen tae me,' said a voice in his left ear. 'If you don't listen, you don't learn – that's whoot my auld faither used tae say tae me.'

'If you don't bugger off, you'll no' have tae worry aboot what your auld faither said tae you,' replied Scott. 'You'll have my trainers up your—'

Before he could finish his sentence, what was now clearly an old woman leaned closer, almost making him retch at the stink of her unwashed body. 'I saw her, aye, plain as day. I wiz only a wean, but I mind it like it was yesterday.'

'Saw who? What the hell are you on aboot?'

Without warning, the old woman stood to attention and raised her right hand in the air, fingers flattened. '*Jawohl, mein Führer*,' she shouted, using the index finger of her left hand to imitate a moustache.

'Bugger me, I'm glad I never had tae spend much time here,' said Scott, his breathing almost back to normal. 'I'd have had tae get my liver wrung oot wae a mangle. Come on, you. Back tae the village and sober up.' He took the woman gently by the arm and tried to lead her back down the road towards the village.

'You will never take me alive,' she shouted in mock German and, with surprising strength, shook herself free of his grip, clambered over a narrow ditch and ran off.

'Aye, right. Well, you're on your own, dear.' Scott waved at her in a gesture of exasperated resignation. 'If you want tae bolt aboot drunk as a laird, that's up tae you.'

Having lost his momentum, the detective turned on his heel and walked, hands in his pockets, in the direction of the hotel. 'There but for the grace of God go I,' he muttered as he overheard the old woman giggling drunkenly at him from the field. A strong gust of wind tugged at his sweatshirt, and he shivered as a dark cloud blocked out the sun.

Kinloch, 1945

The old Austin motor car struggled to the top of the hill, Urquhart willing it on. The fisherman Ranald was beside him in the front, while young Torquil McColl was squeezed into the tight bucket seat behind them.

As they began to putter more easily down the other side, Ranald grabbed Urquhart by the sleeve. 'Doon at the bottom o' the hill, thonder. You can pull the jalopy in at the side o' the road. We'll head o'er they dunes and I'll show you where I found the wreckage.'

Before long, the three of them were wading through soft sand and rough grass to the top of the dune. Urquhart winced at the pain in his thigh, but carried on, following the fisherman and his young charge, who had taken the lead.

'Still there,' observed Ranald, as Urquhart joined him. He was pointing to a scatter of what appeared to be discoloured driftwood that lapped at the white sand of the small bay. 'I reckoned the tide would wash it further ontae the beach. If we take a breenge doon, you can take a look for yoursel', Inspector.'

On closer inspection, the wood was painted dark grey. Urquhart took off his shoes and socks, rolled up the legs of his trousers, and waded into the cold water. He caught hold of a splintered plank and brought it back to the shore. A coil of white paint overlaid the grey, and before he could make an observation, McColl exclaimed excitedly, 'Sir, that's the bottom half of a number three. It must be a Royal Naval vessel, s-surely.'

105

Urquhart looked along the shoreline. Similar pieces of wreckage were visible for about a hundred yards. 'I don't think it's Royal Navy; the lettering doesn't look as it should. Right, McColl, get your shoes off and collect as much as you can and bring it up the beach,' he ordered, noting the rainbow-coloured slick of oil glistening on the water's surface.

Urquhart caught the whiff of pipe tobacco on the air and looked further down the beach to where Ranald was standing, a cloud of smoke evaporating into the breeze. 'I would take a wander o'er here, Inspector, if I was you,' he called.

As Urquhart joined the fisherman, he gestured towards some rocks at the water's edge. 'What would that be floating there?'

'I'll dae the honours this time,' said Ranald, stepping into the surf in his sea boots, seemingly untroubled at the water slopping into them. He bent down and tugged at the dark shape in the water. Soon, the face-down body of a uniformed man was revealed.

Urquhart knelt down and turned the dead man over. The man's eyes were brown and staring, his face was burned black on one side, and his right hand was a bloodied stump. 'German merchant navy.'

'Poor soul,' said Ranald, removing his cap in a gesture of respect.

The policeman rummaged through the pockets of the corpse's uniform until he extracted a cigarette case and another smaller metal object from the left trouser pocket.

'He'll no' be smoking any mair,' observed Ranald quietly, taking a contemplative draw at his pipe.

Urquhart laid the cigarette case on the sand and turned the other item over in his hand. It was slim, silver in colour, with a black swastika embossed on a red roundel.

'Why wid a German merchant sailor have something like that?' asked the fisherman.

'Good question,' replied Urquhart, raising his head to look out to sea. 'And what would he be doing here?' He rubbed his chin. 'That's Gairsay, isn't it?' he asked, pointing straight ahead.

'Indeed it is, Inspector. A fine wee island.'

Urquhart had the feeling in the pit of his stomach that all was far from being right – and he hated that feeling.

By the time Scott made it back to the hotel, winter appeared to have returned to the island of Gairsay. The light rain that had started to fall was now lashing against the window in large drops, blown there by a strong wind. As he looked out at the bay, the sea had turned from an inviting blue to a forbidding grey, the tips of the waves blown into white horses by the strong south-westerly.

'Did you enjoy your run?' asked the receptionist.

'Aye, what I got o' it,' replied Scott. 'That auld woman that keeps getting flung oot o' here accosted me on the road. Well, knocked me doon, to be mair accurate.'

'Oh, old Glenhanity. I'm sorry she spoiled your run.'

'Glenwhat?'

'Glenhanity. That's the farm she grew up on. Folk here often get named after the places where they live – usually the man of the house, but women who never get married, too.'

'Well, she's married tae the booze, that yin,' said Scott, examining the rip in his jogging trousers.

'She's had a hard life, though. Her dad died during the war, and when her mother remarried she didn't choose too well, if you know what I mean. Her stepfather was a horrible man, and when he died she looked after her mother for years. By the time she went, well, Glenhanity was too old to make a life for herself. Sad, really.'

'She'll no' find any solace in the bottle,' said Scott.

'You're not a drinker, I see.'

'Aye, well, no' recently.' He smiled at the woman, then took the stairs back up to his room.

He was about to open his door when he spotted Symington in the corridor. 'Ma'am, how's it going?'

She stopped and looked distractedly at Scott. 'Oh, fine, fine,' she replied.

'Are you sure? You're looking a wee bit pale again, if you don't mind me saying.'

'I'm fine.' This reply was terse. 'We need to have a meeting. I'll see you in the incident room in half an hour.'

Scott raised his eyebrows as he watched her stride down the corridor. 'Who stole your scone?' he muttered under his breath, fumbling with the key to his room.

14

As Daley opened the door to his bungalow high on the hill above Kinloch, his mobile phone vibrated in his pocket. He stepped inside, glad to be out of the rain. 'Symington' flashed on the screen, so he put down his briefcase and answered the call. 'Yes, ma'am, what can I do for you?'

'The weather's taken a turn for the worse here, Jim. They tell me they've had to cancel the bloody ferry, just as the ACC was about to arrive, too.' Daley could hear the irritation in her voice. 'Typical.'

'How's things? Have our team found anything?'

'Yes, it seems so. I don't think I've spoken to as many executive officers in such a short space of time in my career. It gets more bizarre by the minute.'

'They've confirmed that the body is that of Mrs Bremner senior. The Irish Coastguard have organised a search of the area. It doesn't look good for the rest of the family, ma'am.'

She paused for a heartbeat before replying. 'No. And the team here have unearthed some unusual stuff, to say the least. A list of names, Nazis, they tell me, who escaped Germany at the end of the war and were never heard of again. Seems we could have stumbled on something significant.'

'Seems so, ma'am.'

'Listen, Jim. I want you to find out as much about the Bremners as you can. Take it right back to when they arrived on Gairsay. It's impossible to get anything done here: the broadband is patchy, and goodness knows how bad things will get now there's a storm on the way. I'll arrange for the locals to be questioned, of course.' She made her excuses and ended the call abruptly. Daley thought he'd heard the buzz of another mobile in the background.

He picked up his briefcase and walked through to the lounge, pausing at the big bay window. Sure enough, he could see that the loch had taken on the green-grey colour that so often presaged bad weather. The sky was dark over Kinloch and the rain was heavier than ever. He placed his briefcase on the table and took out the leather-covered journal, which was nestled amongst some files and court documents that required his attention. He looked at his predecessor's entry for Monday, 7 May, 1945: *I have collected the belongings of the crew of the U-boat that sank on the causeway. The most interesting articles are these . . .*

Daley peered at a tiny pencil sketch. The years had taken their toll, and, unlike the still-legible handwriting, it was almost invisible. He took a pair of reading glasses from his jacket pocket and looked closer. The drawing was rectangular in shape, showing two sides of what Urquhart described as a cigarette lighter. It took Daley back to the sketches of crime scenes and road traffic accidents he would make in his notebook in his early days as a police officer. With the advent of mobile phones and body cams, these were now things of the past. Instantly, he felt an affinity with the man. The police force Urquhart had worked in almost had more in common with the one Daley had joined than it had with the modern service.

He read on: *These lighters are distinctive. I have a feeling that, judging by the quality and the fact that they both work, despite immersion in seawater, they cannot possibly be general issue. The silver casing and Nazi regalia speak to me of something different.*

Daley could almost hear Urquhart speaking. Certainly, he could follow the inspector's logic. It was the product of a mind trained to be curious; one of a natural detective.

He flicked idly to the final words in the journal. *If my suspicions are correct, then I have come upon something that is as spectacular as it is bizarre and terrifying. I meet with my informants in person for the first time tonight. I have decided not to take McColl, though this has displeased him.*

Daley reached into his bag. The file he withdrew was new but its contents were not. He stared at the faded sepia photograph. The man was wearing a black suit and tie and a white shirt. He had a square face, with high cheekbones and a broad forehead. His hair looked dark in the image, short and slicked back, parted on one side. To Daley, Inspector William Urquhart looked like a man to be reckoned with, though he thought he detected a certain world-weariness, perhaps even melancholy, in his soulful eyes. He was living through tough times, Daley reasoned.

He read the biographical details. Son of a veterinarian, Urquhart was born in Edinburgh and attended the Royal Academy on the outskirts of the city. An unremarkable student, instead of undertaking further education, he had joined the King's Own Scottish Borderers Regiment as a subaltern. Served in the First World War then rose to the rank of captain in the military police. While marshalling troops during the evacuation of Dunkirk, he had suffered a shrapnel wound to his leg, which left him unfit to continue in the army.

Daley padded through to the kitchen, collected a bottle of malt whisky that was almost half full and a squat crystal glass, and returned to the table in the lounge where he poured himself a large measure.

Given his injury, he wondered how Urquhart had been passed fit to join the police, and then reasoned that during the war normal medical requirements would have been less rigorous. Urquhart had investigative experience, albeit in a military capacity. As Daley read on, he discovered that his predecessor was highly competent and well respected by his superiors, despite being thought of as rather aloof and 'not one of the boys'.

'Join the club,' he muttered to himself as he took a gulp of his whisky.

The inspector had been posted to Kinloch in 1944, taking lodgings in a flat in the upmarket Craighardy building, on the edge of town. He was a bachelor, and appeared to have little in the way of personal ties – so opined the superintendent who had written the report, at any rate.

The one black mark that Urquhart had against him stemmed from his time serving as a detective sergeant in Perth, where he had seen fit to punch a senior officer. However, the incident hadn't impeded his promotional prospects – or recurred – and within months of moving to the Argyll Constabulary he had been promoted to the rank of detective inspector.

Daley looked at the photograph again and wondered if anyone would spend time poring over his file in years to come. He doubted it.

'Good luck to you.' He drained his glass and poured himself another whisky.

Dusk was descending over Kinloch now. He watched the red tail lights of a car meandering along the coast road out of town, in the direction of the island at the head of the loch. A murmuration of starlings dipped and soared, seemingly as one, before settling in the swaying trees above the graveyard.

A small fishing boat was making its way to the safety of the harbour, being tossed up and down by the dark, restless waters of the loch.

For an instant he saw Mary disappearing over the edge of the RIB, recalling how he and Scott had desperately clutched at her hands and dragged her from the depths of the broiling whirlpool of Corryvreckan.

Little in the way of personal ties. As these words had applied to Inspector William Urquhart, so they applied to him now.

He turned the page and was surprised to note that large sections of Urquhart's files had been redacted. Page after page, in fact, was blacked out in thick lines. This was highly unusual. Too many years had elapsed for the life of Inspector William Urquhart in Kinloch to remain an official secret. Unless, there was something else entirely . . .

In a darkened room at the heart of the Ministry of Defence building in Whitehall, Timothy Gissing was pointing at a huge screen. Beside him, Naval Commander Parsons was fidgeting.

'Let's go over this again,' Gissing said wearily. 'The body was discovered here, and the Irish Coastguard have picked up wreckage here and here.'

'Yes, sir. They're currently looking through a list of vessels that could be considered as missing – you know, late back to port and so on. It could take some time, I'm afraid.'

'What do we have in the area?'

Parsons bent over his laptop and keyed in some details, then addressed the question. 'We have a minesweeper, *The Devonian,* in the North Channel. Do you want me to ask them to join the search?'

'Yes. Yes, please do that. I need to know as much about this incident as possible – and as quickly as possible. Contact *The Devonian* yourself.'

'We'll have to go through official channels, offer our services to the Irish Republic. I doubt they'll knock back the offer of assistance, mind you.'

'See that they don't. If you have problems, contact me, no matter the hour.' Gissing handed him his card with a sigh. 'What about the weather on the coast of Kintyre?'

'I have the latest forecast here.' Parsons clicked more keys on his computer. 'Looks pretty rough for the next forty-eight hours, at least. It's the tail end of that storm that hit the eastern seaboard of the United States a couple of days ago. I can't remember its bloody name . . .'

'I don't give a damn what its name is. Are you seriously telling me it's beyond our capabilities to land anyone on Gairsay until this clears? I can hardly believe it.'

'Difficult harbour in this type of weather, sir. The wind is coming from south-southeast. Unless it blows round a bit, we're on a hiding to nothing. We do have units on standby with your personnel aboard. As soon as it's practically possible, we'll get over there.'

'What about a helicopter?' asked Gissing, with little confidence.

'Not a chance. There is a small airfield on the island, but it would need a "Winkle" Brown to land anything on it in this weather.'

Gissing snorted. 'Well, keep me up to speed. When do you finish, Commander?'

'I'll be relieved at seven by Childs, sir. I'm yours all night, so to speak.'

Gissing bid Parsons goodnight and trudged down the long corridors to his own office.

'Herr Neyermeyer has been on for you, sir,' said his secretary with a smile.

'What did you tell him?'

'That you were with the chiefs of staff.'

'Good.' He walked into his office and closed the door. He stared for a few moments at his wife's photograph before picking up the phone.

'Hello, my darling. Bad news, I'm afraid. It's going to be an all-nighter, by the looks of things. Sorry about supper.' He listened to his wife's complaints for a while, apologised again, then said goodbye.

He opened the bottom right-hand drawer of his desk. A bottle of brandy rolled to and fro, colliding gently with a glass tumbler. He poured himself a measure, took a gulp of the spirit, and called his secretary.

'Angie, darling, are you busy?'

'No, sir. I'll be in directly.'

He watched as she locked the door behind her. She stood in front of his desk, slowly unbuttoning her crisp white blouse, a strand of dark hair slipping over her right eye as she gazed at him seductively.

In a few moments she had straddled him and was pushing

herself up and down, on tiptoes, her hands gripping the back of his chair on either side of his head, skirt pulled up over her thighs, as he clutched her backside.

His tongue licked her brown nipple as it danced in front of him, leaving it slick with saliva. He pulled her down hard by her shoulders as he groaned with the release of his climax.

As the young woman's movement slowed and she rested her head on his shoulder, he glanced at the photograph of his wife on the desk before him. He turned his head away.

'Now, be a good girl and get me a coffee, would you?' said Gissing, as she eased herself off him and reached between her thighs with a tissue.

Symington's mood had lightened in inverse proportion to the severity of the storm. She was in the incident room, reading some of the hasty translations of the German files found in the Bremners' basement while taking frequent sips from a large glass of wine.

Stürmbahnfurher Hermann Schneider. Hanover, 1973. She scanned the document, discovering that Herr Schneider had lived a quiet life after the war, working as a director of a wallpaper factory. In late 1972, a young female reporter from an Israeli newspaper had turned up at his office, asking questions about his time in the Waffen-SS. The document was straightforward and concise, making no attempt to create a narrative around plain facts.

Symington furrowed her brow as she read on.

It emerged that this file had been written up by Mr Bremner senior. He mentioned a delivery, and then the processing of a parcel.

At first the superintendent couldn't make the connection

between the few lines about Herr Schneider and the mention of the parcel. She wondered – given his profession – if this man had sent the Bremner family wallpaper, that this was the parcel mentioned. Perhaps swatches?

Soon, though, it dawned on her that Schneider and the parcel were one and the same and that Mr Bremner's function had been to arrange the clandestine removal of this man from Germany.

Herr Schneider arrived on Gairsay, and three days later, Mr Lawrence W— was picked up by motor cruiser (H.H.) for transportation to Destination A.

Symington re-read the sentence. The man referred to as Lawrence W. had not been mentioned earlier in the document, so she wondered where he had sprung from. Then there was the question of why either man would have made the journey to the quiet island of Gairsay. Also, what was 'H.H.', and just where was 'Destination A'?

The door swung open to reveal Scott, dressed in a thick Arran jumper and a pair of jeans. 'Good evening, ma'am. Is it no' time you called it a day?'

'Yes, you're probably right. I'm a bit peckish, come to think of it.'

'Come on, and we'll get some scran before the chef buggers off.' Scott rubbed his hands together.

'Are you cold, Brian?'

'Aye, a wee bit. The weather's atrocious.' He nodded towards the window, streaked with rain blown in gusts by the gale-force wind.

'Still, it's quite cosy in here.'

'My old mother was right. I mind her telling my faither, "If you're a heavy drinker, you'll never be cold".'

117

'Sorry?'

'Och, you know what I mean. Since I cut oot the bevy, ma'am, I've been bloody freezing. The doctor says it's quite natural, and my body is adjusting back tae normal. Trouble is, I cannae mind just what normal was like.'

'You're in a much better place, Brian. I'm proud of you – we all are.' She smiled.

'I'm no' accustomed tae hearing that kind of thing, neither. The last time anyone telt me they were proud o' me was when I passed my cycling proficiency test in primary seven.'

'What test?'

'It was a long time ago, ma'am. You're too young tae remember that, likely.'

She closed the file she'd been reading and went to the filing cabinet the hotel had provided. After placing the file in a drawer, she locked the cabinet and looked about for her handbag. 'I'm getting so absent-minded. You can't see my bag anywhere, can you, Brian?'

'Absent-minded? Join the club. It's one o' the pleasures o' getting old. I keep wandering intae rooms and wondering why the hell I'm in there . . . Here, is this what you're after?' He picked up the handbag, which had been tucked under a chair, and handed it to Symington.

'Thanks.' She zipped the filing-cabinet key into an inside pocket of her bag, just as a young waitress leaned her head around the door. 'The chef says he's just about to go, and would you like something before he does?'

'We're just on our way through, thanks,' replied Symington.

The girl paused for a moment, looking at the police officer's bag. 'Is that a real Louis Vuitton?'

118

'Yes, I confess it is,' said Symington, embarrassed. 'I've got a bit of a thing about bags.'

'Me too. I'm saving up for one with my tips. See you in a minute.' She returned to the dining room.

'Brian, I need you to do me a favour tomorrow.'

'Yes, ma'am, nae bother.'

'I want you to get out and about, ask the islanders if the Bremners were in the habit of having guests. If so, how did they get here and how did they leave. I'm sure everyone notices everything in a place like this.'

They left the incident room together, Symington locking the door behind them.

'If it's anything like Kinloch,' said Scott, 'there'll be no doubt aboot it. Worse than MI5 o'er there.' He eyed the window with some dismay. 'I hope the weather clears up a bit.'

15

The man was struggling now. He'd hung on to the piece of wreckage for dear life, eventually being washed up on a rocky shore beneath cliffs, where he was still marooned. His right leg was useless; agony every time he tried to move it. He had called out pitifully for help, but who would come to save him here?

He had managed to drag himself along the sand and was lying in the lee of a huge boulder, drifting in and out of consciousness, his body numb in the biting cold and rain.

He was finding it difficult to swallow now. Though he was drenched, his mouth was bone dry, the taste of the salt water he'd swallowed making him retch from time to time.

He remembered playing in the sand as a child. Sunny days, under blue skies. Buckets and spades. His grandfather building a huge fort in the sand, complete with a moat, into which, through a small channel, sea water flowed. This was where he kept the unfortunate crabs he'd plunder from the rock pools – rock pools like the one he was lying beside. But there was no sandcastle fort here, no sun; just pain, cold and fear.

He'd tried to hold on to her tiny hand, but the rise of the swell had ripped them apart. He had watched her drift away, in and out of sight as he bobbed in the cold sea. He had called out to her, but only moments after her hand had slipped from his, her body had disappeared, consumed by the water and the thick slick of oil that had come from the wreckage of the boat.

As he felt himself drifting off into a sleep from which there was no awakening, he heard voices. Someone was shouting. He lifted his head and thought he saw the flashing of a torch.

He called out as best he could, praying that he could make his voice heard above the churning waves and the driving rain. 'I'm here! I'm here!' he rasped. Then, with one last gargantuan effort, he managed to shout, 'Over here, help me!'

Relief washed over him as he saw the light flash on the surface of the rock pool, piercing the raindrops that fell in a downpour in front of him. He shielded his eyes against the beam as it was directed into his face, trying his best to speak, but could only mouth the words, 'Thank you, thank you, please, help me.'

A dark figure loomed over the stricken man, holding the torch steady, pointing it into his face.

He could hear the croak of the man's voice, but couldn't reply.

Soon the beam of the man's torch was joined by another. 'This is him, no?'

A second figure leaned down over the man lying against the rock, pushing his soaking hair from his bloodied face. He turned to his companion and nodded. 'Yes, this is the grandson. No doubt about it.'

The first man hesitated for a heartbeat, then tugged something from his belt. 'Move out of the way, but keep the light on him.'

He raised the cosh into the air, bringing it down heavily on the injured man's head again and again, the cracking of his skull audible against the noise of the wind and the crash of the sea. Splattered in the dead man's blood, he dragged the corpse into the surf.

Carrie Symington was feeling much more relaxed as she sat at the table with her dining companion. Though she'd known Scott for a few months, this was the first proper opportunity she'd had to speak to him about anything but work, without someone else present. She smiled as he regaled her with yet another story about his early career in Glasgow, and how he and Jim Daley had become friends.

'So, I just says tae this parrot, "Hello, cheeky boy." Sure enough, "I'm fine, Daddy," replies the bird. So, me and the big fella had the pet shop owner bang tae rights. Turned oot he was selling folk fancy birds, then paying this gang o' wee neds tae steal them back a few months later. He didnae reckon on the parrot having learned how tae speak. Liz always found that story funny.'

'Is Liz really that bad? I mean, she seemed so nice when I met her. You know, the model housewife, flour on her hands and the baby on her hip.'

'Och, she's had her moments. Always been decent wae me, but led oor Jimmy a merry dance at times, which didnae endear her tae me, I've got tae say. Mind you, it cannae be much fun living wae him when he's got his teeth intae a case.'

'Which is a lot of the time.'

'Aye, I suppose it is. He gets so involved, you know, like there's nothing else in his life, ma'am.'

'All the best cops are the same. I worked with a guy in the Met like that . . .'

'Aye, but you need tae get a balance. Me, I'm lucky. My Ella's no' interested in the job at all. So, when I get hame we just talk aboot normal things, like where we can go on holiday, or why she's jealous o' the woman along the road who's just had her hoose roughcast. Jimmy's never had that luxury – the pretty yin always had big ambitions for him.'

'The pretty yin? I wish someone would call me that.' She laughed, momentarily wondering just how interesting a conversation about roughcast could be.

'You're no' a bad looker yoursel', ma'am, if you don't mind me sayin'," he said, rather shyly.

'Well, thanks, Brian. And it's Carrie when we're not working. You're as bad as Jim. I've been trying to get him to call me by my first name for ages.'

'Just the way we wiz brought up. I knew John Donald for thirty years, and I would never have thought of calling him by his first name.'

She took a sip of her drink. 'I've read a lot about him, of course. Makes me feel rather inadequate, in a strange way.'

'Eh? Why would you feel inadequate for doing your job well? He'd mair skeletons in the cupboard than Burke an' Hare. So it turned oot, at any rate.' Scott shook his head at the thought. 'Cannae see you harbouring many dark secrets, Carrie.'

'Well, no . . . apart from the brand of hair dye I use.' She reached under the table for her handbag. 'Excuse me for a moment, Brian.'

Scott watched her walk away. And I've been a cop for too long tae miss something that obvious, he thought to himself.

*

Daley was sitting in the dark watching the storm, nursing a glass of whisky. One of the things he'd first noticed about Kinloch was how you lived cheek-by-jowl with the elements. Up until his posting to the town he'd spent most of his life in cities and towns inland, sheltered from all the wild Atlantic could throw at the battered west coast of Scotland. Sure, you got cold in the frost, wet in the rain and hot in the sunshine. However, somehow, a dramatic night like this enlivened the senses and made him feel part of something big, universal – not detached.

Or was it just the whisky?

He stared at the bottle in the shadows, now almost empty. He emptied his glass and placed Urquhart's journal and the files back into his briefcase. He hadn't made much progress, but he had managed to note down a few locations visited by his predecessor, some of which he recognised. He resolved to ask Hamish to take him to the sites.

Urquhart had been searching for answers to something that puzzled him. Daley was used to that thought process, and felt compelled to do likewise.

He walked into the kitchen and flicked the light switch, illuminating the room in a clear white light that made him narrow his eyes after spending so long in the darkness.

After a lengthy search by both Police and Military personnel, no trace of Inspector William Urquhart has yet been found. The last line in Urquhart's file resounded.

He rinsed his whisky glass and opened the fridge. Some gammon and half a round of brie were being kept company by a carton of milk and a half-empty bottle of Chenin blanc. Daley resolved to go to the supermarket the next day. He took out the cheese, closed the fridge door and opened the bread bin. He frowned when he noticed the green mould on the last few slices of bread he'd been counting on as part of his supper. He tried the cheese. It was dry and sour.

Deciding that he'd have to wait until breakfast for any kind of sustenance, he was about to call it a night when the landline began to ring. Back in the gloomy lounge, he could just make out that the number had been withheld. He answered all the same, remembering that Liz had changed the number at their old home in Renfrewshire, determined that he shouldn't have it.

'Hello,' he said wearily, fully expecting to hear the voice of his estranged wife haranguing him about something or other.

'Elliot's boatyard in Belfast harbour.' The voice was male, deep, with a distinct foreign accent.

'Sorry? Who is this, and how did you get this number?'

'Elliot's boatyard,' the voice on the other end of the telephone repeated, before the line went dead.

Daley stood stock still, cradling the phone in his large hand as another gust of wind blasted rain against the window.

16

Brussels

Fifteen men of varying ages, all dressed in formal black tie, sat stiffly around a long, polished mahogany table. The low murmur of voices stopped when the door swung open and a tall man, dressed like everyone else, strode into the room and took a seat at the head of the table. He smiled benignly as he looked around, noting the anxious looks on these faces he knew so well.

'Gentlemen, please. This is not the time for trepidation, but for action. Being fearful that something might happen is unproductive. Stopping it from happening removes that fear. Would you not agree?' He looked at them one by one, seeking consensus, but noted that the man sitting directly opposite him at the far end of the table was shaking his head. 'André, you doubt my logic?'

André sniffed contemptuously. He was in his mid forties, thin-faced with dark hair and darker eyes, almost black; his hair, swept to one side, framed an intelligent face. 'I have been part of this for what – almost twenty years?' He took in the nodding heads of his companions, many of them senior to him in years. 'My father told me about this only when he was forced to. I remember my surprise – shock would perhaps be more accurate. I remember wondering how such a secret could be kept for so long by the few people he named; men from different places, who spoke in many languages, but all of whom I'd known from childhood, and many of whom I see tonight.'

'Thank you for these memories, André. We all have a place in our hearts for your late father. But this is not the time for nostalgia, as I'm sure Pierre would have reminded you, if he was here.'

'He would also have reminded me of the danger of the game we are playing – have been playing for so long. You men have lived with this all of your lives, as did your fathers – yes, and like me, some of your grandfathers. We all knew that something had to be done, and done quickly. But it should have been done before now, as I have advocated for a long time. After all, we now have what we want, safe, with our own people.'

There was a collective sigh from those gathered around the table. As one, they looked at the man who had entered the room last. He was nodding silently.

'Well, Hans?' said André. 'We await your wisdom, as always.'

Hans pushed a lock of grey hair back from his forehead. 'I know that in many ways you have all had reservations about our strategy, but we had no choice. Absolutely no choice! We were born in plain sight, and in plain sight we must continue. It is the way of things, and will always be that way.'

There were nods, shrugs, and the shaking of some heads around the table. He knew that his peers required more to reassure them.

127

'Watch this,' he said, pressing a button on a small handset and turning to face a large screen as it burst into life.

The scene was a crowded street, possibly in Germany or Austria, judging by the architecture. A young man, slim with dark hair, wearing a black leather jacket, was addressing a crowd through a megaphone. He shouted – implored – in perfect German. The cadence of his voice rose and swelled as he made his point. As he finished speaking, the crowd cheered wildly, shouting their approval and waving banners.

The footage clicked off.

'This was filmed last week in Austria,' he said, looking around slowly, fixing each face one by one. 'I think you will agree, gentlemen, regardless of what has passed, we have what we need. Everything else is superfluous.'

There were no longer any shaking heads around the long table.

Timothy Gissing tiptoed down the hall of his Kensington home, hoping not to wake his sleeping wife. He caught a whiff of perfume coming from his shirt collar. He sighed, slipped off his jacket, and made his way through to the kitchen using only the glow of the street lights outside as his guide.

He switched on the light and was startled to see her there, in a white towelling robe, hair dishevelled, holding a large glass of wine. 'You nearly gave me a bloody heart attack,' he said, his hand on his chest.

'Thought you were on an all-nighter,' Lucinda replied coolly, topping up her glass to the brim.

'Sorry, darling, bit of a panic on, I'm afraid. I'll have to pack a bag. Have to head off for a few days.'

'Oh, really. Are you going alone, or is *she* going with you?'

'She? What on earth are you on about? Been on the sauce again? We've spoken about this. You know how bloody difficult my job is, but not long now.'

'I can smell her, you know. Just like I could smell them all.'

'I don't have time for this, Lucinda.' He snatched the bottle of wine from the table and emptied the dregs into the sink. 'I can't help it if you're that bloody sozzled all time your mind plays tricks on you. Go to bed, damn it!'

'That was a rather pointless gesture. It's not as though we don't have plenty of booze in the house.'

'When I get back we'll talk. I don't want to take this shit with us to the Cotswolds. I thought we were going to make the best of our retirement – go for walks, decent holidays, play a bit of tennis. Have a life! Not you staring through the bottom of a glass every night.'

She smiled. 'You have your little crutches, and so do I. Or perhaps crotches would be more appropriate in your case.'

He pulled off his shirt carelessly, sending a button flying across the kitchen floor. Opening the door to the washing machine, he threw the garment inside, then strode out of the room, taking off his watch before running up the staircase.

He stood in the shower, head angled back, eyes closed, mouth wide open, letting the warm water splash over his face. The fear that he'd had in his heart for so long was back at its worst. He could hear his pulse pump in his ears. Yet another fight to keep the truth at bay. Yet another fight to save his own skin, as well as the skin of so many others. Yet another fight to stay out of jail.

The voice he'd heard in his ear only an hour before echoed in his mind, making the noise of the shower almost inaudible.

Fix this and fix it now! Do what you have to do – anything! We can't afford to have your Scottish police stumble on something. We can't trust that they won't realise the truth.

He stepped out of the shower and towelled himself down, wincing at an ache in his lower back. The truth was that this would never go away. He could be in his office, on holiday, at home, in the sack with some giggling girl, having a meal, anywhere in fact. Even retirement was no guarantee. He'd been deluding himself for too long. He felt exhausted. He'd had enough.

He walked into his bedroom. He no longer slept in the same room as his wife, hadn't done for a very long time. More self-delusion. The idyllic Cotswolds home with the roses around the door was nothing but a fantasy. A ridiculous fantasy.

He unlocked a drawer in his bedside cabinet and removed a large manila envelope. With finger and thumb, he eased it open and looked inside. The papers were exactly where they'd been for so long.

He sealed the envelope, lifted a fountain pen from the top of the cabinet and wrote an address on the front, then affixed some stamps from a perforated strip which he left on the counterpane.

He pulled on a tracksuit and bounded back down the stairs and outside, clutching the envelope. He jogged to the end of the street and stopped at the post box, which was set in the wall.

He breathed deeply, then forced the envelope into the box, making sure it was safely inside.

He looked up and down the street. All was quiet. He took the little glass phial from his pocket, slipped it into his mouth, and bit down hard, hearing the glass crack.

In seconds, Timothy Gissing lay convulsing on the pavement, only yards from his home.

The watery morning sun filtered through the blinds in Daley's kitchen. He cursed when he remembered that there was nothing to eat in the house, but decided to brew a pint of coffee in the machine Liz had left behind. He may have to go to work hungry, with a queasy stomach from the whisky the night before, but at least the beverage would wake him up and relieve his thirst.

As he waited for the coffee, he thought about what he'd read the previous evening, and the mysterious phone call.

He padded through to the lounge, lifted the phone and dialled three numbers. 'Yes, business number, please. Elliot's boatyard in Belfast.' He waited for a moment. 'Yes, put me through, please.'

'Elliot's, can I help you?' The woman sounded young and friendly, but slightly distracted, probably due to the early morning call. Daley had been ready to leave a message, but was glad he was actually talking to someone.

He introduced himself, but before he could finish, she interrupted him. 'So have you found our Denny? Where's the stupid bugger ended up?'

Though her voice was bright, he detected a note of anxiety, as though she was determined that their conversation would be positive. Daley had first noticed this phenomenon as a young cop. He would knock at the door of a person who was in hospital, had gone missing, or had been in trouble of some kind – the list was endless – to be confronted by a mother, wife, daughter, father or friend. He knew as well as they did that as a police officer he was there to impart bad, often tragic, news, but so often he felt that those whom he addressed were trying to make sure that they only heard what they wanted to hear. In reality, how often did the police knock at a door to tell someone good news?

'I'm sorry,' he replied. 'I was asked to phone this number by someone last night. I don't know why, or who the caller was. I suppose I'm really wondering if you can throw any light on the matter.'

The woman on the other end of the line was silent for a few moments, then spoke again. 'Kinloch, you said. That's the one across the water in Kintyre, am I right?'

'Yes, absolutely.'

'Denny had a job in your area, well, not far from there. I wasn't supposed to know where he was going, but I had to find the place for him on the satnav before he left. Great seaman, but not too clever with the technology, if you know what I mean. He told me to keep it quiet, but he's been missing for a while now, and we're all really worried.'

'In this area, you say? Where, if you don't mind me asking?'

'Eh, just a wee island. Gairsay. The day before yesterday. He told me it was a rush job, but he was getting crazy money. We had to cancel a couple of jobs, but he said it was worth it.'

'Who was the client?'

'I'm sorry, I don't know. Denny never said.'

'And how much money?'

'No idea. He never told anyone here. He only had time to plot the course and get there – sailing in the dark, too.'

'Is Denny the boss?'

'No, no, that would be his father, Ray. He's not in just now. We've been making sure there's somebody here day and night, you know, just in case the daft bugger turns up. I don't know what the weather's like with you, but it's been hellish here.' Her voice was suddenly flat.

Daley heard her breathe in, and realised that she was clutching at straws. He had the feeling he knew exactly what had happened to the unfortunate Denny, but he couldn't mention it at this stage – not until he was sure, not until he'd been through the process. 'I see. Okay, you've probably been through this with the coastguard already, but can you describe the vessel for me, registered number and the like? The call I received last night was anonymous, so I don't quite know what it was about, but logically it does seem a bit of a coincidence if your colleague was sailing to the coast here.'

Daley listened as the woman described Denny, the boat, and the route that had been plotted.

'Do you think I should call Ray and let him know you've been on?'

'Yes, please do. I'll be back in touch as soon as I've checked a few things out.' He ended the call with a heavy heart. It was unlikely he'd be phoning back. If the boat was the one he was thinking of, another policeman in a different uniform would be knocking on the door of Elliot's boatyard.

Daley dialled Kinloch Police Office. 'Get me the number for the Irish Coastguard, would you?'

17

Kinloch, 1945

'Inspector Urquhart, thank you for bringing this to our attention so quickly. Beats me why this fisherman didn't come directly to us.' The commodore's accent bore the plummy tones of privilege. No matter what the branch of the military, they were invariably the ones who held the top jobs, thought Urquhart once more. It had been the same in the army and it rankled. He longed to live in a world of equality, but doubted he ever would.

'No reason why he should. He spotted wreckage, but didn't know whether it was naval or civilian. The local police station was the natural choice,' he said, in the most congenial tone he could muster.

'Well, what's done is done. We'll take it off your hands now, old chap. This body, it's at the mortuary in Kinloch Cottage Hospital, I take it?'

'Yes.'

'Good. Well, I'll need you to sign the release papers. This is obviously a matter for the Royal Navy. We'll send an ambulance for the remains.'

'No, that won't be necessary, sir. The body was washed up

on the beach, so it remains a civilian matter until my investigations are at an end . . . which they're not, incidentally.'

The commodore settled back in his chair, lit a cigarette and poured himself a whisky, without offering one to Urquhart. 'Now listen, Inspector. I need you to pay very close attention here.'

Urquhart bridled at the man's condescending tone, but nodded.

'This conflict is reaching its conclusion. You're ex-army, you know the form. This is a naval matter, pure and simple. I don't care if this chap's body landed on the church steeple over there' – he waved his cigarette at the window – 'you'll sign the body over to me immediately or you'll be back walking the beat before the next bloody tide comes in.'

Rather than feeling intimidated by the commodore's sudden burst of ill temper and the threat to his career prospects, Urquhart felt a surge of excitement. 'As you say, sir, I'm ex-army, but I'm now a police officer – *a civilian police officer.* The rules and regulations surrounding this situation are crystal clear. The body was found on a beach within my jurisdiction and, as such, will remain in the care of Argyll Constabulary until my enquiries are complete. As you know, a post mortem will be required as soon as possible. This will be performed by our man as soon as he arrives from Oban.'

'Nonsense! Hand over this body, or, I swear, Inspector, I'll have a detachment of Royal Marines go to the bloody hospital and get it!'

'And I'll have them arrested. I've informed you of the situation, Commodore. Now, if you'll excuse me, I have a lot to do . . . as I'm sure you do, yourself.'

'I heard you were a bolshie bugger. Well, you'll hear more about this directly. I'm going to call your chief constable.' He reached for the Bakelite phone on his desk.

'Your prerogative, sir.' Urquhart turned on his heel and left the commodore's office, placing his trilby firmly back on his head and resolving not to go back to the station until after the PM had taken place.

They can't give me an order if they don't know where I am, he thought, a grin spreading across his face. He couldn't remember the last time he'd felt so invigorated.

He wondered about this naval officer, who he'd just watched drain a glass of whisky, then pour himself another large measure. Despite his bluster, he'd looked nervous. Urquhart stored that thought at the back of his mind.

As he walked along the seafront at Kinloch, he observed the usual comings and goings of vessels on the loch. Whether they were the tiny local fishing boats or the colossal warships, they seemed to share a determination of purpose. He was amazed that there were so few instances of collisions in the crowded bay, but the fishermen, the Royal Navy and the merchant seamen seemed to rub along very well.

The sun was beaming down from a blue sky obscured only fleetingly by the odd high cloud. Even the breeze was warm, and the population of the town were taking advantage of the good weather. A young mother, pushing a Silver Cross pram, her hair pinned up beneath a paisley-pattern scarf, smiled demurely at him as she walked past. A group of small boys were kicking a worn leather football along the promenade, socks round their ankles, skinny white legs in long grey shorts yet to catch the colour of the summer sun. A man in a kilt, shading his eyes from the glare of the sun with a folded newspaper, was staring out to sea under the red, white and blue bunting that was stretched between a series of tall poles spaced along the sea wall. As the gulls screeched and tumbled, it was almost impossible to imagine the brutal life-and-death conflict that still raged around the globe.

At the head of the loch, snaking from the shore to the island, he could see the long causeway, proud of the waves now at low tide. The wreck of the U-boat was surrounded by tiny figures, busy dismantling it so that it could be taken away and examined by the Admiralty in London.

He reached into his pocket, feeling the cool silver casing of one of the lighters he'd discovered amongst the crew's belongings. He could feel the shape of the eagle holding the swastika. Why would dead Germans sailors – military and merchant – be in possession of these same items? He should have alerted the commodore to the coincidence, but something in his gut told him that it would have been the wrong thing to do.

He heard the click of segs behind him, and turned to see the kilted man striding towards him.

'Good morning, Inspector,' the man said, holding out his hand. 'Nice tae see you again.' He shook the policeman's hand enthusiastically.

'Sorry, you have me at a disadvantage . . . I don't think we have met.'

'Aye, sorry. I know who you are, but you don't mind me fae Adam.' The man was in his late middle years, clean-shaven with a mop of thick hair, greying now but still showing flashes of the red of his youth. His complexion was florid, and Urquhart could smell the sweet aroma of whisky on his breath. 'I'm Dugald Kerr. I've a wee farm near Blaan. I'm in

Kinloch for supplies. You won't remember, but I was part of the town's welcoming committee when you first arrived with us.'

'Oh, yes, of course.' replied Urquhart, somewhat disingenuously, as all he could recall of that day was a cloying tiredness as he shook the hands of a seemingly endless number of people he didn't know, their faces swimming in front of him. The journey to Kinloch by bus from Perth had been a long one, and he hadn't expected such a welcome.

'Yes, I mind the provost availed us o' some of his excellent whisky, of which I had too much, considering I was up for milking bright and early the next day . . . well, no' very bright, if I'm honest.'

Urquhart laughed politely, and was about to make his excuses when Kerr grabbed his arm.

'Could I have a wee word with you in private, so tae speak?'

'Is it police business, Mr Kerr? You'll understand I'm quite busy at the moment.'

Kerr leaned his head forward conspiratorially, making Urquhart wince at the alcohol on his breath. 'I'm a bit worried that we're no' all pulling in the same direction, if you know whoot I mean?'

'Not really.'

'Put it like this, Inspector. I think there's some folk aboot that would be quite happy if we were losing the war.' He stood back, a concerned look on his face.

'What makes you think this?'

'Everyone has their ain ideas, Inspector. No' all of them coincide, that's all I'm saying.'

'If you suspect any wrongdoing, Mr Kerr, you're duty-bound to make it known to the authorities. Are you saying you wish to make a complaint against a particular individual? Because if you do, it's a serious one.'

'Complaint? That sounds very formal. Mair like pointing you in the right direction, if you know whoot I mean.'

'Well, if you want to get something off your chest, please feel free. I'm all ears.' Urquhart was beginning to suspect that Kerr had consumed more whisky than was good for him, but his natural inclination was to be courteous.

'If you've time, I would like tae meet you for a dram in the County Hotel this evening, aboot five. Trust me, Inspector, I think it will be worth your while.'

Before Urquhart could think of an excuse, Kerr had wished him good day and was striding off down the promenade.

18

Chief Superintendent Symington stepped out of the police car and dashed to the front door of Achnamara farmhouse, as anxious to speak to her officers as she was to get out of the rain and wind.

'DS Scott!' she called.

'Doon here, ma'am. I'll be with you in two seconds.'

Two women in white investigation suits walked past her, acknowledging her authority with silent nods as they did so.

'Right, ma'am. That's the last o' the investigation team oot o' the building. The boss's none too happy. He says he'll meet you at the hotel. I've got tae say, I cannae get my heid roon it, neither.'

'Quite simple, Brian. We've been asked to secure the building and await a party of officers from Special Branch. Everything we have has to be passed on to them. Too big for us, I'm told.'

'And they've just realised that?'

'I think it's taken time, but they've made up their minds now, rather quickly.'

'And how dae they think they're going tae get here? It's still blowing a hoolie oot there.'

'I suppose they'll have to sit it out, just as we'll have to before we can get back to the mainland. A paid break on an idyllic Scottish island, what more could you ask for?'

'Typical, isn't it? The moment I stop drinking, I'm marooned on this rock, no' even able tae enjoy a dram or three.'

Symington bit her lip. 'If the house is clear, I want you to do something, DS Scott.'

'What? I mean . . . aye, nae bother, ma'am. Just say the word.'

'I want you to take this and photograph every document you can down there, got it?'

'Aye, I think so, but—'

'Call it a little insurance, Brian. Don't worry, you're merely acting on orders from me.'

'Whatever you say, ma'am,' replied Scott, examining the smartphone he'd just been handed with no little trepidation. 'I'm no' the worrying kind, unless it comes tae technology.'

'Here, just point and click. It has an automatic flash, so nothing can go wrong. Just try to make sure you frame each page.'

'Are you sure? I'm giving you fair warning. Richard Branston, I'm not.'

'Richard Branson?'

'Naw, no' that clown. I mean a wee mate o' mine fae Partick. Wee Ritchie Branston, he's a real star wae computers and the like.'

'Just get on with it,' she said, shaking her head but smiling nonetheless.

'Nae bother,' he replied, making his way down the hall. He paused and turned back to face her. 'I wonder what happened?'

'What happened with what?'

'Well, you don't send Special Branch up here without good reason. It'll cost a fortune. I might be a dinosaur, but I know it's accountants that are the real bosses these days. Oor boys would have had this wrapped up in jig time, tae, at no extra expense. They must know something we don't, or something they don't want us tae find oot.'

Symington said nothing as she watched Scott open the door in the hall that led down to the cellar. Brian Scott wasn't as daft as he made out, she thought to herself.

The private ambulance with tinted windows pulled slowly away from the pavement of the Kensington street. Two men, one elderly, the other middle-aged, watched it go, their faces expressionless.

Forensic officers in white suits with hoods were busy at the scene. Flanagan, the elder of the two, nodded, and a uniformed police officer lifted the crime scene tape to allow a postman to finally do his job and empty the post box only yards from the body.

'Has anyone spoken to his wife?' asked Iolo Harris, the younger of the two, his voice displaying traces of his roots in South Wales.

'The police have been round to tell her that he's a goner, but we'll have to show face.' Colin Flanagan shook his head. 'Of all the people I expected to off themselves, Gissing was most certainly not one of them. Made a bloody good job of it, too. Hard to think this gesture hasn't been contrived in order to send a message. What a fool.'

'Maybe his wife found out about his, well, dalliances?'

'If it's taken her forty-odd years of married life to discover her husband was a philanderer, she hasn't the brains she was born with. I know she's got a drink problem, but she's no fool. Double first from Cambridge, much better degree than Gissing.'

Harris raised an eyebrow. 'You learn something new every day.'

Flanagan reached into the pocket of his thick overcoat and produced a pound coin. 'Heads or tails?'

'Heads.'

The older man spun the coin and caught it deftly in his left hand, covering the result with his right.

'Don't keep me in suspense, sir.' Harris bounced up and down impatiently on the toes of his well-polished shoes.

'Tails, I'm afraid, Iolo. Job's yours, thank God.'

'Brilliant. No time like the present, then,' he replied, looking at his watch. 'I hate early starts.'

'I have even better news.'

'Oh, great. Don't tell me you want me to spend the bloody day with her by way of solidarity?'

'No, much better than that. You're to be Gissing's successor. I want you at a briefing in my office at ten.'

'Are you serious? I thought Parker was in line for that.'

'He was. But you may have noticed that Tim didn't get the chance to retire. He was in the middle of something, something that needs your deft touch. All bets are off, Iolo. Anyhow, time you were settling into something of a more permanent nature. You're not in the first flush of youth any more, my boy.'

'Cheers, sir.' Harris sighed. 'Anything else I should know about this before I face the grieving widow?'

'No, perfectly straightforward. Get as much from her as you can, maybe take a poke about. Not every day one of our own shuffles off this mortal coil with a cyanide capsule.'

'No. Does indicate premeditation, mind you. He's clearly been thinking about it for some time.'

'Yes. Right, I better be off. Got a meeting with the Under Secretary at the Home Office. Hopefully I'll manage to avoid having to see that awful woman face to face.'

'The Home Secretary?'

'Who else?' Flanagan headed for a sleek black Jaguar parked a few yards away. He stopped in his tracks and turned to face Harris. 'Pack a bag once you're done with Mrs Gissing, Iolo.'

'Holiday?' he replied with a mischievous smile.

'Scotland.'

'Bugger. I was hoping for Barbados.'

Brian Scott was taking the air at the front door of the Gairsay Hotel. Mercifully, the rain had stopped and the wind had calmed down a little, though it still looked stormy. The sea in the bay was an almost luminous green, waves choppy and white-tipped.

'Might get a ferry later,' said a voice from behind, making him jump.

'Aye, maybe. I don't know what my gaffer has in mind, so I'm no' sure if we'll be on it even if there is one,' Scott replied, smiling at the receptionist.

'She's checked you both out, so I think you're on the way back to Kinloch, Sergeant.'

Meanwhile, a dark-clad figure on an ancient bicycle was wobbling down the narrow road towards the hotel. The wind was buffeting the machine, making its rider hastily drag the handlebars from left to right, which sent the front wheel wavering.

'What the fu—' Scott's words were stopped in his throat as the old woman stood on the pedals, facing him and raising her arm, hand outstretched, fingers pointing heavenwards.

'Oh dear, she's early on the go today, right enough.'

'What's that she's shouting?'

The receptionist cocked her head as the old woman's voice carried back to them on the wind. 'I think it's *Sieg Heil*.'

'She's as mad as a box o' frogs. Shouldnae be allowed oot.'

'Oh, she's harmless enough,' said the receptionist benevolently, displaying the united loyalty the detective had noted in the islanders.

'Harmless? She bloody knocked me o'er yesterday.' Scott looked disgusted. 'Ripped a big hole in my Ron Hills, tae.'

'Your what?'

'Running troosers. Cost a small fortune, tae. No' tae mention the big scuff on my trainers and the gash on my knee. I'll gie her bike . . . she should be confined tae Shanks's Pony.'

Scott heard a thudding noise overhead, initially thinking it might be the extractor fan outside the hotel kitchen. However, it was too loud and too persistent. Soon, the dark shape of a twin-bladed Chinook appeared in the sky above the bay, banking left, headed straight for Gairsay.

'They're keen, up in a helicopter in this wind,' observed his companion above the thud of the rotor blades.

'They'll be fine in that big thing,' said Scott.

As the noise became almost deafening, the helicopter hovered above them, then slowly descended to the field in front of the hotel, tilting slightly the nearer to the ground it came.

Soon, the helicopter had landed, and once the rotor blades had stilled, a door in the side of the aircraft opened and a line of men in flight suits stepped onto terra firma.

Symington had also heard the commotion. She knew that the Special Branch team were arriving, but given the strong wind, she hadn't thought they would manage to get to Gairsay until later in the day.

She stared out of the window of her room, counting ten figures as they walked across the field and into the hotel's car park. Though they were all wearing flight suits, they had removed their helmets and handed them to the flight crew as they'd left the Chinook.

She felt a tightness in her chest. The nearer he got, the more familiar he became. She could see him stopping to take in the scene; he was looking straight up at the hotel.

Symington took an involuntary step backwards. She was finding it hard to swallow, and she was perturbed that her legs were shaking so much she had to sit on her bed.

She looked at her reflection in the dressing-table mirror. Her face was deathly pale, and bore an expression that scared her. She almost cried out when a loud knock sounded at the door. 'Who is it?' she asked tremulously.

'Only me, ma'am,' said Scott cheerfully. 'That's Special Branch here. Good news, eh? Didnae think they'd manage up in this weather. That's us off the hook.'

'Give me a few moments, please, Brian.' She tried to compose herself. 'I'll catch you in the dining room in about fifteen minutes,' she continued, trying to sound as natural as possible.

'Aye, nae bother, ma'am.'

She heard Scott padding off back down the corridor. In the bathroom she splashed her face with water and dabbed it with a fluffy hand towel. She began to apply her make-up with shaking hands.

'Pull yourself together,' she said under her breath, as a solitary tear slid down her cheek.

Iolo Harris stood in the bedroom, looking at the opened drawer with a puzzled look on his face. A half-used sheet of first-class stamps was lying on top of a selection of envelopes of various sizes.

He bounded down two flights of stairs, his feet thudding on the thick carpeting.

Lucinda Gissing was stretched out on an expansive sofa. At first, Harris thought she was fast asleep, but she opened her eyes without rising when he approached her.

'Mrs Gissing, sorry to bother you again. I noticed that one of the drawers in the bedside cabinet was open.'

'Tim's bedroom, not mine, Mr Harris.' Her voice was flat, emotionless.

'Your husband's bedroom, I beg your pardon,' replied Harris, glad he'd decided not to refer to Gissing as her late husband. 'When Mr Gissing left to go for his run, did you notice if he was carrying anything?'

She yawned and propped herself up on one elbow. 'What?'

'Mr Gissing, did you notice if he took anything with him when he went out for his run?'

'I don't think so.' She yawned again. 'Could you do me a favour, Mr Harris?'

'Yes, of course.'

'Could you pass me that bottle of whisky on the sideboard, please?'

He frowned. It wasn't quite eight, and in his opinion Mrs Gissing had already consumed a substantial amount of alcohol. He picked up the half-empty bottle of Glenlivet and the crystal tumbler beside it.

'Here you are.' He laid both bottle and glass on the low oak coffee table in front of her, smiling now she could see his face again. 'Are you sure I can't fetch you a cup of coffee, call your family, perhaps? I don't mind, honestly.'

'Oh, spare me that tone,' she said wearily, uncorking the bottle and pouring a large measure into the glass with a glug. 'I get enough of that censure from Tim . . . got, I suppose, would be more appropriate now.' She put the glass to her mouth and closed her eyes as she savoured the spirit.

'Well, time I left you in peace. The liaison officer will pop over and make sure you're okay. They'll be able to take you through what will happen next, help you with the arrangements and so on. And they'll let you know how we'll support you financially through all of this. Tim was a very well-respected member of our team, Mrs Gissing, and we look after our own, and their families.'

'He was a whoring bastard, and you all bloody well know it. I'm glad he's had the decency to bugger off,' she spat, her voice slurred by alcohol and bitterness.

'Nonetheless, you have my profound condolences.'

'Huh.'

'Goodbye, Mrs Gissing.' Harris walked quietly towards the door of the lounge, silently giving thanks that he didn't have to spend any more time with this unhappy woman.

'Hold on,' she said. 'I've just remembered. I think he did

take something with him – one of those big brown envelopes. I saw him through the kitchen door as he was leaving. The last time I'll ever see him.'

Harris reached for the phone in his pocket. 'Excuse me, please, Mrs Gissing.' He hurried from the room, scrolling down his contacts list as he went. 'Sir, we have a problem. We'll have to contact the Royal Mail. Gissing posted something in that box on the wall before he killed himself.'

19

Daley felt quite at home in Hamish's cluttered front room, despite the chaos of the place and, of course, Hamish the cat, who eyed him balefully from his master's chair.

'Are you still off the sugar, Mr Daley?' Hamish called from the kitchen.

'Yes, just black for me, please.'

'Ah, good, for I've nane left.' Hamish ambled through from the kitchen, handing his guest a steaming cup of coffee in an old cracked mug. 'Get that doon ye, you're as pale as a ghost.'

'Thanks, Hamish,' replied Daley, feeling rather fragile after his whisky consumption the previous evening.

'You say you've a few places tae visit.'

'Yes, I didn't recognise the names, but I knew you'd know where they are. Here, I made a list.' He handed the old fisherman a note bearing the names mentioned in Urquhart's diary.

Hamish lifted a pair of steel-rimmed glasses from the table beside him, breathed heavily on the lenses, then wiped them on his thick jumper. 'Let the dog see the rabbit, eh?' He read down the list, grunting and nodding his head as he went.

'Do you recognise them all?'

'Aye, I dae. A lot up the west road – you know, wee bays and the like. Naething aboot Kintyre, or the sea that surrounds it, is a mystery tae me, as you well know,' he said, getting stiffly to his feet. 'I found something that'll likely be of interest to you. Jeest gie me a minute or two, while I remember where I put it.'

Daley watched him plod off, and leaned back in the old armchair, making it creak alarmingly. He looked at the painting of the fishing boat struggling through a heavy sea, which hung over Hamish's fireplace, flanked by two ancient oil storm lanterns. Nothing seemed to change in this room; it was exactly the same as when he'd first visited.

Hamish the cat jumped onto the table his owner had made from fish boxes in the fifties, and, purring deeply, placed one of his large paws on the plaster bust of Winston Churchill which resided there.

Daley sipped at his coffee, observing the animal as it stared out of the dirty window between a gap in the yellow net curtains. He felt comfortable here in a way he could never be in the big bungalow on the hill, which still reflected Liz's tastes. He remembered the joy in his son's eyes as he'd stared at the big tinsel-covered Christmas tree. It seemed like an age away, yet it had only been a few short months before. So much had happened – so much had gone wrong – in such a short space of time.

He heard Hamish coming back down the hall – or the lobby, as he preferred to call it.

'Noo, here we are. I came across this by pure accident last night. I was looking tae find a photograph o' my faither, and kind o' hit the jackpot wae this here.' He handed Daley a yellowed newspaper cutting.

The detective studied it. 'Well, no need to guess which one is your father. He's your double.'

'Aye, folk often say that, though my auld mother – God rest her soul – thought I looked mair like her side o' the family when I was a wean. Och, it's jeest like these women that coo o'er their babies. *Oh, he's like my uncle Stanley, she's jeest the spittin' image o' my granny.* The truth is, a' babies jeest look the same, an' that's a fact. You never know whoot they'll end up like.'

Daley looked closer at the cutting. Hamish's father was on the right-hand side. He had the same slanting eyes and inscrutable expression that Daley was so used to seeing in Hamish. He was wearing a flat cap, a pipe in his mouth.

On the left-hand side of the image stood a younger man, no more than a teenager, Daley reckoned. He was wearing a suit that looked too big on his slender frame. He had a small, round face, and his hair was slicked back in the style of the time. 'Who's the boy?' he asked.

'Noo, I think I'm right in sayin' that's Torquil McColl. I tried tae read whoot it said underneath the picture, but the writing's too small for my auld eyes. Maybes you can make it oot.'

Daley squinted at the caption. 'It just says "Constable T. McColl". Did you know him?'

'Aye, I did. And whoot's mair, I know him still.'

'You mean he's still alive?'

'Aye, he is that. Well on now – must be ninety-odds – but still with us. He's a resident in that big auld folk's home on the hill. Jeest doon fae where you are.' Hamish shook his head. 'They tell me it's lovely inside, you know, a' expensive furniture and oil paintings. No' for the likes o' me, mind. You need tae have money tae end your days in a place like thon. Costs a small fortune.'

'So he's well off. I take it he didn't stay in the police, then?'

'No, I'm sure he did. He was away oot the toon for years after whoot happened. Ended up in the Hong Kong polis. Only came back tae retire, they say. Mind you, that was nearly thirty years ago.'

'After what happened?'

'After the policeman disappeared. Inspector Urquhart, the man you've got the interest in. The boy took it really bad, apparently. His father was the procurator fiscal for years – nae shortage o' money wae him, neithers. Folk say they were cousins o' the Duke o' Argyll, but I'm no' sure if that's right.'

'Wait, you said that Urquhart disappeared?'

'Aye, he did that. No' long after that picture was taken, in fact. My faither was always on aboot it. He telt me there was somethin' no' right aboot the whole thing. The auld fella thought he found something, but you know fine whoot like gossip is in Kinloch.'

'Yes, I do.' Sure enough, in the middle of the three stood a thick-set man, his face shaded by the brim of his trilby; there was no mistaking Inspector William Urquhart, all the same.

Daley thought back to the long black lines, the redacted text in Urquhart's records that had frustrated him the night before. The question that formed in his mind was an obvious one: what was being concealed?

Kinloch, 1945

Urquhart slammed the phone back into its cradle. Speaking to senior officers frequently irked him, but the telephone call from the chief constable had incensed him.

153

'Everything all right, sir?' asked McColl, who was sitting at the other end of the office.

'Does it look as though things are all right?'

'S-sorry, sir. I didn't mean to cause offence.'

Urquhart sighed, reaching for the packet of cigarettes on his desk. 'I'm sorry, McColl, not your fault. Make yourself useful and go down to the pier and find Ranald, will you?'

'Yes, sir. Will I bring him back here?'

'Yes, and tell him to smarten himself up. We've to have a photograph in the newspaper, apparently.'

'We? Do you mean me, too, sir?'

'Yes, I mean you, too. They're making a fuss about finding this body, for some unknown reason. No doubt because we were there before the Royal Navy. Times are changing now the war is coming to an end, thank the Lord. Our chief constable thinks it's time that the military gave way to the civilian authorities. Time to get ready for peace, apparently. Now, hurry up and get down to that pier.'

'Do you think it is . . . coming to an end, I mean?'

Urquhart lit his cigarette, sat back in his chair and closed his eyes. Suddenly, he felt weary. 'Oh yes, I don't think there's any doubt about that. Still a lot of blood to be spilled, though. There's never a shortage of blood to be spilled, trust me on that.'

He watched the young man run out of the office, wondering where his own youthful enthusiasm had gone. It wasn't a conscious diminishment, it had just ebbed away. For a few self-indulgent moments he lamented the loss, and the loss of those who were just as he had been and McColl now was; their youth gone for ever, along with their lives.

*

Daley walked along the white sand with Hamish. He could see Gairsay in the distance, framed by the larger islands of Islay and Jura in the blue haze. He had photocopies of the relevant pages of Urquhart's journal in his pocket.

'Says here that the wreckage was almost opposite Cairney's Rock. Where is that?'

'Aye, Cairney's Rock. A mair than useful navigation point known tae all that sail in these waters,' replied Hamish. 'I'm always amazed when these hobby sailors come up here in their bloody yachts and motor cruisers, and get caught oot because they don't know whoot's whoot. They should be made tae spend time studying the waters where they're jeest aboot tae risk their lives.' He squinted into the distance. 'See thon rock oot there?' He pointed to Daley's right with the stem of his pipe.

'Yes.'

'Well, that's Cairney's Rock.'

When they were directly opposite the landmark, Daley consulted his notes. *The wreckage was spread along the beach, the body caught in a small cluster of rocks on the shore, directly opposite a small outcrop that Ranald tells me is called Cairney's Rock.* Daley looked along the waterline. 'Can't see this little cluster of rocks he refers to. Tide must be too high.'

Hamish stroked his stubbly chin, then lifted his cap and scratched his head with his free hand. 'Wait, noo, till I get my bearings.' His eyes narrowed as he stared out to sea.

'What do you mean?'

'Och, that's not Cairney's Rock. I'm thinking that's the Barrel Stacks. My apologies, Mr Daley.'

'So much for "a navigation point known tae all that sail in these waters",' said Daley, repeating Hamish's comment.

'Sure, things look different fae the land. If I was oot on the sea, I'd jeest have you at the right place within moments.'

'Right, so where is this Cairney's Rock?'

Hamish again scanned the horizon, almost as though he was on a strange shore. 'Damn it!' he said, spitting on the sand.

'What?'

'We're on the wrong beach,' replied Hamish, purposefully not looking at the detective.

'Bloody hell, Hamish! To think I've always felt as though I was in safe hands when I was out with you.'

'Aye, and right you are, tae. There's no' a drop o' water I don't know about aroon this peninsula.'

'Apart from Cairney's Rock,' said Daley, finding it hard not laugh.

'Auld age doesna come alone, an' that's a fact.'

The pair trudged off the beach, back to where Daley's car was parked up on a verge, and drove to what Daley hoped would be the right beach. By his side, Hamish did his best to maintain a dignified silence.

20

Iolo Harris detected an unusual air of panic, or as close to it as the Security Service ever came, as he sat in Colin Flanagan's office.

Three juniors were making their case to Flanagan, whose genial mood from earlier in the morning had changed to ill-concealed rage.

'So, with all the resources we have at our disposal, we were unable to intercept the envelope? I find this incredible.'

'The Royal Mail were very slow to respond to our request, sir. By the time they replied to our email, the item was lost in the system.'

'Oh, I see. So when I asked you to intercept the mail, as a matter of urgency, your response was to jump to it and . . . send an email.'

'Well, yes, sir. I followed our protocols, as always. I—'

'Forget the protocols! You should've been down in the sorting office, making sure my instructions were followed, doing whatever it took. The world doesn't exist in this virtual hyperspace, or whatever you want to call it!'

'Cyberspace, sir,' offered the most junior officer.

Harris winced, guessing what the consequences of this remark were likely to be. He was right.

'Get out,' said Flanagan, staring at the ceiling.

'Sorry, sir?' The young man looked as though he hadn't heard what his boss had said.

'Just get out of my sight!' said Flanagan. 'In fact, go, all of you. I want to speak with Harris alone.'

The three younger men gathered together their papers and laptops and phones and jostled out of the room in an embarrassed silence.

As the door closed, Flanagan shook his head. He turned to the Welshman. 'Three PhDs between them, and they're incapable of the basics. Honestly, I don't know what we're bringing on with this new generation. No bloody common sense. Perish the thought we have to rely on them to defend our nation.'

'What now? Do we have any idea what Gissing was up to or what he posted?'

'That's the thing. I have a basic notion of what was happening, and I'm afraid it isn't good. If I say we're up to our neck in it with the EU and some of their many bloody committees and nooks and crannies, you can imagine how difficult things are going to get. And I'm holding the baby.'

'How so, sir?'

'You're my best asset. This is a close-down job. Gissing and his ilk have been allowed to manage a very difficult situation for years without proper supervision. The whole thing is a bloody mess.'

'What's a mess, sir? If I'm to fix this, I'll need to know what's happening.'

'How good is your knowledge of history, Iolo?'

'Not bad, I suppose. I enjoyed history at Port Talbot Grammar.'

'Well, forget all you've learned. Come with me.' Flanagan stood. 'First of all, we'll have to change your security clearance.'

The pair left the conference room, Harris now thoroughly confused.

Symington hesitated before entering the incident room, closed her eyes in silent prayer, and turned the handle.

Inside, five Special Branch officers were sitting in quiet conversation. The oldest, a thickset man with salt-and-pepper hair, in his early sixties, stood to welcome her.

'Chief Superintendent, pleased to meet you again. I'm Commander Alan Bale, in charge of this lot.' He smiled, holding out his hand for her to shake. 'I think we worked together in Wandsworth nick.'

'You were in charge of the CID there, if I recall,' replied Symington, focusing only on the older man and keeping her tone jovial, 'so I'm not sure "worked together" is quite right. I was only a young copper.'

'Well, it does now. I'll introduce you to our little team. I've sent our forensic boys up to Achnamara to get set up.' He looked across to one of his officers, who had coughed, drawing attention to himself. 'Yes, sorry. You know Harry here, don't you? Chief Inspector Harry Chappell, to give him his full title.'

For the first time since entering the room, Symington glanced at Chappell. He'd put on weight and his black hair had flecks of grey, but there was no mistaking the lop-sided sneer as he stood to welcome her.

'Harry, how are you?' she said stiffly.

'Just fine and dandy, ma'am,' replied Chappell, his Cockney accent still strong. 'Long time no see. Mind you, no wonder with you up in the wilds here.'

A faint smile was the best she could muster. She didn't know what Chappell had told his colleagues about her, but was relieved to note that Bale and the other officers appeared friendly, with none of the little glances and whispered asides she'd been expecting. It was early days, though.

'Now, I've spoken to your ACC. We'd like you to stay on the island for a couple of days, to get us up to speed. Not our usual patch, as you know, Carrie. May I call you Carrie?' asked Bale.

'Of course.' Symington was off her stride. She had expected to take the first available ferry back to Kinloch once she'd briefed the specialist team. 'I have a lot on, so if we can make this as brief as possible, I would be obliged, Commander Bale.'

'Your boss tells me that he has your duties at your division covered. This is a tricky one, from what I've been told. There's a spook on his way from Whitehall. I want to get all of our ducks in a row before he arrives.' Bale looked around the room. 'How do we get coffee in this place, or is it just single malt on offer?' His team chuckled at the notion.

'I'll come with you and you can show me what's what,' said Chappell with a grin. 'We've a lot to catch up on, Carrie.'

She wasn't sure whether she'd imagined it, but she thought she'd caught one of the detectives giving her a knowing smile. 'Sure. It'll be good to hear what you've been up to all this time.' She jutted out her chin, shook Bale's hand, and left the room, Harry Chappell in her wake.

Outside the incident room, she jumped when he grabbed her wrist.

'Nice little display in there, Carrie. Cool as a cucumber, as always. Come here and let me get a proper look at you.' He tugged roughly at her arm, forcing her to turn her face into his. She could smell his breath as he looked her up and down. 'Isn't this nice, ma'am? Me and you in this romantic little hotel.'

She flinched as specks of his saliva hit her face. 'Fuck you, Harry. I'm not surprised that you're here, by the way. I knew you were part of the team. So, if you think you have me at a disadvantage, you're mistaken.' She yanked her wrist from his grip, a defiant look on her face.

'I'm not bothered about having you at a disadvantage, love. Just having you will do nicely.' He stroked her cheek.

'There you are, ma'am,' said the familiar voice of Brian Scott. 'Eh, sorry, hope I've no' interrupted anything.' He cleared his throat awkwardly.

'No, not at all,' replied Symington. 'Harry here has just been sent out to get the coffee. Haven't you, Harry?'

Iolo Harris looked out at the London traffic from the back of the car taking him to Gatwick. 'How long now?' he asked the driver, who informed him it would take at least another hour.

He reached across the back seat and lifted the aluminium briefcase onto his lap. He removed his laptop and typed in his security code. Soon, he was looking at a map of the island of Gairsay. He zoomed in on the satellite image of Achnamara farmhouse. He could see the pattern of the fields and the outline of the coast nearby, the shade of the sea deepening further out.

With his thumb and forefinger, he pinched the screen, making the farmhouse disappear as he accessed the large-scale map. He looked at the Kintyre peninsula, snaking down the west coast of Scotland. Pulling the map to the right, the Antrim coast of Northern Ireland came into sharp focus. He noted how close Gairsay was to Rathlin Island – only a few short sea miles.

He stared out of the window without taking in much of what was passing. Of all the tasks he'd undertaken in his twenty-odd years in the service, this promised to be the strangest, with more potential to blow up in his face than any other.

He took his mobile phone from his pocket, pressed the name he wanted, then waited as his call connected.

'Good morning, County Hotel, Kinloch. How can I help you?'

'Yes, I'd like to book a room for tonight, for a couple of nights, actually.'

'Yes, of course. Wid it be a single or a double you're after?'

'Single, please. The name's Harris, Iolo Harris. I'll be arriving on this evening's flight from Glasgow.'

With his room booked, he sat back, put the phone in his pocket and contemplated the satellite map on his laptop.

His driver cursed and sounded the horn at some errant road user as they made their slow but steady way to the airport.

21

Carpoch Farm, near Blaan, 1945

'You ken fine you're for the market, big fella,' said Dugald Kerr to the wild-eyed Ayrshire bull lumbering around the paddock. He looked across the farmyard to the young man clad in muddy dungarees and rubber boots ambling towards him. 'Andra, get yourself o'er here wae a bit mair urgency! I've an appointment in the County Hotel, as you well know, so we need tae get this big bugger up and intae the float.' He took off his cap and scratched his head as Andra shrugged his shoulders and imperceptibly hastened his progress.

'Haud your horses,' he said under his breath as he neared the farmer.

'I'd rather you were hauding my bull, sonny Jim,' replied Kerr. 'I might be getting on, but there's naething wrong wae my hearing. Get a move on. You're lucky you're no' at the toe-end o' some sergeant major's boot. If I'd no' given you a place here, you'd be in the army, you ungrateful bugger.'

'Whoot dae you want me tae dae?'

'You bring doon the ramp and I'll get a haud o' him. I want tae lead him straight oot the gate and intae the float, so be on your mettle. You ken fine whoot happened tae Tommy Tait last year, so I'd rather you and me didna get crushed like he did, regardless o' you being a lazy swine.'

The farmhand walked over to the float, and on his tiptoes unhooked both sides of the rear ramp, which also served as the door, lowering it slowly to the ground, groaning with the effort.

'Ach, come on, it's no' that heavy,' said Kerr as he put a foot on the second bar of the paddock gate. The animal snorted and stamped towards him, the whites of its eyes flashing. 'Aye, but you're a bad-tempered bugger, right enough. I'll be heartily glad tae see the back o' you. Right, Andra, when I get a grip o' the chain, you get the gate, and I'll fire him up the ramp.'

The farmhand sauntered towards the five-bar gate, ready to lift the latch to enable Kerr to lead the bull from the paddock, up the ramp and into the float, using the heavy chain which was attached to a ring in the animal's nose.

'Right, are you ready?' shouted Kerr, pushing his cap to the back of his head.

On hearing a grunt from the farmhand, he leaned over the gate, tongue poking between his teeth with concentration. With a swiftness of movement and timing born of many years of handling livestock, he caught the chain, jumped to the ground, and pulled the bellowing bull towards the gate that the farmhand was now swinging open.

Kerr tugged at the chain again, and soon the bull was free of the paddock and had taken its first lumbering steps up the stout wooden ramp, which creaked alarmingly with its weight.

'That's it, big fella, jeest you keep going,' said Kerr. He moved quickly, threading the chain through a ring in the float and bringing down a large iron keeper that would hold the animal securely in place as they travelled the few miles to the market in Kinloch. He sidestepped the beast and began inching his way out of the container as the animal snorted and stamped, making the float rock in protest.

Such was the effort and concentration the farmer had put into getting the bull secured, he was only vaguely aware of the encroaching darkness as he tried to jump clear of the beast. But, before he could exit the float, the ramp had been raised and slammed shut.

'Andra! What the fuck are you doing?' he shouted, the panic evident in his voice as he heard the external latches being forced into place. 'Andra!' he screamed as he felt a hefty blow to the back of his leg, which sent him tumbling to the floor with a sickening thud.

His screams were silenced in his throat as the bull brought its right hind leg down on his head, over and over again, sending the bloody pulp of his brain splattering up the side of the float.

Daley looked at the sinister black rocks poking through the waves and the squall of rain passing across the sea, making patterns in the dark water. It was here that Urquhart had found the dead sailor's body amongst the wreckage of the German motor cruiser. He tried to picture the scene as the inspector made his gruesome discovery; the dark clouds added to the brooding atmosphere, and he could visualise his predecessor bending over the remains of the dead man.

He shivered as a sudden cold gust of wind whipped some sand from the beach into his face. Winter wasn't ready to hand its crown to spring just yet. For an instant, he could see Mary, wrapped up against the cold, staring into his face as they stood on the roadside near Blaan, looking at the fire on the hill in the darkness. Part of him wanted the season to remain; it echoed the perpetual winter he had in his heart.

'Does it help you tae picture things in your mind, Mr Daley?' asked Hamish, breaking the mood.

'Yes, sometimes. It's such a long time ago. I can only imagine how different things must have been just after the war.'

'Aye, they were that, fae whoot I can mind o' them at any rate, which isna much. I can still see my faither, mark you, as plain as day in my mind's eye.'

'You've never talked about him much.'

'No. Och, he wisna the man he'd been towards the end of his life. Times got tough at the fishing, and he resorted tae the bottle as a soulmate. Mind, I've been known tae sink a few mysel', so I'll no' haud that against him.'

The two men made their way back along the beach, Daley turning to take one last look at the scene described so well in Urquhart's diary. He had that familiar feeling again: the hunch that said something wasn't right about this situation, the tiny, nagging voice he could not ignore – had never been able to ignore.

'I wonder, this McColl, is he still *with us*, if you know what I mean?'

'He was the last time I saw him,' replied Hamish. 'I used tae go up there tae visit an auld friend of mine. He's deid noo, died nearly a year ago. But Mr McColl was as bright as a button then. Great for his age, in fact.'

'Right, let's go and pay him a visit.' Daley strode off across the machair as Hamish tapped his pipe on the back of his hand, sending ashes flying across the beach and into the restless sea.

Kinloch, 1945

A hush descended on the County Hotel bar as Urquhart walked into the smoke-filled room and sat down. He checked his pocket watch; he was early for his meeting with Kerr. He felt as though he deserved a drink. He liked the calming effect of alcohol at the end of a working day; more often than not he would nurse a solitary malt in his lodgings, using the time to take stock of his day and plan the next – weighing up the many challenges and frustrations he had faced and would face.

For the inspector, the social aspect of having a drink with friends was something to which he couldn't connect – well, not for a few years, at least. He had an unbreakable rule of not entering into friendships within the police, and his role as a police officer meant he was at arm's length from those outside his working world. In any case, those whom he had thought of as friends were either dead or lost in this war that had enveloped the world, each making his own sacrifice in a desperate effort to bring order back to society.

The barman nodded to him while pouring a glass of beer for another customer. There were a few bottles of whisky on display. Kinloch had many distilleries, and though their output had been restricted by wartime rationing on barley, they still managed to keep a smile on the faces of local drinkers by supplying the pubs and hotels with *uisge beatha* – the water of life. The black market in illicit whisky was rife, but in the main the police were advised to turn a blind eye unless business became overt. The much-needed morale engendered by the soothing notes of the amber liquid was more important than the enforcement of a law that the locals would have ignored or found ingenious ways of evading.

For this reason, as well as the fact that few of them had anything seriously criminal to hide, the initial reticence elicited by his unaccustomed appearance in the premises was quickly replaced by a welcoming bonhomie. It soon became clear that the detective's visits were driven by leisure and relaxation, and not duty.

Urquhart had worked in many places since leaving the army and joining the civilian police force, but he hadn't encountered a community as close-knit as that of Kinloch. Everyone appeared entirely at ease with each other. The population of the town was more like an extended family than a group of people who only had their place of residence in common. He had been amazed and strangely heartened by the huge numbers who turned out for local funerals. It seemed as though the whole town wished to pay its respects to fellow citizens on their final trip to the afterlife. It was the way things used to be, Urquhart mused, and none the worse for it.

Also, the good people of Kinloch had coped well with the influx of the military – mainly the Royal Navy – who had more than doubled the population of the West Highland town. Everyone seemed to rub along relatively well. Of course, there were fights between local lads and their uniformed counterparts, but none of the blatant resentment he'd witnessed in other places.

'Can I help you, Inspector?' The barman was wearing a claret-coloured apron over his white shirt, with the name of the hotel embroidered upon it, the sleeves of his shirt held back from his wrists by silver armbands. His bow tie matched the colour of the apron, and his hair was slick with pomade.

'Just a bottle of beer, please, no preference.' Urquhart had realised that it was best to accept what was on offer, rather than to try and find a favourite brew. The barman reached under the counter and held up a bottle of dark beer with a light blue label – a local brew the inspector had enjoyed in the past.

'No' on the hard stuff the day, Mr Urquhart?' asked a stout fisherman with whom he had a passing acquaintance.

'No, Jamie. Just a beer or two will do me.' He smiled and watched the barman pour his beer into a glass, leaving a perfect head. The latter turned to press the big brass keys of the wooden till, which sat alongside a bust of Winston Churchill, staring out grumpily. A wooden plaque bearing the crest of the Argyll and Sutherland Highlanders, the local regiment, took pride of place in front of a small Union Jack tacked across the rear of the serving area.

There were ranks of photographs, too: monochrome, some sepia, but almost all of young men in uniform, either smiling at the camera and holding up glasses of beer or staring earnestly. These were images of the young men of Kinloch, off fighting around the globe. Urquhart thought it a nice touch, as he scanned along the images and remembered his own youth in the army.

'Thank you, Inspector,' said the barman as Urquhart handed him a few coins. 'Great tae see folk wae the right money, so I don't have tae go footering aboot wae change.'

'You'd take a scabby goat as payment, Colin,' shouted the fisherman. 'I mind auld Duncan had a great night oot a couple o' weeks ago wae the three rabbits he brought you.'

'I'm sure the inspector doesna want tae hear aboot that,' replied Colin, clearing his throat by way of emphasis and turning swiftly to attend to the next customer.

Before he could take a seat to wait for Kerr, an old man tapped him on the shoulder. 'They're telling me that you found a boatful of deid sailors up on the west shore the day, Mr Urquhart.'

'That's a bit of an exaggeration,' he said in reply.

'Jeest after they poor buggers on that submarine, tae. An awful business.'

'That wisna a submarine, it was a U-boat, Erchie. Hell mend them's whoot I say,' replied Colin, even though the comments had not been directed at him. 'They were oot tae sink oor boats and condemn all on them tae a watery grave. You shouldna have any sympathy.' This was accompanied by a general murmur of agreement.

Erchie, though, was unbowed. 'You'll likely never have seen a drooning man, Colin. No' wae you being in the hotel trade, an' a'.'

'Aye, maybes not, but I've seen my fair share of dying men. Mind, I served in the last conflict, an' no' as a barman, neithers.'

'Well, I've been at the fishing for a long time, and seen mair than my fair share of tragedy. An' as far as I'm concerned, there's naething worse than dying in the sea. So I'm no' bothered if these men was fae Germany, Glesca or darkest Africa, they deserve oor respect. Mind, it wisna them who started a' this war buggeration.'

Urquhart was surprised how quiet the bar became, but soon realised why: he was living at the heart of a fishing community. Wars would come and go, but the sea was always the enemy for many of the townspeople who made their living in search of fish. In his short time in the town, a number of lives had been lost – not as a result of enemy action, but in the atrocious weather in which fishermen regularly risked their lives.

The silence persisted as Urquhart settled into a seat near the back of the room, as far away from a couple of young sailors as he could get. Kerr had implied confidentiality, so whatever secret he was about to impart, Urquhart reckoned it unlikely he'd wish to share it with the rest of the County Hotel's clientele.

After twenty minutes he looked at his watch. Kerr was now late. However, he reassured himself, this was Kinloch, where folk appeared to operate in an entirely different time zone to the rest of the nation. The old rules of the country still held sway here. The town of Kinloch was surrounded by countryside and the sea; the nearest sizeable centre of population was more than fifty miles away. In places like this, time wore another expression, more imperturbable.

At five thirty the door swung open to reveal a young man in filthy dungarees. 'Gie me a large whisky, please, Colin,' he said, sitting on a stool by the bar. His face was pale, and he looked agitated, Urquhart noticed.

'Aye, son, nae bother. No' like you tae take the whisky. Whoot's up?'

'Bad news, Colin,' replied the youth, almost close to tears.

The murmur of voices ebbed. 'I'm sorry tae hear that, son. Whoot kind o' bad news, if you don't mind me asking?'

The young man took off his bunnet, as though from respect, and bowed his head. 'My great-uncle Dougie's deid.'

Colin placed a small glass, almost full to the brim with whisky, down in front of the man. 'What? He was only in here this morning – my first customer, in fact. He seemed in fine trim. Whoot on earth happened?'

Urquhart put down his own glass, waiting for the reply.

'Killed by a bull. A hell of a sight, apparently. The polis has jeest been tae oor hoose tae tell my mother. I had tae get oot, I didna know whoot tae say.'

Urquhart got up and walked to the bar. After having his photograph taken for the local paper, he had kept away from the office, busying himself with investigations regarding the dead sailor. Nobody had sought him out to tell him. But, if this was a farming accident, the involvement of the police would be minimal. 'You have my condolences, young man,' he said, reaching out to shake his hand. 'Your uncle, what was his full name?'

'Dugald Kerr, Inspector. He had a farm near Blaan. I don't know if you know him.'

Urquhart watched as the lad drank his whisky in one gulp, then coughed.

'Get him another, please,' said Urquhart, feeling cold now, despite the warmth of the day.

22

Daley had driven straight past the large gates to the retirement home, not realising that the imposing sandstone mansion tucked behind a screen of trees was in fact his destination. The tyres of his car popped and cracked their way along the long driveway. Originally the summer home of one of Glasgow's famous tobacco barons, the building was now Kinloch's most exclusive home for the elderly, hidden in the trees, away from prying eyes.

'No' bad, eh?' said Hamish from the passenger seat. 'Only those and such as those get the chance tae end their days here.'

The pair walked up a flight of stone steps under an ornate iron canopy to the front door. A small brass plaque read WELCOME TO STONEBRAE HOUSE. PLEASE RING THE BELL AND WAIT FOR ASSISTANCE. Daley pressed the white enamel button.

They were greeted by a young woman in a smart trouser suit, who introduced herself as Miss Heather Campbell, the manager, and led them through a tiled vestibule towards a lift.

'We do our best to make this more like a home and less of a facility for the elderly,' she said proudly. 'Mr McColl's on the top floor now. He likes the view – sits at the window for hours on end staring at the loch and the hills. Oh, he's happy enough, of course,' she added hurriedly, in case the visitors formed the opposite impression. 'We all have to slow down, and Mr McColl's well into his nineties now.'

The lift juddered to a stop, and she took them down a wood-panelled corridor. Gilt-framed oil paintings adorned the walls, and crystal vases brimming with freshly cut flowers sat on each windowsill. Stonebrae House was at nearly the same elevation as Daley's bungalow, and from the top floor the views across the tops of the trees and down to the loch were breathtaking.

At the end of the corridor was a stout oak door bearing a brass plate with MR TORQUIL MCCOLL etched on it. No room numbers here, Daley noted. Nor was there the odour of disinfectant or unwashed elderly bodies he associated with homes for the elderly. One of Brian Scott's favourite aphorisms came to mind: *Life's a shit sandwich. The more dosh you've got, the less shit you eat.* Here, there was only the scent of money.

A faint voice could be heard in reply to the manager's knock, and soon Daley and Hamish were shown into an airy, high-ceilinged room, home to a comfortable leather suite, grand fireplace and several antique paintings and ornaments. The only clues that this was a care home were a few emergency cords hanging from the ceiling and handrails placed around the walls.

'Mr McColl, Chief Inspector Daley from the Kinloch Police is here to have a wee word. Nothing to worry about, I'm sure. And you'll remember Hamish,' said Miss Campbell.

The old man sitting in a wheelchair by the bay window turned to face his guests. 'Heather, I've been talking to policemen for most of my life, as well as being one myself for more years than I care to remember. Hello, Inspector Daley, and it's nice to see you again, Hamish. I know you're still fishing, because I see your wee lobster boat chugging in and out the loch, through these . . .' He held up a pair of expensive binoculars, rather unsteadily.

Daley studied the old man. Torquil McColl was painfully thin, with wispy hair and an aquiline nose. His hooded blue eyes, washed pale by the years, peered out from a heavily wrinkled face; he very much looked his age, though he smiled at the detective with a steady, determined gaze. Daley guessed that his mind was still sharp, despite a failing body, and pictured the photograph of the three men in the newspaper cutting that Hamish had given him earlier. It was hard to believe that the gangly youth in the oversized suit, standing proudly next to Inspector William Urquhart, was the man now in front of him.

'Can I get you some tea or coffee, gentlemen?' asked Miss Campbell brightly. When they declined, she left the room, reminding them to give her a call when they were ready to leave.

'Lovely place,' said Daley, reaching out to shake McColl by the hand. He was surprised to note the strength of the old man's grip.

'Yes, it is. I'd rather have stayed in Hong Kong, but even then we knew that the Chinese would be back in charge before long, and I didn't want to be left to their tender mercies,' replied McColl. 'Since here and there were the places where I spent most of my life, the choice was s-simple.'

Daley smiled, detecting a hint of the stammer that Urquhart had mentioned in his journal. 'How many years did you serve there, Mr McColl?'

'Most of my career. They had to drag me out kicking and screaming. I was the assistant commissioner by then. But all good things must come to an end. I'm glad I'm not there now, though things have turned out better than most of us thought. I fully expected blood on the streets. We've had some of that, but who would have thought the Chinese could change their ways? Power of money, Inspector Daley, the power of money. Even works on communists.' He coughed, a broad smile still spread across his face. 'Now, you didn't come to hear me babble on about Hong Kong. What do you want from this ancient artefact?'

Brian Scott prided himself on the fact that he knew the workings of the female mind much better than most of the fairer sex were prepared to give him credit for. There were still areas of mystery, of course, like shopping, clothes, soft furnishings and the love of small children, but when it came to things that mattered, he was sure he could penetrate their psyche. He'd watched Symington closely since the arrival of the Special Branch team from London, and though he didn't know her well, he had spotted a dramatic erosion in her confidence – a nervous quality he hadn't hitherto associated with his new boss.

He was watching her again as she looked out of the dining-room window, a small coffee cup poised in front of her mouth, her face bearing a blank expression.

'Penny for them,' he said, making her blink.

'Sorry? Oh, just daydreaming. I didn't sleep too well – all that rain and wind. It reminded me of home.'

'When I think of home I get a' nostalgic. No' the same for you, I see.'

She smiled. 'Nostalgia mixed with a little sadness, in my case.'

'How so?'

'Oh, I had a nice childhood, really. My father managed an estate, and he passed on his love of the outdoors to me. Do you know North Yorkshire?'

'Me and the wife took the weans tae Scarborough once. Long time ago, noo – thon Flamingo place.'

'Flamingo Land. Yes, I went there, too, when I was young. All the fun of the fair, eh?'

'Och, I cannae bear a' that fairground stuff – left that tae her an' the weans. Some nice wee boozers aboot, mind you.' It was his turn to stare out of the window, remembering when alcohol had played such a large part in his life.

'Missing a pint or two, Brian?'

He snorted. 'That's the problem having a conversation wae another cop. The buggers are always trying tae analyse your response, like an interrogation. Oor Jimmy does it tae me all the time. Might as well talk tae thon Keith Floyd bloke.'

Symington decided to let the Floyd–Freud confusion go. 'You're worried about him, aren't you?'

'Who, Jimmy? Aye, I am, a wee bit. He's taken a hell of a blow recently. I never thought he'd leave Liz, like we said. And for that tae happen tae Mary. Well, it would put anyone intae a downer. The bugger thinks too much, though – he's always been the same.' He paused for a moment. 'I'm thinking you might be the same, tae.'

She smiled weakly and took a sip of coffee. '*Touché*, Brian.'

'So, your faither, dae you no' see so much o' him noo?'

177

'He died not that long ago – a couple of years, in fact.' Her expression remained bright, but Scott could see a flash of pain in her eyes.

'I'm sorry tae hear that. I lost my folks a while ago, noo. Never gets any easier, really.'

'That's kind of you,' she replied honestly.

'Oh, aye. Me and my big mooth. Sorry . . .'

'Not at all. It has been hard. Dad and I were really close. And, well, I suppose these days you just don't expect people to die in their early sixties. Everyone seems to live for ever. None of my friends have lost their parents. I feel cheated, somehow.'

'Where I come fae, if you make it tae your mid fifties the bloke fae the *Guinness Book o' Records* comes roon for a chat. We're no' famous for being long-lifers in the East End o' Glasgow.'

'Right. We better get going. I want to have a look at a couple of places on the island. Would you like to come with me? We're kind of kicking our heels until I get the green light to leave, which won't be today.'

Scott's attention turned to the weather. The storm seemed to have blown itself out. The pale green sea was still capped by scudding white horses, but the sky no longer glowered overhead. He even spotted a patch of blue. 'Aye, a wee walka-boot would be grand. Apart fae my wee run, all I've really seen o' this place is that farm, and the inside o' the hotel. Dae you think they'll ever get tae the bottom o' all this?'

'They might, but I don't think they'll be quick to tell us. It's one of the reasons I want to take this walk. That old woman has been bothering me.'

'The old woman? You don't mean that auld soak, dae you?'

'That's a bit judgemental, Brian. She knew the Bremner family well. Strikes me there just might be some information hidden under all that booze.'

'Well, you'll need tae get a deep-sea diver tae swim doon an' get it.' He thought for a moment. 'So you're no' giving up on the investigation, even though the Branch has arrived?'

'No, why should I? This is our patch. We have the right to investigate what we want.'

Scott watched as she shifted uncomfortably. It had taken a while to be sure, but he was now convinced that there was something about the team of investigators who had landed on Gairsay that Carrie Symington didn't like. Well, one of the team in particular, thought Scott, as they readied themselves for their excursion.

Daley was surprised to see tears welling in McColl's eyes. 'He was a good man, Inspector Daley. Oh yes, very brusque, didn't suffer fools gladly and all that. But if he'd not been kind enough to keep me on, my life would have been very different.'

'You'd have found another job, Mr McColl.'

'Yes, yes, of course, my father would have seen to that. However, I'd always wanted to become a police officer – since childhood, in fact. The trouble was, if you'll pardon the sentiment, my father had a very low opinion of the police.'

'Why so?' asked Daley.

'A lot of snobbery in those days. We were distantly noble, if you know what I mean.'

'Man, so it's right,' said Hamish, slapping his own knee. 'Yous are off the Duke o' Argyll, right enough.'

McColl spluttered, then took a sip of water before he could reply. 'Does that hoary old tale still have legs? My word, Hamish, I've not heard that theory for a long time.'

'Oh, so are you sayin' it's no' true?'

'No, no, not in the slightest. I think my great-grandfather had something to do with the duke's estate. But relatives? Not at all. Though my father behaved as though he could have been a belted earl.' He smiled at the thought. 'To answer your question, Inspector, my father had been the procurator fiscal in Kinloch for a number of years. He was a clever man – law at Cambridge. However, in those days, if you wanted to have any success in private practice, you had to have a very large silver spoon in your mouth. We didn't, so he had to settle for life as a junior member of the rural judiciary.'

'He must have come into contact with some interesting people at Cambridge?'

'Oh yes. That's where the stories about our being related to the duke probably come from. He had a number of very influential friends – lords, ladies, even some of the more minor royals. He'd lived in that world prior to the first war. Things were very different, as he kept telling me.'

'In what way?'

'Lots of ways. Part of him could never reconcile the fact that we were at war with Germany for the second time. Always quoting Wellington – you know, about how fine the Prussian military were. They'd been our allies against the French for many, many years.'

'So he was sympathetic to the Germans?'

McColl's face darkened, the smile of recollection disappearing from his lips. 'It was a strange time, Inspector Daley. He wanted me to go into the army but was keen I should wait until after the conflict.'

'So you were fit enough to go? Sorry – for some reason I thought you had some kind of medical condition.'

'Friendly doctor, enough said. For all our disagreements as we were growing up, he didn't want to see me come to harm. Said that the world would be a very different place after the war – a better place. We would finally see the error of our ways in Europe and pursue our collective interests, rather than knocking lumps off each other.'

'Sounds like the Common Market,' said Hamish, still disappointed that his theories as to McColl's connection to the dukes of Argyll had been proven wrong.

'Yes. I suppose so.' He stared out of the window again, the lids of his eyes slowly closing.

'You should have a rest, Mr McColl. Thanks for seeing us. I'll come back and see you again, and maybe I can hear more about Inspector Urquhart.'

'Yes. I am feeling rather tired now. All this reminiscing. Please, do come back soon. Nice to talk to a fellow officer again.' He nodded, smiling, then paused. 'Oh, Hamish, before you go, I have something you might be interested in. Funnily enough, I just looked it out earlier – came across it when I was tidying what's left of my possessions. Can't leave a mess behind and all that – time is short.' He pointed to a chest of drawers on the far side of the room. 'It's a book, on the top there. I know an old sea dog like yourself will give it a good home.'

The dust jacket of the old book was faded. The title read, *The Ring-net Fishermen of Kintyre*.

'Thanks, Mr McColl. Jeest the thing for a wet afternoon. What good luck you came across it before I appeared tae see you,' said Hamish.

'In my experience, luck like that is a regular occurrence. The Chinese have a saying – buggered if I can remember it now. Anyway, I hope you enjoy it. It's a little treasure trove.'

Daley rang the bell, and in a few minutes they were being escorted out of the building.

As the car headed down the driveway, the detective looked across the loch. As always, the big island stood sentinel over the harbour. The tide was low, and the causeway snaked from the shore through the shallows.

23

Iolo Harris sat at the departure gate in Glasgow airport. His Celtic blood was stirred by the change in accents and the friendliness he associated with being at home in Wales, across the water in Ireland, or, as he was now, with his Scottish cousins. Though he'd made London his home, worked there for many years, he'd never really come to terms with the anonymity of the place. Now that it was becoming an even larger melting pot, folk tended to stick to their own. He'd even joined a Welsh choir. That closeness, the familiarity, made him feel closer to the Valleys.

When he listened to his children now, they were English in heart and mind. He recalled the funeral he'd attended in Port Talbot a few weeks before – an old uncle who had lived a remarkably long life. One of his cousins was now working as a computer programmer in Los Angeles. He'd been struck by how American his cousin's children had sounded and behaved. This amused Iolo until he turned to his own son, his eldest, who had also made the trip to pay his respects. He was the spitting image of his father but he wasn't at home amongst the belching steelworks, chimneys and narrow streets of Port Talbot. For him, home was London.

But, in his heart, Iolo knew it would never be his home. He was glad he was going to a seaside town. He'd done some research on the Isle of Gairsay, the Kintyre peninsula, and his immediate destination, the town of Kinloch. Its proximity to County Donegal, where the body of Mrs Bremner had been found, was striking.

Be bold with this, his boss had advised. We've lived with cover-ups for too long. But be discreet.

Being discreet was the essence of his profession. In his opinion, discretion could be defined in a number of ways. Sometimes he had to persuade and cajole; at other times he had to deploy less sophisticated techniques. Threats and the ability to dissemble while remaining an apparent pillar of the state were some of the tools he had to use.

The greater good must prevail. His nation's security was the greater good, and he reconciled himself to the fact that anything he did was justifiable in keeping its people safe, whether they be from Port Talbot or Peterborough, Paraguay or Potsdam.

He'd read the briefing file. He knew what he had to do. How he would do it was another matter entirely.

He hated working with outside agencies. In this case, he would have to deal with officers from Police Scotland and Special Branch; in his view, both agencies had their justifiable detractors. He particularly disliked Special Branch's flat-footed cops who fancied themselves as James Bond.

He'd have to stamp all over that lot.

A voice made him jump. 'Is this the right place for the plane tae Kinloch?'

'Yes, this is the right gate.'

'Thank God for that,' said a small elderly man with heavy stubble, an old-fashioned flat cap and the distinct odour of whisky on his breath. 'Dae you know, I've no' been on a plane since my national service? That bloody road's collapsed at the Rest again, so I've nae choice. Here,' he said, presenting a wrinkled paper bag, 'dae you want a mint imperial?'

Harris was about to politely refuse the kind gesture, unsure as to the hygienic provenance of the confectionery. However, something about this old man reminded him of those of a similar vintage who used to watch him play rugby in Maesteg, and it warmed his heart. 'Right, thanks, buddy,' he said, reaching into the bag and grabbing a mint, hearing himself sound more Welsh than usual.

The old man rubbed his nose on his sleeve and sniffed deeply. 'Is this you away tae Kinloch, Taffy?'

'Sorry? Oh yes, I am.' Harris sat back, propelling the sweet around his mouth with his tongue, feeling, for the first time in a long time, perfectly at home.

Scott and Symington were struggling up a small rise through the heather, their boots squelching in the muddy ground underfoot. Scott seemed to have an ample supply of profanities, fit for any occasion, and Symington was amused that it hadn't failed him on this latest expedition.

'You okay?' she asked, as her companion slipped forward onto the heather.

'Aye, just fine,' he replied, pulling himself back up and examining the mud splattered up his trousers with dismay. 'The going leaves a bit tae be desired, mind you. It looked like a wee jaunt fae the bottom o' the hill.'

185

Symington consulted her OS map, then looked along the rise, only a few yards away. 'Nearly there, I think.'

Soon, the muddy conditions gave way to harder rock, and in minutes they were surveying the scene from one of the higher points of the island. Behind them, with its low hills and sandy beaches, stretched the Kintyre peninsula. In the opposite direction, looking out to sea, was the distant loom of Ireland, and on the other the land masses of Islay and Jura, the latter's peaks silhouetted sharply against the sky.

'We go this way,' said Symington, pointing to her right.

As Scott complained about his muddy clothes, he heard a low noise, a cross between a rumble and a moan, which intensified as they walked.

'Sounds like the hame o' the deid,' remarked Scott.

'Oh, wait,' said Symington, cocking her head to one side. 'Wow, I think that's a snipe.'

'A whit?'

'A snipe, you know, the bird.'

'Oh, right, I'll take your word for it, ma'am. My experience o' birds is kinda limited.'

'Because you're a city boy?'

'Naw, 'cause my missus would string me up.' He smiled to himself. 'What's the other noise – that moaning racket?'

'That, Brian, is the Well of the Winds.' They walked on until, in front of them, amid long rushes, appeared a lochan. The water was grey, the wind rippling its surface. The moan sounded more like a lament for the dead now – a deep wail with no determinate source. 'Creepy, isn't it?'

'Aye, you can say that again. Near as bad as that bloody Rat Stone.' He shuddered at the thought. 'Does everything make a bloody racket here?'

'The difference is that this is an entirely geological feature. It just happened by accident, not the product of some ancient fevered mind. Something to do with the way the rocks are configured and the undergound action of the tides, or so I read last night.'

Just as she finished her sentence, a woman's high-pitched laughter could be heard above the rumble of the Well of the Winds.

Scott groaned.

The small plane landed with a thud on the tarmac at Machrie airport, tyres squealing as the pilot fought to keep the aircraft in a straight line in the strong crosswind.

While other passengers cowered in their seats or let out little yelps of fear, Iolo Harris leaned back and smiled contentedly. The flight had been short, but some of the views from the small window at his side had been spectacular. Little strips of white sand and rocky outcrops reminded him of a recent family holiday in the Caribbean, and the heather-covered hills brought to mind the Valleys of South Wales.

As they opened the door of the plane, the fresh tang of the sea filled the compartment. Harris waited until everyone else had left the aircraft, then crabbed his way along the aisle and down the steps, taking time to return the smile of the air steward.

After a cursory security check in the terminal building, he was soon on his way to Kinloch in an ancient Peugeot now being used as a taxi.

This is where the discretion would begin.

*

'Oh no!' exclaimed Scott as the old woman walked towards them, still cackling.

'Shh.' Symington held her finger to her lips to discourage her colleague from making any other negative comments as Glenhanity strode towards them. She was wearing a woollen skirt, and her bare legs were splattered with mud above capacious old Wellington boots.

'Hello,' said Symington, her voice friendly. 'How nice to see you. It's lovely up here.'

'It is?' said Scott under his breath, still annoyed at the state of his trousers.

'No' many comes up here these days. And jeest call me Glenhanity, every other bugger does.'

'I would've thought this would be one of the tourist attractions of the island,' said Symington.

'Aye, it was, until they dancin' ladies got built.' She pointed south to where the blades of the wind turbines that dominated the island's skyline were turning briskly in the breeze. 'No' forgettin' the auld man an' the auld woman. They're doon there, tae.'

'What's a' this wae auld men and women and dancing ladies? I telt you, ma'am, this one's two bricks short o' a full load,' said Scott, in a whisper just loud enough to be heard over the moaning of the Well of the Winds and the crash of the sea below.

'I can hear fine,' said Glenhanity with a toss of her head. 'You're a thrawn bugger. I don't like you at a'. Folk jeest want tae see big things, like they windmills. They forget the other things – the secrets.'

'Are there any secrets here?' asked Symington.

'There are so. Big yins, at that. Come doon for a wee refreshment, and I'll tell you aboot it.'

'Come on, Brian,' said Symington.

'Come on where?'

'We'll go and have a cup of tea with Glenhanity.' The Scottish name sounded odd in Symington's Yorkshire accent.

'Here, I'm kind of choosy where I eat and drink. You'd need tae get the place fumigated before I neck any tea at her hoose. Aye, and that's if tea's even an option. The only drink she'll likely have will be in bottles wae forty per cent by volume written on them.'

Symington ignored him and fell into step with the old woman.

'The things I've tae dae in this bloody job,' grumbled Scott as he trudged after the two women.

Harris's room was simply furnished with a bed, a wardrobe with a crack which ran its full length, and a chest of drawers. As he opened the wardrobe to hang up his suit bag, he was dismayed to catch the whiff of mothballs, which added another layer of mustiness to the room. He tried to visualise some of his Whitehall colleagues being accommodated in such a place and grinned.

He sat down on the bed and pulled his briefcase onto the bed beside him. After keying in the combination he opened it up and removed two red files, both marked TOP SECRET. The first contained a close-up of the battered face of a dead woman. The purple bruises that covered what was left of her face made her look hideous. As he flicked through the notes, he came across another image, this time of farm buildings surrounded by green fields, the sea visible in the top right-hand corner of the photograph. This was Achnamara farm – his destination for the following day.

He read for a while, reacquainting himself with the case information. He now better understood the need for subtlety and discretion. His boss had given him an outline, but the detail was explosive, or had the potential to be, if it fell into the wrong hands.

He closed the first file and picked up the other. The jowly face of a middle-aged man with dark hair and a neutral expression stared out from an official ID photograph. Harris studied the face carefully. Despite the man's age and the fact that he was obviously carrying a bit of extra weight, he could still discern a strong jaw line and keen eyes. The expression was serious, bordering on melancholic, with an intimidating undertone he suspected few others would have picked up. His wife would have described this man as 'lived-in hand-some', one of the many pro-forma descriptions of people she used frequently. Yes, he thought, you'd be right about this one, love.

He locked the briefcase and slid it under the bed before quickly changing into a pair of black jeans and a sweatshirt. He headed downstairs to see what culinary delights this rather down-at-heel hotel had to offer.

24

Scott looked around the room, aghast, until he caught Symington's eye.

'Your mouth is gaping, Brian,' she said in admonition.

'Is it any wonder?' He made a conscious effort to close his mouth, then continued his perusal of Glenhanity's chaotic home.

The place was dark. The curtains were drawn, obscuring two tiny windows on either side of the room. The walls were covered in what looked like decades-old wallpaper, stained brown by age and nicotine, and slathered with large patches of black damp. Glenhanity had lit a fire, which was now crackling away in the little black iron grate. Above that was a painting of a refined-looking woman in a rather extravagant hat, standing beside the Gairsay Hotel. It faced the police officers, who were perched on an ancient couch, from which straw poked through holes, its wooden frame visible under the threadbare upholstery. Scott's end of the couch appeared to have entirely lost its springs; consequently, he was sitting a few inches lower than his superintendent. He recoiled, a strangled noise in his throat, as he spotted a large silverfish appear from under the picture frame and proceed along the wall above the fireplace.

'Dae you see that?' he whispered.

'What?' Symington replied, her voice equally low.

'That . . . that beastie crawling along there.'

'Oh, be quiet, Brian. You've been in worse places than this. There are some lovely paintings – that woman, those seascapes. An amateur, but a good one.'

'Never knew you was an expert in fine art, tae. And as far as having been in worse places than this, aye, I dare say I have, though I must have put them oot o' my mind 'cause I cannae remember any.' He sniffed the air. 'What's that stench? Smells like something's died. Aye, an' been deid for a while, tae.'

'Dae yous baith take sugar?' Glenhanity's head appeared around the kitchen door.

'Not for me, thanks,' replied Symington. 'Brian?'

'No, no, you're fine, thanks.'

The old woman disappeared again.

'You do take sugar, Brian.'

'No' in here I don't. I dread tae think what's been crawling through it – aye, even if it's sugar at a'. Mair likely dandruff.'

They sat in silence for a few minutes, Scott still following the progress of the large insect that had now reached the mantelpiece and was feeling its way along it using its long antennae.

'Here we are,' said Glenhanity, bearing a tray upon which sat an old brown teapot with a cracked lid, and three mugs, all of which were chipped and bore dubious stains. 'Sorry I don't have any biscuits or the like. I don't get many visitors these days.' She smiled, revealing a row of blackened stumps.

'You don't say,' said Scott, still eyeing the silverfish.

'So you've been in this house all your life?' Symington took the mug of tea she'd been given and warmed her hands.

'I have that. I was born on that couch, wid you believe?'

'Eh, which end?' asked Scott, looking down at the worn fabric he was sitting on in horror.

'You needna worry. The thing's been re-covered a pile o' times since then.' Glenhanity's cackle filled the stuffy room.

'Could you tell us something about yourself, your family?' said Symington.

The old woman sat down heavily, tea slopping out of her mug as she did so. 'My faither was a fine man, missus, the best fermer on the island. Aye, an' the best at the fishing, tae. Wisna a bad painter, neithers. I heard you talkin' aboot his paintings.'

'Oh, so they were painted by your father. He was very talented, indeed.'

'You're right there. He could dae a painting in a matter o' hours. Naebody was interested, mind. If we came fae somewhere else, maybes folk wid have taken mair notice.'

'Oh, I'm sure. He was really, really good.'

'He was a clever man. Read a' the papers front tae back every day. He knew aboot the world, but the world didna know aboot him here on this wee rock. Och, we got along a' the same. We only had this croft, but we put they buggers wae the big ferms tae shame. Folk used tae come fae all over tae get their hands on my faither's cocks.'

Scott, now holding the stained and chipped mug of tea he'd been given as far away from his face as possible, widened his eyes in disbelief.

'I don't know whoot you're staring at, you scunner. Tae hell wae they turkeys, you canna beat a big black cock at Christmas. And my faither had the best cocks aroon. Auld Mrs Gemmill – her family used tae own the island, a way back, that's her in the painting above the fireplace – she widna go back tae London until my faither gied her his best cock, an' that's a fact.'

This latest statement gave even Symington pause for thought, but the bright smile soon returned to her face. 'He was really good at people as well as landscapes.'

'Don't forget his cock,' said Scott under his breath, eliciting another glare from Glenhanity.

'I'm interested in your father's time on the boat. You told me he helped the Bremner family. Did he know them well?'

'He did that. Worked for them. For a whiles, anyhow.'

'So he didn't work for them for long. Why was that?'

'They made the same mistake wae him that they made wae the rest o' the village. They thought we was jeest a band o' yokels that didna know oor arses fae oor tits, if you pardon the expression,' she said apologetically, then broke wind.

'McAuley telt me everybody liked them,' observed Scott, his mug of tea now abandoned on the floor at his feet.

'Aye, sure, that's whoot maist folk were like. My faither saw through them fae the off.'

'Saw through what?' asked Symington.

'Saw whoot they were. On this island everyone's too polite tae each other. We've a' tae muddle through the gither through thick and thin, so it doesna dae tae have any bitterness between folk. Love your neebours, that's whoot it says in the good book, and that's what folk are like here.' She began to cough violently, the strain making her face turn red.

'Are you okay?' enquired Symington, getting up from the couch.

'Fine, dear, jeest fine.' Her cough now subsided, Glenhanity made a rumbling sound deep in her throat, then expertly spat a large glob of phlegm into the fire, where it hissed as it landed on a lump of burning coal.

'Oh, fu—' A furious look from Symington stopped the oath in Scott's mouth.

'Are you member o' the gentry or something?' Glenhanity turned to the policeman, whose face still bore a disgusted expression. ''Cause you sure don't sound like one.'

'You were saying about the Bremners and your father,' said Symington, raising her voice slightly in an effort to end the bickering between her DS and the old woman.

'Aye, they killed him in the end.'

There was a silence in the room for a few seconds, save for the ticking of an old clock on the mantelpiece that the silverfish had mounted and was now feeling its way across, and the crackle of the fire.

'What do you mean, they killed him?' asked Symington.

'He knew fine whoot they were at. They'd been at it the whole war. Helping the Nazis. Aye, and mair besides.'

'They were Jews who escaped the Nazis,' said Scott, making his first real contribution to the conversation. 'Why would they be helping them? They'd get nae help fae that quarter. My grandfaither was at the liberation o' Belsen. He never spoke aboot it. Every time anything aboot the Holocaust was mentioned he just burst intae tears. Aye, an' he wisnae a man prone tae greetin', neither.'

'They was nae mair Jewish than I am,' shouted Glenhanity. 'At the start o' the war they were spies. When the war was coming tae its end, they helped loads o' they Nazis tae escape. Fae this very island, tae. They were treated well. But they'd a bigger secret than a' that, I can tell yous.'

'So they killed your father because he knew this?' asked Symington.

'They did that. Drooned him, they did.'

'That's a very serious accusation, Glenhanity. Do you have proof?'

'He telt me they were going tae dae it, that's my proof!' She held her head in her hands and started to sniffle. 'I was only a wee lassie, but I mind my faither telling me plain as day, efter whoot he saw.'

'What did he see?'

'It was my ain fault,' she wailed. 'I might as weel have drooned my faither mysel.' She looked up at the painting above the fireplace.

'But you were only a little girl. How could it have been your fault?'

'Because I opened my big mooth, that's how. I'd been warned tae say naethin' at the school, but I didna listen.'

'What did you say?'

'I said it once an' it killed my faither. I knew no' tae say it again, or I'd be the next one deid.'

'Is that what you're on aboot when you've had a few too many?' asked Scott.

'I'm no' wantin' tae say any mair,' she hissed at him. 'How dae you know I take a drink?'

'Take a drink? I didnae think you did anything else!' blurted Scott.

'Get oot! Jeest get oot, the pair o' you!' shouted Glenhanity, struggling to her feet, her tear-stained face red with fury. 'Yous'll no' catch me oot that easily. Get oot!'

'Come on, Brian,' said Symington, tugging at the detective's arm as she got up.

The two police officers were just leaving the room when the old woman called out to them to wait. She began rummaging in the drawer of a cupboard by the fireplace. 'Here. Take this if yous don't believe me, but I'm telling you, it's the last help yous'll get oot o' me!' She retrieved something small and shiny, and threw the object towards Scott with no little force.

Scott reached out, catching the object just before it hit Symington. He turned it over in his hand. 'What's this?'

Just over three inches in length, the cigarette lighter was slim and silver, with an eagle holding a black swastika on a red roundel.

'Where did you get this?'

'Jeest get oot!' shouted Glenhanity. 'They never paid my faither for half the things he did, so he took this off them – wanted tae sell it tae get his money. Poor bastard never got the chance.'

'So he took it from the Bremners?' asked Symington.

'Aye, he did that. It never brought him nae luck. I don't know how I kept it for so long. As for the rest, yous are the detectives – get detecting!'

Iolo Harris opted to dine in the bar at the County Hotel. He had enjoyed the starter, a crab cake served with prawn toast, and was now tucking into a thick fillet of cod served with chips and peas.

A variety of drinkers came and went, all of whom, despite not knowing him from Adam, nodded in greeting as he sat at the back of the room.

He took a sip of his pint before attacking the plate once more, glad the portion sizes were more generous than those of the restaurants he frequented in London. The fish was fresh and moist, and he was relieved not to have to consume a fancy foam, pickled broth or drizzled jus. This kind of fare was to his taste: back-to-basics, hearty food of the type he'd enjoyed as a boy in Port Talbot.

The woman who had welcomed him to the hotel bantered with and chastised her customers in equal measure, her laughter and admonishments sounding above the convivial hum.

'Are you all right o'er there, Mr Harris?' she called, standing on her tiptoes to address him from behind the bar. 'Oor chef's made a lovely trifle the day, if you fancy a dessert. Or there's the usual ice cream or sticky toffee pudding, if you prefer.'

'I'm fine, Annie,' he said. 'Bursting at the seams here, so I don't think I'll manage a sweet.'

'We've a lovely cheese board, tae. You canna beat a piece o' Kintyre cheddar, I'm telling you. Folk come fae far an' wide tae eat it. They're selling it in Harrods noo, they tell me.'

'Maybe later.' He beamed a smile at her as she went back about her business.

At that moment a tall, dark-haired man in a crumpled grey suit entered the bar. A corner of his shirt-tail was hanging over the front of his trousers, which he hastily tucked in. Despite the paunch, he still looked intimidating, though his face was drawn and bore deep lines that Harris didn't associate with the age he knew the man to be. Though he looked more careworn than the image in the file, Harris knew who was now leaning wearily on the bar.

He got up from his table, taking his empty plate with him.

'There we are, Annie,' he said, putting the plate beside a water jug. 'Lovely piece of fish. Please give the chef my compliments.'

'Thank you, Mr Harris. Much obliged – glad you enjoyed it,' she said, pushing a small tumbler beneath an optic in order to pour a double measure of whisky. 'There you are, that'll warm the cockles o' your heart.' She turned to the large man at the bar and slid the glass towards him. 'I'll get the money in a second. Can I get you another drink, Mr Harris?'

'Yes, please. Another pint of heavy, if you don't mind.'

'Coming right up.' She removing his empty plate from the bar and placed a pint glass under a beer font in one practised movement.

Harris smiled at the taller man beside him. 'Friendly place, this,' he said, again hearing himself sound more Welsh than he was used to.

'Yes, always friendly in here. Are you on holiday?'

'No, I'm here on business, actually. And, if I'm not mistaken, that business might involve you, DCI Daley.'

'Not your most diplomatic performance, Brian,' said Symington, striding down the hill through the heather.

'Ach, I don't know what you're getting yersel' in such a pickle aboot, ma'am,' he replied.

'You might think she's nothing but an old drunk and not worth bothering about, but it's clear to me that she's one of the only material witnesses we have. Not many of that gener-ation left now.'

'If they a' have lifestyles like her, I'm no' surprised. Hoose o' horror, that place.'

199

Symington stopped in her tracks and turned to face the detective. 'I think we're just about to uncover one of the most important crimes that any of us has ever investigated. That's how important this is, DS Scott.'

'How can we investigate anything? We've been flung off the job.'

'Remember the photos you took of all those documents with your phone?'

'Aye, a bloody pain in the arse it was, tae. Took for ever.'

Symington ignored his grumbling. 'I sent them to someone I know quite well, a professor at St Andrews who's an expert in the Second World War. He's only had time to scratch the surface, but he's, well, he's astonished.'

'Does it matter? It's got cover-up written all over it now Special Branch are on the case.'

'A few years ago, maybe. It's much harder to keep things quiet now. Think of how many of these big internet leaks there have been in the last few years.'

'Aye, but that's all current stuff. Who's interested in something that happened o'er sixty years ago? The past's the past. Might make it ontae the History Channel, but in the end nae bugger's really interested.'

'I'm not sure you're right, Brian. From the off, I've been under pressure from more senior officers than I regularly speak to in the course of a year, and that's just in the last few days. Why would they send a team from Special Branch up here in so much of a hurry? You saw the weather they landed in – there's an urgency about this.'

'The only reason I can think of is that there's something that might be important now, but what fae then could have any impact these days? Unless . . .'

'Unless what?'

'Och, you know yersel', unless somebody wae a big job an' lots o' money has got something tae lose.'

'Or maybe more than one person?'

'Noo, that would be even mair like the thing.' Scott chewed his lip. 'You know, one o' these days, I'll investigate a case wae a good auld-fashioned ned at the heart o' it. I swear, things are mair complicated now than they've ever been.'

'You swear quite enough already,' she replied with a laugh.

They continued their progress back to the hotel, both police officers now deep in thought.

25

Brussels

He stared at the screen and sighed. Timothy Gissing was dead.

He'd trusted Gissing, as he'd trusted his father before him. Safe pairs of hands in a country he had always known had never fully signed up for their project. First to help keep the Soviets at bay, then to stop the world from discovering their mutual secret – their insurance, as it was often called.

He sat back in his chair, angling his head towards the ceiling. The Project. That had been its original name, so, so long ago. It had been his job to make sure that the secret at its heart was protected. Now, he and the guardians faced the most significant problem they'd encountered in a generation.

He dialled the number that was imprinted on his mind.

'I'm in need of help,' he said in German when the phone was answered. He waited, hearing various clicks on the other end of the line. Eventually he heard a voice: frail, feminine. Despite this he shivered involuntarily. 'We have to meet.'

'Is that wise?' A pause. 'If this is something to do with the Greeks, I'm not interested. I see them snivelling on the television almost every night. I'm sick of it.'

'This is nothing to do with the Greeks. I can be in Munich this evening. Where and when can we meet?'

He could hear a wheeze in her throat as she contemplated his proposal. 'How long has it been?'

'Almost eight years,' he replied. 'You've lived longer than you thought.'

'I've stayed alive because I've had to. Who will keep things together when I'm gone? You?'

'Things will be kept together until so much time has passed that no one will care. Regardless of whether you and I live or not.'

'I wish I shared your optimism. Things are a mess – not just the Greeks, everything. But our grip is strengthening. And when the rest of the world knows, then it will be our time again.' Her voice had regained strength and force – become almost manic.

'Where do we meet?'

'Not here. Not in Munich – not in Germany. There are too many cameras now; these phones that everyone has. There is no privacy any more.'

'There are people with phones everywhere, not just in Germany.'

'We meet in Linz.'

'Are you sure?'

'We meet in Linz, twenty-four hours from now. You know the place. I'll be there at noon.'

Before he could reply, the phone went dead. He shuddered.

Near Blaan, 1945

Inspector Urquhart was on his hands and knees, examining the cattle float; the young farmhand was watching him in silence. McColl was in the yard making a sketch of the scene, as he'd been ordered.

'What's your surname, Andrew?' asked Urquhart, still busy with his task.

'Mitchell, Andra Mitchell.'

'And how long have you worked for Mr Kerr?'

'Near five years. I came here when I left the school.'

'And what age are you now?'

'Nineteen. Whoot's that got tae dae with anything?'

'Just answer the questions.'

Urquhart looked around the float in disgust. The smell of dung was overpowering in the cramped space. Red blood and gore was splattered across the straw bedding and up the walls. White matter, shot through with dark arterial blood, lay congealed at his feet. The remains of Dugald Kerr's brain.

'We'll go through it again.' He heard the farmhand sigh behind him. 'And again, and again, if I feel it's necessary. Is that clear?'

'Aye, perfectly,' replied Mitchell wearily.

'You were in the barn, you heard screams and you ran out. Am I right?'

'Aye. I was busy sorting oot some bailer twine when I heard him.'

'Was it normal for Mr Kerr to handle the bull by himself? It's a huge beast, surely it would be a two-man job?'

'Depends. The auld boy thought he knew it a'. He was

always daein' stuff he shouldna. Thought he was too clever tae let yin o' the beasts get the better o' him.'

'You don't sound very fond of him, Mr Mitchell. Nor do you sound very upset by his death.'

'That's jeest how I am, ask my mother. Never cried when my auld man got killed in the war. Whoot good does it dae?'

Urquhart ignored the farmhand and stepped down the ramp. 'You say the door was in this position when it happened. Yes?'

'Aye, jeest the way it is noo.'

The detective leaned forward, pulling at a brass ring that was set in the door. It was loose. 'Is this the keeper for the catch that secures the ramp when it's closed?'

'Aye. Why dae you ask?'

'Because the screws are loose. And these marks look like hoof imprints to me. A bull kicking back at the door with its hind legs, trying to batter it down. Loosening the catch, even?'

'Ayrshire bulls. They're really bad-tempered. The big bastard was a'ways trying tae batter doon the door. Naethin' unusual aboot that. That's jeest their nature.'

'And Mr Kerr never asked you to fix it?'

'No' recently. Here, whoot are you trying tae say?' said Mitchell, suddenly realising the implications of Urquhart's enquiries.

'When you saw him he was inside being trampled by the bull?'

'Aye, he was. Screaming, it was horrible.'

'Right.' Urquhart wiped his hands carefully. 'I want you to come to Kinloch with me. I have a few more questions to ask you.'

'Whoot? Are you arresting me?'

'You're helping with enquiries, Mr Mitchell. A man has died here. I want to be sure that we get all the facts right.' He walked away from the float and turned to face the farmhand. The bull, back in the paddock, was snorting, dried blood on its nose where the ring had been pulled frantically by Dugald Kerr. 'Tell me. Did Mr Kerr mention where he was going later in the day?'

Mitchell shrugged his shoulders. 'I canna mind.'

'Try and *mind*, Mr Mitchell.'

'Och, I think he said he'd tae go intae the toon. Away drinking in the County, likely.'

'Oh, so he said he was going to the County?'

Mitchell swallowed hard. 'No, but he went there near every day. Jeest a wild guess.'

'Come with me, Mr Mitchell. McColl, have you finished the sketch?'

'Yes, nearly.'

'Hurry up, then.'

Urquhart stared thoughtfully at the young farmhand as he escorted him to the car.

As they drove into Kinloch, Urquhart was surprised to see bunting being stretched across Main Street by two council workers standing on wooden ladders on either side of the street. Other workers were busy erecting a large podium outside the town hall.

'What on earth is going on?' he asked, turning to McColl in the passenger seat.

'It's the c-celebration of Hitler's death, on tomorrow. M-my father was telling me about it last night.'

'Organised by whom? It's the first I've heard of it.'

'B-by the provost, I think. S-surely it will be the end of the war, sir?'

Urquhart sighed. 'As I've told you before, if anyone thinks the Germans will lie down and die just because Hitler's dead, they have another think coming. I dread what will happen to the POWs, for a start.'

'B-but the Geneva Convention – surely they'll be safe?'

'Do you really think the Germans care about that? You mark my words, there are horrors we've yet to discover.' Urquhart gripped the steering wheel, trying to control his irritation.

'Dae you no' like them, then?' scoffed Mitchell.

'I wonder, why is a fit young man like you not off serving his country in the hour of its greatest need?'

'I'm a fermer,' replied Mitchell, staring defiantly at Urquhart in the mirror. 'Who would feed the country if a' the fermers was away fighting wae the army?'

'You tell me, son. I'm quite sure there are old farmers – women, too – who can work the land. In my view, if you're young and fit, you should be helping win the war.'

He suddenly realised that McColl was staring at him from the passenger seat. He thought of apologising, but didn't; he didn't feel like giving the grinning farmhand in the back of the car anything else to sneer about.

They drove up the hill and were soon through the gates of Kinloch Police Station.

Daley studied Iolo Harris's ID. They were now sitting at the back of the bar, Daley's normal perch.

'You've done your homework, Mr Harris.'

Harris smiled. 'It's my job to be one step ahead, Chief Inspector. I needn't tell you the challenges our nation faces these days. I'm paid to keep us all safe, as are you. We're on the same side.'

'So, you thought you'd just come here and hijack me, rather than use the normal channels?'

'I'm all for the friendly approach, Jim. May I call you Jim, by the way?'

Daley shrugged. 'If I can call you Iolo.'

'Nice little hotel, this. Good grub, too. Can't stand the bloody fancy stuff I keep getting put in front of me in London.'

'I couldn't stand living in London.'

'No, I'm not that fond of it, either. But, you know, you get used to it. Been there for twenty-odd years now.'

'Working with the MOD?' It was Daley's turn to smile.

'Somebody has to. You had a bad experience with us, then? I know you're not ex-military.'

'You're a spook, Iolo. Plain and simple. You might be working for the MOD, but you might as well have MI6 tattooed on your forehead.'

'Not true, Jim. My job is only to investigate incidents that come within the remit of the ministry.' Harris surprised himself at how easily he could lie. It hadn't come naturally. Unlike some of his colleagues, for him it was the least appealing part of the job.

'When are you heading over to Gairsay?' asked Daley.

'Tomorrow. I have to liaise with a Special Branch team over there.'

'Yeah, the guys who replaced our investigation team.'

'Wasn't my decision, I can assure you of that. I can't stand those bloody cowboys.'

'Why the stopover in Kinloch? You'd have made the ferry after your flight here.'

'I need something from you.' Harris casually lifted his pint glass and drained it in a couple of gulps. 'Can I get you another?'

Daley shrugged. 'Sure. I've nothing to rush home for, but you'll know all about that, I'm quite sure.'

Ignoring the mild barb, Harris got to his feet. 'Large one?'

'What do you want from me?'

'I think you can answer that question yourself.'

'The journal?'

'Got it in one. Now, give me a minute, and I'll do my best to tell you why.'

Daley watched Harris go to the bar. Despite his friendly, informal manner, he detected a formidable individual at work. He could have arrived unannounced in Daley's office and demanded Urquhart's journal. The fact that he hadn't proved that he at least wasn't hidebound by protocol.

Even so, Daley knew he had to be on his guard. Harris's appearance confirmed that there was much more to the disappearance of the Bremner family than met the eye.

26

Urquhart pushed the big key into the lock of the grey cell door and opened it. Mitchell, lying curled up in a rough blanket, didn't move. The inspector walked over to him, prodding him gently with the tip of his shoe to rouse him.

'Time to get up, Mr Mitchell. You're free to go.'

The young man jolted awake and stretched. 'Och, longest lie-in I've had for ages. How come you had tae keep me here o'ernight, though?'

'If you go to the sergeant at the bar office, he'll give you back your things,' said Urquhart, ignoring the young farm-hand's question.

'I'm off the hook then.' Mitchell yawned and got to his feet.

'You're in exactly the same position as you were yesterday, son. I'm investigating the death of Mr Kerr, and I'm not sure that I have the full picture yet.'

'He was unlucky. I telt you, he was always taking risks wae they beasts. No' jeest that: up ladders wae nae stops, or naebody standing at the bottom. Never breaking his shotgun when he was climbing fences. He was asking for an accident.'

'I believe Mr Kerr's nephew is taking charge of the farm today.'

'Aye, mair than likely. That's me oot o' a job, then.'

'I'm sorry to hear that, Mr Mitchell. One tragedy after another. Now, go and get your things.' He watched as Mitchell lurched down the corridor, yawning and stretching. 'Oh, and don't go leaving the country. If you're thinking of going anywhere, I want you to let me know.'

Mitchell turned, nodding his head in reply.

Urquhart had to admit, for such a young lad, he had remained unruffled. But he knew something else. The farm-hand was lying, and all he had to do was prove it.

He walked to his office, where McColl was typing up Mitchell's statement, sighing as his finger, yet again, caught an unwanted key.

'Leave that for now, McColl. I'll let the sergeant finish it off.'

'I'm sure I won't be too much longer, s-sir,' apologised the young man.

'I have something else for you to do. You can drive, yes?'

'Yes, sir.'

'Good. Andrew Mitchell is just about to be released. I want you to take the car and follow him. Be discreet. Don't let him know you're following him. I want to know what he does, where he goes, and who he talks to and when. Do you think you can do that?'

'Yes, sir. N-now?'

'Of course. Off with you!'

He smiled as McColl nodded determinedly and dashed out the room. Maybe they'd make a policeman of him yet.

*

Daley wasn't surprised to see Harris the next morning, waiting for him at the entrance to Kinloch Police Office. He escorted the MOD man to his office, and fished around in his bag. He was about to hand over Urquhart's journal when he hesitated.

'What if I chose to make something of this?'

'Your choice,' replied Harris, looking relaxed as he sat back in the chair opposite Daley.

'Okay. Well, in that case, maybe I'll just hold on to it for now. You don't mind, do you?'

'Me? I don't really care, DCI Daley. Though the question will be asked: how did it come into your possession in the first place?'

'I found it.'

'Yet you didn't include it in the productions uncovered at the farmhouse?'

'Oversight. You know what it's like for us overworked cops. And, as you know, I've had a lot of personal issues to deal with.'

Harris chuckled. 'You know what, you keep it. But the approach won't be as softly-softly when my superiors get their teeth into it.'

'What is it about Urquhart? This diary appears to be too hot to handle, and his file is redacted beyond anything I've ever seen. I'm missing something, but don't think I'll miss it for ever. That's the thing about us lower-level law enforcement guys – chips on the shoulder breed a determination to succeed.' He slid Urquhart's journal across the desk.

'Thank you, DCI Daley. Oh, by the way, I know about Feldstein.'

'Know what?'

'More than you, I think. Instead of worrying about Inspector Urquhart, I'd delve into the present, if I were you.'

'Meaning?'

'Meaning that the past is the past, in every way. But people like Feldstein, though they operate in the present, are an unpleasant echo of things that would best be left alone.'

'Unpleasant, how? He seemed quite friendly to me. More helpful than those who are supposed to be on my side, in fact.'

Harris stood up, tucking the journal under his arm. 'Ask yourself why the Bremners disappeared with such apparent haste, Jim.' He turned to walk away. 'And take another look at Mrs Bremner's face – what was left of it – and ask yourself why she ended up dead where she did.'

'So, you think Feldstein had something to do with this?'

'You and me aren't kids any more, Jim. We both know the game and how it's played. As far as I'm concerned, there's enough to worry about in the present without harking back to the past. All sorts of nutters trying to blow us all to kingdom come.'

'Everything has its starting point though.'

'Yeah, that's right, but remember, Jim, I'm on your side, no matter what you think.'

'Well, good luck on Gairsay.'

'Thanks. I enjoyed our chat last night.'

Daley watched the door closing behind the Welshman. He drummed his fingers on his desk, reflecting upon what had just passed between them. Urquhart, the Bremner family, Feldstein, and now the Security Service. Whatever Harris said about ignoring the past, there appeared to be a lot of interest in it. Too much interest for it to be laid to rest. And he'd laid enough to rest in the past few months. He was glad he'd copied every page of Urquhart's journal.

Kinloch, 1945

The preparations for Kinloch's celebrations were now well advanced. The podium, soon to be supporting the great and the good, stood solidly in front of the town hall, flanked by two limp Union Jacks. The bunting was stretched across the road all the way down Main Street.

Urquhart looked at the town's notice board bearing the details of the event. It was due to start at seven that evening. KINLOCH WELCOMES THE DEATH OF THE FÜHRER was scribbled in bold white chalk. He raised his eyebrows, still concerned that people were being lulled into a false sense of security by the death of the German leader.

He waited for a horse pulling a cartload of beer to pass before crossing the road. A man in a brown dustcoat waved to him from the ironmongers, smiling broadly from a gap in the heavily taped windows – protection against the unlikely event that a German bomb should shatter them. A military lorry chugged past, a knot of kilted soldiers leaning out of the back, waving and shouting at passers-by.

Urquhart turned down a back street, past a church, and then into a leafy square where he found himself facing a large sandstone building fronted by a neatly trimmed hedge. The garden was surrounded by the rusting stumps of railings – a testament to the war effort and the need for iron. He'd been told that most of this recovered metal lay in huge warehouses across the country, and had only been collected to show that things were being done. In the early days of the war, when it looked as though invasion was imminent, those small gestures had meant a great deal.

Straightening his tie, he walked up to the door and knocked three times. An elderly woman in a checked blue apron, her hair scraped back in a severe bun, soon answered the door.

'I'd like to speak to Colonel Blair, please. Inspector Urquhart from Kinloch Police . . . He knows me,' he added, noting her grim expression.

The woman looked him up and down, then shrugged her shoulders. 'He's having his afternoon nap, Inspector. Could you no' come back later?'

'It is rather urgent, if you don't mind.'

He was led down a dark hallway and into a room stuffed with dust-covered aspidistras in brass pots, redolent of the Victorian age.

'Take a seat. I'll let the colonel know he has a visitor.'

'Thank you.'

'I'm no' saying he'll speak tae you, mind. He's regimental aboot his naps. Says that's why he's lived tae such a great age.'

Urquhart took a seat in a high-backed winged armchair. On the walls were many paintings and photographs, mostly military scenes. In one old sepia photograph, he recognised a young soldier, dressed in desert fatigues and a pith helmet, standing beside an Indian orderly. Though the face was fresh and unlined, Hector Blair's features were easily recognisable.

After a few minutes he heard a noise from behind the door. The familiar voice, though not issuing the booming commands he was used to, made him smile.

'Break out the cake, Mrs McKay, and the Darjeeling. Heaven knows we get precious few visitors here. Number one rations, what?'

A stooped old man with mutton-chop whiskers and an impressive moustache entered the room. Over red-and-white striped pyjamas, he wore a silk smoking jacket, piped with gold braid, that afforded him a somewhat eccentric air. The cane he was leaning heavily upon was ebony, with a silver handle. At the sight of Urquhart, he waved it in the air, a wide smile becoming apparent under his fulsome facial hair.

'Bless my soul, young subaltern Urquhart, as I live and breathe. Thought you'd never find the way to this house. How long have you been in Kinloch now? Too long not to have paid court to your old major, I bloody well warrant.'

Urquhart stood to shake his old commanding officer by the hand. Here was the man who had taught him the ways of the army and the leadership of men. Here was the man who had saved his life – more than once.

'Sorry, sir. Not been here that long, actually. Just getting embedded, if you know what I mean.'

'Embedded with this lot in Kinloch? I doubt anyone who hasn't been born here has ever done that. Fortunately, I have that dubious privilege.' He grimaced as he sat down on a chaise longue opposite his guest. 'Sit yourself back down, man. We're not in the old regiment now, more's the pity. That housekeeper of mine will lavish some of her magnificent fruitcake on us shortly. She's a dismal old bint, but she bakes like a dream. Now, what can I do for you?'

'Well, of course this is mainly a social call—'

'Social call! You forget I know you of old, William. You're one of the least sociable men I have had under my command. Always had your nose to the grindstone. Your brothers-in-arms would be happily whooping it up in some bloody dive, while you'd be head down writing to the families of the fallen. And no shortage of them in the last dust-up, sadly.'

'No shortage this time around, either, sir.'

'No, indeed. Could all have been so easily nipped in the bud, too. Adolf Hitler would have been found dead on the streets of Munich, where he bloody well belonged. No more a military man than I'm a painter and decorator.'

'He's gone now, of course, sir.'

'Gone? What do you mean, gone?'

Urquhart cleared his throat. He'd been impressed by the mental acuity of his old commanding officer, but now wondered if that had been an entirely accurate appraisal. 'Killed himself, sir.'

Colonel Blair twiddled one of his whiskers impatiently. 'Hmm. I met Schicklgruber once, you know,' he said, using the unflattering nickname Hitler had been given by Churchill. 'A coward and a madman.'

'You were the military attaché in Berlin for a while, weren't you, sir?'

'Over ten years. Met them all. Nazi High Command. Opportunists, bloody civilians dressed as soldiers. Dangerous bunch, though, like any fantasists.'

Urquhart listened to the old man rant about the Nazis. Very few people in Kinloch knew that in their midst lived a man who had met not only Hitler, but just about every senior member of the Nazi Party, and on numerous occasions. Indeed, when Deputy Führer Rudolph Hess had made his doomed trip to Britain in 1941, eventually crash-landing in a Scottish field in Eaglesham, Blair had been taken to Buchanan Castle in Stirlingshire to verify that the man was indeed who he said he was. By all accounts, Hess had welcomed him like an old friend, much to the consternation of the senior army officers present.

Even Prime Minister Winston Churchill at times sought the advice of the man who had seen Germany fall under the spell of the Nazis. Feeling his age and fearing the worst, Blair had taken his leave of Germany in 1936, to settle down to retirement in Kinloch. Few had listened to the old soldier who warned anyone who would listen about the charismatic German chancellor and his ambition to dominate the world.

'The thing that still gets me is all those fine, brave men lost their lives in the trenches, and that charlatan escaped to heap misery on the world again. Sometimes there is no justice, Urquhart.'

A tap on the door announced the arrival of Mrs McKay, bearing a tray on which sat a silver teapot, two china cups and saucers, a sugar bowl and tongs, and a tiny milk jug, alongside several portions of fruitcake. She placed it on the table between the two men.

'Will I be mother, or do you gentlemen want tae pour yourselves?'

'I'm sure we'll manage, Mrs McKay,' said Blair. 'Thank you. Another magnificent fruitcake, I see.'

She smiled, despite herself, and left the room. As he listened to her footsteps padding back down the hall, Colonel Blair reached into his pocket and produced a silver hip flask.

'She's a fine housekeeper, but she's Wee Free. Frowns at a decent dram. Do the honours, would you, Urquhart?' He handed the inspector the flask. 'One of those French philosophers, I think, said, "A day without wine's like a day without sunshine." Well, I feel the same about the fruit of the barley.'

Reclining comfortably with his cup of Darjeeling tea, complete with a large splash of whisky, Blair looked at the policeman. 'So, tell me why you're really here?'

'I'd like you to look at something, sir.' Urquhart dug into his trouser pocket and handed the silver cigarette lighter to the colonel.

Blair produced an ancient pair of half-moon spectacles from his smoking jacket and peered at the object with rheumy eyes, the bottom lids of which sagged like the pockets of an old, well-worn jacket.

'I'll be damned. Where did you lay your hands on this, William?'

'I have two in my possession: one from the crew of the U-boat we found in the loch; another one, this one, I found on the body of a dead German merchant sailor.'

'I've seen something like it before. Not the same, mark you, but similar. The senior members of the party used to be given them – badge of honour or something. Expensive, too, made by some excellent German silversmiths. Very fond of their cigarettes, those Germans. Can't smoke a civilised pipe or cigar. But then, what would you expect from such beasts?'

'So, in the possession only of those and such as those, you reckon?'

'Certainly the case in my time, Urquhart. Changed days over in Berlin now, mind you.'

The old man returned the lighter. 'Think I'll help myself to another bumper. Care for one?'

Urquhart declined politely, citing being on duty. The two men chatted companionably about old times and old faces for a while. Urquhart began to feel guilty that he hadn't paid a visit before now to the man to whom he owed so much.

But, as Blair had remarked, he wasn't the most naturally sociable of men.

During their conversation, a small part of Urquhart's mind kept sparking, returning to the distinctive cigarette lighters and what he'd just been told. He tried to keep the thoughts at bay, but knew he'd have to let them surface soon, to analyse them and draw some kind of conclusion as to why they were now in his possession and not in the hands of some senior member of the Nazi Party.

Probably sooner than was courteous, Urquhart made his excuses.

Colonel Blair, somewhat unsteadily, showed Urquhart to the door. 'Are you officiating at these celebrations?'

'Oh, I'll probably have to show face, sir. Are you coming to cheer the death of Hitler?'

'Not a chance. Seen too many flags waving and heard too many pipes skirling in celebration over the years. You know damn well some poor bugger is getting a bullet in the head at this very moment. It's not over yet, not by a long chalk. We'll have the Russian bear at the bloody door next.' He took Urquhart's hand for a moment. 'Do you still miss her, William?'

'Sorry, sir?' replied Urquhart, playing for time, knowing full well who the colonel meant.

'I thought so.' Blair smiled. 'We were lucky to make it out of the trenches, my boy. Only normal to have regrets. If you want my advice, you'll find yourself someone to keep you warm when you get to my age. Bloody well wish I had.'

'Yes, sir,' said Urquhart. He had only two things on his mind as he strode purposefully back into town: the lighter he could feel in his trouser pocket and the dark-eyed girl standing beside a river in Normandy.

27

Scott and Symington were examining the silver lighter in the latter's hotel room, avoiding the incident room which was now crawling with officers from the Met.

As Scott took some pictures of the object, Symington's mobile buzzed.

Though she kept up a smile during the call and barely spoke, Scott noticed how pale her face had become. When the call ended, she did not say who the caller was; all she told the detective was that tonight would be their last on the island.

'We'll catch the mid-morning ferry tomorrow. I'll have Jim send a car to pick us up from the ferry terminal,' she said brightly – too brightly for Scott's liking.

'It'll be nice tae get back to civilisation,' he replied. 'I want tae see how oor Jimmy's getting on. Might go and stay with him for a few days, if I'm welcome, that is.'

'Why wouldn't you be welcome?'

'Och, the big fella's always in one o' his moods these days. Just wants tae stare into space and feel sorry for himself, if you ask me. He'll realise I'm having none o' it.'

'Yes.'

Scott could see his colleague's mind drifting off to something else. Judging by the slight tremor of her hand, combined with the anxious expression on her face, something else was giving her cause for concern.

'Dae you mind if I ask a question?' said Scott.

'Sorry? No, yes, please do,' she replied, flustered now that she realised he'd caught her in an unguarded moment.

'You've not been yourself since they guys fae Special Branch arrived. If I was a betting man, I'd say you're getting a hard time from them, or maybe just one of them?'

'Don't be ridiculous, DS Scott. You don't have to apply your detection skills to me. In fact, I'm having a drink with some of the boys tonight, by way of wishing them good luck.' She leaned forward. 'Of course, we'll continue our own private investigation into events when we're back in Kinloch.'

'Listen, Carrie, I've been around women all my life. I know fine when something's no' right. It's like the times I gie my missus a Christmas present and she opens her eyes wide an' tells me she loves it.'

'What do you mean?'

'When you've been married for as long as we have, every change in tone, tip o' the heid and blink o' the eye means something. I can see you're as happy going oot for a drink wae these buggers as Ella was when I handed her that *Fast Diet* book last Christmas.' He stood up. 'Och, she tried tae tell me that it was just what she was after, but I could tell it was just a front – aye, despite her goin' on aboot it a' year.'

'Bit insensitive, Brian.'

'We decided a long time ago that Christmas was for the weans. We'd buy them decent presents, have a nice meal and a few bevies, but keep oor gifts tae each other as simple as we could.'

'Right, and . . .'

'Well, I swear, see ever since? She's no' been happy wae what I've dreamed up tae gie her.'

'No? I wonder why?'

'Anyhow, the look I saw on your coupon when you were on the phone there is the same as her indoors when it comes tae Christmas: putting a brave face on it.' He looked down at her. 'Tell me I'm no' right.'

She swallowed hard. Just as she was about to speak, her phone buzzed again. 'It's Jim. I have to take this.'

'Okay.' Scott shrugged.

'So, you'll rubber stamp this freedom of information request, ma'am?' Daley listened for a few moments, then replied, 'Good, good. I'll get that car up to you in time to meet the ferry.'

As he ended the call, he looked at the photocopy of the sketch Urquhart had made: the eagle with a swastika between its talons.

His mind turned to Torquil McColl, gazing out of that high window, waiting for his life to end after years spent on the other side of the world. Everything had changed so much since McColl had been a young detective, sitting in this very station. To Daley, a child of the sixties, the war seemed distant: a thing of black-and-white films, the Airfix models he'd made, and the comic books he'd read. Yet the time between the end of the conflict and his birth was scarcely twenty years. Now that he was middle-aged, twenty years didn't feel anything like it had when he was a boy. He was closer to the events that had shaped the modern world than he had thought possible.

The phone interrupted his thoughts.

'Who? I've never heard of him,' he said with more than a hint of irritation to the lad manning the office switchboard. 'Oh, just put them through.'

When he said hello and asked if he could help, the voice on the other end of the phone wasn't that of a stranger, as he'd been expecting.

'Why not just give your name, Mr Feldstein?'

There was silence for a few moments, then the caller replied: 'To safeguard you as much as myself, Mr Daley. I know how efficient you policemen are at logging calls – to whom and from whom and where from. You'll want to keep any association with me in the shadows, I assure you, especially when you realise what is to come. I want to meet with you, but somewhere that no one will see us. I hope you understand the need for secrecy.'

'The last time we met you pointed a gun at me. Why should I trust you?'

'Yes, indeed I did. But, please understand, the metaphorical gun you now have at your temple is much more dangerous then the little pea-shooter I threatened you with. After our meeting, I think you will understand this.'

Daley racked his brains. Kinloch was a difficult place in which to be anonymous. 'Do you have a good memory, Mr Feldstein?'

'Yes.'

'Well, here's where we'll meet . . .'

Brian Scott was sitting alone in the dining room of the Gairsay Hotel. On the other side of the bar he could hear the raucous chatter of the Special Branch team – expletive-ridden tall tales of heroic and not so heroic occurrences, the meat and drink of a night out with the boys in blue. Now and again he could hear Symington's awkward laugh, but not very often. He still had the feeling that she was a reluctant participant, that she was putting a brave face on it.

As the barman came through to the dining room, he was shaking his head and rolling his eyes. An elderly couple, sitting opposite Scott, looked outraged at the language and were tutting to each other.

Scott had noticed that the boss of the Special Branch contingent, DAC Bale, had taken his leave early – no doubt, like most senior officers, due to a mixture of discretion and fear of embarrassment at the antics of his junior colleagues. The only man Scott had ever seen buck this trend was the late and not much lamented John Donald. The late chief superintendent often let his façade slip on a night out with the boys, returning rapidly to type as a boorish, condescending bully. It was DCI Harry Chappell who reminded Scott of his dead ex-boss.

He picked at his fish, swilling it down with the dregs of an unappetising glass of warm ginger beer and lime.

'You want another?' asked the young barman, spotting his glass was empty.

'Aye, son. Maybe something different this time. What dae you suggest?'

'Coke?'

'Aye, I suppose so,' replied Scott without any enthusiasm, wishing earnestly he could partake in a pint of decent lager instead of the succession of fizzy soft drinks he had to rely on to slake his thirst.

As another burst of laughter issued from the other room,

the barman brought his drink to the table. 'You no' joining your mates?'

'No mates o' mine, son. Rowdy lot, eh?'

'Aye,' replied the young man cautiously. 'I didna think the polis would behave like that.'

'Bad apples in every barrel, my boy. These guys are from the Met. No' good honest Scottish cops like myself.' He grinned.

'Do you want to see the dessert menu?'

'Aye, go on. I might as well get my chops roon a decent sticky toffee pudding.'

As he waited for the menu, he looked out of the dining-room window. It was dark now, a bright moon casting a silver sheen across the still waters of the bay.

The elderly woman smiled at him as she and her husband made their way back to their room, having finished their meal. 'Not exactly the quiet wee break we were hoping for,' she said to Scott.

'Sorry about that, ma'am,' replied Scott.

'Oh, it's not your fault, son. It's good to see that some policemen are still polite and sober. Goodnight.'

As he watched the couple go, he almost laughed out loud at the thought of being considered polite and sober. Out of the corner of his eye, he spotted a shadow passing the window. He was sure that it was Symington, and wondered where she was going in the dark. She didn't smoke, so it wasn't as though she was off to shiver in the designated smoking area, a little nook beside the hotel entrance that was blasted by the elements.

Another figure passed the window. This time, he was sure that it was DCI Harry Chappell.

'There you go,' said the barman, placing a laminated list of desserts on the table.

'Och, I've changed my mind, son. Think I'll go and get a smoke then watch a bit o' telly up in my room before I hit the scratcher.'

'No bother.'

'Here, take this, son,' he said, handing the barman a five-pound note. 'Get yoursel' a drink later on. You'll be needing it, having tae listen tae this mob for the rest o' the night.'

Scott squinted at the bar area. Sure enough, though a noisy huddle of Special Branch officers were seated around a table covered in crisp packets and pint glasses, there was no sign of Symington or Chappell.

He walked out into the hotel lobby and through the front door, shivering at the chill in the evening air. The flash of his lighter briefly illuminated his face in the darkness. He took a long draw of his cigarette and stared up at the flickering scatter of stars in the velvet blue sky, savouring the moment of tranquillity.

The anguished scream of a woman pierced the still night air.

28

Daley opened the gate that led onto the strand by the causeway. The smell of seaweed was strong, and a breeze ruffled his hair, prompting him to remember that it needed a trim. He had let himself go since Mary's death, he knew it. He no longer had that guiding female hand, first provided by his mother, then his wife, and for all too short a time the young woman he would never see again.

Again, he fought the good fight against the sadness that had plagued him for so long. He suspected he'd chosen the wrong job, and indeed married the wrong woman, and to have any chance of eradicating this deadened sensation from his life, he was going to have to draw on some resources he wasn't sure he had. Even when he'd had the chance to start again, an opportunity to feel renewed with Mary, it had ended in tragedy. He longed for the blessed release of alcohol – the numbing of pain that a few glasses of whisky could temporarily provide. Then he remembered the haunted look in Brian's eyes when his friend had been at his lowest point. If Brian, with his ebullient nature, could descend so far, only managing to drag himself clear of the abyss in the nick of time, what hope was there for him?

He was distracted from these depressing thoughts as the clear beam of powerful Xenon headlights flashed over his head and a car drew up in the layby on the roadway above. Daley heard the dull clunk of an expensive car door closing, followed shortly after by the creak of the gate that he'd just come through.

In a few moments, Feldstein appeared in the darkness, silhouetted by torchlight, which flashed briefly in Daley's face.

'What made you think of meeting here, Mr Daley?'

'I don't know, to be honest,' replied Daley. 'If things are as you say, and meeting with you is so toxic, then we have limited options.'

'This place plays a big part in what you are seeking.'

'How do you know what I'm seeking?'

'I know. You might not have realised yet, but you will. Whether what you find will be something you can believe is another matter. Have these.' He handed Daley a folder. 'Things are worse than we thought. We have so much to defend. Our world has changed so little in the last seventy years, Mr Daley. Much less than you think. Powerful people hand things down the line. They've learned to hide their intentions by peaceful means, not undercover of the horror of war.'

'You're talking in riddles, Mr Feldstein.'

'Imagine this. You fight to bring a criminal to book for years – most of your life, in fact. After a battle that not only nearly destroys you, but your own people, too, you have them. They are removed from society, never able to wreak the havoc they have created.'

'Sounds like my life.'

Ignoring the detective, Feldstein carried on. 'Then, just as the last of them die, you discover that the snake has a long tail. A tail that will grow for ever, encircling the world. And you are too old to fight any more.'

'I don't understand. Please, you have to be less melodramatic. I don't have time for this,' Daley replied testily.

'Ask yourself why your investigations into a missing family on a tiny Scottish island have been usurped. Not only by Special Branch, but now your Security Service.'

'How do you know this?'

'Eyes and ears, Mr Daley. In my organisation, in yours, in Special Branch, even in your precious secret services. It's how the world works.'

'And why on earth would what happens in this little corner of the world have significance, especially given the nature of the things you describe?'

'Quite simply, everything is connected. More now than ever before. But everything has a starting point.'

'And an end point?'

'Not necessarily.' Feldstein walked slowly towards the edge of the shore as the waves withdrew from the shingle. 'This is where Urquhart died.'

'How do you know?'

'I've seen his file.'

'So have I.'

'Yes, but the one I have – and you now mostly have – is not redacted.'

'And if I find something – *if* – what can I do, if things are at the levels you say?'

'You'll find a way. I have read much about you, Mr Daley, about your determination and courage against the odds. To fight someone like Visonovich and win, even temporarily, is an achievement.'

'You are well informed.'

'It won't last for ever. Everyone is in danger. You must already realise that the Bremner family have been removed – destroyed by their own. What chance do we stand?'

'I'm sorry, this is messing with my head. I'm in charge of a quiet police station in a quiet town, in a quiet part of the world. How can this affect me?'

'Quiet now, but not always so quiet, I think.' He reached out, shook Daley by the hand. 'I wish you good luck, the very best of luck. Wait a few minutes before you leave this place. We won't meet again, Mr Daley.'

'You seem very sure of that.'

'When you've lived as long as I have, you learn to see into the future – your own, at least. Like the little boy with his finger in the dam, you can only hold back the black water for so long. In the end, it consumes us all.'

'And may I ask how you can access the backdated files from my police force, and I can't?'

'Who said it was a police file? Read it, Mr Daley. Read it and understand it, for the struggle now passes to you.'

Mystified, Daley watched Feldstein disappear into the darkness. The vehicle soon sped away.

Just as Daley was about to walk back onto the road from the strand, another car drove past, its lights flashing across the fields. Clutching tightly the thick file that Feldstein had given him, he shivered.

At the far end of the car park, a flash of movement caught Scott's eye.

He could hear a strangled voice pleading, 'Get off me, you . . .' A male grunt, the sharp slap of a hand across a face, followed by another squeal, made Scott sprint towards the voices.

He could now see two figures, one pinned by the other to the bonnet of a car, in a commotion of flailing legs and arms in the moonlight.

He pulled at the clothes of the uppermost figure, who spun round.

'What the fuck do you want?' said Chappell, just before his face contorted in pain as Scott kicked his right knee with all the force he could muster.

Instead of falling to the ground, Chappell growled, squatted forward, making himself low, then forced his head into Scott's solar plexus, expelling what little breath the detective had left and sending him tumbling backwards in the darkness. Chappell jumped heavily on top of him.

'Not spent much time in a rugby scrum, have you?' growled the Englishman. He caught Scott a glancing blow across the bridge of his nose with his forehead, sending yellow flashes across the Glaswegian's vision.

Chappell straddled his victim and lifted his balled fist high above his head, ready to bring it down on Scott's unprotected face. Scott was quicker. He freed his arms, clenched his fists together and, pushing with all his might, brought them up sharply under Chappell's chin, sending his head flying back. The Cockney reeled backwards, giving Scott time to wriggle from underneath his bulk, and get painfully to his feet.

Scott could feel someone tugging his arm, and in the heat of the moment, full of adrenaline, he raised his bunched fist in order to defend himself.

'Brian, enough!' shouted Symington, her voice shrill, face ashen.

Chappell was struggling onto his side now, trying to get back to his feet. Before he could do so, Scott caught him again with a sharp kick to his lower back that left him spread-eagled on the gravel.

Scott knelt over him, grabbed a handful of his oily hair, and pulled his head back. 'You're right, you bastard. Never played rugby in my fucking life, but I grew up in a scheme in the East End o' Glasgow. You rugger boys should gie it a go – might improve your game.'

'Brian, for the last time, *stop*! That's an order!'

Scott stood up, dabbing at the blood he could feel streaming from his nose, and turned to his chief superintendent. 'What the fuck is going on, ma'am?' he wheezed. 'If you'll pardon the expression.'

Feldstein had left the lights of Kinloch behind when he noticed something in his rear-view mirror. A vehicle was speeding up behind him, as though about to overtake. As he was manoeuvring his own car along a series of tight bends, he knew that this was impossible, so he clutched the steering wheel and braced himself for a collision.

Sure enough, as the blinding headlights filled his mirror, he felt the first nudge of something hitting his rear bumper. Though he couldn't be sure nothing was coming in the other direction, he couldn't see any oncoming headlights, so tugged at the wheel with his right hand, sending his car careening sideways.

As he did this, the car that had been behind him – a bulky SUV – tried to draw level with his, ploughing along the embankment at high speed. Feldstein took a deep breath. He would have to brake, suddenly and hard. He'd been trained in aggressive driving techniques long before cars were managed by the complex computer-based systems they now boasted, but this manoeuvre was still a dangerous one, the outcome of standing on his own brakes at this speed while slaloming the car around the winding road uncertain.

He felt another nudge from the SUV, steel on steel. The wheel was almost dragged from his grip, but he managed to hold on, trying to ready himself for emergency braking.

A few things happened at once: as he counted down in his mind to the point when he would apply the brakes, the SUV hit him another glancing blow to the side, this time making him lose control of his car. As he fought with the wheel with all his strength, he saw a dazzling flash of lights – this time, oncoming. A truck loomed ahead.

Before he had the chance to take evasive action, the two vehicles collided head-on with sickening force, instantly sending a ball of red flame into the night air.

The SUV slowed slightly, then sped on into the darkness.

29

He parked his car outside the mustard-coloured three-storey building. Even though he'd been here before, he shivered involuntarily and tried to compose himself.

He knocked on the door and waited. A young man dressed in blue overalls answered, looking him up and down suspiciously.

'Can I help you?'

'Frau Weber, please. She's expecting me.'

'Ah, yes, of course. We have to be careful. We are plagued by – well, you can imagine – certain unwanted visitors.'

He was led through a workshop and up a wooden staircase. Everything was painted a utilitarian grey. They walked past a small canteen, where other men in blue overalls were sitting at a large table, reading newspapers, drinking coffee, or staring blankly at mobile phones.

At the end of the corridor they reached a large oak door. The young man knocked sharply three times, cocked his head to listen for a reply, and on hearing a weak voice reply, turned the heavy brass handle and strode into the room.

'Your visitor, Frau Weber,' he said, standing to attention.

An elderly woman was sitting in a high-backed, ornately carved wooden chair. Her hair was long, straight and parted in the middle, framing her round face and pale, shrewd eyes. She peered at him through frameless spectacles and smiled.

'Hans, how lovely to see you again. You have put on some weight, no?' She turned her attention to the younger man. 'Leave us.'

Hans scanned the room. It was wood-panelled, with thick carpeting and dark red wallpaper – exactly the same as it had been on his last visit, almost ten years before.

'Don't stand on ceremony, Hans. Take a seat.'

He nodded, then sat down opposite the old woman on a leather couch, perching on the edge. This house, indeed this old woman, made relaxation impossible.

'You are not taking care of yourself. Too much time in Brussels, I think.'

'Yes, I spend most of my time there now. I've grown to like the city.'

'Why?' The question was sharp. 'A horrid little town in a horrid little country. Barely a country at all – nothing, in fact.'

'The centre of all we've achieved.'

'A flag of convenience. I hope I live to see the day when things will be run from Germany, as they should be.'

'I don't think that will be popular in Berlin. They have enough on their plate.'

'Ach, no wonder, with that hausfrau in charge. I will never trust her – *we* can never trust her.'

'Yet she continues to bring prosperity to Germany.'

The woman eyed him with no little disdain. 'The German people bring prosperity to Germany – as they have always done, and will always do.' She paused. 'Ah, did you know I've learned something new?'

'What?' he asked, confused by the sudden change of subject.

'YouTube!' She beamed. 'I watch it all the time now. Most entertaining.'

'I take it you're not watching cute cat videos.'

'Ha! I was watching a young man we know – well, not personally. You know who I mean.'

'I do.'

'As the father and grandfather were sadly unimpressive – uninspiring – he is not.'

'No, indeed.'

'We have it now. Strength from the past. The beginning of it all – from where the flames spread. Brussels, Maastricht, Paris, Rome, London – take them all!'

He sat back for a few moments, making no comment, as Frau Weber ranted on. When he was at home in Brussels, in his own environment, he was in control. Here, he was like a fish out of water, and the past that he spent so much time trying not to think about harried him, roaring in his face, like a spectre only he could see and hear. Despite her age, she was still formidable.

'And what about these people who are flooding our country and the rest of Europe? Tell me, what will we do with them?'

Eventually, he forced himself to intervene. 'We have things to discuss, do we not? I have to know what to do, what to say to our colleagues.'

His interruption quietened the old woman. She sat staring at the ceiling for so long that he began to fear she'd had some kind of seizure.

She turned to him. 'This is the hard time we knew would come. These times always come. Only Germany is holding Europe together. Our banks, our money; we are already buckling under the strain. This is no reward for the determination of the noble German people. We risk disintegration. Absolute failure of the great plan. We must get back on track. That is why we have had to take independent action.'

'You should have asked me – at least given me warning. You know that Gissing is dead?'

'Yes, I know. But what is one man?'

'He and those who came before kept the secret. They weren't happy, but they did it. Without him . . .'

'There are others.'

'But can they be trusted?'

'Gissing is not the only one to pass. Feldstein is dead.'

For a moment he was so shocked it almost took his breath away. This man had been in his mind for so long. At best, an irritation; at worst, his nemesis.

'How? I mean, how did he die? Naturally, I hope.'

'A tragic traffic accident. The kind that happens every day.'

He stood up so quickly he felt faint, and a pain shot through his lower back. The woman before him was in her nineties, his senior by two decades, but often he felt too old to bear the burden. First the Bremners, now this.

He watched her pick up a newspaper and start reading as though he wasn't there.

Her time is short, he thought. She has done all the damage she can.

Quietly, Hans took his leave of the woman he'd known for so long, knowing he'd never see her again.

*

Symington was sitting on the edge of the bed in her hotel room, shaking violently. Her face was smeared with rivulets of mascara and tears.

Scott was in front of the wardrobe mirror, doing his best to stem the flow of blood from his nose with a couple of wads of cotton wool plugging each nostril. 'You don't need tae say anything, Carrie. You don't know me very well, but I'll tell you this, I've a fair few secrets up here in my noggin that naebody will ever find oot about.' He tapped his head.

'I don't suppose it matters now. I'm quite sure Harry will make certain of that.'

Scott turned to face her. She looked so small, so vulnerable. Nothing of the confident persona she projected as a division commander remained. He sighed, silently giving thanks that his rise in the ranks had been less than meteoric.

'This bastard, Harry, you've known each other for a long time. I can see that.'

'Yes,' she sniffed. 'Too long, much too long.'

Scott thought for a moment. Subtlety was not his strong suit. He tried to think how Daley, much better at interviewing the fairer sex, would approach what was clearly a delicate matter. Yes, the best course of action was softly, softly.

'So, was you shagging this bloke behind his wife's back or something?'

'What?' She sounded genuinely astonished.

'I mean, this is the twenty-first century. Folk get o'er these little piccadillies every day.'

'Peccadilloes,' she said.

'Aye, that's the one. I knew fine I'd heard John Donald come oot wae something like that.'

'I don't know what to say, Brian.' She cradled her head in her hands and sighed. 'I can tell you one thing, though. You'll have a new boss very soon, I guarantee it.'

'Och, enough o' the subtle approach.'

'That was you being subtle?' She smiled wanly.

'Women are a law unto themselves. Just ask the wife. Everything done on a nod or a wink – I can never get my heid roon it. It took Ella aboot six months tae tell me she was going through the menopause, and even then I didnae see what a' the fuss was aboot. I mean, it's no' as though we was planning any mair weans. Fuck me, she cried for near three years . . .'

'It's our primary function, though – well, for most women.'

'What? Roaring the place doon 'cause you're no' bleeding every month? I wid have thought it wid be a chance tae pop the champagne corks. It wid be, if it was me.'

'It's a primeval thing. It's like a death, or so I'm told. The end of your reproductive years is a hard thing to get your head round.'

'Oor Ella still gets loads done – she's right productive. Bugger me, she painted the hall and papered the kitchen last month. How much mair productive dae you want?'

'Oh, Brian . . . I'm worried you'll get into trouble for this.'

'For what? Stopping a woman fae getting assaulted? I dinnae think so.'

She looked at the floor. 'He knows things about me. Has done for years.'

Scott knew when someone was about to unburden themselves. 'Look, tell me aboot it, Carrie. I swear tae you, I'll no' breathe a word o' it tae a soul.'

'I was a young cop, in Wandsworth at the time. We'd been on a shift night out. I used to enjoy them in those days.' She shrugged and smiled wryly at Scott. 'We'd gone to Epping Forest – you know, a little jaunt, somewhere different. I had the car, an old Mini. Terrible thing to drive . . . I was drinking soft drinks, well, I thought I was.'

'Was you slipped a Mickey Finn?'

'Nothing so sophisticated. One of the guys on my shift had been slipping vodka into my orange juice. I just didn't taste it.'

'Hardly the crime o' the century. You mean you got behind the wheel after a dram or two? Fuck me, there wouldn't be many cops left fae my generation if they'd binned every bugger that used tae dae that.'

'I was stupid. I heard them all laughing when we pulled off, you know, back to London. I was just happy – young, happy and stupid. We came round this corner, I wasn't even speeding, and there was this thing, this shadow in the dark.' She hesitated.

'Go on. You might as well spit it oot,' encouraged Scott.

She looked him straight in the eye, her face devoid now of any emotion. 'I'll never forget his face. He came round the corner on a moped, just a flash of white in the darkness. He was on the wrong side of the road by miles. High as a kite, so they discovered in the PM.'

'But you was still o'er the limit?'

'He hit me straight on. The windscreen shattered when he hit it with his helmet. He broke his neck.' She looked out of the window into the darkness beyond, the events of that night long ago playing across her mind. 'It was then the arsehole who'd been spiking my drinks spoke up. It doesn't take much booze to put you over, you know, especially when you don't even know you're drinking it,' she said defensively. 'He'd been really smart,

241

only putting in small amounts of vodka when I wasn't looking. Of course they all thought it was a laugh. Until—'

'Until you'd got a young lad splattered across the bonnet o' your car.'

'The traffic cops from the nearest division attended. When they found out the guy was dead and we were all in the job, they sent for their sergeant.'

'Don't tell me, Harry Chappell?'

'The very man.' She began to sob uncontrollably.

'You don't need tae tell me any mair,' said Scott, colour appearing in his cheeks. 'He ignored the fact that you was o'er the limit, and it was a' just a tragic accident. Am I right?'

'Yes, such a cliché, isn't it? I should've come clean there and then. I was young – doing the job I'd dreamed of. They all persuaded me. But they don't see that boy's face every night. I still see him, you know.' She reached out to Scott, who embraced her gingerly.

'I was in my flat, just round the corner from the nick, and it was a Friday night – I always remember that – a few months later, after the court case. There was a knock at my door.'

'Harry?'

'Yup.' She lowered her head. 'I remember he was stinking of garlic. Been out for a curry with the boys, he said.'

'He forced himself on you?'

'He didn't have to. He told me . . . He told me that if I didn't come across with, you know, he'd spill the beans. Tell the gaffers that he'd been put under pressure to ignore the fact that I'd had a drink. He told me I'd go to prison!'

'Aye, a fine specimen, right enough,' said Scott, patting her on the back. 'You should've let me get a few mair kicks in while he was on the deck.'

242

She sat back, her tears suddenly stopping. 'I deserve what's coming to me, Brian. I'll never get over this . . . never. It's haunted me ever since. He'll never stop.'

'But it wisnae your fault.'

'But I should've told the truth. It's my job, Brian. It's my job to uphold the law.'

'How long did this go on for? You know, wae happy Harry oot there.'

'Years, on and off, until he got bored. I toughened up, moved up the ladder. Almost forgot all about him, or tried to, at least. Until a few days ago. He's a vindictive bastard, though.' She looked at her DS again. 'But, then again, I deserve all I get, don't I?'

'Ach, don't be so hard on yourself. Just you get some sleep, ma'am,' said Scott, 'and leave that bastard tae me.'

'Brian, don't get involved. Please don't do anything stupid.'

'Me, dae something stupid? Chance would be a fine thing.'

30

Kinloch, 1945

The Kinloch Pipe Band were a mismatched lot: youths – boys, merely – with fluffy faces yet to see a razor, marched alongside men, most of whom were well into retirement. The elderly faces glowed red with the strain of blowing the pipes and parading up the Main Street at the same time, despite their proceeding at a snail's pace. The young men who would normally have been the heart and soul of the band were scattered across the world, fighting for their country in the global theatre of conflict they all prayed would come to an end.

Behind the pipe band marched a company of Royal Marines, magnificent in their dress uniforms, dark blue with brass buttons, and boots that gleamed with polish. Many of them were grinning at the sight of the bandsmen ahead, manfully struggling up the gentle slope to the top of the street.

Outside the County Hotel, a group of men in flat caps had gathered, glasses of varying sizes and shapes held aloft in their hands, a blue fug of tobacco smoke gathered above their heads.

On the edge of the pavement, waving small Union Jacks and cheering with unrestrained joy, many holding on to small children, were the womenfolk of the town, hallooing and calling out to encourage the procession on its way. For them, the tall, straight-backed Marines were the personification of the servicemen who were their loved ones: their husbands, boyfriends, sons and sweethearts. They symbolised the men they prayed for every night, the reason for their rush to the door when the letterbox rattled, hoping for a few scribbled words to bring some comfort and dreading news of another kind.

The young women, lips scarlet with beetroot juice in place of lipstick, cheeks nipped red to make up for the absence of rouge, smiled and cheered the loudest of all, trying to catch the eye of the handsome men in uniform. Tanned legs were the product of gravy browning, some of which was smudged and streaked in places, but was all they had to give their legs some colour after the cold dark winter and the absence of nylons.

A drunk old man, his nose bulbous and pitted by a lifetime of over-indulgence, capered in front of the band, his arms aloft in an attempt to dance the Highland fling. The flat cap slanted on his head covered one of his eyes, and from time to time his right hand crept into the pocket of his patched tweed jacket, which bulged with the half bottle of whisky that was stowed there.

'Gie us "Cammeltoon Loch"!' shouted a man in a striped butcher's apron, a streak of rabbit's blood slathered up the white coat he wore as a badge of office. Yet another uniform in a world of uniforms, where everyone had to be seen to be contributing. His shop had so little meat to sell, many of his customers simply took to the hills or the sea to harvest the sustenance they needed. However, with the help of his brother-in-law and his shotgun, he was able to stock some provisions.

Yet, even here, far away from the bombs of the Blitz and the horrors of the latest weapons of terror, people were thin, pallid and tired; their clothes were threadbare and owed more to the thirties in style than the midst of the decade in which they lived.

The Reverend McLintock, Minister of the Wee Free Church, looked on with tight-lipped distaste, though the blush of whisky was plain on his cheeks if you stood close enough.

An old woman in a rickety wooden wheelchair sniffed quietly as she watched the Marines, remembering the three sons she had lost in a previous conflict.

A man in tartan trews and a Tam o' Shanter raised his eyes to the heavens and sang the Gaelic words to the tune the band were asthmatically wheezing out.

A young boy, standing at his young mother's side, ran the back of his hand along his dripping nose, then wiped it on her bare leg, leaving a white streak where the gravy browning was erased.

Across the street, the coloured bunting flapped in the gentle evening breeze, as though waving to the townsfolk below, sharing in their joy and celebration.

Urquhart took in all of this with a jaundiced eye. Crowds – any large group of people – took him back to the beaches of Normandy, and the desperate struggle for survival. He turned the silver lighter over and over in his palm, trying hard to keep the memories at bay, trying to share the joy of the people amongst whom he was standing, but from whom he felt devastatingly apart.

He watched the Kinloch provost clamber onto the platform, a sheet of white paper clutched in his hand, ready to make his speech.

Someone flicked a switch and the Tannoy squealed into life over the skirl of the pipes and the roar of the crowd. A man in a brown dustcoat stepped in front of the box microphone and mumbled one-two-three into it, but succeeded only in making the squeal more ear-splitting.

Urquhart felt a tug at his sleeve, and spun round, his mind back in Kinloch, no longer absorbed with his own horrors.

'Sir, thought you'd b-better see this,' said McColl.

'I told you to keep an eye on Mitchell,' boomed Urquhart in reply.

'Y-yes, that's what I've been doing. Look over there, s-sir.' He stood on his tiptoes, pointing over the heads of the people, across the street to the Post Office. A group of local young men were leaning against the whitewashed walls, sharing a joke with two kilted soldiers, who appeared to be handing out cigarettes.

'What is there to see?' asked Urquhart, slightly irritated by McColl's inexplicable excitement.

'D-do you not see him? M-Mitchell, I mean, he's on the left.'

Urquhart scanned the knot of young men. Not just any gang of local lads; he noticed the son of one of Kinloch's prominent businessmen, the nephew of the sheriff, and young MacAllister, heir to the lairdship of Glen Loss. They were all smartly dressed and confident, in trilbies, not the flat caps of their less illustrious peers. The suits and raincoats they wore were new and of a fashionable, modern cut. Try as he might, though, he couldn't spot the young farmhand.

'Why on earth would Mitchell be with those boys? Out of his league, I would've thought.'

'In the grey trilby, sir.'

There he was. The thick-set youth was laughing loudest. He was wearing a gabardine raincoat over a suit. He turned momentarily in Urquhart's direction, but didn't spot him in the crowd. Andrew Mitchell was no longer in filthy corduroy trousers, tied at the bottom against vermin by nicky tams. He was clean-shaven, well dressed, and in the company of Kinloch's most well-to-do sons.

'I lost him for an hour. D-disappeared out of sight. I was about to come and tell you when I s-spotted him again,' shouted McColl, the screech of the Tannoy system now so deafening that some of the townsfolk were gesturing wildly at the podium.

'Come with me, McColl.' Urquhart forced his way through the crowd and crossed the street by the Post Office, in front of a battalion of the local Boys' Brigade.

Mitchell was gesticulating, his accent sounding loud over the more refined tones of his associates. 'She's got a big pair, I tell you, I saw her at the barn dance in Blaan. Jeest a cracker. Hey, what the—' He yanked his arm from Urquhart's grip, then turned, and on realising it was the detective, looked sheepish.

'Having a good time, Andrew?'

'Whoot's it tae you?'

'I want a word, up at the station. You're coming with me.'

Urquhart hauled Mitchell away from the company as his erstwhile friends purposefully turned their backs on their unfortunate companion.

Forcing their way through the crowds, Urquhart, McColl and the nattily dressed farmhand made their way back up the hill towards Kinloch Police Station.

31

As Daley stood by the roadside watching Feldstein's wrecked car being towed away, he remembered the swish of the vehicle speeding past the strand the night before. The body had been taken to the local hospital, but had been dead on arrival.

This had been no accident. According to the lorry driver, who had managed to jump to safety from his burning vehicle, another car had been involved, driving recklessly, and had failed to stop, despite the collision.

After a few words with the investigating traffic officer, Daley made his way back to Kinloch, going straight to his office and not even acknowledging those who wished him good morning.

He removed the file given to him by Feldstein from the holdall at his feet and settled behind his desk. He no longer cared that he was looking at material unauthorised by his superiors; he only cared that yet another life had been lost, another face to add to the spectral parade throughout his career. The dead girl, lying in a pool of her own blood on a shabby bed in an even shabbier room, loomed in his mind. She had been the first. He wished she had been the last.

He read a report that had been typed on an old-fashioned machine and corrected by Acting Constable McColl in

1945. He thought again of the wizened man staring from the high window in Stonebrae House. It was hard to picture him clattering away at a typewriter.

Inspector Urquhart intimated to me that he was meeting with someone at the causeway. He didn't tell me who he was meeting, and I knew not to press him on the matter. The Inspector was very determined that his orders be followed to the letter. He always was.

At this point, Daley spotted a hand-written note at the bottom of McColl's statement.

Insp. D. Gloag. NB: Though McColl doesn't mention it in this statement, he expressed a feeling that this meeting had something to do with Andrew Mitchell, main witness in the Kerr case.

Inspector Gloag had signed this off with a flourish, though as Daley scanned the rest of the file, he saw no further mention of the observation.

The copies of various files and documents were stamped, but the mark was so faded that Daley couldn't make it out. Only when he came to a file marked TOP SECRET did he realise that the stamp read PROPERTY OF THE STATE OF ISRAEL.

He'd always known that Feldstein was a member of some group dedicated to flushing out the dwindling numbers of war criminals, but not an agent of Israeli Intelligence. This realisation made his heart race. How could the disappearance of a family in the twenty-first century – despite their historical Nazi connections – be of any interest to modern Israel?

He thought more about Feldstein. What did his death mean for the rest of those trying to make sense of the disappearance of the Bremners?

He thought about the deceptively easygoing Iolo Harris, the Special Branch team on Gairsay with Scott and Symington, the cellar of the old farmhouse filled with pictures and documents from the war, the photographs he'd seen of Urquhart, his solid and dependable predecessor.

He felt as though he was taking up the cudgels of an investigation that had ended with the inspector's untimely death – as though, with his last breath, Urquhart was trying desperately to tell him something. It felt like the man was shouting to be heard in the next room – across decades.

The glass box in which Daley sat would have been unrecognisable to Urquhart, but they were united by elements of an investigation that he could follow up. He decided to take up what he could of Urquhart's last case, but he felt alone – and distinctly uneasy.

The door was rattled by a sharp knock.

'Sir,' said Sergeant Shaw, his face anxious. 'It's the old boy, Hamish. He's been attacked. He was found outside his house by someone out jogging early this morning. He's in Kinloch hospital.'

'How is he?'

'Pretty bad, sir.'

Without waiting to hear more, Daley flung on his jacket and within minutes was at the wheel of his car, screeching out of the yard.

Harry Chappell examined his bruised and bloody face in the harsh fluorescent light of his bathroom. His lip curled at the thought of the rough-looking detective sergeant who had bettered him in a fight.

He walked stiffly to his bed, working out what he'd tell his superior while planning revenge: revenge against the man who had left him battered in the car park, but most of all, revenge against *her*. It seemed she'd found another champion – someone who would try and protect her from his advances. But he was different now, more powerful. He was part of Special Branch, a chief inspector. No Scotch DS with heather in his ears would get the better of him.

He picked up the mobile phone from his bedside table and scrolled down to his boss's name. He would tell the truth – well, mostly the truth. How the Scotch detective was out of control when he found himself and Symington having an intimate moment in the car park. How he'd been completely unprepared for an attack, especially one from a fellow officer. He knew he'd have to give something away as to his past with Carrie, but his boss was old school and wouldn't hold up his hands in horror at the thought of a liaison between officers.

As for Symington, well, she'd be bound to keep her mouth shut. He had her where he wanted her, no matter how much she tried to twist from his grasp. She would never risk the exposure of being responsible for the death of a young man and then being part of the cover-up.

He might get a bit of stick from his colleagues, perhaps even a reprimand from the boss, but who cared?

He was about to press the call button when he heard a tentative knock at his room door.

'Who is it?' he called, rather suspecting that it would be Symington, anxious to concoct some excuse in order to protect herself from any implications of the fight. She'd want to apologise, keep him sweet.

'Maintenance!' The voice was local, high-pitched and effeminate. What was it about the hotel industry that attracted so many mincers, he thought.

'Can you come back later? I'm busy.'

'Och, dearie me,' came the sing-song voice in reply. 'It's jeest that we've had a right bugger wae the boiler for the central heating. If I don't get to your radiator, I dread to think what might happen. Water everywhere, I shouldna wonder.'

'Bloody hell!' cursed Chappell as he got up from the bed. 'Save me from these yokels.' He opened the door wide, expecting to find the camp boiler-suited maintenance man he'd seen sashaying around the hotel, but his mouth fell open when he realised who'd come to call, and he tried frantically to close it. He failed when a sharp kick to his abdomen sent him flying backwards onto the carpeted floor with a heavy thud.

'So you're up and aboot,' snarled Scott, kicking the door shut with a back-kick. 'I hoped you'd maybe given up the ghost last night.' He loomed over the stricken man as he tried to get up.

'I'll make sure you lose your miserable job, you Jock bastard,' panted Chappell, still winded.

'Will you? Fuck me, that'll be interesting. Especially when I tell your gaffer that you've been raping a female colleague for years. Exposing shit like that's worth losing my job for. Anyhow, I'm no' bothered. It's high time I was out of this, tae be honest.' Scott knelt down over Chappell, grabbed him by the shirt collar, and whispered in his ear, 'Noo, listen tae me. You'll tell your boss you had a wee tumble last night – too much to drink. Then you'll tell him you're gettin' right bad heidaches an' you need tae call it a day and go off the panel.'

'What if I refuse?' wheezed Chappell, his throat constricted by Scott's grip, his face crimson, a vein pulsing blue in his temple.

''Cause. I'll kick you good-looking, ya prick. Doing time for sexual assault and corruption will be the least o' your worries. I'll make sure you never see the inside o' the jail, don't worry. Inside o' the crematorium, mair like.'

'So, she told *you* about our little secret—' Chappell was stopped speaking mid sentence when Scott caught him with a sucker punch under the chin.

'Whit secret? Dae you know one? I don't know any secret. Just leave her alone fae noo on in. I'll find you. I don't care aboot my career, but I think you've a good bit mair tae lose than me, *Chief Inspector*.' To finish off, Scott punched him hard in the stomach and stood up, straightening his tie. 'Now, you have a good day. If you're no' off this island on the next ferry, I'll make sure you find another route hame – in an ambulance. See ya.'

Scott sauntered out of the room, leaving Chappell gasping for breath.

'Lovely day, Mr Scott,' remarked the chambermaid as she pushed a trolley loaded with bed linen along the corridor.

'Aye, no' bad at all, dear,' he replied, pulling the hotel room door firmly shut behind him.

Hamish was lying on a bed, a drip feeding into his arm, connected to a monitor that bleeped in time with the old man's heart. A woman was sitting at the bedside, holding his hand, while two young men, dressed in rancid dungarees that stank of fish guts, towered over her.

'Annie, how is he?' asked Daley.

'Och, is this no' jeest a wile thing. Who wid attack an auld man, especially oor Hamish? Widna hurt a fly, so he widna,' replied the hotel manager, tears in her eyes.

'He's been responsible for hurtin' a few fish o'er the years, mind you,' said the youngest of the two fishermen, his belly bulging beneath his dungarees.

'See if you canna say anythin' that's no' stupid, jeest say naething, Erchie,' the older fisherman replied. 'No' hurting a fly is a figure o' speech – it doesna mean he's actually no' hurt a fly, you stupid—'

'How did this happen? I mean, who found him, Annie?'

'Wee Tina, Michael Kerr the baker's daughter. She's on a health kick. Goes oot jogging early every morning before she goes tae the shop.'

'Aye, then she stuffs her face full o' they Danish pastries and pineapple whirls. It's a wonder she can run the length o' hersel' wae an arse the size o' a lobster boat.'

'Erchie, will you shut up!' protested Annie. 'Can you no' see that your great-uncle's struggling for his life here? I don't know whoot gets intae you boys.' She gave him a withering look.

'Anyhow, is it no' your job tae tell us whoot happened tae Hamish, Mr Daley?' the older man said pointedly.

'You be quiet an' aw, Tony. Mr Daley's jeest found oot whoot's happened. You'll find the culprit, sure you will,' implored Annie.

'Yes, of course I will,' he replied, still shocked to see the man who had saved his life in such a state.

A doctor, accompanied by a staff nurse, entered the room and asked the visitors to leave.

As Annie and Hamish's great-nephews trooped out, Daley hung back. 'How is he *really*?' he asked the doctor.

'Taken quite a beating, sir. For the life of me, I don't know who would do such a thing. We're getting him stabilised, then he's for the helicopter to Glasgow. He'll need to have an MRI scan, and he'll be better off up there in case, well, in case he suffers any complications.'

'But you think he'll regain consciousness?'

'Oh, he was semi-conscious when he was brought in. Even spoke a few words.'

'What did he say? I'm sorry, I have to ask. I need to find who did this, and it may help.'

'I doubt it, but it was strange. He kept on saying the same thing over and over again, sounded like gobbledegook.'

'Which was?'

'The well of the winds. He said it over and over again. Now, if you don't mind, I need to examine my patient.'

Scott was enjoying a kipper in the dining room when Symington arrived for breakfast. She'd done a good job of disguising her pallor with foundation, but he could see that her eyes were red-rimmed and puffy. She looked relieved when she realised that the only other diners were the elderly couple, not any Special Branch personnel.

'Morning, ma'am,' said Scott, trying to sound as cheerful and as natural as possible. 'It's a lovely day.'

She sat at the table and summoned a weak smile. 'How are *things*?'

'Just dandy. You should try one o' they kippers. Lovely, so they are.'

She looked nervously around the room as the young waitress who had admired her handbag came to the table to take her order.

'Good morning. What would you like today?'

'Oh, just coffee and a croissant, please,' said Symington. 'I've had too many hearty breakfasts over the last few days.'

The girl smiled and padded away.

'Here,' said Scott. 'Don't you know breakfast is the most important meal o' the day? I keep trying tae encourage oor Jimmy tae eat a proper breakfast, but no' him. If you eat well first thing, you're no' wanting tae nibble away at rubbish for the rest o' the day. My auld faither didnae gie me much good advice, but that was a pearler.'

'What other gems did he pass on?' said Symington, beginning to relax a little.

'Never eat yellow snow, and pretend you're another bugger when the sheriff officers come tae the door.'

'Bailiffs, where I come from.'

'Aye, whatever. It was quite an education seeing my auld fella when they came knocking at the door, I'll tell you.'

'How come?'

'He was a maister at it. Even pretended he was French once. Put the big bugger right off. "I am not knowing zees Meester Scoot." The works. Aye, he was classic at it.'

'So he saved the day?'

'Naw, no' really. They took the telly and my mother's hoover, but it was still entertaining.'

Suddenly, Symington flinched in her seat. When Scott turned to see what had prompted this, he noticed one of the Special Branch team enter the dining room, visibly bleary-eyed from his over-indulgence in the bar the night before.

'Morning, guys,' he said cheerily. 'Ain't that sun bright? Nightmare.'

'Big heid the day?' asked Scott.

'Yeah, something like that, mate.' He chuckled. 'Not as bad as Harry, mind you.'

Symington made a noise, a cross between a whimper and a cough, her eyes flashing wide.

'Oh, what's wrang wae him, then?'

'Big girl's blouse, mate. He had so much to drink last night he fell down the stairs. Made a right mess of himself. He's off back to the smoke. They just gave him a lift to the ferry. The gaffer's not best pleased, but that's what you get when you can't handle your drink. You both look quite fresh.' He smiled.

'I don't touch the stuff,' replied Scott, hearing the words but still not quite believing them.

'Good on you. I could've signed the pledge this morning, I can tell you. Still, unusual for you Jocks, isn't it? I thought you was all mad for it up here.'

'Just shows you shouldnae make sweeping judgements based on race. Like these buggers you hear talking aboot us no' being understood doon south. Pain in the arse. I've never had any bother making folk understand what I mean . . .'

The man shook his head and wandered off to a table.

Symington's phone rang. 'It's Jim,' she said.

Scott looked on as she answered the call. When she was finished he looked at her with a puzzled expression. 'Is who all right?'

'Your friend, the old fisherman Hamish. He was beaten up last night, apparently. He's in a bad way.'

'What!' Scott was shocked. 'He's just a great auld bloke. Oor Jimmy'll no' be happy aboot that. Right fond o' him, so he is. Me and a', come tae that. Is he going to be okay?'

'He's being taken to Glasgow in a helicopter.' She lowered her voice so that the Special Branch officer, now seated at the other side of the room, couldn't hear. 'And Feldstein was killed in an RTA last night.'

'The shit's going to hit the fan noo, then.'

'Why do you say that?'

'It doesnae take a genius tae figure oot who he was working for, does it?'

'Meaning?'

'Thon Israeli mob, Mossad. That's what they're called, isn't it?'

'Very astute.'

'Up here's for thinking' – Scott tapped his head, then pointed underneath the table at his feet – 'an' doon here's for dancing. This Bremner case has just reached the next level, would you no' say, ma'am?'

She nodded, then looked round the room again with a sigh.

32

Iolo Harris sniffed the air as he stepped off the ferry onto the Isle of Gairsay. He watched a gull circle lazily above the bay, then dive into the water. A few moments later, it bobbed back to the surface, the silver flash of a wriggling fish clasped tightly in its beak. As though curious to see what was going on, a seal poked its head from amongst the bladderwrack floating near the shore. It yawned, then turned its head to study the bustle surrounding the ferry: passengers jostling to get on board, drivers on the jetty switching on their engines, sending clouds of blue exhaust fumes into the air.

He watched as a large man with a bruised face limped down the slipway and onto the vessel. A grinning crew member gave the passenger an exaggerated salute, seemingly unperturbed by the contusions on his face.

'I think you're going my way,' Harris said to the driver of a white minibus with GAIRSAY HOTEL printed on the side.

'I will be if you're going to the Gairsay Hotel,' replied the driver.

'I am that,' he replied, jumping into the vehicle. 'Busy this morning, eh?'

'Aye, the place has been going like a fair since that family disappeared. Policeman and journalists – och, jeest a' sorts. Are you here for that, yourself?'

'Here to admire your windmills, buddy,' replied Harris.

When the minibus eventually pulled into the hotel car park, Harris heard his phone beep. The message from Flanagan was brief and to the point: *Landscape changed. Call ASAP*.

In a few moments, he heard the familiar voice of Flanagan. 'Listen, Iolo, we have to think on our feet here. A senior Israeli diplomat, if you get my drift, was killed in a road traffic accident in Kintyre last night. I have a meeting with the minister in half an hour, and as you can imagine, Tel Aviv is up in arms. The Americans too, predictably.'

'What about Brussels?'

'The hell with Brussels. I think we might be about to change sides. Any residue of what happened on this little island has to be removed. No need to spell things out. We have to be seen to be squeaky clean in all this. '

As he hung up, Harris tried to picture just what changing sides might entail. One thing was certain: though this was a tiny island off the remote Scottish coast, what was about to happen would have global ramifications. Ultimately, high politics was not his business. He concerned himself with much more practical things. He knew what he had to do.

Daley was trawling through CCTV footage taken across Kinloch the previous evening. DC Potts was assisting him in the search for any sign of Hamish and how he might have come by the injuries he'd sustained.

As they'd been informed, he'd left the Douglas Arms, crossed the car park in the square and headed onto West Row. Daley watched the flickering image of Hamish stop now and then, look in a few shop windows, and then carry on in his habitual style, hands in pockets, head held high, as though sniffing the air. The detective caught the glimpse of a smile on his old friend's face, which made him smile himself, then quickly become angry. Who would hurt a harmless old man in such a callous way, and what on earth did they have to gain by it? Daley reasoned that his association with the fisherman was at the heart of the matter, and it made him feel sick to his stomach.

Well of the winds. Hamish's words echoed around his head.

'Look at this, sir, this vehicle here.' Potts pointed at the screen. A dark SUV was driving up West Row past Hamish.

'What about it? It's just a car driving through the town,' replied Daley, more irritably than he'd intended.

'But here again,' said Potts, sending the image flickering forward at high speed, making Hamish look as though he was power-walking along the road. He paused the footage. 'See, would you not say that's the same vehicle, sir?'

Daley stared at the screen; yes, the SUV was driving past Hamish, this time heading back into the centre of Kinloch.

'Worth a look. Can we make out the registration?'

'No, sir, not without augmentation, I don't think. But look, here again.'

Daley leaned forward. Hamish had turned into Main Street and headed down towards the loch. The SUV – definitely the same car – was making its way slowly back up the street, its lights flashing into the CCTV camera as it turned back into West Row.

'Why would he be cruising about at that time of night, sir? I mean, it's not one of the local lads looking for girls – not in that kind of motor.'

'Get this footage up to the tech boys and have it enhanced. Good work. Let's hope we can get an ID on that plate.'

He went into his glass box, sat down heavily, making the big leather chair squeak in protest, and called the front desk. 'Sergeant Shaw, the lorry driver who hit Feldstein mentioned another vehicle. What was its description?'

He listened as Shaw tapped the keys of his computer terminal.

'Dark-coloured SUV, sir. Possibly a Merc or similar, but not a Range Rover.'

Daley walked back to the CID suite. 'Let me see that footage again.' He leaned over the back of Potts's chair, remembering with a pang that the last time he'd done this was when Mary was busy operating the terminal. No smell of strawberry shampoo now, just the slight odour of sweat from the young man who had been working through the night.

'Here we are,' he said, pausing the footage to show the best screen grab of the SUV they had.

'What model would you say that was?'

'Looks like a Merc to me, sir. Not sure which model, but I can check.'

'Please do,' replied Daley.

Alan Bale wheezed as he leaned down to switch on the computer in the incident room at Gairsay Hotel. He hated having to liaise with the spooks, but at least this chap seemed approachable, not one of the high-handed ex-public schoolboys he was more accustomed to dealing with.

'Here we are, take a look.'

'Well, there's no doubt what he's doing, but who is he?'

'One of the Kinloch plods. A DS Scott, I think.'

Harris looked on as the screen image revealed the detective photographing page after page of documents in the cellar of Achnamara farmhouse, somewhat inexpertly, he thought.

'Get this!' shouted the man onscreen. 'I'm fucking Lord Beaverbrook, me.'

'I have no idea what he means,' said Bale, brushing a strand of grey hair away from his forehead, his cheeks flushed.

'Means Lord Snowdon, I reckon,' replied Harris, trying to hide his smile. 'You know, the photographer who used to be married to Princess Margaret.'

'Oh, very good. Anyhow, as you can see, he's taken a picture of nearly everything in the place. Not sure how you want to approach this?'

'Just how did you come across this footage?'

'Hidden cameras everywhere. The local boys missed the lot, inside and out. Took us ages to find them.'

'Have you found anything else? I mean apart from this copper taking snaps of all the documentation, that is?'

'There was a computer in the bungalow, but it's encrypted. Might be some kind of record of what went on down there, but we don't know yet how long for. We pinged the files down to London.'

'Okay, thanks. Let me know the minute you hear anything.'

Bale exhaled loudly.

'What's wrong?' asked Harris.

'Just want to get things straight. I'm not one for beating about the bush . . .'

'No, indeed,' replied Harris, exasperated that the policeman was doing exactly that. 'Just spit it out, man!'

'Well,' Bale began cautiously, 'frankly, I'm too high a pay

grade to be an office boy to you. If you're taking charge up here, well, at least have the decency to tell me, so that I can deploy somewhere else. It won't be news to you, of all people, that we are just keeping our heads above water with all the security threats we face in this country at the moment.'

'No need for concern, sir. It's your pigeon. I'm just an observer.'

'Oh, yes, well, if you say so,' replied Bale doubtfully.

'This DS Scott, is he still on the island?'

'Yes, he and his chief superintendent – Symington's her name – are here. Leaving today, I think. They've been helping with the handover. Not too happy about us taking charge here.'

'Yeah, never easy, is it?' Harris replied blandly. 'I'll go and have a word before they take off.'

'Be careful. Symington's a smart cookie. Don't know for the life of me what she's doing up here in the back of beyond. Waste of a clever cop, if you ask me.'

'You never know. Maybe they need clever cops up here, too,' replied Harris before taking his leave.

As he walked through to the hotel reception, he reflected on his encounters with police officers over the years. He'd met a few – very few – who were dedicated and selfless. The great majority, though, were not; especially those in the senior ranks. He'd spent half of his career trying to cover for preening officers who'd been promoted beyond their capabilities and had made a hash of the jobs that had been entrusted to them. He longed for the day when the police would emerge from the dark ages and put in place a dedicated officer class: executive ranks chosen for their expertise, not their ability to brown-nose or handshake their way to the top of the tree. He thought of Daley. He certainly possessed some of the defensiveness and watchfulness of his kind, but he also appeared to have a soul and a quick mind. Not that he would ever reach the rank of commander or beyond: he was too straight, too intelligent, lacked the requisite naked ambition. Daley would have been better doing a job like his. The ability to twist and turn was constant, but remaining grounded, knowing which way was up, as an old mentor of his once said, was just as important.

He wondered in which direction up might be found when the spirals of this case eventually unravelled. He wondered if Daley would orient himself in that direction, too, or would he need help?

'You have a Ms Symington staying in the hotel. Could you get a message to her, please?' he asked the receptionist.

33

Kinloch, 1945

Andrew Mitchell's face was beginning to swell where Urquhart had landed him a punch. There were tears in his eyes as he faced the inspector in the spartan interview room, only a rickety table between them. A stony-faced constable stood by the door, arms folded.

'I'll ask you again: how did you come by the fancy clothes? From your new friends?' barked Urquhart, his face still red with fury.

'Whoot business is it o' yours?'

The inspector flew at him across the table, grabbing him tightly by the collar of his shirt. 'I told you. I'm investigating the death of Mr Kerr. I know you know much more than you're letting on, so just tell the truth.' He pushed the farm-hand backwards with such force that the younger man almost toppled off his chair.

Mitchell looked pleadingly at the constable, but got no response.

'I think you locked Mr Kerr into that cattle float and made sure he was trampled to death. I couldn't work out what you had to gain before, apart from losing your job, but when I saw you with your new pals, well, things started to become clearer.'

'I don't know whoot you mean. I jeest treated mysel' tae the suit an' that fae my savings, if you must know. Is it a crime tae wear a nice suit, noo?'

'And how much did it all cost?'

'A few quid, I canna remember.'

'Let me see,' said Urquhart, picking up his notebook. 'The suit's Savile Row, London, as was your shirt. The shoes are from Milan. Just where did you purchase these, for a few quid?'

'I paid a frien for them.'

'And this frien is?'

'I'm no' saying'. I don't have tae answer they questions.'

Urquhart stood up suddenly, making Mitchell cower. 'In that case, I have no choice but to charge you. Can you note this down, Constable McLennan?'

'Yes, sir.' The constable took his notebook from his top pocket, placed it in the palm of his left hand, and licked the tip of his pencil. 'Ready when you are, sir.'

'Andrew Mitchell, I am charging you with the murder of Dugald Kerr at the premises of his farm on the day of—'

It was Mitchell's turn to stand up. He yelled at the top of his voice, 'No! You canna dae this!'

'I can do what I like, son. Of course, you know what the penalty is for murder.'

'No! You're no' hangin' me. I never done it!'

'Put the cuffs on him, MacLennan.'

'Get your hands off me!' shouted Mitchell, making a bid for the door. MacLennan caught him in the midriff with a punch that made the farmhand double over.

As Mitchell was handcuffed by the burly constable, Urquhart bent down and said, 'You'll die for this, son. Pity, really. I'm not even sure you did it, but, if you did, I know somebody put you up to it. In fact, that's why you were working at the farm, wasn't it? To keep an eye on him.'

'I'm no' sayin'. They'll kill me!' screamed Mitchell as the constable pulled him upright.

'Now we're getting somewhere. Who'll kill you?'

'I canna say!'

Urquhart stood up straight, rubbing his hands together as though wiping them clean. 'Well, you're going to hang anyway, so my job is done. Take him away, Constable.'

'Haud on! I want tae say somethin',' shouted Mitchell, his eyes wide in desperation.

Symington apologised to Harris for the lack of biscuits.

'No problem. I'm sad to say that I suffer from the same problem that afflicts so many of my countrymen: short legs, long backs and the ability to put on pounds at the drop of a hat.'

Symington smiled politely. It hadn't taken long for Harris to take in the shadows under her eyes and her air of distraction. Despite the occasional deployment of a toothy smile, here was a woman under extreme pressure.

'So, when can we expect to see DS Scott?'

'He won't be a moment, Mr Harris. Just writing up some case notes before we head back to the mainland.'

'Good . . . You've not been up here in Scotland for long, have you?'

'No, not long at all. I arrived in November last year. It's all been a bit of a blur, really.'

Harris recalled the details of Symington's file. She'd already been part of a high-profile case involving a wealthy local family. Here she was again, on the edge of something even more significant.

'I must admit, it makes a pleasant change from traipsing around Whitehall. The sea air and the scenery.'

'I can hear you're a Welshman, from what part?'

'Port Talbot, also by the sea, but not the same clean air as up here in the Highlands.'

There was a firm knock at the door and in strolled Scott.

'What's this aboot a spook?' asked Scott. Only Symington was visible to him as he came up the short hallway. 'Last thing we fuckin' need – spooks and Special Branch, eh?' The look on Symington's face made him hesitate, and as he turned to his left he spotted the dark-haired man in jeans and a sweatshirt sitting on the end of the bed.

'Detective Sergeant Scott, I presume,' said Harris with a smile. 'Been in the wars, I see.'

Without thinking, Scott touched his bruised face.

'Aye, well, you know how it is when you're a polisman – there's no shortage of rough and tumble.'

'Funny, I saw a man getting on the ferry this morning. His face was in a worse state than yours. Dangerous island, is it?'

Harris noted the glance that passed between Symington and Scott. If he hadn't known better, he'd have been convinced that they were having an affair. But even at this brief exposure to the chief superintendent and her rough-and-ready DS, there was something about the dynamic that didn't seem right. A shared secret, perhaps, but nothing sexual.

'If we could move things along, please, Mr Harris,' interjected Symington. 'We're heading back today, and we've a few things to do before we catch the ferry.'

'Well, I'll get on with it.' He turned to Scott. 'I'm interested in your photographic skills.'

'Eh?'

'You know. Point and click – taking pictures on your phone. In this case, in the cellar of the farmhouse. Achnamara, isn't it?' he said, finding the word difficult to pronounce.

Another exchange of glances.

'What do you mean, Mr Harris?' asked Symington coolly.

'Unbeknownst to you and Lord Beaverbrook here, the entire cellar was covered by CCTV. Special Branch have just discovered it.' He looked at Scott again. 'I'll need you to hand over all the images you have and make sure they're deleted from any other devices you might have. This is a matter of national security, and it will be followed up.'

'Wait a minute,' said Symington, getting to her feet. 'Sergeant Scott was acting on my orders when he took those pictures, and just to let you know, it was prior to the arrival of Special Branch. As the investigators in charge we had every right to make notes regarding the locus, and photograph anything we liked.'

'Of course you had,' replied Harris. 'But now you don't. So, before you head off back to the mainland, I'd like to see the device which was used to photograph the documents, and I need an assurance from you, Chief Superintendent, that all copies have been destroyed and are not in anyone else's possession.'

'My phone was used. I'll let you have it once I've removed any information that is personal or irrelevant to this case.'

Symington gestured towards the door, indicating that in her opinion their meeting was at an end.

'Excellent. And what about the copies?'

'None were made. I asked DS Scott to take the pictures to make sure we had a record of exactly what was found at the Bremner property before they disappeared. I have to tell you, I'm very unhappy at the way this case has been passed from pillar to post. This is my patch, and, at the very least, I should be kept in the loop.'

'So you made no copies, and neither did you distribute any?'

'That's correct, Mr Harris. Now, if you don't mind, we have a ferry to catch. I'll leave the phone with you before I go. I'll need a signature, of course.' The toothy smile was switched on again, but her eyes were cold.

Harris bade the two police officers a good day and left the hotel room. He had some sympathy for Symington and the high-handed way the local force had been treated, but he also knew when he was being lied to.

Kinloch, 1945

Urquhart was doodling absently on the blotting sheet in front of him. McColl was typing away in the corner of the office, working through the report he'd been asked to file.

As the inspector had suspected he would, Mitchell had caved in. Heavy-handed tactics, which he'd deployed in the military police, always left a bad taste in his mouth, but in this case the end had justified the means.

Yet he felt as if there were too many ends and no discernible beginning. He shouldn't have been surprised to discover that there were elements of every community who didn't support their own country in this hellish conflict. He recalled being shocked when a general, full of rich food and port, had casually mentioned the abdicated king's admiration for the Third Reich. The thought had left him profoundly depressed; that this man to whom he had pledged his allegiance was in awe of Hitler was insufferable.

'I know these p-people,' remarked McColl, having reached the part of Urquhart's report where locals were mentioned.

'Good. You can tell me all you know about them, and their families. At the same time, you can also forget what you've just read and never mention it to a soul. If I discover you've whispered a word of this to your father, or anyone else for that matter, I'll have you charged with treason.'

McColl gasped slightly and turned back to his typewriter, shoulders hunched, hands shaking slightly as they hovered over the keys.

Urquhart headed through to the back of the station. He nodded to Constable MacLennan, who took the keys from his belt and unlocked the cell.

Huddled in the corner, covered by a grubby grey blanket, Mitchell looked frightened. 'Look whoot you've done tae me,' he protested, touching a weal on his cheek, upon which the blood had almost congealed.

'Get up,' said Urquhart, catching Mitchell's shin with a kick, which caused the farmhand to cry out in pain. 'You know the trouble you're in, I needn't tell you that.'

Mitchell whimpered and nodded his head.

'I can help you. Save you from the noose. You'll do time, but what happened to Mr Kerr could have so easily been an accident.'

'It was jeest an accident—'

'Shut up and listen. Get cleaned up, go home, and get a good night's sleep. From now on, you'll do exactly what I tell you.'

'An' jeest whoot's that?'

'Well, Andrew, you're going to get yourself a new career.'

'Oh aye,' groaned Mitchell, looking doubtful.

'Yes. Deviate in any way from what I tell you to do, and you won't see many more dawns – that's a promise. Get back here tomorrow morning, seven, sharp!'

34

Daley had decided to go back to basics. He was constructing a timeline of events in the old-fashioned way, on a board, with lines and squiggles and messy handwriting, the way he'd been taught so many years ago. He still preferred the hands-on paper-and-pen experience to that of computer, spreadsheets and databases. Recently, he'd come to feel he was existing in some intangible virtual reality – a world from the pages of some dystopian fantasy. He had mentioned this to Brian, who had opined sagely on the efficacy of sucking a peppermint in order to cure dystopia.

He stuck a photograph of Achnamara farm at the centre of the board. Radiating from it were red lines drawn with a marker pen. At the end of one was the small vessel from Elliot's boatyard that had vanished, and which he assumed had been used by the Bremners to make good their escape – an escape that had gone tragically wrong, for reasons that were yet to be explained.

Another red line ended with the drawing of the head and shoulders of a man: Feldstein. From that radiated depictions of a book – Urquhart's journal – and the SUV.

Underneath the farm, a dotted red line meandered to the faded image of Urquhart himself. Next to this was a copy of one of the inspector's drawings of the cigarette lighter.

He was drawing Stonebrae House when his phone rang.

'Sir, Royal Infirmary in Glasgow for you,' announced Shaw.

As Daley asked for the call to be put through, he could feel his heart sink. He'd heard the helicopter taking Hamish there, and he knew how frail the old man had been when he'd last seen him.

'DCI Daley?'

'Yes, speaking.'

The doctor confirmed that he was calling about Hamish. 'Tough old guy, took quite a battering. But he's starting to speak now. Says he has something to tell you and only you.'

'I see. I'm a bit pushed here, in the middle of a serious investigation. Can he speak on the phone?'

'No, not yet. But he seems to want to see you. I get the impression that you're a friend of his, as well as investigating the circumstances behind his attack. It would do him the world of good to see someone. He's becoming quite agitated, actually.'

'Okay. I'll try to get there as soon as I can. Please tell him I'm asking for him.'

Daley felt guilty, remembering that the old fisherman had once saved his life. He deserved his attention. He called Symington.

'Hi, Jim, sorry I've not been in touch. We'll be over later today, just winding things up here.'

'You heard about Hamish?'

'Yes, I did. DS Scott was outraged, as you can imagine.'

'Well, he's regained consciousness and wants to see me. We're full on, as you know, but I think I should go. He has information, apparently. I owe it to him, you know? There could be some reason he was targeted in this way, that it wasn't just some random mugger. I was wondering if you could get the chopper to lift and lay me – it would save time.'

'Yes, no problem. I'll put the request in now. Do you have any idea what he has to say?'

'No, not really. But when he was found he kept muttering something over and over again.'

'Yes?'

'Well of the winds.'

'Oh,' said Symington, surprised. 'Now, that *is* a coincidence.'

Kinloch, 1945

Urquhart was startled by the sound of an explosion. From his window, which overlooked Main Street, he could see the tell-tale wisp of white smoke rising above the loch. The blast he'd heard was the call to arms of the local lifeboat crew and could be heard across the town. It always amazed him how quickly these dedicated men – mostly retired or working fishermen – got to the boat and launched. He watched as a man in huge gumboots raced down the street in the direction of the pier, soon followed by others.

'Ranald is here, sir,' said McColl, poking his head round the door. 'He wants to see you, urgently.'

The fisherman's tanned features were obscured by the cap he wore, pulled down over one eye. He had a small boy by the hand, who could only be his son, such were the slant of his blue eyes and the proud way he held his head.

Urquhart walked to the other side of his desk and knelt down in front of the child. 'What's your name, son?'

277

The boy – barely more than a toddler – looked up at his father, who smiled encouragingly.

'Hamish,' he replied in a tiny voice. 'Whoot's your name?'

'I'm Inspector Urquhart. Here, this is for you.' He fished into his trouser pocket and brought out a sixpence, which glinted in the sunlit room.

Hamish's eyes lit up, but still he looked up at his father before he took the money on offer.

'Whoot dae you say?'

'Thank you, mister,' replied the child, studying the coin closely, as though he was seeing money for the first time.

'Thank you, Inspector Urquhart,' said Ranald. 'You didna need tae.'

'Happy to. Now, what can I do for you?'

'You'll have noted that the lifeboat's away oot.'

'Yes, I did.'

'Well, they tell me there's been an accident jeest off Gairsay, no' far fae the beach where we found that poor soul. My friend tells me there's somethin' no' right aboot it.'

'In what way?' Urquhart looked puzzled.

'Och, jeest that. A collision o' Gairsay boats. Hardly the weather for that kind o' thing. And, well, it jeest makes me feel uneasy. That's a' I can say.'

'Uneasy, how?'

'Well, now, you see, if I knew that, I'd be a rich man. Och, sometimes you jeest get a feeling, you know, in the pit o' your stomach.'

'Do you think I should take a look?'

'Aye, I think maybe you should. I'm mair than happy tae take you. Need tae gie me an hour or so, before we can set off.'

'Can I get a poke o' jujubes wae this?' said Hamish, still mesmerised by the sixpence.

'I dare say you can, son.'

Daley was soon being whisked into the air, the thud of the helicopter blades pounding through his headphones as the aircraft dipped its nose and headed out over the loch, gaining height as it went.

As they approached the island that guarded Kinloch from the worst the sea could throw at it, he looked down. The causeway was visible now that the tide was ebbing. Soon it would again fulfil its ancient purpose, and tourists and locals alike would be able to walk across it.

He remembered doing just that with Liz, not long after he'd first arrived in Kinloch. The feeling of walking across the water had been unsettling, and his recollection of the sensation matched his mood today.

He wondered if old Mr McColl, stuck in his wheelchair at the high window, was watching the helicopter from his room in Stonebrae House.

The sea darkened as they flew over the island and out into the sound; the waves, choppy and tipped with white, were more restless than they had been in the sheltered waters of the loch.

Soon they had left the Isle of Arran behind, passing over small islets and skerries before they reached the Ayrshire coast and its patchwork of fields, dotted here and there by sheep and cattle, then small towns and villages. The urban sprawl of Glasgow lay ahead.

Though he was, in fact, coming home, it didn't feel like that. He wasn't quite sure when he had lost the feeling of the city being his home. He supposed that the death of his parents and his move with Liz to the leafy Renfrewshire suburbs had all played their part in the process. These days, nowhere seemed to qualify as home. Kinloch was as near as it came, yet it was already filled with the ghosts that had followed him from the place over which he now flew.

The tinny sound of the pilot's voice in his headset announced that they were landing, and he was soon led from the aircraft and into the hospital.

Sitting in a corridor, waiting for someone to take him to see Hamish, he watched the medics bustling to and fro. A doctor, who seemed impossibly young, jogged past, looking at her watch and muttering under her breath. A few moments later, a distinguished-looking man in a pinstripe suit underneath a pristine white coat strolled past him, followed by a gaggle of trainees clamouring for his attention.

As always when he visited hospitals, he was forced back to the times when he'd gone to see his mother, before cancer finished off what was left of her. This place was more modern, with bright landscape paintings on the pastel walls and an air of cleanliness and efficiency.

The stuffy warmth was making him feel drowsy. He could feel the touch of his mother's cold weightless hand on his, see the anguished face of the woman he had loved. There had been no words, no need for awkward platitudes, just a silent, drawn-out farewell between a mother and son bound together by blood and unconditional love. One life full of endless, fascinating potential; the other dwindling. It was a final goodbye he played over and over in his head.

'Chief Inspector Daley, isn't it? Please come with me. Your friend is just down at the end of the corridor.'

He accompanied the nurse to a private side room off a large ward, where the only noise came from bleeping, buzzing and humming machines. Only one bed here, though, and one patient.

Daley gasped when he saw Hamish's face. Such was the swelling around both eyes, yellow, black and purple, it made the old man virtually unrecognisable.

The nurse gently shook her sleeping patient's shoulder.

'Have we hit a shoal?' Hamish looked around, bewildered; his body in a hospital bed, his mind in a fishing boat at sea.

'This is the policeman from Kinloch you asked to see, Hamish. He's come all this way.' She smiled as the old fisherman tried to focus on his visitor through his puffy eyes.

'Och, I wisna expecting you tae come a' the way up here, Mr Daley.'

'Well, no signs of memory loss, anyway,' said the nurse to Daley. 'I'll leave you to it. See you in a wee while, Hamish.'

'Aye, she's a good wee lassie, that yin,' said Hamish, smiling up at Daley. 'There's this other yin wae an arse the size o' a small country and a voice like the Pladda foghorn that I'm no' too keen on.'

'How are you feeling?'

'Och, nae worse than if I'd been oot on the batter for a few nights. A sair heid and I canna feel my right arm very well, but that'll come back, so they say.'

Daley felt his temper rise – a rush of anger, as though he was rising off the floor. He fought to keep his expression neutral. 'Have you remembered anything about what happened? They tell me you kept saying "well of the winds". What's that about?'

281

'Damn me, I canna remember a thing aboot it. You needna worry. I'm no' the first poor soul who's taken a hiding, and that's a fact. No, whoot I have tae say is much mair interesting.'

'The Well of the Winds, it's a place on Gairsay, right?'

'No. Well, aye, but it's no' that I'm blethering on aboot.'

'What, then?'

'It's a boat. Well, used tae be a boat. They said it was an accident, but I know that it wisna.'

Daley began to worry that his old friend was confused and that his journey had been a wasted one. He'd hoped that Hamish had remembered something that would identify his attackers. Instead, his mind appeared to be wandering.

'They Bremners you're looking for – they did for him. Aye, and mair besides. It jeest came back tae me, efter all these years, tae.'

'Who?'

'Glenhanity. Och, he'd a real name, but I've never known whoot it was. He was a fisherman on Gairsay. They killed him tae shut him up. Folk will tell you it's a rumour, but I mind different.'

'Who did this? The Bremners?'

'Aye, try an' keep up, will you? Have you had a dram or two the day, already? You're away wae the fairies, so you are.'

'So why did they want to shut him up, and how do you know?'

'What they didna know wiz my faither's friend, auld Malky Lang, was oot on his wee lobster boat. It was a nice day, and Malky was mair a crofter than a fisherman, so he liked tae stay well intae the shore. He was just at the mouth o' the burn when he saw whoot happened . . .'

35

'Haud your horses,' mumbled Glenhanity as she heaved herself out of the chair where she'd been fast asleep. Someone rapped on the door again. Though her first step was unsteady, she got into her stride after the third, and was soon opening the front door – more to berate her visitor than bid them a good afternoon.

'Oh, it's yourself? I don't often see you at my door. In fact, I canna remember when I last set eyes on you.'

That had been two hours ago, and since the visit she'd stared greedily at the bottle of cheap whisky that now sat on her mantelpiece. It wasn't often she was gifted something. She eyed the bottle again and scanned the room. Sure enough, an old enamel mug was sitting on the carpet next to the couch. It was the one she'd given to that cheeky detective the other day. The contents appeared untouched. She considered giving it a rinse, but on reflection, couldn't be bothered going to the kitchen. She merely tipped the mug upside down and emptied the cold tea onto the carpet before running her dirt-engrained forefinger around the rim.

Glenhanity then shuffled over to the fireplace, mug in hand, unscrewed the bottle and poured herself a generous measure of whisky. 'Miserable soul,' she muttered, replacing the bottle on the mantel. 'Leaving the bloody price on – Greeks bearing gifts, so yous are.'

The bitter taste of the whisky hit her tongue, followed by the familiar burning sensation in her throat as she swallowed. She took another swig. There was a scorching feeling in her throat, an agonisingly intense sensation. She coughed to try and clear her throat, cursing the cheap spirit, but within seconds her eyes were streaming and she was struggling for breath.

Glenhanity let out a howl as she staggered towards the kitchen for some water, reaching desperately for the old brass tap, but a convulsion shook her body and she collapsed on the floor. A bright light flashed before her eyes, then dimmed for ever.

Kinloch, 1945

They had left young Hamish with an aunt before taking to the sea in Ranald's skiff. The water was calm as they got underway, though Urquhart felt a chill he hadn't expected as they passed the island at the head of the loch. He could see one of the area's famous wild goats making its way steadily up a precipitous slope, stopping only to gaze down on them from a narrow ledge. The animal was chewing vigorously, but appeared unfazed by the chug of the old diesel engine as the vessel made its way out into the sound.

As they neared Paterson's Point, Ranald caught the inspector's attention by pointing ahead. 'That's the lifeboat,' he called above the rattle of the engine. 'They're likely on their way back fae the accident.' He stood at the prow of the boat and waved his arms.

The blue lifeboat with the small wheelhouse angled her course towards them until the vessels were almost touching, side by side, held in position by the skill of the mariner at each helm.

'How ye, coxswain?' shouted Ranald. 'I'm hoping things aren't as bad as I've been telt.'

The coxswain, dressed like Ranald in a thick fisherman's sweater, dungarees and a flat cap, puffed on his pipe as he leaned on the gunwale. 'No' good at a', Ranald. I've got Glenhanity aboard, deid – poor bastard.'

Ranald removed his cap, prompting Urquhart to do likewise with his hat. 'Och, whoot on earth happened?'

The coxswain drew deeply on his pipe and stared at Urquhart as he answered. 'I'm no' right sure, but I'll tell you this, Inspector: if you're investigating this, you'll need tae have your wits aboot you – aye, an' someone wae a good knowledge o' the sea at your shoulder. There's something jeest no' right, but it's no' my job tae have an opinion.' The other crew members looked on, subdued. 'I've failed at my job. Make sure you succeed at yours. Noo, I'll need tae get this poor soul tae Kinloch, if you'll excuse me.'

The lifeboat's engine growled into life, and the powerful vessel made her way back to Kinloch.

'Dae you want tae carry on or go back tae the toon, Mr Urquhart?

'I think we'll keep going, Ranald. I'd like to see what happened.'

'Very good,' replied the fisherman, as he steered a course around Paterson's Point and headed for the Isle of Gairsay.

*

Daley was glad he'd seen his friend, and relieved that his injuries hadn't broken his spirit. The doctor had intimated that he would likely make a full recovery and should be able to come home soon. He'd watched Hamish's reaction to this, noting something he hadn't seen in the man before – fear. He thought about what Hamish had told him as he flew back over Goat Fell on Arran in the police helicopter, heading back to Kinloch.

He now had the familiar, almost comforting, feeling that accompanied his immersion in a challenging case. It was as though his mind was becoming cold and analytical – divesting itself of any peripheral worries and concerns to dedicate itself to solving what confronted it.

He remembered the first time he'd experienced this sensation. It had been not long into his career in the CID. He had stared at the body of a dead girl lying on her bed. The child's face had been porcelain-white and her eyes had stared in horror, the imprint of the last moments of her short life etched for ever upon her features.

There was a tiny chair, like the ones that parents are forced to sit on when visiting a primary school, a splash of colourful cartoon characters across the wallpaper, a bright red bedside light, plastic dolls scattered on the floor, the wrapper from a chocolate bar discarded on the carpet; all of which fitted, were meant to be there in a child's bedroom, but were heartbreakingly at odds with the lifeless body on the rumpled bed.

It was then he'd felt his heart harden for the first time as the need, the desperate need to bring the person who had done this to justice, rose in him.

As the loom of the Kintyre peninsula appeared, he had that feeling again. All thoughts of Mary, Liz, his son, his future, his self-induced misery, faded away. He could see the board in his office, the cellar at Achnamara, the face of the Bremner family's matriarch, the swastika on the notepaper with the neatly typed German script – 'H.H.', then a scribbled signature at the end.

H.H. He berated himself. The conclusion he'd come to was too obvious, lazy, in fact: Heil Hitler. What if it meant something more than just an empty salute to a madman?

'We'll be landing in five minutes, sir,' announced the crackling voice in his headset. He didn't reply. 'Sir, are you okay?'

'Yes, I'm okay, and, yes, I heard you.' He didn't care how terse he sounded. He was now determined to solve this case. The future – his future – could take care of itself.

He could barely make out the causeway, now almost submerged beneath the waves. But, in his mind's eye, the stern face of Inspector William Urquhart was as plain as day.

Gairsay, 1945

Urquhart studied the tall, powerfully built man. He had a chiselled face, tight blond curls cropped close to his head, and grey-blue eyes. His wife was younger, petite, dark-haired, and waspish in appearance, very much the more vocal of the pair.

'You were on his boat, *Well of the Winds*, yes?' asked Urquhart.

'Yes. My husband has already made this clear, no?' Mrs Bremner fixed him with a steely look.

'This is the first chance I've had to talk with your husband, Mrs Bremner. So the answer is no, he hasn't made this clear – to me, at least.'

Mr Bremner spoke. 'I apologise, Inspector. This has been a shock to us all. Glenhanity was our friend, as well as our employee.' His accent, like his wife's, was distinctly German, but less shrill.

'You had been out in the bay attending to lobster creels?'

'Yes, I am learning this. Since we came here, we are trying to make a living as best we can. Support ourselves and help the community. This is uppermost in our thoughts. We are most grateful to this island, its people. We have our farm now,' he continued, holding out both hands as though showing off his property. 'It doesn't look much now, but we have a second chance in our life, yes?'

'Back to this morning, Mr Bremner.' Urquhart ignored the man's description of their family circumstances, much to the annoyance of his wife, who snorted in derision and spoke to her husband in rapid German.

'No, Mrs Bremner, I don't work for the army or the government intelligence. This is Scotland, not Germany.'

'You speak German, Inspector.' Mr Bremner seemed calm, but his wife's face betrayed a sudden flash of panic, rather than the irritation she had displayed since his arrival.

'I fought in the last conflict. I became a liaison officer just before the Armistice.'

'So you hate the Germans as much as we do!' blurted Mrs Bremner.

'No, not true. I have great admiration for the German people. I was disgusted by some of the punitive measures placed upon the country by the Allies. The sanctions were, in my opinion, a mistake, and have led to the tragic situation in which we find ourselves.'

'I see,' replied Mrs Bremner, doing her best to look unimpressed, but remaining watchful. 'But the situation, as you call it, will not last much longer, I think.'

Urquhart ignored her, turning his attention back to her husband. 'You were attending to the creels, then what happened?'

'We could not get the creel from the water. It was stuck – the rope had become caught. We couldn't free it. Glenhanity said we should fetch his boat, we would pull from both ends, try and free the rope.'

'Then?'

'I took him across the bay. He boarded his vessel and we returned to the creels.'

'So how did he end up trapped underneath your boat?' Urquhart spat out the question, deciding to speed things up, catch Bremner off guard; it was a technique he'd learned in the military police.

'He disappeared. I looked around and he was gone.' Bremner swallowed hard. 'The boats had come together. I think he'd been trying to push off my boat while I was busy with the creel. He must have lost his balance.'

'And what did you do?'

'I-I looked over the side, the space between the boats. Though it is a calm day, there was a swell, so the vessels were drifting apart.'

'When did you see him?'

'His hand, I saw his hand first. His fingers were gripping underneath my boat. I only noticed them because he moved. He was trying to bring himself up to the surface, but he was stuck.' Bremner's face crumpled.

'How long did it take you to pull him up? Surely it was just a case of grabbing his hand and pulling him up from the water?'

'No, no, he had become trapped. I did manage to catch his hand, but I couldn't get him to move.'

'Did he grip back?'

'Yes, I think he did. I don't know!' he shouted, standing to emphasise the point, his wife shushing him at his side.

'Can't you see that my husband is upset by this? How can you carry on with this questioning?'

'I want to see his boat,' said Urquhart, ignoring her pleas.

'I will take you.' Bremner was calmer now.

They walked along a path between fields, Bremner taking the lead, his wife by his side, holding his hand and talking to him quietly. Urquhart followed behind, Ranald at his side. The fisherman hadn't spoken since they'd arrived at Achnamara, though Urquhart noted that he was absorbing everything, his face a picture of concentration under the peak of his cap.

Two small boats were tied to a small stone jetty which consisted of a collection of large rocks that sat proud of the water. The larger of the two vessels was painted bright blue, well maintained, brass rowlocks shining. A pile of lobster creels was stowed neatly at the stern.

The smaller boat looked shabby in comparison. The varnish covering the wooden planks of the clinker-built hull was patchy and in need of retouching. The vessel was a shambles of nets and white buoys. One thick glove, greasy-looking and missing a finger, sat on a bench seat beside a penknife and a bodkin, which was used to maintain the boat's nets.

Urquhart stood at the stern, Ranald by his side.

'Can you take a look, please, Ranald?'

'This man isn't police,' said Mrs Bremner sharply.

'He is working under my instructions and on my authority, Mrs Bremner. Carry on, Ranald.'

The fisherman looked at him, about to ask a question which Urquhart silenced with a shake of the head. Expertly, he jumped from the jetty onto Glenhanity's boat, then rifled around under nets and fish boxes.

'*Yente*,' said Urquhart quietly, though loud enough for the Bremners to hear above the lap of the waves, the squawking gulls and the noise made by Ranald's rummaging. He paused, looking at the couple. Their gaze remained fixed on Ranald as he ran his hand along the floor of the vessel.

Urquhart pursed his lips.

At the prow, in peeling paint, the name of the small boat was still legible: *Well of the Winds*.

36

Iolo Harris was sitting alone outside a little restaurant on Gairsay, a converted boathouse overlooking the bay. He had intended only to have a light lunch, but had enjoyed the starter of smoked mackerel pâté on rye bread, served by the chef no less, so much that he was now indulging himself with a dressed crab salad.

He was enjoying the sights and sounds. The ferry, which plied its trade back and forth all day between Gairsay and Kintyre, was roughly halfway through another outward journey. A bespectacled middle-aged man and a scruffy old Jack Russell terrier were making their way along the white sandy beach. The little dog was snuffling and pawing at the sand. As the dog went about its business, the man read passages from the paperback he was carrying.

Only feet away, a great black-backed gull eyed Harris intently, the end of its yellow beak a splatter of red. As the pair stared at each other, Harris amused himself with the notion that they were in silent communion: the intelligence officer and the intelligent bird. He tossed a bread crust, which the bird caught in mid air and gulped down greedily.

A seal, its head just visible above the grey water, looked about, sniffing the air, as the raucous laughter from a couple of fishermen on a small boat out in the bay carried across the calm sea.

Harris's phone vibrated and he reluctantly pulled it from his pocket and clicked on the email icon.

Though his face remained impassive, what he read surprised him. Timothy Gissing had left a mountain of problems behind, dating back to the previous incumbent, by no coincidence, his father, the late Sir David Gissing.

Harris often puzzled over the behaviour of the English upper class. Though things were changing – very slowly – the country, by no means an international minnow, despite the loss of empire and influence, was still controlled by the Establishment. These men – and they were largely men – were the product of a handful of schools and universities, a privileged elite who stretched back over generations and centuries, families who treated access to prestigious positions as a matter of right.

David Gissing had been Her Majesty's unofficial conduit between the fledgling Common Market, the trade organisation that had sprung from the ruins of Europe to become what many thought would eventually be a superstate, with the ability to challenge the USA, or even the seemingly unstoppable economic powerhouse of China.

Reading this email, it appeared that the Gissings had not only seen themselves as mere functionaries, but pivotal decision makers. One other name stood out: Hans Neyermeyer, who was known as 'The Father'. The Father. Harris allowed the title to echo in his head. He was an old hand at reading between the lines – especially the subtle ones placed there by Civil Service mandarins. There was something hidden in all this, he was sure of it.

As Harris took his final mouthful of crab, he ruminated on the fluctuating nature of the world, and, more pertinently, his place in it. He clicked off the email and scrolled down his contacts until he found the name 'J Daley'.

'You've got tae wonder what goes through their heids.' Scott was leaning over the side of the ferry as Symington took pictures on her phone. They were approaching the mainland.

'Who?' replied Symington, still focused on the moving tableau as the ferry slid through the waves.

'Fish. What dae they think aboot? Swimming away a' day, a' their lives, come tae that. Must be a right bugger – don't think I could cope.'

Symington looked at him askance. 'I wouldn't worry too much, Brian. You know the chances of your being a fish, well, they're pretty slim when you think about it.'

'Ach, it's just a' this time I've got on my hands, you know, wae me off the bevy. Your mind starts working overtime.'

'Yeah, well, I understand that. But you've done the right thing – saved your life, most likely.'

'Aye, you're probably right, ma'am. Takes a bit o' getting used tae, mind you . . . Fuck me, I used tae drink like a fish, noo I'm wondering what they get up tae a' day.'

Symington studied him for a few moments. He had a nasty bruise over his right eye, a lump under his left, and his lip was split. He'd certainly taken a battering.

'Jim will want to know what happened to you.'

'I wouldnae worry too much aboot that. I'll just tell him I got intae a wee argument wae one o' they Special Branch boys. It's no' as though it's the first time.'

'Yes, but I don't want you getting a hard time for helping me. Which I'm still very grateful for, but not very comfortable with, incidentally.'

'Why? What's the problem? If you're worried that Harry will spill the beans, I don't think you've anything tae worry aboot.'

'You seem very certain about that.' She eyed him with suspicion.

'Aye, och, just my instincts,' he said, clearing his throat.

'I think I'm going to tell him the truth – Jim, I mean. I'm going to tell him about Harry and the whole sorry business.'

'I wouldnae dae that, ma'am,' replied Scott in a rush. 'Oor Jimmy's no' himself, you know that. No telling how he'll react tae something like that. You've got tae understand, he's no' like me – he thinks too much. Though he's made his fair share o' mistakes and a', mind you.'

'So you think he would put it on paper?'

'I'm no' sayin' that. Mind, we're just over a' the shit John Donald was up tae.'

'Come on! You're not putting me in the same category as him, are you?'

'Naw, naw, cool your jets, eh, ma'am,' replied Scott, wincing at the expression. 'Let me tell you, it doesnae matter what your heid's telling you. We've sorted the problem oot. The mair people know aboot it – no matter who they are – the mair chance you've got o' problems. Trust me.'

'You're probably right,' said Symington, snapping some guillemots as Scott stared back at the sea, pondering the plight of fish.

Urquhart was thinking how quiet Ranald had been since they left the Bremners on Gairsay. He angled his face towards the sun and closed his eyes. He'd learned a lot about Germany during the last conflict. The diversity of people, places and cultures that now made up the united Germany – the enemy they had been fighting so long – was greater than many in Britain realised. The Jews, persecuted, and if the stories he'd heard were to be believed, now victims of unimaginable cruelty, had made a big impression on him.

As the Armistice was negotiated, he had come to know a German Jewish family; the father had been his counterpart in many ways. He'd been invited to dine with them on a few occasions and enjoyed being part of a family at a time when he was still mourning the loss of the woman he loved, and missing home.

Everyone welcomed him without demur, thankful, as he was, that the horrors of the trenches were now behind them. Everyone bar one: old Frau Lansky. Though Jewish, she was fiercely protective of her country, and still regarded Urquhart as the enemy.

Her family – behind her back – had a name for her, a Yiddish name. *Tell the yente this . . . don't tell the yente that.* 'Yente' meant 'she devil' or 'harridan' in English.

When he'd said that name in front of the Bremners, there had been no response: nothing. For a woman with the redoubtable nature of Mrs Bremner, the insult would have been obvious. She hadn't turned a hair, though there could be no doubt that she'd heard him.

It had confirmed his suspicions that the Bremners were no

more Jewish than he was. So who exactly were they and why were they lying?

He believed that he knew the answer, but if he was to expose them he had to be sure of his facts.

'What did you think of what Mr Bremner said about the accident, Ranald?' he shouted above the putter of the engine.

The fisherman removed his cap and scratched his head, pipe in hand. 'Can I be honest wae you?'

'Yes, of course. That's exactly what I want.'

'I canna see how an accident like that wid have happened as he said. Poor seamanship's the only excuse, an' I tell you, whoot I know of Glenhanity, he was a good mariner.'

'Meaning?'

'He wid never have put himself in danger's way like that. When you dae somethin' a' your life, you get used tae how you have tae dae it. Mr Bremner might be new tae the ways of the sea, but Glenhanity certainly wisna. Aye, an' it's him that's away tae lie on the mortuary slab.' He sniffed loudly. 'Jeest my opinion, mark you.' He put his cap back on and stared back at the sea, and their route home. 'Oh, aye, and another thing.'

'What?' asked Urquhart.

'There was a wee stow box under the bench seat o' Glenhanity's boat.'

'Is that unusual?'

'No, no' at a'. Used tae keep stuff in, like your charts and baccy an' that. You're sitting jeest above mine. They're a' lead-lined. I line mine wae oilskin, tae – it works efter a fashion.'

Urquhart reached down and felt the wooden sides of the box that fitted neatly under the seat.

'Yes, but what was so unusual about the box aboard Glenhanity's boat?'

'I didna say naething at the time. I wisna sure if you wanted me tae, you know, in front o' they Germans.'

'Tell me what?'

'Well, somebody's taken a jemmy tae the box. The lid was pulled clean off – freshly done, tae. The splinters were still sharp, and the wood was fresh, and the sea hadna got at it, which would happen quickly on a wee boat like that.'

'Was there anything inside?'

'No, not a thing. I had a poke aboot, but I don't think they twigged.'

'Thank you, Ranald.' Urquhart watched as a guillemot dived into the water like a missile.

So the Bremners had been searching for something. The question was: what?

Scott followed Symington into Kinloch Police Office. Though Special Branch had taken over operations at Achnamara, Daley had a team of young detectives investigating the disappearance of the vessel from Belfast that appeared to have been used to effect the family's escape.

Symington leaned over DC Potts, who was scanning CCTV footage.

'Anything to report?'

'Yes, ma'am. Found this a couple of hours ago.' He sent images tumbling backwards as he looked for the item he had to show the chief superintendent. 'Here we are.' He stopped the footage as the correct frame number appeared in the corner of the screen.

'I cannae see anything,' said Scott, peering through his half-moon glasses. The image appeared to show a boatyard. A jumble of masts, buoys, lifebelts and general sailing paraphernalia was strewn about the space; a few boats bobbed beside a small pontoon on the left-hand side of the image.

'Wait.' Potts tapped the keyboard repeatedly, making the image enlarge around a particular area. Soon, two figures could be made out: one, a tall man, was handing something to the other. The transaction over, the former turned on his heel and ducked into a large black SUV, which sped out of shot.

Scott peered closer, his nose almost touching the screen. 'Cannae make oot that guy's face. Can you, ma'am?'

'Talking of faces, what happened to yours, Sergeant?' asked Potts with a grin.

'Shut up, the pair of you! I'm trying to think here.'

'Dae you think it's Feldstein? It looks a wee bit like him.' Scott looked up at Symington.

'I'm not convinced. But it's somebody, and whoever it is, I'm willing to bet he's organising the Bremners' escape. Look at the car. Where's DCI Daley?' asked Symington, noting the door to his glass box was open, with no sign of its occupant inside.

'He left about half an hour ago, ma'am. Not sure where he went.'

'Here's DCI Daley to see you again, Mr McColl.' Heather Campbell patted the old man gently on the shoulder, making him flinch. 'Sorry, were you asleep?' She swung the wheelchair around slowly as McColl blinked his almost translucent eyelids.

Daley noticed he was much paler and more tired-looking than he had been on his previous visit. The old man smiled at his guest as the manager caught Daley's eye and mouthed, 'Not too long,' out of sight of her charge.

She made her excuses and left the room.

'Not feeling so great today, Mr McColl?' asked Daley.

'When you get to my age, you're just happy to be breathing.' He coughed.

'I've just discovered something I thought you'd like to know.'

'Oh, if it's about your friend Hamish, they told me – at least the local minister did, when he was here praying for my soul. Terrible thing. You know, I've lived through some of the worst times the world has ever seen – and saw some rough stuff in Hong Kong over the years – and things like that still shock me. Poor man, how is he?'

'He'll survive. But, I agree, it shocked me, too.'

McColl licked his lips. 'Could you pour me a glass of water, Mr Daley?' he asked, pointing to a jug on the table. 'Sorry I can't offer to make you a cup of tea. Heather should have offered you one.'

'She's got enough to do,' replied Daley, pouring water into a glass. 'I'm not staying for long, I can see you're not feeling too well today.' He handed the glass to McColl, who grasped it with trembling hands.

'Please, stay as long as you want. I do get tired, but it's part and parcel of being in this condition. Time is heavy on my hands, Inspector. Ironic, really, when you consider how little I have left of it.'

'I've discovered something about Inspector Urquhart that I thought you'd like to know.'

'Oh.' McColl's eyes widened. 'Strange, I was just thinking how much you reminded me of him. You're taller, of course, but people are taller now, aren't they? Even in China. Who would've thought it?'

'Better nutrition.'

'And a better world, if you find yourself in the right place, that is. I thought Hong Kong would fall apart when the Chinese walked back in. It appears that I was wrong.' A strange look passed across his face; a mix of surprise and regret, Daley thought.

'Would you have stayed, if you'd known things would turn out the way they have?'

'I might've considered it. But, och, better you die where you were born. It's the natural way of things. As much as I loved Hong Kong, I didn't want to spend the rest of eternity under the soil there – not under the communists. Buggers would just build a bloody great skyscraper on me, anyway . . . Sorry, I'm rambling. What did you want to tell me?'

'Information has come into my possession about Inspector Urquhart's disappearance.'

'Oh, I see. How s-strange. How did you come by this?'

'Can't say, I'm afraid, but I know how he died and where it happened.'

McColl dropped the glass of water. 'W-what?'

Daley watched as the tumbler rolled on the thick carpet, the water turning the carpet a darker shade of red.

'I-I'm sorry, Mr Daley, bit of a surprise after all this time.'

Daley regarded the old man, mentally cursing, not for the first time, his lack of tact. He had thought that McColl would be intrigued to find out what happened to his mentor, so long ago. He hadn't considered that it would be so upsetting for him. All of a sudden, McColl looked exhausted, and he'd stammered again, something Daley had noticed on his previous visit.

'Look, let me get the nurse. Do I press a button?' He looked around the room for an alarm.

'N-no. Tell me, what is it that you know?'

Daley sighed. 'Are you sure you want to know?'

'Yes, yes, please go ahead.'

Daley thought he detected a momentary high-handedness that was characteristic of someone with McColl's background, as well as the time he had spent in the officer class of the Hong Kong police – much more like the army in its structure than its UK equivalent, with indigenous lower ranks largely overseen by patrician ex-pats.

'He was murdered. On the strand over there, near the island.'

'I knew it!' declared McColl. 'He took too many risks, wouldn't share his workload or his theories. He was trying to expose influential people, Mr Daley. Very influential people. I tried to tell him . . .'

Daley watched the old man's head sink to his chest.

37

'Make it go away, Iolo. We have what we need – the leverage we require. The last thing we want is for this bloody place to end up as some kind of curiosity shop, a damn museum.'

'Can't we just dismiss the Branch and shut the investigation down on a nod and a wink?'

'No can do. Special Branch have already tried to ring-fence the whole thing. They know the significance. Just do the business, then we can let the locals deal with the aftermath, which of course they will be singularly unable to do.'

'Wouldn't bet on it, sir. Couple of sharp minds up here – more so than that collection of supercops.'

'They have nothing to go on. Bits and pieces they shouldn't have, that's all. We'll shut it down at their HQ. Goodness knows there's been enough strife in the short time Police Scotland has been in existence. The top brass there won't want any more bad headlines. Whatever comes of this – and more will – we won't be implicated.'

The call ended and Harris immediately dialled another number.

'Alan, I would like to have a sit-down with you and the team – a partial debrief, if you like . . . No, best if it's everyone. You know how it goes with operational inclusivity these days. We'll be on Skype to Whitehall, so a good chance for you to make your point to the suits.' He listened to the response, smiling at the altered tone on the other end of the line. He could almost hear the Special Branch commander purring at the thought of communion with senior members of the intelligence community. 'Good. Make it for about six? We can have a run-through at five, if you want.'

Harris took a deep breath, pondering on the subtle arts of pragmatism and discretion.

'You're looking a bit peely-wally,' said Scott, sitting opposite his old friend in his glass box.

'Peely-wally? You look as though you've gone ten rounds with Mike Tyson. What happened to your coupon?'

'Long story, buddy. Suffice tae say, I was a knight in shining armour on a big white horse.'

'The closest you've ever got to a white horse is drinking it. Tell me that whatever happened isn't going to rebound, Brian. I'm not in the mood for any complications right now.'

'Nah, just a storm in a teacup. The other guy's off wae a worse-looking coupon than mine. Aye, an' a flea in his ear, tae boot.'

Daley scrutinised his friend as he was speaking. He knew he was being spun a yarn, but he had neither the strength nor the inclination to probe further. Brian was a big boy now; whatever he'd been up to, he'd have to get on with it.

'Our new gaffer looks distinctly furtive, too. What gives there?'

'Och, you know, wee bit o' man trouble. You know yoursel', the heart's a sair maister, eh? As my dear auld mother used tae say.'

Daley sensed that Scott was trying to bring this conversation to an end, so decided to let him.

'We've got a guy handing something over at that boatyard in Belfast, so we can assume that he was part of the effort to extricate the Bremners.'

'Yes, and driving a vehicle that bears more than a passing resemblance to the SUV that was crawling round Kinloch on the night Hamish was attacked.'

'Aye, bang on, Jimmy. Ever get the feeling there's somebody at the back of all this, just pulling strings?'

'Yes, but why? Pity we haven't got access to all of the files from the Bremners' place.'

'Who says we haven't?'

'What have you done?' Daley looked dismayed.

'Me? How come naebody ever says, "Aye right, Brian, well done!" Naw, for me it's always the opposite.'

Daley looked unconvinced.

'I'm pleased tae say, Jimmy, my auld mate, I was following orders to the letter.'

'Indeed he was,' said Symington with a smile, entering the room.

Daley looked at her. She was presenting the same façade – head held high, authoritative but friendly manner – as she walked into his office, but he detected something else. He'd seen it when they first arrived back from Gairsay. There was always something to be found behind the eyes. Maybe he was just looking for things that weren't there, overthinking everything. If that was the case, though, he'd been overcomplicating things to solve crimes his whole career, so he saw no reason to doubt his judgement.

'Here, tell him about they photos you had me take, ma'am,' said Scott.

'You mean the ones I had to surrender to Special Branch?'

'Aye, they ones.'

Daley was thoroughly confused; not just by what Symington and Scott were trying to tell him, but by the strange familiarity that was now apparent between them. The visible manifestations of bonds forged in adversity, he thought. He remembered Scott's constant difficulties with John Donald. The pair had barely managed to tolerate each other for years. Now, it seemed, his friend's relationship with Donald's successor was of an entirely different nature.

'I want us to pool all we have,' said Daley. 'Everything you picked up on Gairsay, and what I've got, plus what's happened in the interim . . . if you think that's appropriate, ma'am?'

'It's still our patch. We've managed to salvage enough evidence to try and make sense of things, so I think we should try.'

'Tae what end? I mean, even if we discover what they Bremners were up to or what happened tae them, what good will it dae? That Welsh spook's there to make sure the whole thing gets covered up – trust me,' said Scott, grimacing as he took a gulp of cold coffee.

'Okay, here's my overview,' offered Daley. 'We have a family embedded on the island for decades, clearly spies, and possibly for other, more obscure purposes.'

'Like spiriting away Nazis at the end of the war, for instance,' remarked Symington.

'Yes, undoubtedly, but I'm sure there's more to it. Something's nagging away at me. If you have access to the paperwork from the cellar, we can maybe make progress on that front.'

'I have an expert looking at it all. We'll have to keep it quiet, but I can trust him.'

'So, we stand a chance of discovering what happened over a number of years. But it doesn't answer the question as to what changed so suddenly to encourage an entire family – three generations of them, remember – to up sticks and flee at the drop of a hat. What on earth could prompt it? Even if the activities of senior members of the family during the war had come to light, surely the impact on everyone else would be minimal?'

'Unless they was still up tae something – the whole lot o' them,' said Scott.

'But what could that possibly be?' said Symington. 'And you say this Harris wants to meet with you, Jim. I wonder why.'

'No idea, ma'am. He called earlier – all very mysterious.'

'That mob are always mysterious – that's why they're called spooks, Jimmy.'

'We'll get our heads down and try and join our dots.'

'Here, is it quiz night at the County the night?' asked Scott, the master of the left field. 'Need tae gie the grey matter a wee break. You, too, by the look o' things.'

'I've always thought your grey matter was very well rested,' quipped Daley.

'And it's something tae dae when you cannae get plastered o' an evening.' Scott smiled knowingly.

As they prepared to review what they'd managed to glean, both in Kinloch and on Gairsay, Daley's mind drifted to the journal of Inspector William Urquhart. No matter how bizarre he thought the idea, he had convinced himself that the fate of his predecessor was the key to making sense of what had happened to the Bremner family.

Kinloch, 1945

Andrew Mitchell was sitting on the rocks, staring at a large warship making its way out of the loch via the navigable channel on the other side of the island. He could see sailors going about their business on deck, amid a flurry of ropes, shouts and whistles, as they prepared to enter the sound and the mighty Atlantic beyond.

He never thought he would envy these men. In the early part of the war, as more and more servicemen appeared in Kinloch, turning it from a sleepy county town into a bustling naval port, he'd often wondered why on earth anyone would volunteer to get themselves blown to smithereens. He'd wrapped his sandwiches in brown paper and cycled dutifully to the farm every day, thankful that his life didn't offer up the horrors that these men faced.

Now, though, he did feel envious. His life had become so complicated and dangerous, he would have happily swum out to the big ship and stowed away, faced any danger in order to escape the misery that was now his existence.

An oystercatcher's mournful cry yielded a counterpoint to the deep rumble of the warship's engine. The bird disappeared across the undulating water of the loch, which was changing colour as the sun sank into the Atlantic, invisible to him across the other side of the peninsula. The white dots of sheep and the occasional wild goat began to take on a golden hue as they grazed on the steep slopes of the island to his right.

Though he heard the crunch of the pebbles, he didn't turn round to see who was coming. He knew.

'Mitchell, what do you have for me?'

He remained silent for a while, too miserable to reply. He was being forced to play a game he'd never wanted to be part of, and had absolutely no aptitude for. He couldn't think, he couldn't breathe, could hardly feel. He was content dealing with cows and sheep – not so much pigs, but even that was better than what he was actually doing.

When he tried to sleep, all he could hear were the blood-curdling screams of Dugald Kerr being trampled to death by that beast. There had been death, and there would be more, and there was nothing he could do about it.

'Answer me when I talk to you!' Urquhart's voice was stern. 'You've dragged me here to tell me something. I want to know what it is, now!' His raised voice echoed across the causeway, over to the island and back again.

For the first time, Mitchell looked up at the policeman. 'They want to meet you.'

'Who wants to meet me, and why? If you've told them about our agreement, I'll arrest you now, and you'll hang before the summer's out. That's a promise.'

'I'm jeest passing on a message. I dinna know whoot they think, or whoot they know. It didna come fae me. I jeest got telt tae pass it tae you.'

'By whom?'

'A man. I've never seen him before.'

'What does he look like?'

'Och, I don't know. Big chiel, thin, posh.'

'And he asked for me by name?'

'Aye.'

309

'Out of the blue? You had nothing to do with this, and you don't know him?'

'No! Like I telt you, I've never seen him afore. He just asked me tae pass this on tae you, somewhere quiet, like.'

'And what do your fancy new friends say?'

'Oh aye. Whoot freens? Naebody wants anything tae dae wae me.' He stood up. 'I jeest want tae get away fae here – get this o'er an' get away fae this place. I've done whoot you asked, kept an eye on things, no' said naethin'. That was the deal, right?'

Urquhart had put Mitchell under pressure intentionally. He wasn't really surprised that whoever was using the susceptible young farmhand had been able to see he was being pulled from both sides.

'When do you speak to this man?'

'I don't know. I've jeest tae wait until he contacts me.'

'Tell me what you need from me.'

'He wants a time an' a place, somewhere quiet tae meet you.'

'Very well. In two nights' time. Here will do, down by the causeway. Tell him I'll meet him here.'

'Aye, an' you've no' tae tell naebody.'

Urquhart didn't reply.

'Whoot if he doesna get in touch wae me before you want tae meet, I mean?' There was a sudden panic in the young man's voice.

'He's hardly likely to send you here to ask the question, then not follow it up. He'll contact you, don't worry.' Urquhart looked down at Mitchell; he looked young and scared, like so many men in this war and the last. The way he had been. He couldn't help but feel a certain sympathy for the lad. 'Do yourself a great service, son. Leave here, get a job far away. Make a life for yourself, and be thankful you still have a life to do something with. Far too many young men like yourself don't have that luxury.'

'And you'll jest let me go?'

Urquhart shrugged. 'I think you've played your part. Take the chance while you have it.' He dug into his trouser pocket and withdrew a five-pound note. 'Here, take this.'

'Whoot's this for?'

'Just say it's for services rendered. Use it to make a new start. What happened to your raincoat, by the way?'

Mitchell ran his hand over the rip in the gabardine. 'Caught it on my bike.'

Urquhart lit a cigarette and drew deeply on it as he watched Mitchell tramp back along the rocky shore, then up over the machair to his bike, which was propped against the fence by the road above.

38

Special Constable McAuley switched off the till and walked across to the shop's door, turning the notice on it from OPEN to CLOSED.

It had been a quiet day. He'd already tallied up, so was looking forward to taking the narrow stairs up to the flat above the shop, having dinner, a small glass of whisky, and putting his feet up in front of the TV for the evening.

Just as he hefted the cloth bag of coins, he heard movement from behind.

'I'm just on my way up, dear,' he said to his wife, as she appeared, bird-like, at the back of the counter. 'Do you need anything from down here before I set the alarm?'

'Set the alarm! Listen to you,' she replied. 'Has there ever been a robbery at this shop – in fact, anywhere on the island?'

'You know what's been happening at Achnamara. Gairsay is quiet, but I tell you, dear, you never know what will happen next. Wearing my police hat, I've seen things – aye, even here – I never thought I'd see.'

'Och, you and your hats.'

'Metaphorically speaking. I wasn't saying that I can only think about my various duties if I have the right hat on. That would be childish.'

She smiled. 'I know fine. I'm only teasing, love.' She bit her lip, a worried expression crossing her face.

'What's wrong?'

'Och, just a thought. I haven't seen Glenhanity today, or yesterday, come to that. Have you?'

'Now you mention it, no, I haven't. I suppose I just assumed that she'd been in when you were down here in the morning, as usual.'

His wife shook her head. 'It's no' like her, that's for sure. She's normally regular as clockwork, coming in for her cider.'

'I hope you're not selling alcohol before ten. We've spoken about that,' he chided.

'I have not.' She looked indignant. 'I know fine when I can sell booze and when I can't. Even if I did, what could happen? You're not going to get the appropriate hat on and arrest me, are you?'

He frowned at the dig, but chose to ignore it. 'I'll give the hotel a call. I'm betting she's sprawled across the bar as we speak.'

'I'll get your hat,' she said, smiling at his obvious annoyance.

The three detectives were in the dining room at the County Hotel. It was just after five and they had decided to have a meal prior to having a go at the quiz.

'They always do lovely fish in here,' said Symington. 'I had lemon sole the last time I was here. It was delicious.'

'Widnae be up tae much if they couldnae manage a decent fish roon here,' replied Scott, swilling his ginger beer and lime around the glass with a distinct lack of enthusiasm. 'The loch is just at the bottom o' the road. No' many food miles involved up here. Bloody things can near jump on the plates.'

'Food miles?' remarked Daley.

'Aye, all the rage noo, Jimmy. The further your dinner has tae travel tae get on your plate, the worse it is for the planet.' Scott nodded wisely. 'It's a' aboot seasonality and local produce these days, that's for sure.'

'And you know all this, how?'

'Every bugger and his friend knows aboot it. See if we all ate what grows near where we live, or gets reared on local farms, the world would be better a'together. A' that carbon footprint stuff, you know, the energy it takes tae get your scran halfway across the planet. That's a bloody disgrace.'

'Do you have the Food Network at home?' asked Symington.

'Aye, we got it a few weeks ago wae oor new satellite package. Right interesting, so it is. Thon Hugh Fearnley-Whitshisname is a right canny bloke.'

As Daley eyed his friend with amusement, the redoubtable Annie bustled in with three plates of food, one of them balanced in the crook of her arm.

'Right, noo, here's your lemon sole, Ms Symington. And your steak and chips, Mr Daley.'

'Thank you,' said Daley, looking down at the large cut of rib eye, still sizzling on the plate.

'And here we are, Brian, one kangaroo burger, jeest how you like it.'

'Spot on, Annie, I'm fair ravenous the day. It's a' this sailing yous have got me at again,' he said, digging his knife and fork into the juicy burger.

'Lots of kangaroos where you live, Brian?' asked Daley.

'Eh, here, this is bloody good,' replied Scott.

'Are yous taking part in the quiz the night?' asked Annie.

Symington looked up. 'Oh, yes, a little light relief, then back to the grindstone.'

'Grand. We've got a team fae the lawyers coming in the night, an' the fire brigade, tae. Hope it'll no' be a grudge match,' she said, leaving her charges to their dinner.

McAuley buckled his belt, making sure that his handcuffs and baton were located just where they should be. He looked at himself in the long mirror, adjusting the angle of his hat. He was always amazed just how different wearing a uniform made you look and feel. There had been no sign of Glenhanity in the hotel, and he was now getting ready to pay her a visit at home.

'You be careful, Malcolm. You know fine how nasty she can get if she's on a right bender.'

'Don't you worry, dear. I'll go up on the quad bike. That road up past the Well of the Winds is almost impassable now with all the mud. Hopefully we'll get a decent summer – dry the place out.'

She wished him well as he thudded down the stairs, then listened to him kick-start the bike. He was soon chugging away on the machine.

She pushed her last boiled potato around the plate in a pool of melted butter, then pushed the plate away, reaching across the table for the phone.

The number was a long one, but she knew it off by heart. She waited as the phone clicked and bleeped, then listened intently as an unfamiliar tone pulsed in her ear.

'He will find her soon,' she said, without preamble, when the call was answered.

'Good. You will have time once they have removed her body. Use it well.'

Nothing else needed to be said.

*

315

Iolo Harris sat in the centre of a ring of Special Branch officers. Each of them had made their point and he had dutifully taken notes, trying to appear as engaged as humanly possible.

'Right, so any more questions?' The reply was a collective shaking of heads. 'In that case, we'll go live to Whitehall in a few moments. Just enough time for a coffee, do you think, Alan?'

'Yes, absolutely.' The Special Branch commander stood up and stretched. 'Do you think they'll be impressed?'

'Oh, I should think so. You've found a lot of things the unit from Glasgow missed completely. That micro CCTV network monitored from the bungalow, for a start. Major feather in the cap.'

The burly English policeman put his arm around the shoulders of the slight Welshman, taking him to a corner of the room, where he adopted a more conspiratorial tone. 'I wouldn't be averse to a late career change, if you know what I mean, Mr Harris.'

'Please, Alan, Iolo. Let's not stand on ceremony. Is life in the Branch not treating you well?'

'Well, no, I wouldn't quite say that. This is a high-profile case – could hardly be more so – but one has to take one's chances when they present themselves, I'm sure you agree.'

What Harris thought and what he said in reply were two very different things. Still, he reasoned, this pompous oaf's sails would soon be spilling wind.

'One must indeed take the chances while they're there to take.'

39

McAuley brought the quad bike to a juddering halt in the yard at Glenhanity farm. A pile of black plastic refuse sacks were propped up against the wall beneath what he knew to be the kitchen window. An emaciated hen, bald patches on its wings, was pecking hopefully at the muddy ground. An ancient bicycle, originally black but now more rust than paint, had been abandoned near a stretch of dry stone wall which looked very much as though it was ready to collapse. A crow hopped along its length, regarding him with a beady black eye.

That this was called a farm really was a joke. The dwelling house was nothing more than a hovel, the parcel of land barely large enough to be thought of as a croft. The owners of Gairsay, way back in the mists of time, had renamed it 'farm' in the hope that someone would take the place on. No one ever had, so it had remained in the possession of the old woman who spent her days boozing; physically there, but living only in her tortured, alcoholic mind.

He grimaced at the thought of ending his days in such a way. He had the lease of the shop and the flat above, but had been giving more thought recently to what he would do when he and Jean retired and were forced to make way for younger shopkeepers. In the back of his mind, he really wanted to leave the island, the place he'd spent most of his life, to experience something new and different before he was too old to care. He wasn't sure his wife would share the notion, but it was a discussion they would have to have soon.

The caw of the crow echoed across the yard, returning him to the present, and his duties.

'Hello! Anybody there?' The question sounded forced, but for want of something else to shout, it would have to do. He realised that he was again looking for someone in a place that looked as deserted as Achnamara. While he hoped the outcome would be different, he had decided as he bounced across the hillside on the quad bike that if she was lying drunk and most likely abusive, he was going to call for the community nurse. Helping geriatric alcoholics was not in the remit of a retained police officer, as far as he was concerned.

He turned the handle of the front door, unsurprised when it creaked open. The stench of the house, a mix of unwashed skin, cat piss and general decay, almost made him choke.

'Glenhanity?' He entered the living room, noticing a bottle of whisky on the mantelpiece, its cap cast onto the carpet. He'd been here many times before, helping the old woman with her groceries, but it definitely looked worse than normal. There were ashes in the hearth, and the old clock was almost two hours slow, its tick sounding hesitant and hollow, like a diseased heart about to stop.

He stared at the painting – the only thing in this house he had ever admired. The woman smiled from the front of the

Gairsay Hotel of old. He walked towards the fireplace and looked more closely. The frame was soot-black, but when he put on his reading glasses, he could make out a small brass plate with something etched into it.

He'd never had the chance to examine the painting at close quarters, so took the opportunity to run his finger across the brass, revealing the name more clearly: *Well of the Winds*.

That didn't make sense. Though the subject was on Gairsay, the scene was of the village, and nothing to do with the tiny loch on the hillside not far from here.

He shrugged his shoulders, tutting when he looked at his blackened finger, which he rubbed on the greasy velveteen arm of the couch as he walked by.

'Glenhanity, where the hell are you?' he called again, this time with more urgency and exasperation.

The door into the tiny kitchen was ajar. This, of course, was his destination when he delivered the groceries – such as they were. Usually a loaf, some potatoes, a few tins of beans and some sausages, always complemented with gut-rot whisky and cans of head-splittingly strong cider.

For a while, when he'd first taken on the shop, he'd wrestled with his conscience, concerned that he was profiting from the old woman's misery by selling her booze. Then, his wife, not for the first time, made him see sense. Would Glenhanity not just buy her alcohol somewhere else if they didn't provide the service? One thing was for sure, if she was forced to buy whisky from the hotel – the only other outlet on the island, and much more expensive than the shop – the meagre list of foodstuffs that she could afford would dwindle to nothing.

He wrinkled his nostrils at a new smell, even more offensive than the general odour of the place that assaulted his senses every time he visited. He pushed at the door with the toe of his boot, and had to grip the door jamb to prevent himself from collapsing when he saw Glenhanity.

The linoleum tiles were slathered with a grey-brown pool, upon which the body lay, propped up between the sink and the door. Her face was ashen, angled up to the ceiling, a look of abject horror in her staring eyes. A green sludge had trickled from the corners of her slack mouth and down the front of her clothing.

He rushed out of the kitchen, doubled over and retched. He felt the room starting to spin. Amid his panic and revulsion, he resolved to resign his position as special constable forthwith. However much he enjoyed wearing the uniform, parading about the island when it was full of tourists, the events of the last few days had opened his eyes. If this was real policing, he was happy to leave it to the professionals.

He straightened up, took another deep breath, and was about to make for the front door and fresh air, when he felt something hit him. He twisted his neck to look down at his shoulder, along which a large silverfish was creeping, antennae twitching.

Special Constable Malcolm McAuley felt the world slip away as he fainted, landing on the sticky carpet with a thud.

There was a crack, almost like thunder, but lacking the resonance.

Mrs McAuley heard it as she stirred the soup for tomorrow's lunch on the stove.

The fishermen, hauling creels from their lobster boat in the bay, heard it, too, and looked up into the clear blue sky, wondering from where the noise had come.

In his kitchen at the boathouse restaurant, the chef jumped, slicing the tip of his thumb with his Sabatier knife, sending a splash of red blood across the carrots he was about to julienne.

A visiting golfer on the beautiful nine-hole course swung his club and connected only with fresh air, his score now spoiled by the bang, which still echoed across the bay.

At the fish farm, a worker poured too much cleaning solution into the holding tank, the sudden crack having made his hand wobble.

Across Gairsay, people emerged from their homes and places of work, looked about, and wondered what on earth had happened. Was it an explosion? It sounded like one.

In the hotel, looking out at the gathering darkness from the bar, Harris quietly sipped his drink and watched the young barmaid as she swept up the remnants of the pint glass she'd dropped. He smiled at the attention she was being given by the Special Branch officers who were asking her if she was okay.

Alan Bale walked across the room, a large glass of red wine in his hand. 'What on earth was that? Sounded like a bomb going off.'

'Yes, I thought that, too. But why on earth would anyone set off a bomb here?'

'We better get on to the local boys. Don't want to be standing around here in the hotel if something's kicking off. There's a special on the island, but better call the main office in Kinloch. I'll do it. I'm the senior police officer here, in any case.'

'By quite a long way,' said Harris under his breath as he watched Alan head to the bar, in search of the number for Kinloch Police Office.

On the floor of Glenhanity's cottage, McAuley was regaining consciousness. After a moment of confusion, he remembered where he was and forced himself to his knees, wincing at the pain in his shoulder, which he'd knocked when he fell.

Breathing rapid, shallow breaths, he crawled from the room, out of the cottage, and into the blessed relief of fresh air. The phone in his pocket began to ring, just as he spotted something in the gloaming.

A thick pall of dark smoke was rising from Gairsay. Though he couldn't see the source of it, he knew that he was looking across the fields in the general direction of Achnamara.

'M-McAuley,' he said, scrambling to his feet and answering the call without checking who was on the other end.

'It's Sergeant Shaw at Kinloch Police Office. We've had reports of an unidentified explosion coming from the island. Can you have a look?'

'No, no, I can't. I resign. Now, in fact. I would get someone over here quick smart, if I was you.'

He put the phone back in his pocket, pulled the hat from his head, and stamped it into the mud.

40

'Question one!' yelled Annie. She was sitting in front of the bar in the County Hotel, brandishing a redundant microphone, which squealed in protest if she spoke too loudly. 'Whoot place is further north, Kinloch or Newcastle?'

'Might have known,' said Scott. 'Obsessed wae themselves. Is every question going tae be aboot Kinloch? If so, we're buggered.'

'Oh, shut up, Brian,' replied Symington.

Daley took a sip of his beer. He noticed that his chief superintendent, after a good meal and a few glasses of wine, had relaxed. Looking at her and Scott, his face bruised and battered, he wondered again just what had passed between the pair on Gairsay.

'Question two! One for you boys in the fire brigade, I'm thinkin'. Name the firemen fae *Trumpton*.'

'Fuck me, it'll be Muffin the Mule next,' said Scott.

'That's contrary to Section Two of the Animal Welfare Act, isn't it?' said Daley.

'Just you get your thinking cap on, Jimmy boy. Wae a' they books you've read, surely some o' the words will have stuck. Was wan o' them no' called McGrew?'

'I don't even know what *Trumpton* is,' said Symington with a hiccough.

'Easy!' shouted a thick-set red-headed man who sported the weathered complexion that Daley associated with fishermen and farmers. Daley reckoned he knew him, but couldn't quite place the face.

'Sit down, Kerr,' shouted Campbell the lawyer. 'If you're trying to put us off, you won't succeed.'

Kerr – the name rang a bell. Daley recalled that the farmer he'd read about in Urquhart's journal who had been killed by the bull had the same name, and red hair. Yes, he'd had a farm near Blaan. It couldn't be a coincidence.

'Question three! Name the odd yin oot: a blue whale, a sperm whale, a minke whale an' a killer whale.'

'Here, how can there be an odd yin oot when they're a' whales?' shouted one of the fire brigade's team.

'Whoot wid be the point o' me telling you that? It's a quiz, no' *Look and Learn*. Jeest put doon an answer.'

Daley eyed the red-haired man.

Kinloch, 1945

It had been almost forty-eight hours since he had given Mitchell the message, and there was still no reply. Urquhart questioned the wisdom of giving the farmhand money. He'd given him a hard time in an attempt to find out the truth, but he'd felt sorry for him. Though he knew someone had closed the gate to the cattle float, leaving Kerr to his fate, he wasn't convinced it was Mitchell, though he was sure he had been present. In any case, all of it would have been almost impossible to prove.

There were more sinister forces at work, of that he was sure.

For some reason, he hadn't felt like going home this evening. He rarely felt this way, but at the moment, rather than shunning his fellow townsfolk, he felt as though he needed company, so had headed to the County Hotel.

As he was being served, he looked through the serving hatch at the vestibule beyond. A woman in a tatty coat, headscarf knotted under her chin, was standing there, a battered cardboard suitcase at her feet. She could have been almost any age, from thirty to her mid fifties, but the inspector reckoned that she was younger, and that some problem –an illness, or perhaps just a hard life – had worn her down.

The child at her side, a little girl, most likely only four or five, seemed unnaturally quiet, as though, like her mother, she was at the mercy of some overriding sadness. A red curl had escaped from under her grimy white beret, and he could see she'd been crying, yet she studied the noisy drinkers behind the hatch with no little fascination.

Urquhart cursed his compulsion to analyse everyone, even if they weren't suspects, or of interest to the police. It was a habit he couldn't break.

'Here you are, Mr Urquhart. Have that one on me. Ranald said you'd had a hard day the other day. He said nothing mair, mind you, just that.'

'Thank you,' replied Urquhart, lifting the dimpled pint glass from the bar.

'I see you looking,' said the barman, leaning forward. 'That's the lassie who just lost her man, you know, on the lobster boat at Gairsay. She's booking in. Has to make the arrangements, take possession of the body and gie it tae auld Kennedy the undertaker. Sad business, the poor lassie.'

'Can you look after that for me for a moment?' said Urquhart. He left his pint on the bar and walked out into the vestibule.

The first ten questions had been asked – a third of the quiz – so Annie was taking a break, allowing her customers to recharge their glasses. Daley walked to the bar, waiting patiently to be served behind a throng of customers.

Standing next to him was Kerr. The man smiled at Daley, nodded in greeting.

'Some tough questions, eh?' said Daley.

'Aye, I knew fine Annie widna make them easy. As long as she doesna get too intellectual, whoot wae a' they lawyers.'

'What gives you the idea that lawyers are intellectual?' remarked Daley with a smile.

'I reckon you'll know a' aboot that, whoot wae your job, an' a.''

'Could I have a quick word with you? Nothing important, daft, really.'

'I've never been asked questions by a polisman that didna have some reason behind them. Och, but I've naethin' tae hide, so ask away.'

'If we can step out here, just for a second or two.' He led Kerr into the hallway outside the bar.

'Here, this is gettin' serious. I didna dae it, whootever it is.'

'I'm trying to piece together the life of one of my predecessors. Just a hobby, really. The inspector who was here at the end of the war. He was called—'

'William Urquhart was his name,' interrupted Kerr. 'He investigated the death o' my great-uncle Dougie. Aye, then disappeared himsel', the poor bugger.'

'Oh, so you know all about it.'

'I widna say that. There was a bit o' a stink at the time, you know, him disappearin' jeest after Dougie was killed. Terrible death it was – crushed by a great lump o' a bull in a cattle float.'

'Yes, it sounded horrible. I've been reading all about it. Everyone blamed the farmhand, a man called Andrew Mitchell, I think.'

'Aye, they did that, but we never believed it – the family, I mean. No' for many years, anyway.'

Daley was surprised. 'I thought it was pretty open and shut.'

'No, not at all. He left a note, well, no' a note addressed tae anyone in particular. My faither found it in his papers a few years later. He moved in exalted circles, auld Dougie. He had freens in high places, the laird o'er at Glenlargie, for one. He was on the local council an' that. Got mair than he bargained for. So my faither reckoned, anyway.'

'So you don't blame Mitchell?'

'Well, in the note, Dougie wrote aboot how he'd found somethin' oot. Some secret that scunnered him o' a' they dignitaries he kept company wae. He was worried that he was in danger.'

'Yes. I know he'd arranged to meet Urquhart on the day he died. Do you know what he was worried about?'

'No, no' really. Just that it was something tae dae with the war. The story in the family was he found a spy, but, och, that's likely fanciful. He wrote it for his wife, but she never got tae see it. For some reason it jeest got lumped in wae his belongings when he died. My faither found it when he was clearing oot an auld loft at the farm.'

'Did he report it?'

'Naw, this was nearly twenty years later. Naebody was bothered by that time. Maist o' the folk that would have been involved were deid, anyhow.'

'Did you hear any more about Mitchell? He left town, according to Inspector Urquhart's journal.'

Kerr looked puzzled. 'No' the story I heard.'

'Oh. What did you hear?'

'They found him deid. Flung himsel' off the rocks near Machrie – roon the coast, anyway.'

'Funny that the inspector didn't mention that.'

'You're the man wae the records. I'm thinking he disappeared no' long after Mitchell topped himsel'. Mind you, that's jeest a notion.'

They heard the microphone squeal back into life in the bar. 'Yous have two minutes tae get back intae your teams. We'll be here till four in the morning at this rate.'

'That'll be fine!' Daley heard someone shout.

He walked back into the bar, deep in thought. He'd broken the rules of investigation, many of them his own. He had read Urquhart's description of his meeting with Mitchell, how he'd given him money to help him leave the area and make a new life. He'd assumed that the younger man had taken the advice and gone. Daley had failed to check the records of the time to see if anything could be gleaned from them. It was a basic mistake, but it annoyed him nonetheless.

He returned to the table where Scott and Symington were looking at him expectantly.

'Did you forget your wallet, Jimmy?' asked Scott, a withering look on his face.

'Sorry?' replied Daley, mystified.

'He means, where are the drinks?' said Symington with a broad smile.

Daley headed back to the bar, deep in thought.

Kinloch, 1945

'I'm sorry to bother you. I'm Inspector Urquhart.'

Before the woman had a chance to reply, the little girl piped up. 'We're fae Glenhanity croft on Gairsay, an' my dada's deid, all 'cause o' the evil woman an' that wean.'

The mother pulled her daughter roughly by the arm, instantly making her burst into tears. 'Whoot did I tell you aboot that mooth o' yours!' she shouted, then fought to regain her composure. 'Sorry, Inspector, my daughter hasn't worked oot yet when tae speak an' when tae keep quiet.'

'You have my condolences. I'm investigating what happened to your husband, and I can assure you—'

'My husband drooned!' she shouted. 'Drooned, plain an' simple. You've naethin' tae investigate.' Despite her protestations, he could see she was frightened.

'Sorry, I didn't mean to upset you.'

'I've a lot tae deal wae. I jeest want tae get the wee one settled, and dae whoot we've got tae dae the morrow and get back home, so if you'll excuse me . . .'

Urquhart turned round, seeing the receptionist was back at her post, brandishing the room key. He watched the mother sign the hotel register and take the key. After a nod of thanks to the receptionist, she picked up her suitcase and made her way up the staircase. The luxurious thick red carpet made the mother and child look pitifully out of place.

The little girl turned round to take a last look at the policeman with her big dark eyes, before rubbing her nose on her sleeve. 'How did you no' tell the man aboot *Well o' the Winds*?' she exclaimed.

The woman tugged at the girl's arm, almost making her topple over. 'Shut up!'

Urquhart walked back into the bar and drained half of his drink without returning to his seat. The last thing he'd wanted to do was upset the grieving woman, but he'd been surprised by her reaction. Grief could do strange things to a person – he knew that – but she had seemed genuinely terrified.

The big doors of the bar creaked open. Though Urquhart didn't bother to turn round to see who came in, he soon felt a tap on his shoulder.

'McColl, what do you want?'

'Sir, a letter for you. Someone posted it through the front door of the station.'

Urquhart looked at the plain brown envelope. It read: INSPECTOR W. URQUHART. PRIVATE.

He untucked the envelope flap, read the contents of the note inside, and then stuffed both into his pocket. 'When did this arrive, and why is it open?'

'Not sure, sir. A constable brought it to me a few minutes ago. I thought you might be in here, so I thought I'd bring it down. What is it?'

'I have an appointment in a couple of hours or so.'

'Shall I come with you, sir?'

'No. You get home, get some rest. I have a feeling you won't be getting very much in the foreseeable future.'

McColl looked crestfallen.

'Don't be so precious, McColl. This is a job I need to do alone. As you progress in your police career, you'll realise it's the only way sometimes.'

'V-very good, sir. I'll s-see you tomorrow.'

Urquhart watched the young man walk off, not without a touch of petulance, which, he reasoned, was no bad thing. Perhaps his young charge was beginning to emerge from the long shadow of his father after all.

Mitchell had done his job. Maybe now he would be able to get to the bottom of things.

41

Gairsay's part-time fire service had done its best to save the farmhouse, but the explosion had torn out the heart of the dwelling and virtually nothing was left, save for a few charred timbers and a mass of blackened, melted detritus – the remnants of furniture, cooking utensils and electrical equipment, the stuff of domesticity.

Commander Bale looked under the arc lighting that had been erected by the fire brigade from the mainland, who had arrived as quickly as possible to aid their island colleagues. 'Whoever did this made a bloody good job of it. Nothing left – absolutely nothing.'

'Yes, looks as though the charge was set in the cellar, so it's in even worse shape. You guys will have plenty images, though,' said Harris, his hands stuffed into the pockets of a thick winter jacket.

'We have what we have, sir. Couldn't legislate for this happening – well, *we* couldn't.'

Harris contemplated the smouldering wreck of what was once Achnamara farmhouse and stroked his chin. 'What are you suggesting, Commander?'

'Me? Nothing, apart from the fact that it was convenient we were all taking part in your debrief when this happened.

Normally, we'd have had somebody there round the clock, but you wanted to speak to us all. So what is it my grand-daughter comes out with? Ah, yes, "just saying".'

'That's a very serious accusation. I hope you'll be making that official, because if you don't, I most certainly will.'

'Now, hang on—'

'No, you hang on!' shouted Harris, his face only inches away from the senior policeman. 'If you're insinuating that I have something to do with this, I want that accusation followed through. The government can't have that sort of thing hanging over its head now, can it?'

'I don't know . . . just circumstances. I'm not saying I suspect something, just that it looks suspicious.'

'I'll raise your concerns with my line manager. I'm sure they'll want to make sure that this is all whiter than white. I'll also mention it to the local officers when they get here.'

'Local officers?'

'Yes, this is their domain now. There's nothing for you boys to investigate, is there? It's all up in flames. In fact, if I were you, I'd start winding up the operation. Once you've given your statements and put everything you have to bed, I imagine it'll be back to the Big Smoke for you tomorrow.'

'Very well, I'll put those wheels in motion,' replied Bale coldly.

'That fireman, him over there,' said Harris, pointing at one of the members of the island brigade.

'What about him?'

'Didn't I see him in a police uniform earlier?'

Jean McAuley wasn't used to the quad bike, and riding in the dark with the big headlight shining its bright beam along the rutted path made it even more difficult, but soon she drew up outside the Glenhanity croft.

She struggled off the machine and hesitated, searching in the deep pocket of her anorak for the powerful little Maglite torch. She took a deep breath and pushed open the rickety door.

The smell was overpowering. She knew that the owner was still lying dead in the kitchen, but she wasn't interested in that.

She cast the beam about, first onto the couch, then up onto the mantelpiece. She looked at the painting in the torchlight. The woman smiled down at her, cheeks pink against a pale complexion. He'd been a good painter, she thought. Could have made something of himself if he hadn't been marooned on this island, struggling to make a meagre living from root vegetables, chickens and whatever fruits of the sea he could glean. The life of the crofter in those days – before grants and encouragement – was a tough one. Life was just bloody tough anyway; even now, she reasoned.

She directed the beam along the mantelpiece. There it was, just what she was looking for. She picked up the bottle, went into the kitchen, where she poured the contents down the drain, and tucked it into her pocket.

It was strange to think that the woman she'd known for so long was on the floor, dead. She wondered how far they would take the investigation of her death. After all, everyone on Gairsay had been predicting it for years – it was a miracle that she'd lasted so long. A life of loneliness and drunkenness had reached its natural conclusion, regardless of how unnatural the final moments of that life had been.

She cast the beam about one last time. The torchlight flashed off the brass of a small photo frame. She walked across to the mantelpiece and picked it up in her gloved hand, squinting at the image of a little girl in a white beret. It was an old monochrome photograph that had been coloured at a later date. The little girl's cheeks were too pink – a bit like the painting above – and the lock of hair which curled from under her hat was red too.

She replaced the photograph and left the house, the old front door creaking in protest as she closed it behind her.

She tramped through the heather, cursing in Gaelic as she stumbled over clumps of thick grass and rocks in the darkness, the only light that of her torch and the pale moon. She could hear distant voices carrying from Achnamara, across the hillside, on the still night air.

She thought of her husband. His panic when he'd returned home, desperate to change from his police uniform into that of a fire-fighter, off to tackle the blaze caused by the explosion at the farmhouse.

He'd asked her to call in Glenhanity's death at the Police Office at Kinloch. She would do it when she got back home. With everyone's attention focused on the Bremners' place, she'd have plenty of time. First the family, now the house had disappeared.

She remembered how much she'd loved old Mrs Bremner. How the woman had always taken an interest in her, teaching her how to bake, what to read, how to think, and how to hate.

Her traipse through the heather was over. She stood at the edge of the small, dark loch and took a deep breath. The moon was a limpid disc, the reflection rippling on the black water. She was momentarily startled when an oystercatcher swung low over the water, its piercing cry echoing across the hillside.

She pulled the empty whisky bottle from her pocket, swung her arm, and propelled it far into the water, watching as it bubbled away into the Well of the Winds, like the votive offerings of old.

Glenhanity would no longer be a problem. The old woman was silenced for good.

42

Daley stood on the deck of the ferry as it made its way across the narrow sound towards Gairsay, Scott at his side, shivering in the cold night air. Even from this distance, he could see the flashing blue lights of the emergency services as they attended to the incident at Achnamara Farm.

They'd been pulled from the cosy conviviality of the quiz night at the County Hotel, which pleased him, in a way. In his current state of misery, nights lasted for ever. They were long, lonely, silent times, with only the beat of his heart in his ears for company. He couldn't concentrate to read, watch TV, listen to the radio – all the things that normally acted as a balm for his racing thoughts.

Recently, only the journal of Inspector William Urquhart offered any kind of solace; an absorbing, intriguing break from the heartbreaking reality of his life.

He'd reached the last part of the journal. Looking out across the dark waves, he remembered the words written in the inspector's neat hand.

> *There is always a time in one's life when the need to know is greater than the need to be safe. I have experienced this before, and it is as much of a surprise to me now as it was then.*

All of us have the capacity to hasten our own end – the conclusion of our lives. But what are these lives, if lived only as a battle against the forces that will bring about our demise? There must be something more important – something greater than that.

I have seen good men – and at least one good woman – die in this way. Better specimens of humanity than me have made the journey from what we know to what we don't.

This war – as did the last – has taken so much hope, promise and youthful potential away. We will never know what those who have fallen may have done with their lives. It would be naïve to think that none of these poor souls had the capacity to change the world for ever – for good, or bad; so, where does that leave us now?

We are living in a world that isn't what it could be – or even what it should be. Each death is a personal tragedy approximating calamity, not for the one, but for us all.

All we – I – can do is carry on the struggle to save lives and right wrongs.

Why the philosophy? I don't honestly know, but, in a strange and totally unexpected way, I feel as though, having witnessed so many endings, it is time for my own.

I will do what I have always done. Fight against the darkness.

Kinloch, 1945

Inspector Urquhart took the coast road out of Kinloch, along the bay and towards the island. The car's headlights, mere slits to comply with blackout regulations, gave only the barest glimpse of the road ahead. Wispy clouds scudded across a full moon. The warships on the loch appeared as one solid, dark mass, dotted here and there by a light on a mast or the spark of a cigarette on deck.

He wondered what Kinloch would be like in peacetime. The war had brought the world to this remote Scottish coastline – sometimes welcome, sometimes not – and had changed the community irrevocably.

He fought a wave of sadness. He had made mistakes – should have done things differently. Maybe there was still time. He'd always favoured prevention over cure; most of the time, though, this was an impossibility. The people with whom he was now dealing had their roots in the highest echelons of society. They had witnessed the events of Britain in the thirties and not liked what they had seen. The levers of power had begun to grind in a different direction.

He found it hard to imagine that some of his countrymen would take up arms against their own nation, but the reasoning was sound. How deep had this gone? He knew there were many who favoured reconciliation with what was left of Germany, rather than staying in bed with Stalin and the mighty Russian bear.

His mind slipped back to France and the weeks before the Armistice. As a young officer – Wellington would have called him a galloper – he was tasked with taking a sensitive missive from the front line to command HQ, located in the relative luxury of a bombed-out château, almost five miles back. He wasn't irked by the fact that colonels, major generals and the ranks above quaffed wine and ate fresh meat while their men were slaughtered in the trenches – it was the privilege of command. Why on earth would any army risk the lives of those who directed its course? No, he was reconciled with that notion. What shocked him was a chance meeting.

He had been asked to remain seated in a corridor, and he was looking up at an ornate plaster ceiling, waiting to be called. He could hear laughter emanating from the dining room, a few yards away, and smell the pungent aroma of cigar smoke.

Two mirrored doors swung open. A general – identifiable as such by his red-and-black formal uniform – tumbled from within, his right arm draped around a companion, who was guffawing at something, chattering away in a language Urquhart did not then understand.

The man's uniform was grey-green, and he carried a spiked helmet in the crook of one arm. It was Urquhart's first sight of a German officer at close quarters, and the experience unnerved him. It wasn't that the man scared him – no, it was the camaraderie that clearly existed between this man and the English general. Young privates – many of them his friends – were being blown to smithereens, yet here the enemy was welcomed with open arms and a fine cognac.

The German gave him a withering look, then the two continued on their merry, companionable way.

Urquhart wasn't naïve – certainly no more than most at his then tender age. He knew that communication between enemies must take place, back-channels to peace. But the feeling of revulsion had never left him. It made him feel as though the whole war had been some sort of hellish prank played upon millions of innocents.

Why could disputes amongst nations not be decided over the dining table at the outset, thus avoiding the need for a murderous entrée of tragic, unnecessary death? If that was how things were ultimately resolved – old men blathering over wine and canapés around a large table, why not just skip to the dessert?

As Urquhart neared his destination, he supposed that this was, in some small way, what he was trying to achieve.

'I never thought I'd be back here a few hours after I left,' Scott grumbled. 'At least the boss didnae make a fuss when you said it would be better for her tae hold the fort.'

'She was pissed,' said Daley with a laugh.

'What's the scoop when we get there? Glenhanity or Achnamara?'

'I'm guessing we won't be able to do much at Achnamara. By all accounts, there's bugger all left of the place and Special Branch are still in charge. We better make Glenhanity our priority.'

'Carrie's dying tae get her teeth stuck intae Special Branch tomorrow. Tells me she's going tae pull together what you found oot fae this diary, and what this professor has for her. You never know, we might solve this yet, Jimmy boy.'

'You never know, and none of us have been shot at, half drowned or impaled – that makes a nice change.'

'Aye, but I'm still on a boat,' grumbled Scott.

43

Kinloch, 1945

Inspector Urquhart pulled into the layby above the causeway. He could see its dark serpentine shape meandering through the waves, revealed intermittently by the moonlight. All was quiet, save for the distant calls of sailors across the loch. As he reached into the pocket of his raincoat for his torch, the faint notes of an accordion melody were carried on the air. 'Clair de Lune' – the tune made him smile and feel melancholy at the same time. It had been her favourite.

As he opened the gate and made his way across the machair and down onto the rocky strand, he thought of her. Somehow, she seemed nearer now than at any time since her death. She'd been cut down by a carelessly discharged round fired by an inebriated soldier celebrating the end of the war. How ironic, his commanding officer had said, to have survived the conflict, only to be killed on the first day of peace. It hadn't felt ironic to him; it had felt horrific, and something good had ended that night.

He heard something scurrying across the pebbles and pointed the torch in the general direction. He could make out the figure of a man, the cut of his expensive raincoat instantly recognisable, despite the shadows.

He walked nearer, directing the beam straight at the man. 'What in hell's name are you doing here?' He sighed, wishing that, for once, someone would heed his advice.

There was no reply, and he turned to face the water's edge to stare across the black loch. He needed to do this on his own.

As he grabbed at his trilby to stop it being blown into the sea, he felt an arm snake around his neck. Before he could react, a cold, agonising pain shot through his chest. He tried to draw breath, but could only hear a rasping noise in his throat.

Suddenly, lights flashed across his vision: white, green, red, in vivid patches and patterns. His panic mounted and he felt himself falling backwards. The lights faded, and the last thing he tried to do was call her name. He felt such profound sadness that he couldn't give it voice.

Hans Neyermeyer read and re-read the document in front of him. It wasn't like anything he'd ever written: not one of the myriad memos, instructions, press releases, blanket communications to bureaucrats across the continent, or advice to members of the commission, council, or parliament. No, this was more akin to a death warrant for the men he had known; figuratively, if not literally. Yet he suspected many would take the route that he was about to tread, rather than the alternative – the shame, censure and prosecution that was inevitable.

One line was etched in his mind: 'That from evil, good can spring.'

It was a bastardised quote from Saint Augustine, his Enchiridion: musings on faith, hope and love. He hoped it would lend the missive some kind of scholarly respectability.

Good could and did spring forth from bad. However, when bad remained at the heart of something good, it sullied it.

It was ironic that the European Union was now facing the most challenging time since its inception. Member states were in a clamour of discontent, with threats of referendums across the continent. Old rivalries, hidden for years behind a façade of peace, unity and shared interests, were re-emerging. Germany at its heart was struggling to maintain order, to keep the dream alive.

He felt a sudden surge of pride for the nation of his birth. His homeland *was* Europe – soon they would all see this and fall back into line.

Then he thought of the old woman in Linz. After all these years, she was still sitting at the centre of the web, twisting and controlling the strands of their existence, keeping her dream – the nightmare – alive. She'd survived everything: the assassin's bullet, exposure by the press – even the revulsion of an entire people – but still she prevailed.

He looked again at the document flickering on the screen. This would end it – finish her off for sure. Not just her, either. The future would no longer be assured. The continent would roll on – whichever way – but all the ghosts of the past, and present, must be put to rest. The present must be left to take care of itself.

He reached over to the large tankard he kept on his desk, flipped open the ornate lid, and extracted a Cohiba cigar. He ran it under his nose, smiling at the way the aroma already made him feel, before it was even lit.

He reached into his pocket, feeling the heft of his father's silver lighter, and looked at the inscription: *Oberst Neyermeyer, mit bestem Dank, Adolf Hitler*.

He lit the cigar and inhaled deeply.

'You're in for a treat here, Jimmy,' said Scott from the back seat of the Land Rover. They were being driven by a Forestry Commission worker, bumping up the muddy track that led to the smallholding that was Glenhanity. The dawn was breaking cold and grey across the island.

Daley, huddled into his jacket, looked out of the passenger window at the glistening lochan beside them.

'That's the Well o' the Winds. Me and the gaffer were up here for a wander.'

'You and the gaffer seem to have had a great time,' replied Daley.

'Aye, well, it wisnae a' fun and games.'

'No, your face is testament to that. Do you ever intend to tell me what happened?'

'Nope, and I don't think it's fair for you tae keep pressing me, neither. Fuck me, it's no' as though I haven't kept a few o' your secrets o'er the years.'

'Fair enough.'

'That's us here,' declared Scott.

Perfect timing, thought Daley. 'Looks pretty run-down – the house, I mean.'

'Run-doon? This place makes run-doon look like the Ideal Home. I'm telling you, there's creepy crawlies in there that thon Attenborough wid be shocked tae see, an' that's before there was a stiff lying in the hoose.'

The Land Rover pulled up in the yard, and both detectives got out.

Scott swore profusely as he stepped straight into a puddle. He pulled off his shoe to drain off a dribble of filthy water. 'See what I mean? And we're no' even in the hoose yet. When dae you think the SOCO boys will arrive?'

'On the first ferry. They're on their way down the road from Glasgow now.' Daley reached into his pocket. 'Put these on,' he said, throwing a small bag at his DS. 'We'll have to tread carefully here.'

'You could've gied me these before I jumped intae that puddle,' said Scott, struggling to put on the cover-shoes that would help preserve any forensic evidence. Daley did likewise, and they entered the house.

The smell hit Daley instantly. He knew that when he eventually had the courage to leave this job, the most visceral of his memories would be tied in with smell: rotting corpses, the metallic stench of blood, shit and vomit. Not for the first time, he wondered why on earth he was still exposing himself to this cavalcade of misery. He braced himself and scanned the living area.

'Dee whad I mean?' said Scott, holding his nose.

Daley's eyes were drawn to the painting above the fireplace. The woman in the old-fashioned clothes, in the bright scene, was completely at odds with the chaotic, stinking room. He wondered why anyone would put such a cheerful work in such a dismal frame. It appeared to be made of some kind of dark wood and was covered in soot. For a second, it crossed his mind that the painting looked in much better condition than the frame, but this thought was banished by a cry from Scott.

'Oh, for fuck's sake! Just when I didnae think things could get worse.'

Daley followed the voice into the kitchen. The dead woman was slumped against a cupboard on the kitchen floor. She sat amid a dark pool that Daley knew would be a disgusting mix of blood and faeces. Her open eyes looked heavenward, her mouth gaped, and her chin was slathered with thick green vomit. A bluebottle was buzzing around the corpse and, as the detectives looked on, it settled on her cheek.

Daley felt nausea washing over him in waves.

'Come on, Jimmy, let's get oot o' here. I know you've got a weak stomach, and I feel as if I've just woken up after fourteen pints and a vindaloo.' He tugged at Daley's sleeve.

'I don't like this. This old woman just dies in the middle of all this Bremner business? It doesn't feel right.'

'Don't tell me we'll have tae deal wae this as well, if she didnae die fae natural causes?'

'No, we're too stretched with the Bremner case. When SOCO get here they'll pass their findings up to Division. If there's anything about your friend here to be investigated, they'll have to do it.'

'No friend o' mine, God rest her soul.'

Daley looked around the kitchen. Two of the Bremner family found dead – the rest probably dead at the bottom of the Atlantic – and now this. He wasn't certain that Glenhanity hadn't died of natural causes – after all, she was a chronic alcoholic – but, as always, doubts, questions, buzzed in his head.

'It's a miracle she didn't keel over long ago, mind, with her drinking,' said Scott. 'They telt me at the hotel that she'd got a lot worse recently. She was always a boozer, but she only started tae make a nuisance of herself in the last wee while.'

'I wonder why?'

'Oh! Oh, ya wee bastard!' Scott rubbed his head vigorously.

Something fell onto the linoleum. Daley watched as a large insect with long antennae scurried across the floor in a series of little clicks.

Both policemen hurried out of the cottage to wait for the SOCO team in fresh air.

44

Symington sat behind Daley's desk in his glass box, running her tongue around her parched mouth. She had a pounding headache, brought on by too much wine – far too much wine. She'd taken some painkillers and was desperate for them to take effect.

She lifted her mug of coffee shakily with both hands and thought never again. She wasn't a regular heavy drinker by any means. Hangovers got worse the further she progressed into her thirties. Today, especially, she could easily envisage the day she would swear off alcohol for good.

The phone on her desk rang.

'Ma'am, Superintendent Nelson at Complaints and Discipline for you. He called HQ and was redirected here.'

Her head was spinning, and her chest felt tight. This could be the end of her career – the beginning of the end, at any rate. Her mind flashed back to the fracas in the car park on Gairsay.

'Chief Superintendent Symington, Bill Nelson. I don't think I've had the pleasure of meeting you, as yet.'

'No, indeed, nor I you. What can I do for you?'

'It concerns one of your detectives – Detective Sergeant Brian Scott, to be precise.'

'Yes.' She felt the phone shaking in her hand against her ear.

'We've had a back-channel – unofficial, if you like – contact from the Met. Not a complaint, as such, but it could turn into one unless we handle it carefully. Apparently, he was involved in some kind of altercation with a Met detective recently – a chief inspector from Special Branch, no less.'

'Oh, I see.' Symington felt her face burning, the way it always did when she was in an awkward situation. 'What are the details?' She closed her eyes in readiness for the onslaught.

'That's just it. The details are very patchy. The Met hinted that if we administer the veritable boot to the arse we can nip this in the bud. As you'll be aware, because of due process, although I know about this, I don't know, if you get my drift.'

'Yes, yes, I see.'

'If I have to turn this into an official discipline enquiry . . . well, you know the score, I'm sure.'

'Oh, I do.' She thought for a moment. 'Anyone else we know involved?'

'All I know is that there was some kind of contretemps. There are murmurs of another senior officer behind it all. Whether it's one of theirs, or one of ours, I don't know.'

'So, what would you like me to do?' she blurted.

'Well, given it's best that we keep this low-key, I was hoping you would deal with Scott and lay down the law. He needn't know that a lid can be kept on this, so we have some leverage.'

'Right, well, leave this to me. I'll make sure that DS Scott is in no doubt as to what is expected from him in the future.'

'Thank you, Carrie. Good luck. I'm afraid DS Scott has one of the bleakest disciplinary records of any cop on the force. The boot you administer may need to be a firm one – and take a good run-up before you do it.'

'I'll let you know how I get on.'

'I'll leave you to handle it, but, one word of advice, if I can be so bold?'

'Yes, most welcome.'

'Keep your boot on Scott's throat. He's a bloody menace – always has been, despite his many successes. I've always thought that tolerating his behaviour was too high a price to pay. After all, he's not the only talented detective we have on the books.'

'I understand.'

'Trust me, give him too much rope, and it will be your head in the noose – not his. You can't rely on Daley to keep him on the straight and narrow – hand in glove, that pair, too close personally to be working together. You'll be tired of hearing about John Donald, I dare say, but only someone with his, well, let's say skill set, could cope with that little nexus. Anyway, I hope you don't think I'm standing on your toes,' he said, ending on an upbeat note.

'No, not at all. I'm grateful for the advice. He and Daley do have an unusual professional relationship.'

Symington ended the call, her hand still trembling as she placed the receiver back on its cradle. This had all the hall-marks of another lucky escape. If she wanted to keep the career she'd coveted since being a girl, she would have to keep the lid firmly closed.

She thought about Daley and Scott. Maybe it was time for a bit of space to be inserted between the two detectives.

The email alert on her mobile sounded. It was the professor who was studying the Achnamara documents. Taking a deep breath, she decided to take her mind off her personnel woes and read on.

Daley sat in the lounge of the Gairsay Hotel, nursing a mug of steaming coffee. The dawn had broken into a magnificent spring morning, and he was looking absently out of the big bay windows across the sound, which shimmered blue in the sunshine. Two fishermen plied their trade in a small lobster boat, while gulls wheeled above their heads in the gin-clear sky.

He'd had a message from the records department at HQ. They'd found a statement from the shepherd who had discovered the body of Andrew Mitchell. He was found in a crevice above the Goat Rock, a tall pinnacle of granite that jutted from the very edge of the peninsula, as though pointing an admonitory finger towards Ireland.

The report was dated two days after the disappearance of Inspector William Urquhart. But, then again, what Daley knew, and the records department did not, was that the inspector hadn't simply disappeared: he had been murdered. The fact that this incident had remained redacted, covered up for so many years, was testament itself to something unusual. The war would always be used as an excuse, but, as far as Daley was concerned, at least, it wasn't a legitimate enough one.

He read again Urquhart's last journal entry. The man had known he'd been dealing with something untoward. People – powerful people – would always influence events in their favour. Daley pondered how much more significant the power of privilege would have been at the end of the Second World War.

On examination, though, it seemed likely that, despite Urquhart's leniency and efforts to help the wretched farmhand, Mitchell had turned on the policeman. Daley wondered what pressure had been placed on the young man. A simple farm worker, caught in a web of danger and intrigue, manipulated by men whose lives the young man would have found it hard to imagine. It had been sufficient to bring about the end of Urquhart's life and drive Mitchell to suicide – or was that too neat? He'd read the archived shepherd's report when it arrived. It would make no difference to William Urquhart, who had given his life, so long ago, trying to make a difference, but at least he would have an answer.

Daley felt more of an affinity with his predecessor, who had died long before he was born, than he did with many of his contemporaries. Times had changed and he had a feeling of being left behind. And it wasn't the first time he'd felt this way.

He'd miss Inspector William Urquhart.

'You wantin' an egg roll, or something, Jimmy?'

Daley hadn't heard Scott enter the room. 'Yeah, why not? Don't forget the tomato sauce.'

'Aye, nae bother. Free range, or grain fed?'

'Sorry?'

'Just joking, buddy. I'll bring it on a china plate, tae. Earl Grey do the trick?'

'Cut it out, Brian.'

Scott shook his head. He knew there was no point in talking to Daley when he was in a mood like this. Whatever was bothering his old friend, he was so deep in thought that only something concerning the case would rouse him.

'Oh, just tae keep you up tae speed.'

'What?'

'Latest on Glenhanity.'

'Yes.'

'I've just been talking tae the forensic boys. They're no' happy the old dear just died o' natural causes. She's going up the road for a post mortem. The Crime Squad are investigating, seein' as we're all oot o' resources, Jimmy.'

'Yet another mystery on Gairsay.'

'Aye, looks like it. They're just finishing off. They'll come doon and gie us the heads up in an hour or two. In the meantime, I'll away an' get oor scran.'

'That can wait.'

'Eh? Where are we going?'

'Back to the house, Brian.'

'No way, no' on an empty stomach. I'm only feeling well enough tae get something tae eat noo.'

'Come on, we'll pick stuff up on the way. Something's bugging me.'

With an ease of movement that belied his bulk, Daley jumped out of the chair and bounded out of the room, Scott in his wake.

'Bring oot your deid,' muttered Scott under his breath.

45

Harris was packing a bag in his hotel room at the Gairsay Hotel. He'd achieved all he could here, though the fallout from the Bremner case had the potential to spill into the national – perhaps international – consciousness. Most fortuitously, in fact. If things did get hot, the Bremners could be consigned to the realms of the conspiracy theorists – a whole world of the unexplained reduced to twenty-second YouTube grabs.

He looked out of the window. DCI Daley was hurrying across the car park, tucking his shirt into his trousers as he went.

Harris had heard that a mad old alcoholic woman who lived in the hills had been found dead, but had paid it no heed. Now, though, there was something about the chief inspector's urgency that piqued his curiosity. He was doing what he was trained to do: observing and making connections that others could not.

Perhaps he wouldn't be catching the afternoon ferry with the Special Branch contingent, after all.

Daley hesitated outside Glenhanity cottage and sniffed the air, deep in thought.

'Aye, nae wonder you're taking the chance tae get a breath o' fresh air, big man. You'll suffocate in there.'

'Have you ever painted, Bri?'

'Aye, Ella and I just finished the kitchen and the hall a couple o' weeks ago.'

'No. I mean painted as in van Gogh. Painted a picture.'

'If it wasnae the morning, I'd swear you was on the sauce. The last picture I mind painting was in primary five. The teacher – she was a right auld bitch – took one look at it and flung it in the bin. "You stick tae the welding when you get older, Brian Scott," she says tae me. So that was kind o' the end o' my artistic career.'

'But if you did – let's try to imagine,' said Daley, his brow furrowed. 'When you gave your painting a title, you'd name it appropriately, yes?'

'Like the *Mona Lisa*?'

'Well, yes, in a way. You'd name it after the subject, or at least what's going on in the picture.'

'Aye, sounds reasonable tae me. What you getting at?'

'Come with me.'

Daley strode towards the house, just as a man in a hooded grey coverall exited the front door.

'Okay to go in, like this, I mean?' asked Daley.

'Yes, sir. We're just about done – wire in.'

Daley walked straight into the stench and darkness of Glenhanity's lounge. Ignoring the blue tape, and a SOCO officer packing away his fingerprint kit, he loped over to the fireplace. Scott was behind him, peering up at the ceiling for any stray insects that might try to make a bid for freedom onto his head.

'What are you after, big man?'

Daley was studying the painting in the filthy, old frame. 'In Urquhart's journal, someone – the Bremners, he'd deduced – were looking for something on Glenhanity's boat, *Well of the Winds*. His daughter, the old woman who died here, had put them on the trail by saying something at school. They broke into a strongbox, and likely killed the father, just to have a look. It was so important to them that they were willing to take the risk of killing a man to find it.'

'And that means we're in here, why?'

'The boat was called *Well of the Winds*. It was painted by the man who used to live here, and who was also responsible for this picture.' Daley indicated the painting of the smiling woman.

'Aye, the auld yin was never done goin' on aboot him. How she got him killed an' that. Steaming when she said it, mind. You don't think there's something in it, dae you?'

The bright morning light was diffused into a dull grey by the tattered net curtains shrouding Glenhanity cottage. In this pale glow, Daley walked towards the fireplace, reached out, and ran his finger across the small brass plate at the bottom of the picture frame.

'See, it says, *Well of the Winds*. You've been there – can you see it in this painting?'

'No, I cannae. That's the village, is it no'?'

'Give me your penknife, Bri.' Daley reached out, knowing that his friend never went anywhere without the Swiss Army knife his father had given him as a teenager, and which had proved useful over the years. He pulled the painting from the wall and laid it on the couch.

'I'd ca' canny on there, big man. The auld yin was born up that end.'

357

Daley ran the sharp knife around the edge of the painting. Soon, he was peeling the picture of the smiling woman away, like removing the film cover from the screen of some new electronic device. Another painting was being slowly revealed as Daley rolled back the original.

Minutes later, they could see the second painting underneath. It looked fresh, unsullied by dirt, dust, the stain of nicotine or bleaching from the sun. In fact, it looked as though it had been painted the day before.

Five figures stood on a dark windswept hillside, beside a stretch of water.

Instantly, Daley recognised one of them from the photographs at Achnamara. The tall figure of Bremner was unmistakeable: the blond hair cut close to his head, the square jaw and grey-blue eyes.

Two other men in dark trenchcoats bookended the scene. In the middle stood a young woman holding the hand of a toddler swadddled in a thick coat and bobble hat.

Daley stared at the painting. The woman had blonde hair, and the artist had been careful to paint her face with the same detail he had Bremner's, as though anxious to portray their features precisely. The other subjects – including the child – were less well defined.

He noted that her eyes were blue and slightly hooded, giving her a languid expression. She had a peaches-and-cream complexion.

'Fuck me, Jimmy,' said Scott, breaking the spell in his own inimitable fashion. 'I wonder who that is. Glenhanity's wife, and the auld yin as a wean?'

'Not a girl, I don't think, Brian. Look at the clothes the child's in – all blue.'

'Right enough. Blue for boys, pink for lassies. My auld dear was a stickler for it.'

'They all were at the time. No, that's a wee boy.' Daley rubbed his chin. 'You'll recognise the location though.'

'Aye, it's the Well of the Winds. No mistaking it. I was only just there wae Carrie.'

'Yes, Well of the Winds,' repeated Daley, the words a quiet incantation.

'Beats me why this place is so important,' said Scott, inter-rrupting Daley's train of thought.

'See that out there?' Daley pointed out the window towards the sea and the islands of Islay and Jura, which looked almost close enough to touch.

'It's the ocean, you don't need tae tell me that. I've been oot on it enough since we came doon here.'

'Not just any ocean – the Atlantic. It's an ideal route to flee mainland Europe.'

'Aye, but mind, this place was crawling wae the navy in nineteen forty-five. Wid they no' be suspicious aboot a bunch o' guys in jackboots cloaking o'er the water towards them? You're reading too many o' they books, Jimmy. What are you on the noo – David Icke?'

'I know what you mean about the navy, but what do you think the Bremners were doing here? From what I've seen, I think it's clear: they spent the first part of the war spying on naval manoeuvres, and the end of it helping spirit away Nazis. Why is that not possible?'

'Aye, right,' said Scott doubtfully. 'So, what's this lassie and the wean in the painting a' aboot?'

'I don't know. Something and nothing.' Daley studied the figures in the painting again.

'And?'

'What do you mean?'

'I know that look, Jimmy. What else are you thinking?'

'That woman. There's something familiar about her. I just can't place it.'

Scott peered at the painting. 'Is she no' a bit like the wee lassie that used tae work in Donald's office in Paisley – you know, the wee blonde yin?'

Daley shook his head. 'No, Bri, I don't think it's her.'

Mrs McAuley watched her husband as he pulled away in the red Post Office van, off to make his deliveries across the island. He'd take the time he always took – about an hour. She shut the shop door and flipped the sign to CLOSED.

She picked up the phone and dialled the long number from memory. As usual, the phone was answered after three rings by a young man, who politely asked her to hold. The voice of the old woman she'd known for so long boomed on the other end of the line.

'You have done what we talked about, yes?'

'Yes. All traces have been removed.'

'Good, good. You have done well – everything that was needed.'

'Thank you.'

'It is time to put into action what we have been discussing for a long time. Now the family have gone, you too must leave. It will become too dangerous.'

'I understand.'

'Money and further instructions will be sent through the usual channels. Be ready.'

The caller hung up. No farewell.

Mrs McAuley walked back to the door and turned the sign back to OPEN. Now she would have to persuade her husband to leave the island. As usual, she would succeed. To succeed was what she had been trained to do.

The European Parliament, Brussels

When the security officers arrived, he was sprawled face-down on the desk, lifeless blue eyes staring unseeingly at the letter with the silver lighter on top, a small but effective paperweight.

The security chief was called for, and he arrived, panting through the door, in a few short minutes, his jowly face red and shiny.

He sniffed the air and coughed.

'Pierre, the smell, what is it? I can't place the odour.'

'Almonds, monsieur. Most distinct. Cyanide, I would guess, but that is only speculation.'

He looked at Hans Neyermeyer. Bubbles were visible at the corners of his blue lips.

'What is it with these people? Who would have thought it? Neyermeyer of all people. They send messages, even in death. But what is the point? We will clean up this mess, have a death certificate issued confirming this man died of a heart attack brought on by too much work, then quietly dispose of the nonsense he has written.' He shrugged.

'May I interject?'

'Yes, if you must, Pierre.'

'In this instance, monsieur, it will be more problematic to dispose of what was written. It is not a mere suicide note.'

'How so, Pierre?'

'There's this hard copy' – he nodded to the letter on the desk beside the dead man – 'but he also emailed it.'

'Where? To whom?' The security chief's face became more flushed, and a large bead of sweat trickled down his forehead onto his long nose.

'To this address, monsieur.' He pointed to the recipient's address.

'Who is this?' The bead of sweat now slipped off the end of his nose, plopping onto the document with a tiny splash.

'We do not know, monsieur. A journalist, perhaps, a colleague, friend. We are looking into it.'

'Find out, Pierre. We must find out.'

The security chief picked up the silver lighter, then pulled a packet of Gitanes from his trouser pocket.

'But, monsieur, the regulations!' cried Pierre.

He didn't reply. He flicked the lighter into life, igniting his cigarette and inhaling deeply, and examined the eagle embossed on the side with narrowed eyes.

46

As soon as Daley stepped back into his glass box, he detected a change in atmosphere. Symington held up her hand, not lifting her eyes from the document she was reading.

Daley and Scott stood in silence; the former irritated that he was being silently ordered to shut up in his own office, the latter with a puzzled frown on his face.

After scribbling her signature across the bottom of a letter, Symington looked up, her expression neutral.

'You're back, gentlemen. I trust your trip to Gairsay was a fruitful one.'

'You want tae hear this one's theory, Carrie,' said Scott, angling his thumb in the general direction of Daley.

'Chief Superintendent Symington, or ma'am, when we're in the office, please.'

'Sorry?' replied Scott, momentarily mystified.

'The correct designation, please, DS Scott.'

Daley watched as Scott's face took on a deflated expression.

'In that case, may I ask when I'll get to sit back behind my desk in my office, *ma'am*.' Daley was furious at the offhand way she had put his friend down.

'As soon as I'm finished here, which won't be long,' replied

Symington, stopping Daley's protests in his throat. 'I need a few minutes with DS Scott, please.'

Daley gave an irritable sigh, turned on his heel and left the office, attempting to slam the door in his wake, which simply glided shut in a glassy, insubstantial protest.

'What's going on?' asked Scott.

'There are ramifications after our little problem the other night.'

'What?'

'The bosses know that you were involved in the assault of a fellow officer,' she said, a slight tremor in her voice.

'Oh aye. Well, it's his word against oors, and there's two o' us, *ma'am*.' An angry tic appeared beneath Scott's right eye. 'This is Scotland, and you'll have heard of corroboration, ma'am?'

'Even so, I have to be careful. I'm getting pressure from higher up and you don't seem to have a lot of friends in high places.' She exhaled. 'Listen to me. This little misdemeanour can be overlooked. I can fix that. As you say, there were two of us. But we can't treat this like some scrap in the playground, trust me.'

'Meaning I'm aboot tae get the order o' the boot?'

'No, I'm not saying that. Just keep your nose clean from now on, for both our sakes!'

'And what about Harry boy?'

'He says he's happy to overlook this if he gets a written apology.'

'And I've tae write the letter?'

'Just do it. It'll be better for both of us, Brian.'

'Detective Sergeant Scott, if you don't mind – us being in the office, ma'am . . . Right, I get the picture. You'll get your letter.'

Symington closed her eyes and tried to convince herself she really hadn't had a choice.

Daley flicked through the old microfilm records. Almost everything was digitised now, but the process hadn't quite reached the forties.

He wasn't happy at the way Symington had spoken to Brian, but he supposed he shouldn't be too surprised. It was unlikely that the young woman had reached her rank so early in her career without possessing the tools of all the other executive officers he'd encountered during the course of his long time in the police. He was disappointed, though.

The search seemed interminable, but searching through yards of microfilm came more naturally to him than perusing a database, so he soon reached the dates he was looking for.

There it was. The statement was dated two days after the death of Inspector William Urquhart, just as he'd been informed. He read on. Suddenly the expression on his face changed. He pushed the chair away from the desk and hurried from the room.

At last, it all made sense.

Scott pounded down the road to the County Hotel, still smarting from his encounter with Symington. It was mid afternoon, and the place was peaceful. Annie was sitting on a stool behind the bar, polishing glasses with a pristine white cloth. The vacant look on her face indicated that this process was automatic, her mind elsewhere. A solitary old man was sitting in the corner, his chin resting in his hands as he flipped through a newspaper spread across his table.

'Should see a bit o' tumbleweed rolling through here any time now,' quipped Scott.

Annie jumped, almost dropping the glass she was holding. 'Near scared the life out o' me there, Brian. What can I get you?'

She seemed to have lost the carefree, down-to-earth spirit he'd become accustomed to over the years. Despite having her mind on the job of pouring him a glass of ginger beer and lime, she still looked distracted, a bit depressed even.

'No' you, tae. What is it wae people today? Naebody's behaving normally.'

'Och, sorry,' replied Annie, tears welling. 'Jeest had a bit o' maist unwelcome news, a few minutes ago. Knocked me for six, so it has.'

'I'm sorry tae hear that. Anything I can help with?'

'Nope. If you was a surgeon, aye, maybe, but I'm thinking that it's the polis that's tae blame for this.'

'Eh, what on earth are you on aboot?'

'Just had Hamish's nephew in. The auld fella's taken a turn for the worse – Hamish, I mean.'

'I'm sorry tae hear that, aye, right sorry. But oor Jimmy telt me he was on the mend, just waiting for the green light tae get hame.'

'Aye, so he was. That was the plan. But the auld bugger got up this morning – likely tae go tae the toilet or something. You know him, proud man, he widna be wantin' tae pish in a cardboard potty.'

'What happened? Did he fall?'

'Naebody really knows. Whoot I've heard is that he was found slumped on the flair out for the count. Poor Hamish. He doesna deserve this.'

'What's it got tae dae with us, the police, I mean?'

'You know whoot they're sayin' in the toon, Brian?'

'No, enlighten me.'

'That it's a' 'cause o' his involvement wae the polis. You know fine, he's never done helping yous. He was out wae Mr Daley the other day. Everyone puts two and two the gither. He got battered on the heid 'cause o' something Mr Daley found.'

'Well, I hope he improves. I know Jimmy will be upset when I tell him. He was quite cheery – for the first time in ages – when he came back tae the toon and telt me Hamish was getting better.' He swirled the ice cubes in his glass. 'You mind and tell any o' his relatives that come in here we're asking for him. Everyone up at the office.'

'Maybe if he'd stayed away fae the office, he widna be in the state he is,' she replied indignantly. 'But, aye, I'll gie yous a shout if anything changes.'

Having failed to gain any kind of cheer, or even a shoulder to cry on, Scott left the County and headed onto Main Street in search of an alternative, just in time to see Daley's car speeding down the road. He waved, trying to catch his colleague's attention, but Daley was looking straight ahead with a grim look on his face.

Some poor bastard's in for it, thought Scott.

47

Daley skidded to a halt outside Stonebrae House, sending an arc of gravel into the rose bed bordering the immaculate lawn. He hastened up the stone steps to the front door, and in minutes he was being accompanied along the familiar corridor to Torquil McColl's suite.

The young Czech nurse in front of him tried to make conversation, but she elicited only grunts from the big policeman.

McColl's wheelchair was sitting as always in the bay window, its occupant looking across the broad vista of the loch, only the back of his small, wispy-haired skull visible.

'Mr Daley for you, Mr McColl. Your new friend?'

'Thank you, Darina. I'll ring if we need any refreshments,' said McColl weakly, still not turning to face his guest.

'Are you sure? It is no problem to bring coffee now.'

'It's fine!' Suddenly there was strength in McColl's voice as a little buzzer sounded and the motorised chair swung round. 'You people never listen.'

The carer made her excuses and quickly left.

'Back again, Chief Inspector,' said McColl. 'Can't keep away, it would seem.'

'I'd like to talk to you about the events surrounding the disappearance of Inspector William Urquhart,' said Daley, forgoing any social niceties.

'So I assumed. But I don't know how I can help you further,' replied the old man, his voice more assured than Daley remembered.

'Andrew Mitchell. He was blamed for killing the inspector and disposing of his body, then, a couple of days later, he himself was found dead, having apparently thrown himself from the cliffs at the Goat Rock. I think I'm right so far, yes?'

'Just so, Mr Daley. As I remember it, anyway, from such a distance.'

Daley walked across the room and settled into an armchair facing McColl. He rubbed his temples with the thumb and forefinger of his right hand.

'You look tired, Chief Inspector, if you don't mind my saying. No medals to be gained by wearing yourself out. Trust me, you'll get no thanks.' The old man looked rueful.

'Did you manage a lot of time off in Hong Kong?'

'Not with the triads with their fingers in everything – no, not likely. We had our work cut out, I can tell you.'

'I've been thinking, Mr McColl. You spent most of your life there – why did you come back?'

'We've had this conversation. Everyone is from somewhere, and I'm from these parts. You come home to die.'

'William Urquhart didn't get that opportunity.'

'No, no, he didn't. But, well, bad things happen, as you well know. Police officers see this more than most – past and present.' He smiled, red cracks showing on his thin, dry lips. There seemed to be a steel about him, a resolve Daley hadn't noted until now. He said nothing.

'You clearly have something on your mind. Spit it out, man.'

'I know what really happened. On the strand, down there.' Daley nodded at the window.

'And that would be?'

'I looked through the records – still on microfilm, most of it.'

'Microfilm, now those were the days.'

'Indeed. I read the shepherd's statement. It was dated two days after Urquhart disappeared. So Mitchell instantly becomes the likely culprit. He already has some sort of involvement in Kerr's death, though nothing can be proved. He has many fancy friends – wealthy young men whose idea of right and wrong he doesn't necessarily share but is so keen to please – and he goes along with them. People who would rather side with the remnants of the Third Reich than our ally, Russia.'

A flash of anger passed across the old man's face. 'And they were right! Look what happened. A whole continent riven in two for years. The brink of global nuclear destruction not long after. All this from a country that should have been on the bones of its backside, were it not for what they plundered from Germany.'

'I'm not sure the majority would share that view, Mr McColl.'

'They should. I came into daily contact with communism. An evil, evil doctrine. Subjugated, starving peasants and landowners alike. No one safe. Look at Stalin's purges. Mao was worse!'

'But you didn't just form these views in Hong Kong, did you?'

'I have no idea what you mean, Chief Inspector.'

Daley walked over to McColl and leaned on the window frame. He looked down at the old man. 'What was he like, really like, I mean?'

'You mean Urquhart? . . . He was convinced that he was right. Arrogant, you may say.'

'Yet he stood up for you against your father. Gave you your chance to become a detective, which gave you a career for the rest of your life.'

McColl was unmoved.

'Why did you go to Hong Kong? I know I've asked you this before, but I'd like to hear it again.'

McColl shrugged. 'Everything after the war was grey and drab. Kinloch returned to being in the middle of nowhere when the military left. I didn't want to spend my life in a one-horse town. My father had influence and got me the position in Hong Kong. One of the few good things he ever did for me.'

'But that wasn't the reason you left.'

'What?'

'I have it here – printed it off the microfilm. We can do that now.'

'What is it?'

'It's a newspaper article. It accompanied the case on the disappearance of Inspector Urquhart, but this portion had been redacted for years. When it was available again, nobody bothered to take a look. Dead farmer, dead farmhand, missing police inspector, presumed dead. All too long ago for anyone to bother about.'

McColl pursed his lips, the skin on his face so translucent it was easy to picture the skull beneath.

'Although the discovery of Mitchell's body was reported two days after Urquhart disappeared, the shepherd had discovered it before then. He told the newspaper, quite plainly. I'll read it for you.

'"The lad's body was trapped in a gully at the Goat Rock. I wasn't able to reach it, though I did try. As soon as I could, I travelled into Kinloch to report what I'd found. It was the lambing season though, and because my ewes needed me more than a dead boy, I had to delay my journey there for two days."'

'What on earth has this to do with me?' There was now a distinct tremor in McColl's voice.

'In the absence of a proper investigating officer at the time, statements – including that of our shepherd here – were taken by the only person available. You. You signed it off. Your signature is still visible on the microfilm. The hand of an awkward young man, but yours, nonetheless.'

'I made a mistake! Everyone thought Urquhart was off investigating something. He d-did things like that. I was left on my own to take statements. I had no experience then. It was a s-simple mistake!'

'But you must have known that Mitchell's body was discovered before the inspector disappeared – some six hours or so, as it turns out – so there was no way he could have been responsible for Urquhart's death.'

'Who talked about his death? He d-disappeared – was never found. No body, no m-murder.'

'That was another thing that was covered up. I know that Urquhart's body was never found. Because of suspicions as to what was happening at the time with German "escapees" – let's describe them as such for now, shall we? – the American Secret Service took an interest. They even found his journal.

Long after the war, they passed on what they had to Israeli groups looking to bring war criminals to justice. Still, nobody made the connection. Not until one man, a Mr Feldstein, thought he smelt a rat. But even they had traitors in their midst, and some of this evidence disppeared. Feldstein was tenacious, though. Tracked it down, and much more besides. Took him half a lifetime.'

'This is fantasy. Utter f-fantasy!'

'Solving this puzzle was easy, when I had all the pieces. I have read Urquhart's journal several times.'

'S-so?'

'Only two people knew where he was meeting the men he thought were responsible for collaborating with the Nazis – rich, influential men, rather like your father.'

'Huh.' McColl waved his hand dismissively.

'There was the unfortunate Mitchell, who we know couldn't have had anything to do with Urquhart's death, as he was dead himself, and one other: you, Mr McColl.'

'T-too much of a leap, p-pure conjecture. It would never stand up in court. Never!'

'He mentions telling you. States quite clearly that he doesn't want you there as he has to do this on his own. You bring him the letter, in fact. Protecting you from the people you grew up beside, his reward for that was being murdered by the young man he thought he'd taken under his wing. But you weren't at odds with your father at all, were you? You were working for him and a group of like-minded fascists. The poor, stammering, oppressed-son routine was just that: an act.'

McColl's head flopped forward. His breath rasped in his chest.

Daley bent over the man he had just revealed as the murderer of Inspector William Urquhart. 'What can I do? Shall I get the nurse?'

'Please, no. Just pour me some water. M-must take my pill.' McColl fumbled in his cardigan pocket as Daley poured mineral water from a bottle into a small crystal glass.

'Here.' Daley held the glass to the old man's lips as, with a shaky hand, McColl slipped something into his mouth.

'I knew this day would come,' he croaked.

'Drink this, quickly,' said Daley, pushing the glass nearer to McColl's lips.

'Now you must bear the burden.'

At that moment Daley heard the tiniest of cracks. As the scent of almonds permeated the room, McColl's body convulsed in his wheelchair, his long and duplicitous life brought to an end.

48

From the bay window, Daley watched the body of Torquil McColl being taken into the ambulance in a body bag. There would have to be a post mortem, but the detective knew he'd witnessed the man taking his own life with a cyanide capsule.

'This will do nothing for the reputation of Stonebrae – of the franchise,' wailed manager Heather Campbell, wringing her hands.

'I'm sorry, Miss Campbell,' replied Daley. 'If I were you, I would keep the press away as long as you can. I'm afraid this won't end with the report of Mr McColl's death.'

'What do you mean?' She looked puzzled.

'Nothing I can tell you about at the moment. Unfortunately, though, I suspect your recently deceased resident may well gain some notoriety in the near future. I can't say any more, but be prepared.'

Daley took the lift to the ground floor, deep in thought. Everything had fallen into place. The Bremners weren't the only people working for the enemy; they'd had some level of support in the community.

As he was about to step into his car, he looked out across the loch. Two people were walking across the causeway, oblivious to the sad events that had taken place there during the war. He wondered how many people who were still alive did know. Very few, if any, he reasoned. Still, he felt strangely unburdened, relieved that he'd been able to get to the truth of what happened to his predecessor; he was now finishing the job Urquhart thought he'd be unable to complete.

His phone rang. Symington.

'Are you ready to come back to the office, Jim?'

'Yes, on my way,' he replied, noting that her insistence on correct usage of job title from Brian Scott didn't extend to him.

He drove back through the centre of Kinloch. As usual, he waved to a couple of casual acquaintances, but was mildly surprised when his greeting was returned with scowls.

Back in the office, Shaw told him that Symington was waiting for him in the AV suite with Scott.

He made his way there, and on entering the room immediately sensed the heavy atmosphere. His colleagues were sitting in silence. Scott's arms were folded, and he was staring determinedly at the ceiling while Symington was keying a message into her phone.

'Everything in order at Stonebrae?' she said, looking up at him.

'Yes, ma'am. I can fill you in on the details if you like.'

'Later, Jim. I'm just waiting for a video call from Professor Carr at St Andrews University – you know, the chap who's been looking at the documents we photographed at Achnamara.'

'I hope he's discreet. I have a feeling this is about to become a major news item.'

'Oh, he is, don't worry. I know him quite well. A good friend, in fact.'

Scott glanced sidelong at Daley, and the latter guessed that whatever had passed between sergeant and chief superintendent had not been reconciled.

Before Daley could comment, the large screen began to flicker into life, revealing a slightly dishevelled man in early middle age sitting in front of a beautiful stained-glass window.

'Carrie, how are you? Lovely to see you – even slightly pixelated!'

'You, too. How are the good people of the Kingdom of Fife treating you? I know how hard it is starting a new job,' she said, smiling rather nervously, Daley thought.

'Fine, fine. New challenge, and all that . . .'

As this idle chit-chat continued, Scott turned round in his chair, curling his lip in disdain. The last time Daley had seen him make this surreptitious gesture was behind John Donald's back.

'Let me introduce you to my investigating officers, Nigel,' Symington announced. 'DCI Jim Daley' – she waved in Daley's direction – 'and his number two, DS Brian Scott.'

Scott turned back to face his friend, mouthing the words 'number two' with a sardonic look.

Symington asked Carr what he'd come up with.

'Oh, a veritable treasure trove, Carrie. I'm compiling a detailed report for you, of course, but I thought I'd give you the heads up on the bare bones. We have a major find, here. I've traced the Bremner family – well, Mr Bremner – back to pre-war Munich. His name is Bremer – a subtle, most convenient Anglicisation. He was originally a member of the SA, then the SS, but disappeared from the records before the commencement of hostilities in the late thirties.'

'Planted on Gairsay,' observed Daley.

'Indeed, forward thinking, and by no means unusual. We're discovering that the Nazis placed a surprisingly large number of observers around the coast, particularly the Atlantic approaches. I must say, the Bremers were in an excellent position to observe shipping movements on the North Channel, and beyond. Also, they made contact with fellow agents on the west coast of Ireland. Seems far away to us over here on the east, but no more than a hop, skip and a jump from Gairsay.'

'So,' said Symington, 'we have reports of shipping movements and so on, but what about as the war neared its end?'

'That's where things get interesting. Nothing too unusual about planted agents passing on details of naval manoeuvres, but the next part of their operational lives involved the spiriting away of senior Nazis through Scotland and Ireland to various locations – usually South America, but a few to the United States.'

'And there is documentary proof of this?' asked Daley.

'Yes, there is. They have used codes, but we broke them some time ago, so we've been able to identify some of the individuals, many of whom were thought to have been assassinated by the Russians; not so the Bremers. The whole thing was quietly forgotten about at the end of the war. After all, a defeated, humbled Germay was no longer the enemy. It lay further to the east. Let sleeping dogs lie seems to have been the watchword. It will come out now, don't you think, Carrie?'

'I have no idea,' she replied.

'Do we have any information about the local groups who aided and abetted this?' asked Daley.

'Most people don't realise, or have conveniently forgotten, that support for the Nazis was not confined to certain members of the royal family and the aristocracy. There were many who admired the Third Reich and despised the Soviets, including nationalists, right-wing conservatives, business-men who spotted an opportunity, some religious sects, union members, even some masonic lodges – in short, many more people than you would imagine, and some of whom supported the organisation known as die Herzen der Helden. Hearts of the Heroes.'

'I think I've heard that phrase before, Professor Carr,' said Daley.

'Still in existence. An organisation initially dedicated to the removal of Nazis from under the Russians' noses, then in later years a source of support to their children and families living in exile. The founder, Frau Weber, is still alive, in fact.'

'And what about those whom the Allies helped escape to the USA? Like Wernher von Braun, for instance.'

'Yes. There is no doubt that certain war criminals were assisted in their escape. Remember, German technology was cutting edge. It's unlikely that Neil Armstrong would have walked on the moon had it not been for the genius of the same man who was responsible for the doodlebugs. It's a sobering thought.

'Oh, and another thing – these little cigarette lighters, the silver ones with the eagle insignia . . .'

'Yes, where did they come from?'

'As you know, the bottom was falling out of the German economy and money was becoming worthless. To incentivise those people from whom they needed help, they had to think of something else. These lighters were issued to the highest-ranking members of the party.'

'Then used as a type of currency?' asked Daley.

'Different days, Chief Inspector. All of Europe – including ourselves – was on its knees. Goodness me, Hungary in 1946 suffered the worst inflation *ever* recorded. In those postwar days, certain items took on a more precious significance.'

'And that's it. Long gone and forgotten about.' Daley watched the professor shrug. 'But if this was all so neatly swept under the carpet, with everyone conveniently ignoring the truth, why the interest from Israel? Why all this cloak-and-dagger stuff with our security services?'

'That, Mr Daley, is a question I am unable to answer.'

Daley and Scott adjourned to the County Hotel. It was early evening, and the usual suspects were dotted around the bar, at favourite tables, or sitting on stools near to the point of purchase.

'Evening, boys and girls,' said Scott, in his customary breezy manner.

Instead of the normal, good-natured greetings, many customers turned away from the policemen, or pretended not to have heard him.

'Mr Daley, Brian,' said Annie. 'The usual?'

'Yes,' said Daley. 'And you can also tell me who's died.'

Scott winced. 'Sorry, Jimmy. I should have kept you up tae speed,' he said under his breath. 'Wae all that's been goin' on, well, you know . . .'

A thick-set fisherman sitting at the bar got off his stool. Daley recognised him from his visit to Hamish in the hospital – it was Erchie, one of the old man's nephews.

'Dae us a' a favour an' dae your drinking elsewhere.'

'Sorry?' replied Daley.

'You heard,' he continued, to a murmur of agreement. 'My uncle's near at death's door, and a' yous can dae is get drunk. If it wisna for you, he'd likely be in here having a dram himsel'.'

'I didn't have time tae tell you, Jimmy. The auld man's taken a turn for the worse.'

Daley turned to ask Annie about Hamish, when a blow caught him on the back of the head, sending him staggering forwards.

'Right, you,' shouted Scott, making for the man who had caught Daley a glancing blow with the bar stool. He was too slow, though.

Daley turned and sprang forward in one smooth movement, his outstretched fist connecting with Erchie's chin. The big man fell backwards, crashing across a copper-topped table, from which glasses tumbled to the floor, to the protests of the drinkers sitting there.

Daley lunged across the bar and made to go for the man again.

'Jimmy, enough!' shouted Scott.

Daley swung round, both hands bunched into fists, a wild look in his eyes. The blow had enraged him. His vision was flickering and flashing red, and he felt as if he were floating above the floor.

Scott held out his hand, fearful that his friend was about to lash out at him. 'Come on. Let's get you oot o' here.'

He nodded to Annie as he led his boss from the hotel, expecting a look of concern or a word of goodbye from her. Instead, she turned on her heel and leaned across the bar, silently wiping it with a cloth.

Once outside, Scott stopped, taking deep breaths. 'You lost it there, Jimmy.'

'Why didn't you tell me about Hamish?'

'Didnae get the chance, big man. We was straight intae that call fae the prof when you came back in.'

'There's always an excuse, isn't there, Brian?'

'Eh?'

'You heard me. I think I preferred you on the bevy, do you know that?'

'That's a cheap shot, Jim.'

'The hell with you. I'm going home.'

Scott watched in dismay as his best friend stomped down Main Street, almost knocking a pair of hooded youths flying as they passed on either side of him, catching the big policeman with their shoulders.

A black crow cawed overhead as it flew down Main Street in Daley's wake.

49

Daley helped himself to a large measure of the finest malt he had. It was a mild evening, and, desperately needing to clear his head, he decided to sit on the decking at the front of the house.

To his right, the town was spread out before him, lights twinkling in the twilight; the distant rumble of traffic was punctuated by the occasional car horn, used as a greeting, rather than as a warning.

He couldn't stop thinking about Hamish. He'd been pleased to see the man apparently return to health after his brief visit, and wondered what had gone wrong. He felt a lump in the pit of his stomach at the thought of his friend's relapse. He considered calling the hospital, but couldn't face it until he'd had another soothing dram. It had been that kind of day; it had been that kind of year, in fact.

The dark island loomed to his left, silent and indomitable as always, the guardian of the loch around which the town had sprung. The man who had dominated his thoughts for the last few days had been the same: William Urquhart, the silent and indomitable protector of the good people of Kinloch, some of whom had so callously engineered his end.

He was surprised to see a car's headlights coming up the long gravel drive towards his bungalow. Scott, he assumed, anxious to make amends; he should really apologise.

In the semi-darkness, though, he could see that the vehicle was a local taxi, and he listened as the passenger got out of the vehicle and paid the driver.

Daley was still sitting on the decking when he heard the chime of the doorbell. He wearily hauled himself to his feet to answer the door.

'Now then, boyo. Haven't you been busy?' Standing on Daley's porch was Iolo Harris.

With a sigh, he admitted his unexpected guest, showing him onto the decking and offering him a drink, which the Welshman accepted gratefully.

'I love this malt. They sell it for an outrageous price in Harrods, did you know that?'

'I'm not in Harrods very often,' replied Daley. 'Thank the Lord.'

'No, me neither, Jim. I read it on the internet. My favourite shopping destination is Neath Market – faggots and peas to die for, boy. My kids hate them. But then again, they hate anything that's not London.'

'Symington has copies of the documents, you know,' said Daley.

'Yeah, I knew she would have. She's a good liar, that woman.'

'Aren't we all?'

'I know I am – have to be, really. It's half my job.'

'Try not to do it to me, if you don't mind.'

'No, no, that's not why I'm here. I know what you know, you see, and I think it's fair to say that you know a lot.' Harris smiled benignly and took a sip of the whisky.

'I must admit, I've discovered things in the last few days that I would never have thought possible.'

'Oh, Jim, you know as well as me, anything is possible. How many times have you found that the least likely scenario is the one you were looking for? Maybe it doesn't happen so much in the police, but it does in my line of work.'

Daley picked up the bottle from the table and poured another two generous measures for himself and his guest.

'So, then, what's the least likely scenario here?'

'Apart from your DS and chief super's little cabal? Well, as always, there is one truth, but two ways to go.'

'The truth being?'

'You tell me, Jim. I know you solved the Urquhart mystery, and the result is lying in the morgue at Kinloch hospital now. Strange thing, death by cyanide. Looks instantaneous, but apparently it's agonising.'

'I won't ask how you know that.'

'No, best not. You know us chaps from the Security Service – waterboard you at the drop of a hat, we will. Worse, too.' He grinned wolfishly.

'Okay. I know that Urquhart was killed by a group of Nazi sympathisers, a group of influential locals. I know that the Bremners – the Bremers – were spies, then became part of something called the Hearts of the Heroes, as Nazis were spirited away at the end of the war. I'm certain that our friend Feldstein was from some Israeli spooks' network and lost his life because of what he knew, as did poor old Glenhanity and her father before her.'

'Yeah, all good. You've heard the phrase "collateral damage". There always is some, Jim. I wouldn't feel too sorry for Feldstein. He's laid a few to rest by less than judicial means. The old woman, well, I feel more sorry for her. She was harmless. But, tell me, what else do you know?'

'Well, I suspect a German submarine got into difficulties, just out there, behind the island, delivering more customers to the Bremers on Gairsay.'

'Interesting.'

'These people were taken to Gairsay, and those who transported them there – the sailors – had an unfortunate accident not long after. Maybe hit a mine, who knows? Possibly because they knew too much. There's nothing in the records about it, but Urquhart did find a body, and wreckage, come to that. It's in his journal.'

'And your reasoning behind this theory?'

'The lighters – the silver ones being used by people whose currency was worth nothing, to barter for their freedom, or for help. One was found on the body of a drowned German merchant sailor, just across from Gairsay, as it happens.' He paused, taking a sip of the malt and savouring it. 'But I don't think they were just being used instead of currency.'

'Hmm.'

'I reckon they were more like a calling card – like a Masonic handshake, though much more secure, as only those and such as those could have them in their possession.'

'It's an interesting theory, Jim.' Harris smiled knowingly.

'My question is: why carry on this charade? The war is long gone. And in any case, it's been conveyed to me that we've known about people like the the Bremers for years. Well, your people have, at least.'

'How very insightful, as an old boss of mine would say.' It was Harris's turn to savour the fine whisky. 'It's a complicated time, as you'll be well aware. Perhaps we should just leave it at that . . . The problem is, if this was all to be revealed we may well be thrown back into the horrors of the past more easily than you imagine. Things are in a fragile enough state as it is, especially regarding Europe. You know how sensational things become, what with social networking and all. We all spend our lives only seeing part of the picture – and sometimes that's for the best.'

'And that's all there is to it? People have devoted their lives to a cause long gone, and continue living in the shadows, even though everyone knows the game was up a long, long time ago.'

'As I say, nobody knows the full picture.'

'Indeed. Just as well, as we know that some have lost their lives because of it – recently, too, as far as the Bremers are concerned.' He searched Harris's features for the truth. 'But it all just has to go away?'

'As away as it's going to get. I truly believe it's time for us all to move on. I have to say, Jim, you're wasted in the police. Seriously, give me a call when we've resolved this little mess – if resolution is forthcoming. You've done so much better at joining the dots than half the Oxbridge boffins I have to deal with every bloody day.'

'Well, I had a little help from Inspector Urquhart.' Daley stared levelly at Harris. 'But, one last thing: why did they use this route?'

'Quite simple. It was the last place anyone was looking. Most of the Nazi officers were escaping from the west coast of France, or Spain. Who would ever have thought of making a run for it from dear old Blighty?' Harris eyed Daley. 'Don't worry, Jim. It will come out one day – nearly did during the Falklands War, but that's another story. No doubt, in time, we'll get the full, well-spun, sanitised tale.'

'Yeah, when nobody cares any more. Men like Urquhart – their sacrifices – all forgotten.'

Harris shrugged his shoulders. 'What can I say? Here's to him.' He raised his glass.

'To William Urquhart, to them all,' echoed Daley.

The two men fell into a companionable silence, as though allowing what they had discussed to drift away on the breeze.

'I'd better go, Jim. Early start. I'll see myself out. Nice night for a walk, too,' said Harris eventually, draining his glass and offering his hand. 'It's been a pleasure. I mean it.'

Daley accepted the Welshman's hand. 'Likewise.'

'Don't be too hard on your DS. He's a loyal man. But beware of those with ambition – that's all I'm saying. Goodnight, Jim.'

50

Daley remained on the decking, with only his whisky and the fading view for company. The lights of Kinloch still twinkled beneath him.

He kept looking at his mobile phone, knowing he had to make the call, but dreading it too much to follow the act through.

He remembered Scott's face when he'd come to tell him about Mary. He felt the pain in his heart, he felt it every day. All those who had gone – all the familiar, much-loved faces in his life.

He thought about Symington. Young, personable, approachable, but he had detected her steely ambition from the start. He knew he'd probably never get to the bottom of what had happened between her and Brian on Gairsay, but reasoned that he knew too many things that burdened him already, so what was the point in adding to the misery?

He thought of his son, his wife, the tatters of his personal life. Was he too old to start up the treadmill again, or were lonely nights like this all that there was in store? Maybe he should get in contact with Harris. Perhaps it was time his life took a different direction.

He must have dozed off, because he was startled back into wakefulness by the buzz of his phone.

Seeing the caller's number, his heart sank. It was the hospital.

'Jim Daley,' he said, a slight waver in his voice.

There was an agonising pause.

'It's yourself, Mr Daley.' Hamish's familiar tones were unmistakeable.

'Hamish, you're on the phone!' Daley felt a huge weight lifted from his shoulders.

'Aye, well, I know that fine since it was me as called you. Well, wae the help o' my wee friend here, Nurse Hogan. Did you think I was deid or something?'

'No, don't be daft,' replied Daley, having thought exactly that only moments before. 'I'd heard you had a fall – a wee bit poorly, that was all.'

'I gied myself a dunt, right enough. Och, but once I got a wee rest and a few o' they magic pills doon my throat, I was back tae normal. Takes a lot tae knock an auld seadog like me on the heid. Anyway, this insna a social call. I've found something you might be interested in.'

'Really, what?'

'Dae you mind that auld Mr McColl gave me a book on the fishing? It's been in my jacket a' this time.'

'Yes, I remember. But there's something I need to tell you about him—'

'Jeest haud your horses,' said Hamish resolutely. 'Here was me fair enjoyin' a story aboot the ring-net fishermen, when something fell oot the book.'

'Oh, what?'

'A photo. I have it here. Must have been pasted inside the cover, by the looks o' things. Mr McColl must have forgot a' aboot it. Quite interesting tae see him young again – aye, an' his faither. I only mind him as an auld, auld man.'

'Right,' said Daley, frantically thinking how to tell Hamish that McColl was no more.

'Remind me o' the number o' this fancy phone o' yours. The nurse says she'll send you a photo o' it. They come oot wae such terms these days.'

Suppressing a smile, Daley did as he was bid and gave Hamish his number, which he heard the old man repeat painstakingly to the nurse at his side. He was so relieved that his friend was in the land of the living, he would have happily listened to his voice all night.

'Right. She's sending it noo,' declared Hamish triumphantly.

'Now, I've got something to tell you on this subject,' said Daley, deciding it best he break the news of McColl's death, rather than have Hamish hear it from some gossip. As he listened to the old man mumbling something to Nurse Hogan, he idly clicked on the image she had sent him. As the old black-and-white photograph was revealed, his jaw dropped.

'Wow!' he said, astonished. The faded image revealed three adults. There was McColl, slightly younger than the last picture Daley had seen of him with Urquhart – no more than a young teenager, in fact. And there was an older man whom Daley assumed was Mr McColl senior, as Hamish had just described, and a woman holding a baby. She was instantly recognisable, her hair falling over one of those distinctive hooded eyes. The broad smile on her pretty face looked strained, however, as though she was posing with this father and son for the sake of the picture, nothing else. The smile was a false one.

'Are you still there?' asked Hamish.

'Yes, yes, I am. Can I ask you a question, Hamish? Is there anything written on this photograph?'

'Aye, there is. Can you read that out, Nurse?'

There was a pause, then Daley heard the woman's voice. 'With Unity Mitford, Inch Kenneth, 1940.'

'Is that all?'

'Aye, that's it,' replied Hamish. 'Tell Mr McColl I'll bring this back hame wae me. He'll likely be wantin' tae keep it, whoot wae his faither in it, an' a.'

Daley knew he should have told Hamish of McColl's fate there and then, but, after telling his friend how glad he was that he was on the road to recovery, he hastily ended the call, claiming there was somebody at the door.

He'd found the woman in the painting. It was Unity Mitford.

He stared in disbelief at the laptop on his dining-room table. He had been prepared for the fact that Britain had harboured more traitors than he'd ever thought possible – Harris had confirmed that – and of course neither was he surprised that McColl and his father were amongst their number.

As he read on, though, he could hardly believe the story that was emerging.

Unity Valkyrie Mitford, one of six sisters from that famous family, had first travelled to Germany in 1933 where she witnessed the Nuremberg Rally. Having become infatuated with Adolf Hitler, she made it her objective to meet the man himself; they did, in fact, become close companions and she was widely regarded as being his lover, much to the exasperation of Eva Braun.

After the declaration of war with Germany in September 1939, it was reported that Unity, distraught, had shot herself in a Munich garden. Surving the suicide attempt, she returned to Great Britain under safe passage from the heart of Nazi Germany to recuperate from her injuries at home. During a visit to the family's home on the remote island of Inch Kenneth, she collapsed and eventually died in Oban in 1948.

He read on.

Early in the new millennium, a journalist had uncovered evidence pointing to the possibility that on arrival back in Britain, rather than being taken to a hospital for the treatment of her wounds, she was taken to a remote Oxfordshire house normally used as a private maternity clinic. The assumptions were obvious.

Though missing any hard evidence, the idea that the young woman who had been painted so carefully by Glenahinty senior, and now stared out at him from his mobile phone, had been pregnant with the child of Adolf Hitler made Daley gasp.

Glenahinty senior was well read – Symington had told him that. Had he actually recognised this woman who had been splashed all over the papers, and taken the time to record what he had witnessed?

He thought of the Bremers; of their child, Randolph, who had been brought by a friend to safety in Gairsay, and educated by a German tutor. The quiet, lonely boy, who had turned into a sullen, awkward adult. He recalled the painting; the windswept scene where a little boy held the hand of Unity Mitford.

Daley sat back in his chair and slammed down the lid of the laptop. Somehow all the questions that had plagued him had now been answered. He felt sick to his stomach. Now, and certainly not for the first time, he wondered if he truly knew anything about the world, if everything was just a web of lies and deceit.

Had McColl really handed over the book, forgetting about the image concealed within? It was plausible, given his age. Or, as Daley now suspected, had the events at the end of the war weighed so heavily on him for decades that he knew it was a chance as he neared the end of his life finally to unburden himself?

No wonder they had been unable to trace the youngest member of the Bremer family. He hadn't just left after a family rift; he'd been spirited away.

The big detective lurched from the table like a parched hero staggering from a bone-dry desert, desperately searching for the water of life, despite being sickened by its darkest, hidden secrets.

Afterword

Present-day Vienna

The bright lights shone on the young man's black leather jacket and slicked-back dark hair as the unruly crowd in the hall roared its approval.

'We can no longer stand by and watch our nations being destroyed from within by those to whom we have given safe harbour!' His voice boomed through large speakers on either side of the stage. 'For us, all that is left is to rise, to rise against the tide that threatens to drown us all. One people, one Europe!'

Alois Bremer stepped back from the microphone and drank in the cacophony of adulation that greeted the speech from the country's most promising young star of the far right.

As he looked around the room, nodding his approval, he swept back a strand of hair and folded his arms.

The crowd bayed for more.

A Note from the Author

Campbeltown at war

Like many, I have an interest in the history of World War Two. As with the fictional Kinloch in this book, the real Campbeltown played its part in the conflict. As discussed in previous notes, the town makes for a perfect port. It is sheltered from the fury of the Atlantic by its location on the east side of the Kintyre peninsula, in the natural haven of the loch, itself protected from heavy seas by Davaar Island at its head. Many have been fooled by the calm of Campbeltown Loch only to find much more restless waters in Kilbrannan Sound beyond. Add to this easy access: to the Atlantic approaches (where much of the naval war played out); the great shipbuilding River Clyde; the Hebrides and north in the direction of the Baltic; as well as the ports to the south in England and beyond. It is no surprise that the Royal Navy was so prominent there between 1939 and 1945.

For the people of Campbeltown the war quickly became ever present. Huge warships dominated the loch; work was taking place at HMS Landrail, then occupied by the Fleet Air Arm, later to become RAF Machrihanish, and HMS Nimrod, a submarine training school. It was located at what was then Campbeltown Grammar School, but became part of Castlehill Primary, where I spent many a happy day as a young pupil. The population of the area almost doubled, thronged as it was by servicemen and women.

In the main, despite its strategic significance, the distance between Campbeltown and Nazi-occupied Europe meant it was difficult for enemy bombers to range, though many heard the ranks of Luftwaffe planes as they made their way to blitz Belfast – part of the Nazis' attempt to disrupt ship-building there. Occasionally, the Luftwaffe would attempt to drop mines on Campbeltown Loch and just beyond in an attempt to hamper naval movements, but these efforts were mercifully few and far between, and occurred mainly in the early part of the conflict. However, on one such raid the mines missed their target, hitting houses on the shore at Low Askomil. One of the casualties was the local procurator fiscal.

In the most conspicuous raid on Campbeltown in November 1940, a lone German aircraft set about its savage business, causing damage to the Royal Hotel and destroying the clock tower of the Victoria Hall next door. Indeed, bullet holes can still be seen in the sandstone brickwork of the hotel, damaged as the pilot strafed the seafront and Main Street with bullets, sadly leading to a small number of fatalities.

One tall tale as to why this single plane set upon Campbeltown has it that the pilot, having been schooled in the area in the 1930s, fell in love with a local girl who rebuffed his advances. He bore such a heavy heart that he decided to wreak vengeance on the town. This story, amongst others, has been discredited. It is more likely that this aircraft formed part of a squadron attacking a secret installation on Rhum that same day, and the pilot became disoriented. As related by Campbeltown native and now BBC journalist Jamie McIvor on the online Kintyre Forum, a mention by the infamous Lord Haw-Haw the next evening of damage to Kinloch Castle was taken by locals as being a reference to the attack. However, the damage was done to the castle on Rhum and had nothing to do with Campbeltown and its long association with the name 'Kinloch'.

Unity Mitford

A member of the famous Mitford clan, Unity was somewhat overshadowed by her older siblings. Looking for her niche, she – like many of the aristocracy at the time – embraced the ranting of Adolf Hitler, seeing him as a defence against Communism spreading from Russia under the tutelage of Stalin.

So obsessed did she become, that she made it her business to travel to Germany in the years before the war in order to meet the Führer. Using her undoubted good looks and resourcefulness, she did, by making sure she was in the right coffee shop at the right time.

However contrived their meeting, she and the German chancellor went on to spend a lot of time together, and Mitford was frequently mentioned as being 'Hitler's girl', suggesting some kind of relationship. There were even reports that his long-time partner and eventual wife, Eva Braun, developed a visceral hatred of the young English socialite, further fuelling the fire as regards a potential affair.

The accepted history was that, eventually discarded by the Führer, Unity Mitford tried and failed to kill herself with a bullet to the skull. As a gesture of goodwill, she was given safe passage in 1940 to return to Britain to be looked after by her family.

Writing in December 2007, journalist Martin Bright cast doubt over this version of events. To cut a long story short, he uncovered details that appear to indicate that Unity Mitford was smuggled from Germany and taken to a private nursing home in the English Home Counties. You would be right to assume that there is nothing unusual about someone recovering from injury to be admitted to such a place. However, this establishment was a private maternity clinic, lacking both the facilities and expertise required to treat a patient suffering from the trauma of a bullet wound.

There are photographs of Mitford arriving back in England on a stretcher in the early weeks of 1940. She's sitting up, looking coyly at the camera, covered by a blanket, but with no obvious signs of injury to her head – not even a bandage. Indeed, for someone who has just attempted to take her own life by such means she looks remarkably healthy.

Guy Liddell, then number two at MI5, doubted that she had tried to kill herself. Despite his best efforts, he was never permitted the opportunity to interview the young woman. In itself this seems strange, given that she had just returned from Germany and was a known intimate of Hitler. Surely she would have known much that would have been of interest to British Intelligence as war raged across the globe.

Whatever the truth, Unity Mitford disappeared from sight and died on the family's estate of Inch Kenneth, a small island near Mull, in 1948.

For further reading, see the article mentioned above:

'Unity Mitford and Hitler's Baby' by Martin Bright, published in the *New Statesman* on 13 December 2007.

In this latest of Daley's investigations, much of the action is set on the fictional island of Gairsay, in fact the beautiful Isle of Gigha. With its white sands, beautiful gardens and sweeping vistas across the Atlantic towards Islay and Jura to the west and Kintyre to the east, it is well worth a visit. The ferry ride takes less than half an hour; I guarantee that in those thirty minutes you will be transported to another world.

D.A.M.
Gartocharn
March 2017

Acknowledgements

As always, my lovely family, Fiona, Rachel and Sian, who make this all worthwhile. My publisher Hugh Andrew and all at Birlinn/Polygon; editor Alison Rae (the magnificent); and my inspirational agent Anne Williams of KHLA.

To the staff of Campbeltown Library for their help with research on the town in World War Two, and John Martin, a man with a foot in both camps, being a native of Campbeltown as well as a long-time resident of the beautiful Isle of Gigha. His colourful memories of both places helped immensely. Incidentally, Hamish owes more than a nod to Mr Martin, as you can see for yourself if you are wise enough to visit the bar of the Gigha Hotel, where he can occasionally be found holding court while sucking on an unlit pipe.

To Alex McKinven for his memories of old Campbeltown. Freddy Gillies, another ex-pat Campbeltonian Gigha resident, whose book *To Campbeltown Once More* (Ardminish Press) is a treasure trove of stories. Also some of the many works of Angus Martin, the true historian of the area. My gratitude, too, to Professor Gavin Bowd of St Andrews University. His book *Fascist Scotland* (Birlinn) contains fascinating glimpses of disturbing goings-on during the war right across society. Also, of course, the books by the late

Angus MacVicar, particularly his autobiographical works – repositories of endless delights.

My late father and mother, Alan and Elspeth Meyrick; and my granny Margaret Pinkney (née Macmillan), all of whom regaled me with stories of times past, from childhood onwards, and are the reason I write in the first place.

Finally, to the people of Kintyre, the place I still and will forever call home, God bless you.

I'm so heartened to hear from an amazing number of readers who have made the trip to Campbeltown after reading the DCI Daley books. Please sign up to my Twitter feed and Facebook page to discover more about what's going on in Campbeltown and its environs, plus some great places to stay.

The DCI Daley thriller series

Whisky from Small Glasses

DCI Jim Daley is sent from the city to investigate a murder after the body of a woman is washed up on an idyllic beach on the west coast of Scotland. Far away from urban resources, he finds himself a stranger in a close-knit community.

Love, betrayal, fear and death stalk the small town as Daley investigates a case that becomes more deadly than he could possibly imagine, in this compelling novel infused with intrigue and dark humour.

The Last Witness

James Machie was a man with a genius for violence, his criminal empire spreading beyond Glasgow into the UK and mainland Europe. Fortunately, James Machie is dead, assassinated in the back of a prison ambulance following his trial and conviction. But now, five years later, he is apparently back from the grave, set on avenging himself on those who brought him down. Top of his list is his previous associate, Frank MacDougall, who, unbeknownst to DCI Jim Daley, is living under protection on his lochside patch, the small Scottish town of Kinloch. Daley knows that, having been the key to Machie's conviction, his old friend and colleague DS

Scott is almost as big a target. And nothing, not even death, has ever stood in James Machie's way . . .

Dark Suits and Sad Songs

When a senior Edinburgh civil servant spectacularly takes his own life in Kinloch harbour, DCI Jim Daley comes face to face with the murky world of politics. To add to his woes, two local drug dealers lie dead, ritually assassinated. It's clear that dark forces are at work in the town. With his boss under investigation, his marriage hanging by a thread, and his side-kick DS Scott wrestling with his own demons, Daley's world is in meltdown. When strange lights appear in the sky over Kinloch, it becomes clear that the townsfolk are not the only people at risk. The fate of nations is at stake. Jim Daley must face his worst fears as tragedy strikes. This is not just about a successful investigation, it's about survival.

The Rat Stone Serenade

It's December, and the Shannon family are heading to their clifftop mansion near Kinloch for their AGM. Shannon International is one of the world's biggest private companies, with tendrils reaching around the globe in computing, banking and mineral resourcing, and it has brought untold wealth and privilege to the family. However, a century ago, Archibald Shannon stole the land upon which he built their home – and his descendants have been cursed ever since.

When heavy snow cuts off Kintyre, DCI Jim Daley and DS Brian Scott are assigned to protect their illustrious visitors. But ghosts of the past are coming to haunt the Shannons. As the curse decrees, death is coming – but for whom and from what?

*

All of the DCI Daley thrillers are available as eBook editions, along with the novella and three short stories below.

Dalintober Moon: A DCI Daley Story
When a body is found in a whisky barrel buried on Dalintober beach, it appears that a notorious local crime, committed over a century ago, has finally been solved. DCI Daley discovers that, despite the passage of time, the legacy of murder still resonates within the community, and as he tries to make sense of the case, the tortured screams of a man who died long ago echo across Kinloch.

Two One Three: A Constable Jim Daley Short Story (Prequel)
Glasgow, 1986. Only a few months into his new job, Constable Jim Daley is walking the beat. When he is called to investigate a break-in, he finds a young woman lying dead in her squalid flat. But how and why did she die?

In a race against time, Daley is seconded to the CID to help catch a possible serial killer, under the guidance of his new friend, DC Brian Scott. But the police are not the only ones searching for the killer . . . Jim Daley tackles his first serious crime on the mean streets of Glasgow, in an investigation that will change his life for ever.

Empty Nets and Promises: A Kinloch Novella
It's July 1968, and redoubtable fishing-boat skipper Sandy Hoynes has his daughter's wedding to pay for – but where are all the fish? He and the crew of the *Girl Maggie* come to the conclusion that a new-fangled supersonic jet which is being tested in the skies over Kinloch is scaring off the herring.

First mate Hamish, first encountered in the DCI Daley

novels, comes up with a cunning plan to bring the laws of nature back into balance. But as the wily crew go about their work, little do they know that they face the forces of law and order in the shape of a vindictive fishery officer, an exciseman who suspects Hoynes of smuggling illicit whisky, and the local police sergeant who is about to become Hoynes's son-in-law.

Meyrick takes us back to the halcyon days of light-hearted Scottish fiction, following in the footsteps of Compton Mackenzie and Neil Munro, with hilarious encounters involving the US Navy, Russian trawlermen and even some ghostly pipers.

Single End: A DC Daley Short Story

It's 1989, and Jim Daley is now a fully fledged detective constable, working in the heart of Glasgow. When ruthless gangster James Machie's accountant, known as the Magician, is found stabbed to death in a multi-storey car park, it's clear that all is not well within Machie's organisation.

Meanwhile Daley's friend and colleague DC Brian Scott has been having some problems of his own. To save his job, Scott is persuaded to revisit his past in an attempt to uncover the identity of a corrupt police officer. But there's a problem. To do so, he must confront Machie and his cohorts. Brian Scott is soon embroiled in a deadly game of cat and mouse with his childhood friends.

As Daley seeks out his old mentor, Ian Burns, to help save his friend and find out who is telling the truth, it becomes a desperate race against time.